Remnant

A Novel
about a tribe of Israel

by
Beth Josephson

With the exception of historical figures, whose philosophies are discussed herein, the characters in this novel are fictional composites, products of various life choices. Any resemblance to specific living persons is coincidental.

Cover and illustrations by Donna L. Thomas.

Published by Atitlán Publications
Aloha, Oregon

Printed in the United States of America
Library of Congress Catalog Card Number: 97-75229
ISBN 0-9660467-1-4

"And it came to pass"

Cover and Illustrations by Donna Lacey Thomas

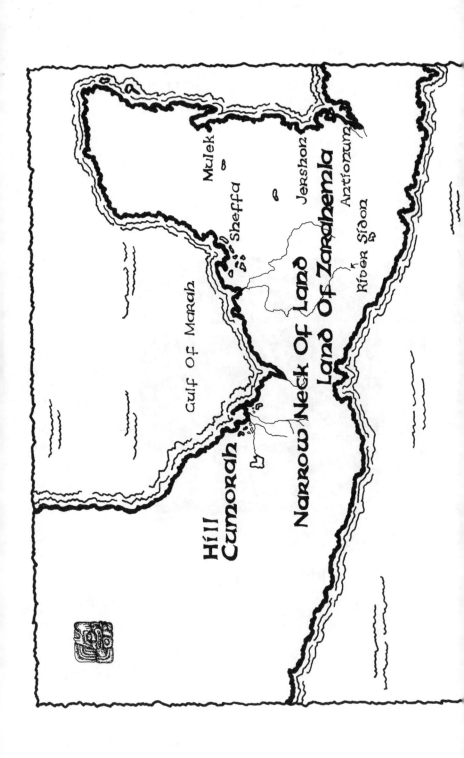

Família Benamoz Genealogy
(Tribal Ancestry in the House of Israel)

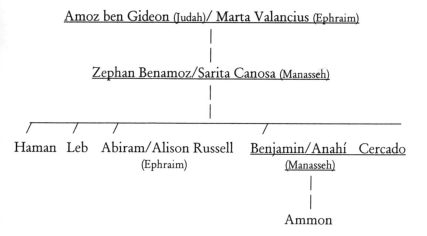

Amoz ben Gideon (Judah)/ Marta Valancius (Ephraim)

Zephan Benamoz/Sarita Canosa (Manasseh)

Haman   Leb   Abiram/Alison Russell   Benjamin/Anahí   Cercado
                       (Ephraim)   (Manasseh)

                                                        Ammon

JUDAH. Son of Jacob, who was son of Isaac, son of Abraham. History of the descendants of Judah found in the Holy Bible.

JOSEPH. Younger brother of Judah, sold into Egypt, where he had two sons, Manasseh and Ephraim. Joseph's father, Jacob or Israel, deliberately crossed his hands, thus giving the birthright blessing to Ephraim, the younger son. Jacob, also a younger son and recipient of the birthright, repeated this type-scene when he gave the birthright to Ephraim. At that time, Israel prophesied that Joseph would be a fruitful bough by a well, whose branches would run over the wall, even unto the utmost bounds of the everlasting hills (Gen. 49:22 KJV), and that the seed of Joseph would become a multitude of nations. Isaiah also said, For out of Jerusalem shall go forth a remnant. (Isaiah 37:32 KJV) In fulfillment of these prophecies, tribal descendants of Joseph were led out of Jerusalem to the western hemisphere in 600 B.C., where they established two mighty nations, whose descendants currently live in Central America. The smaller nation was Christian. Though it became extinct, it left a history of its people, named in the Bible as the stick of Joseph. (Ezekiel 37:16 KJV)

To Carol

Parte Primera

Cumorah

2067, A.D.

The Book Of
Amoz

Fiery Serpent

THE BOOK OF AMOZ

1

Black Sea Democracies
2067, A.D.

Afternoon shadows followed a boy who crept into the steelyards. He hurried past great furnaces which, day and night, rumbled their thunderous complaints toward the sky. Benjamin, grandson of Amoz ben Gideon, made himself small as he edged over to his father's office. Black smoke streaming from towering structures, an incessant roar of angry heat — none of it was as frightening as going home with Grandma gone.

Papa was not in his office. Ben paused before a door which bore a large poster:

CENTRAL COMMITTEE DIRECTIVE:
Political Holiday March 13
Deployment of Troops for Foreign Wars

With powerful strides Amoz ben Gideon reached the door and tore off its poster. Then his face softened. "Benjamin. How is my youngest grandson today? Come in!"

Ben started. Cloaked in shadows behind his grandfather, a figure stood motionless. There, behind the desk. The electric light was not on.

Amoz flicked on the light and turned to the intruder. "Now see what you've done, Andrei, lurking around like that! You've frightened my boy."

Andrei stepped forward. He was of medium height, solid build, wide shoulders. He had close-cropped hair, graying at his temples, with a broad, square face, flat nose and cheeks, as if he had been pressed against a wall many times. "A thousand pardons, young man," he said softly.

"Ben, meet Andrei Kovac, Secretary of Agitprop." Amoz gave a wry smile. "In other words, political officer, informer, meddlesome bureaucrat."

"Come now," Andrei said. "That loose tongue of yours will get you into trouble from which even I cannot extract you."

"These days your kind imprison a man for every word he speaks, but you look away from truly important matters, like government corruption," Amoz said. "We're not in the Eastern Empire, you know!"

"Not yet."

"We may be living in the twenty-first century, but nothing has changed. Every century has its tyrants. Vladimir is drunk, but not with liquor. It's power, that's what."

"I wouldn't criticize Vladimir if I were you."

"Vladimir is only one person, Andrei, and he will join the parade of tyrants through history. But we must remember the prophets. And prophets always say the same thing. It is a pattern, Andrei. Don't you see it?"

"Not really. Everybody is different, and things just happen. You like to think everything is planned so you can feel more secure. At times I almost believe it myself. We're getting old, Amoz. Everything runs together when you get old."

"History is older than we are, Andrei, and human nature does not change. In every era, men want to rule the world." Amoz crushed the poster. "Wo unto them who decree unrighteous decrees!"

"You know how the Committee feels about your quoting a Bible!"

"Precisely. They want to govern our every move! Why is the Committee not bound by the law in our land? "

"Because the Committee answers to the order of Voltaire. You know that." Andrei sat on a desk corner. "But don't be alarmed. Voltairism is a global strategy. An alliance with the order of Voltaire will protect us from aggression."

Amoz wadded the glossy poster into a tight ball and received a paper cut from its sharp edges. He tossed it into a wire wastebasket. "Aggression. Oppression. All the same. Bureaucracy closes my business to promote their agenda, but allows me no time to mourn my wife. Voltairists do not worship the same God as I do. We do not share the same standards of morality, admire the same heroes, nor celebrate the same holidays."

Andrei opened his mouth and then shut it. "But you will get time off from work," he said slowly, "next month. For now you are expected to reconsider your views." He paused. "You still don't understand, do you?"

Amoz groaned. "No, Andrei. It is the Committee who does not understand. When politics overpower a man's work, his family, and his religion, that's going too far!"

"Well, everything *is* political, isn't it?" Andrei paused. "Amoz, I think you are mistaken, but I respect your right to disagree."

"Then why are you a bureaucrat?"

"Because I am a negotiator."

Amoz put an arm around the boy's shoulder. "Come, Benjamin. I will submit a letter of protest to the newspaper."

"It will never get through," Andrei called after them.

2

Ben hurried with his grandfather along crowded streets. Tanks and other military equipment jockeyed into formation. Young men and women dressed in smart gray uniforms and pale blue caps marched in neat squadrons, their legs rigid, with booted feet thudding in rhythm on the pavement.

"What are they doing, Grandpa?"

"A parade tomorrow. A new Youth Service Corps is recruiting with extreme forcefulness. But I do not trust them."

"Why, Grandpa?"

"It is too much like the programs of The Third Reich. One of my ancestors was torn from his family and put in another home because he would not enroll in the Voluntary Youth Program."

7

"At school they say it's all done to help other people, but we can't graduate unless we do it. I suppose it isn't really voluntary, is it?"

"So much talk about compassion, but it is compulsory. It is not the Lord's way. Here we are." Amoz walked into a drab office building and took the stairs two at a time.

The editor's office was filled with reporters. Everyone crowded around a stranger, a big man with a voice to match. Benjamin immediately recognized the western style of his apparel, including cowboy boots.

"And how is the nation accepting this order of Voltaire?" the man was saying.

"Everyone is enthusiastic," said Gutis, the pasty-faced editor, "except for this man."

All eyes turned to Amoz ben Gideon as he entered the room.

"He does not trust anything our leaders tell us," Gutis continued in a tight voice. "Amoz, meet Dan MacRay, correspondent from the West. Now don't say anything that will embarrass us."

Amoz grinned. "Don't mind them," he said to the visitor. "Their sole purpose in life is to abstain from truth."

Dan MacRay laughed and gave Amoz a hearty handshake.

Taking Amoz' letter, Gutis thrust his jaw forward and turned down his mouth. "So what do you have this time, Amoz?" He held an edge of the typewritten sheet between thumb and fingers, scanning it. "It will never get through."

"You mean, past the censors?"

With a furtive glance at MacRay, Gutis shuddered. "Shh! This publication has to keep its doors open!"

"This is a kept press," Amoz said to MacRay.

"Amoz!" Gutis wrung his hands. "Do you realize how long our journalists have been waiting for housing? We can't offend the Central Committee!"

Amoz kept his eyes on the visiting correspondent. "I survived the Empire's prison camps for four years during the War due to mistaken identity, Mr. MacRay, and he worries about apartments."

Gutis sniffed. "Just because you suffered at the camps you try to force your biased reactions on the rest of us! What an ego!"

MacRay's eyes widened; his mouth fell open.

"Tell me, Gutis," Amoz said. "What is wrong with my letter to the editor?"

"You quoted some Western writer who said when people turn from God, they lose their liberty to a rising tyranny. You called this 'the law of history.'"

MacRay leaned forward in his seat.

Gutis lifted his nose. "This God of yours is ideologically incorrect, you know. Nothing about this is found in the approved histories."

"Written by kept historians," Amoz retorted.

"Stop saying that!" Gutis wiped his forehead with a handkerchief. "You are so uncaring! Here we are trying to celebrate a new order, and you keep throwing your twisted view in our faces. You are unkind! Why aren't you happy we are starting something new? You do not love the people!"

"Are you through?" Amoz said.

"Yes. And you are, too." Gutis dropped Amoz' letter in the wastebasket and rubbed his palms with his handkerchief. "Meeting adjourned."

Chairs scraped on a dark brown tiled floor. Reporters filed out past dingy yellow walls and high, tiny windows.

The editor offered a sweaty hand to Dan MacRay. "You can see we really are very progressive," he said. "How can anyone dislike this new world community?" Gutis rolled his eyes. "But then, Amoz has always been radically opposed to change."

"Very educational, thanks." Dan rose to his feet. "In my country we are obliged to report objectively, so I must interview the opposition." On the stairs Dan caught up to Amoz, who slipped him a note and hurried away with his grandson.

3

After lunch on the holiday Ben set out with his grandfather to spend the afternoon at the park. They lingered near a lake to watch the ducks. Ben saw a man approaching them. "Look, Grandpa! The man from the West!"

Amoz glanced around quickly. "So it is! Wait here, son. I will be right back."

The two men nodded to each other and spoke softly.

"I don't believe I was followed," Dan MacRay said.

Amoz smiled. "Our country isn't that bad yet. But the Empire has plans. At this very moment the Central Committee studies ways to destroy our freedom. You have already seen how the intelligentsia is driven by propaganda and economic threats. The order of Voltaire. is just another tool of deception."

"Most of your people seem to buy into this new order," Dan said.

"We are faced with a deadly dilemma. If we accept the new order, we will be stifled by a world despotism. But for hundreds of years we have had in our midst underground bands of organized crime and terrorism from the Tartarean empire. Our people are understandably afraid of escalating power in these bands, so they turn in desperation to promises from the order of Voltaire."

Dan stared out over the lake. "Unfortunately, the West has been ambiguous. We give lip service to freedom, but also send immense donations to Tartarean Empire —"

"— the same big money which sustains slave labor camps for political prisoners."

"The same big money which supports the new order, which criticizes prisons in my own country for human rights abuses. But our prisons are like resorts for murderers, and our people resent it." Dan shook his head. "Our world is webbed with contradictions."

Amoz skipped a rock over the water and gazed at its ripples for a long time. "Indeed, a paradox. In my country the underworld grips us; in your land you have freedom, and Egalitarians openly teach and promote the doctrines of Voltaire. If you are not careful, the underworld will swallow your country, too. Your people must be warned, before these secret networks get above you. I have for you a story and a poem." He pulled two small computer disks from his breast pocket. "And something here for Mitchell Hunt."

Unlike the passive masks on citizens in this closed society, Dan's face telegraphed his emotions in full play. "Are you sure? He is —"

Amoz put a finger to his lips.

"With your literature, I promise you I will reach as many people as I can," Dan continued, "but we also have a kept press, and I don't wish to raise unrealistic expectations."

"I understand."

Dan pulled a small book from his briefcase. "I deeply value your friendship, Amoz. Please accept this gift."

Though he tried to concentrate on the ducks, Ben could not keep his eyes off his grandfather. Grandpa handed the man some of his manuscripts. How exciting! He saw Mr. MacRay sign a small brown book and give it to Grandpa.

The two men shook hands and embraced for a long moment, then turned and walked away from each other.

4

Not long after, Ben and his grandfather headed for the city center to catch a bus. By this time the main square seethed with people, all crowding in to see the parade.

A boy and an old man went one way; everyone else, it seemed, pressed with urgency against them. Past a bakery they walked, past a pharmacy, past a postal station. Soon they came to a school. Masses of children Ben's age, all in uniform, streamed out the school doors.

The drill sergeant, a husky man who frowned with his whole body, paused a moment to size up Benjamin. "Mister! Why is this boy not dressed for the march?"

"We choose not to do that."

"What? Not join the new Egalitarian Youth Service Corps? You will not come over to our side?" The man's voice was cold and calm. "Your child belongs to us already. What are you? You will pass on. Your descendants, however, now stand in the new camp. In a short time they will know nothing else but this new community. It is the only way for world peace." The man looked upon Ben.

Ben stood still, but feeling strong at his grandfather's side, returned an unblinking gaze. Ben felt a collective stare from hundreds of eyes as the boys and girls crowded around their leader.

Amoz smiled down at the sergeant. "You have your world, and I have mine." He stepped aside and walked on, and did not look back.

"Traitors!" the man shouted after them.

"Traitors!" the children echoed.

"Fall in line!" the sergeant bellowed. "March!"

Clomp, clomp. Their boots pounded the pavement. "Trai-tors!" they chanted. "Trai-tors! Trai-tors!"

Darkness caught up with the boy and the old man when they boarded a bus. The bus slowed to a crawl in a street thronged with people. At length it stopped; the driver stood and announced, "I can go no farther until the crowds disperse. If you do not care to wait, you will have to walk."

"Let's go, Ben. Stay close to me so I don't lose you in the crowd."

Ben needed no coaxing. Everywhere stern soldiers jostled agitated people. It was scary. Must get home and close the door against this . . .smoke. And this endless chanting. Fire. A bonfire. Newspapers, books, tossed into the fire. Bibles, too? "Grandpa, are those. . .?"

"Yes! Two blocks and we are home. Come!"

5

Nine days had passed since Marta's funeral. Amoz ben Gideon looked at his son Zephan and his family, now without their mother and grandmother. Zephan had been devoted to his mother and had always honored his father. He had married well, too. Sarita had escaped severe crippling from a childhood disease, but she continued to fight chronic pain while working tirelessly for her family. Their four young sons were each different. Fortunately Haman and Leb, at sixteen and fifteen, were too young to be conscripted into Empire forces. Those were a rebellious duo, though, to their parents' grief. Maybe a military life would settle them down. Amoz grimaced. No. Not the Pax military.

In contrast, Abiram was a serious, industrious lad. Already, at thirteen he was helping Zephan at the metalworks. And Benjamin, only twelve, had been Marta's pet. Perhaps Amoz loved the boy so much because he resembled his grandma. Over and over he saw Marta in the boy's easy smile.

But Ben was not smiling now. Though he stood very straight, being large for his age, his lip quivered. He tried hard to be a man and blinked away stubborn tears. His expressive round eyes, sometimes gray, were now blue windows. Amoz sensed the boy inside sometimes glimpsed a world unseen by those around him.

"Was Grandma gathered home to the arms of our Father in Heaven, like it says in the Bible?" Ben managed, his voice cracking.

"Yes, Benjamin, like this." Amoz held the boy a long time, and his own tears formed dark rivulets on the back of Ben's faded shirt.

Amoz shepherded Zephan and Sarita into the office. Everything was so strange and empty without Marta. When she became too ill to move, the family had gathered around her bed. Since her death, Amoz avoided spending time in her room, so devotions were conducted in the office.

This tiny room had been his haven. In it, he had spent many a late night, writing. But his was a voice in the wilderness.

Amoz looked lovingly upon his ancient word processor. He had steadfastly resisted upgrading. He couldn't afford it anyway. He resented company policies which refused to service their non-technical customers with parts for low-end word processors. According to computer manufacturers, if you weren't spending thousands of your hard-earned money every year to buy the biggest, fanciest, and most costly computer and software on the market, then you weren't worth bothering with. Long after his colleagues had discarded their early vintage computers, Amoz clung to his antiquated machine, keeping it in good repair with care and generic components from the hardware store. In the face of others' scorn, he would quietly reply: "Use it up. Wear it out. Make do, or do without."

But the wily old writer had method in his stubbornness. He had developed a private code based on ancient Biblical types which even the most sophisticated hacker could not crack. The ruling regime would never understand the language of the Spirit.

As mandated by the ruling party, Amoz' shelves were overstuffed with books on political doctrines. Behind them were stashed disks of his many manuscripts. Not the best place to conceal his work, perhaps. But it had survived a decade. How much longer could it last? He stirred a small fire crackling in the fireplace. It was only a matter of time.

With a sigh he lifted a heavy Bible from the shelf, turned to a passage in Ezekiel, and asked Zephan to read it.

"Moreover, son, take one stick, and write, For Judah. Then take another stick, and write upon it, For Joseph. I will take the stick of Joseph, which is in the hand of Ephraim, and the tribes of Israel. I will put them with the stick of Judah, and they shall be one stick, and they shall be one in my hand." Zephan looked up. "You know what this means, Father?"

"Now I do. May God forgive my stubbornness. All these years you were right, my son, but I was too blind to accept it." He reached over and patted Sarita's hand. "At least when this choice daughter brought you the truth, you, Marta, and the children were not as hardhearted as I."

Zephan leafed through the Bible with reverence. "This is the stick of Judah, Father, the record of your people. I understand how you feel. The Bible has come through much tribulation, and some plain and precious parts have been lost over the centuries. While many Gentiles have revered the Bible, others have not understood, and I can see how you would be skeptical of the truth, especially when it comes to you through the Gentiles."

Amoz ben Gideon took down a small brown book and turned it over and over. "This book is yet another Messianic testament, from another whole people — descendants of Joseph of Egypt, the brother of Judah. All their prophets, too, testified of Christ. I cannot reject their testimonies. Zephan, this testament has led me to the true Messiah, at last."

"That's wonderful, Father!"

The older man shook his head. "But just like my more obstinate ancestors, I looked beyond the mark and would not accept the living prophet. Only written words of past prophets would satisfy me. I hope someday to meet our present prophet."

"In Cumorah, in the West, resides Joseba Bianco, an Apostle of the Lord. Like the chief prophet and his fellow Apostles, he is sustained as a prophet, seer, and revelator. I'm sure we will get to meet him."

"I hope so." Amoz retrieved a wood-carving knife from his desk drawer and looked down at his hands, dry and rough from preparing metals, from shaping metals into weapons. He grasped the knife and cringed inwardly at what he was about to do.

He sliced the cover off the little book and cast it into the fireplace.

Zephan gasped. "Father! What are you doing?"

"This is the stick of Joseph, record of the tribe of Joseph. If you know its title, it would only further endanger you."

"Why, Father?" Sarita's eyes were wide.

"You already know how much the Tartarus Empire hates Jews and the Bible. While the Jewish state is tiny, this, the house of Yeshurun, includes peoples from nations world wide," Amoz said. "The Empire does not know about this hidden giant. Descendants of Joseph, themselves, are largely unaware of their own identity. But the covenant people have transcended the ages. Yeshurun is real, with living oracles, just as in ancient times, and with prophets, even among the Gentiles."

"I understand," Zephan said. "Already in this land, agents of Tartarus destroy Bibles."

Amoz riffled some pages in the book of Joseph, then read a verse. "This book names the order of Nehor as an abominable force among all nations, which oppresses people of faith and binds them down with an iron yoke. The words are exceedingly plain. According to this book, the order of Nehor requires reverence for doctrines of men, and it enforces those doctrines with the sword. The book of Joseph also warns of bands of robbers called Gadiantons, who plundered the people with the consent of their governments.

"These same evils exist today," Amoz said, "only with different names. Gadianton robbers still abound in the Tartarus Empire; they continue to plunder and terrorize the nations. But agents of Tartarus have donned faces of philanthropy, and call themselves Egalitarians. Today the works of Nehor are carried on by the order of Voltaire."

Sarita's mouth formed a surprised "O".

Amoz smiled. "But our enemies do not know about our secret weapon."

"What is that, Father?" Sarita asked.

"The word of God is sharper than a two-edged sword." He became brisk. "First, we must leave. We go to a land of liberty. Listen to this. . ." Once again caught up in excitement over his discovery, Amoz read aloud. "'If they will serve God and keep his commandments, it shall be a land of liberty unto them, and they shall never be brought down into captivity, save by their own iniquity.'

"So my people became a hiss and a byword because of their iniquity," Amoz continued. "Now, these times are the fullness for Gentiles." He read on, "'But in the day when the Gentiles shall be lifted up in pride above all nations, and shall be filled with lying, murders, hypocrisy, priestcrafts, and secret abominations,' says the Holy One. . ."

Moving his finger rapidly down a page, Amoz continued reading, "'Then shall my people who are a remnant of Jacob be among the Gentiles like a lion in the forest, and he will go through and tread down and tear in pieces, and none can deliver. All their enemies shall be cut off.'" He tapped the page with his finger. "This, my children, is why this book is dangerous. Anyone possessing this book, if found by agents of Tartarus, will be charged with treason. And if the regime finds anyone to identify as the remnant. . ." His voice trailed off.

"We must be very careful," Zephan finished for him. He took the little book and gazed at the pictures. It was in English. He tried to recall words from his arduous studies in school.

Amoz watched fire consume the book's cover, seeing something far away. "I pleaded with God to spare my precious Marta to journey with us, but he saw fit to deliver her from the evils in this world. Now, my children, listen carefully."

Zephan inched his chair forward on the hardwood floor, closer to his father.

"In eight days I travel to the land of Cumorah, in the West, to meet with Jaime Canosa concerning a shipment of ore. These are days when people suspect even their own kin, but Canosa can be trusted. Our weapons manufacture has opened a door for me there. The Empire is infiltrating Cumorah, and I am to supervise assembly and maintenance of weapons among the insurgents there. I told the authorities you and your family will be visiting your Aunt Naomi on the Balkan coast, but in reality you are going with me, and Naomi has already left for the West. Zephan, you followed my instructions to ensure passage on the plane?"

"Yes, sir."

Amoz shifted in his chair and leaned forward. Suddenly he felt a great sadness well within him. "I must demand strict obedience to what I say next. If anything happens to me, do not try to defend me. If the authorities discover my writings, you will not be able to help me. You must hide and escape. Get on that plane for the West at all costs. Then find Canosa. I will join you as soon as possible. Do you understand?"

Zephan nodded, his face gloomy.

"But Father, we couldn't leave you!" Sarita trembled with emotion. For a long moment she held the old man's blue-eyed gaze.

"What would be gained by giving one more family to this beast which devours our land?" Amoz read again from the small brown book. "The time will come when God will avenge his people, for he will not always suffer their cries from the dust." He put his arms around Sarita and held her tight. "No, my daughter, you must take the children and live for freedom. If I am taken, I will be counting on ·you."

6

Each day which followed was filled with anticipation. After school, Benjamin would retreat into his grandmother's bedroom to study the coverless little book. In his mind he could see Grandma's hands ironing crisp white curtains, remember her face on a flowered pillow, and feel her presence.

Evenings he would read aloud to his grandfather, questioning about meanings, surprising even himself with his speedy grasp of the language.

"You have fared well with English, son." Amoz said with grandfatherly pride. "You improve every day. Maybe you even surpass your father."

"I feel as if I stand in the place of those who wrote this book, Grandpa."

"It is a gift you have, my son."

"I know this book is true," Ben said. "I feel. . . compelled to read it, Grandpa. It is so familiar to me, as if I had always known it."

The day before the journey, Benjamin rushed home from school for his usual activities, almost ritual since his grandmother's death. First, a glass of milk, just as Grandma would always give him after school. Extra milk rations were a luxury given those families on the State's "valued service" list. Next he toured the house, mentally saying farewell: to the kitchen, where Grandma had shared many afternoon conversations and helped him with his studies; to Grandpa's office, where he had lost himself in so many good books; to the bedroom he shared with Abiram, where he visually reviewed the few articles he would take to Aunt Naomi's house. For security reasons, he was not to pack anything until the last moment. Skipping his homework, he hurried with the little book to Grandma's bedroom to await Grandpa's arrival from work in late afternoon.

Mama had taken his brothers to the dentist. Papa said it would be a good cover. A visit to the dentist office was such a normal thing to do, no one would suspect they were leaving the next day, never to return. Ben grinned. He had just been, so he didn't have to go. They would be gone for hours, and he could say his goodbyes to his home in peace. Haman and Leb wouldn't be here to mock and torment him as they were wont to do. Besides, Haman had already fought several times with Papa. Haman didn't want to leave his friends. And Leb copied Haman in everything.

Ben smiled. It was another good reason for Haman to have his mouth filled with a dentist's fingers. Then he couldn't say something he shouldn't. Maybe he would even have fillings in his teeth, so his tongue would be numb, and he couldn't use it to lash out and insult Papa.

Papa would be at work until after dark. One more day.

The front door opened and closed. Ben heard weary steps in the hall and Grandpa puttering in the kitchen.

Ben finished one more chapter and placed the book under his shirt. No more sounds came from the kitchen. The boy glanced out the window and saw a secret police vehicle pull soundlessly up in front of the house. He stifled a cry, bolted for the door and ran into Grandpa, standing there in silence.

"Benjamin, my son," he whispered. "This could be dangerous. The secret police must have followed me here, so if I do not meet them, they will search until they kill us all. In here. Quick!"

In the closet was a false wall with a crawl space behind it, and the boy quickly slipped inside. He watched his grandpa's face disappear behind the wall, heard a rustle of Grandma's few clothes being arranged on the other side, and then slow steps toward thunderous pounding on the door. That was the last time Benjamin ever saw his grandfather.

Ben heard angry voices. From the office, he could hear sounds of bursting glass, objects crashing to the floor. Down the hall came a thud of heavy boots.

Thumping, creaking, tearing. Again, shattering glass. Steps reached the closet. Hearing a scrape of hangers on metal, Ben flattened himself against the floor and wrapped his arms over his head, scarcely daring to breathe. He heard footsteps retreat, grateful for their heaviness, so his pounding heart might not be heard.

With sweaty fingers he touched the small book lying open and pressed beneath his chest. Ben half-expected the book to be damaged from his thumping heart. That book was now his only link to Grandpa. Grandpa! His childish heart cried without voice into darkness.

At last all was still.

Long after the footsteps were gone Ben allowed a sob to escape. He struggled with the door, but could not open it. At length he slept without rest, seeing only an evil black car, and his grandfather vanishing into the night.

7

Zephan's step was almost jaunty as he hurried home. He had forced himself to work hard until the last minute, even giving extra time so his superiors would not detect his excitement. Now the hour was almost seven. Only hours till departure, and freedom!

Strange. Sarita and the children must be delayed at the dentist. Had Ben gone with them after all? And where was Father? The house was dark. Seeing the door splintered and ajar, Zephan skipped a breath. He stood very still, listening. Nothing. Before entering, he carefully extracted the heaviest of Father's tools from a box beneath a front step. Though all civilian weapons were banned when the ruling party came into power, Zephan had learned how to defend himself when necessary.

The electric light did not respond. He groped in darkness for a candle off the coat closet's top shelf. Everywhere he saw destruction, revealed by eerie patches of candlelight: furniture crushed and upended, cupboard contents broken and scattered on the floor, windows broken, food pilfered, glass everywhere. In the office, books had been thrown on the floor; the shelves were empty. Father's manuscripts lay smoldering in the fireplace. Desk drawers were pulled out and overturned. Father's ancient computer, which he had kept running for decades with tender care, as well as his fine wooden desk —— both had been hacked to pieces with an axe.

The boys' rooms were less damaged. Bed coverings lay on the floor, trampled by muddy feet. Someone's angry boot had smashed Ben's wooden carvings. Benjamin.

God in Heaven, are You there? Please help me find my little boy.

Mother's room. The child would study on her bed. No place to hide there. No, please. Not that.

Bed overturned. Window broken, curtains slashed. Lamp thrown to the floor, axed. Family photos torn and hurled across the room. "Inhuman beasts!" he said aloud.

19

There, from the closet. A whimper? Suddenly remembering the hiding place, he secured the candle and moved the false wall.

The boy staggered out from his cramped position and threw himself into his father's arms.

No words came. Zephan could only hold and stroke the sobbing child and try to calm him. Dear God, do You remember us?

One lone book remained behind the wall. Zephan picked it up with his free hand and peered at it. The "stick of Joseph". It was flattened at the spot where it had lain beneath Ben's body. In flickering candlelight, Zephan caught a few English words. "Behold, the Lord hath redeemed my soul. . .I have beheld his glory, and I am encircled about eternally in the arms of his love."

8

At his mother's side, Benjamin kept his eyes on his father's firm, square shoulders. The family waded through one line after another of bureaucratic stampings, signings, scrutiny, and interrogation.

With hat pulled down, Zephan mechanically displayed upon demand Amoz ben Gideon's passport. Zephan had the same wide brow, deep-set blue eyes, full mouth and strong chin as Amoz. The passport's heavily stamped black-and-white photograph confirmed the resemblance.

The boy glanced at Haman and Leb, who scowled at their mother in swollen muteness. Ben's mischievous little wish had been granted, but he felt a twinge of sympathy for his brothers. No denying their pain. Then, seeing the approach of yet another official, Ben was relieved that Haman could not say something spiteful which could endanger the family.

Seated at last in the plane, with engines roaring, Ben faced straight ahead, unable to look upon an empty seat between him and the window.

A woman in gray slacks and shirt, bearing a ubiquitous Empire badge, stopped at every seat, checking tickets. Her hair was pulled back severely, revealing a face pinched by a lifetime of grudges. She took Zephan's ticket books and studied them for a long time.

"Amoz ben Gideon?" Her voice was gravelly and mannish.

Zephan nodded.

"And where is Zephan?"

"He was delayed to another flight. He will meet his family in the Balkans for a vacation on the coast."

The woman said nothing, but continued to stare, first at Zephan, then at the photo. Pivoting, she marched toward an exit, taking the passport with her.

The engines were shut off. Twenty minutes passed. No announcement was made concerning the delay. No one showed curiosity. Although these passengers were mostly government and military officials, citizens did not customarily question each other.

Zephan wiped sweat from his forehead, then reached down and scratched his ankle.

Forty minutes had passed. The woman returned with a stocky, square-faced man. Andrei. Had he betrayed Grandpa? Andrei Kovac arrived at Zephan's seat and nodded at the woman, who moved on to remaining passengers.

Andrei returned the passport, but it fell at Zephan's feet.

"I'll get it," Andrei murmured. He leaned way over Zephan's lap, blocked curious eyes with his hindquarters, reached into Zephan's sock and palmed a wad of currency. With a grunt the man stood up. Andrei glanced at the passport and thrust it into Zephan's lap.

Ben searched Andrei's face, but the man's eyes were inscrutable.

"Everything seems to be in order," the official said quietly. Andrei waited until the woman made her exit, then followed her back down the aisle.

Once again engines started, and the jet finally lifted off. Gray land receded in afternoon mist as the aircraft turned west and headed toward the sea.

Sarita felt Zephan's hand close over hers, but she could not hide her grief.

9

Zephan pulled the coverless book from his satchel among his carry-on articles. He turned to the last section and again looked at a short note written to his father and signed, Dan MacRay.

To my cherished friend, Amoz. . .

He must find this Dan MacRay.

Zephan turned to the first chapter and began to read about an ancient family's flight from Jerusalem to the new world. It spoke of

21

a land of promise, choice above all other lands, set aside in covenant for the family of Joseph and to any children of Israel led out from captivity by the hand of the Lord.

Voices from a young couple in front of him interrupted his reverie. Zephan strained his ears in attempt to understand snatches of animated Spanish.

The young man's hair was long and filthy, he had a huge beard, and his clothing was torn and ragged. He must have been lost in the wilderness for a long time. The woman's clothing was as scant as her companion's was shabby. Her eyes and lips were heavily painted, giving her a forward and wanton look. She must have been lost from home. The young man repeatedly mentioned another individual named Cabrios, boasting about Cabrios' revolutionary activities in a land called Antionum.

How brash. A revolution? And who was Cabrios? Perhaps some insurgents Father had talked about. Zephan's Spanish was a bit sketchy. He probably misunderstood them.

He shrugged. Instinctively, however, he clasped the book to his bosom, as if prying eyes or evil officials might wrest it from him.

To his left, Leb's boisterous protestations filled the air. Haman was cheating at cards again.

For Zephan the night was long and filled with memories. He would never see his father again, and as he looked out the window, black emptiness beneath them yawned its indifference. One more life was crushed to earth by the Tartarus Empire and its iron yoke. Helpless but for his own flickering faith, Zephan was hurtling through mists of darkness. Tomorrow would bring his family to a mysterious, unknown land.

All at once, daylight, and mountains topped out like islands over a foaming sea of clouds. Along wide beaches, palms in dense rows brushed bellies of fat woolly clouds. Breakers trimmed the sea like white lace on his mother's emerald green Sunday dress. White houses nestled in luxuriant vegetation and bright plantations stretched to the mountains. Poinciana trees waved brilliant red flags; lavender orchids crowded narrow roads. Zephan's heart was captured. Indeed this was a choice land, but beneath him mighty nations slumbered in the morning hours, unaware of their greatness.

When the aircraft touched down, Aurelia and Jaime Canosa were waiting with a big, polished antique car called a Thunderbird. Among shining modern automobiles crowding the colorful streets, Benjamin marveled to see many vintage cars that looked like new.

"Where are the police to check our bags?" Zephan asked.

Jaime and his wife exchanged glances but said nothing.

The Canosas pulled up to a broad drive at their home in a small village called Ammonihah. What a contrast to winter dullness left behind: rain-washed fruit trees, bougainvilleas in crimson pillars, and pale orange tiles on white Spanish architecture.

Ben stared at the spacious entrance and ventured through an arched doorway to a huge dining room. Through large windows sunshine poured in, flowing through multiple crystals in a chandelier to create colored patterns upon the wall. A big basket of fresh fruit rested on a lace tablecloth.

Ben picked up an orange. So that's what an orange felt like. Round, bumpy. He sniffed it. Delightful scent.

"Go ahead, Ben," Aurelia said. "Eat it."

The boy sunk his teeth into the whole thing, and was puzzled at a burst of bittersweet.

Everyone laughed. Even Haman and Leb. Aurelia quickly peeled and sectioned his orange.

Ben savored white and golden fruit and smiled at this agreeably plump woman with a plump and agreeable heart.

She tossed an orange to Zephan, and began peeling fruit for Sarita and the children, but Haman and Leb did not want any.

"I have not had an orange since I was a young girl," Sarita said softly. "The children have never tasted it."

"Let's take them out to the plantation, Aurelia," Jaime said. "We have plenty of time before supper."

Sugar cane fields neighbored a simpler plantation home. Outbuildings with modern equipment surrounded the house. Small orange and avocado groves flanked the farm. Various fruit trees shaded a courtyard, and a stable bustled with activity. But the largest fields were pineapple.

Ben asked to ride horses, so the animals were led out for a ride around the grounds. Mounted on a small mare, Ben imagined himself riding beside a valiant captain in an ancient land. Abiram rode double with Zephan.

Haman and Leb chose to ride around in the Thunderbird convertible with Aurelia and Sarita.

Jaime reined in next to Zephan. "Want to talk about it, *joven?*" he asked quietly.

The younger man looked around.

"It's all right, Zephan," Canosa urged. "You're safe here. I understand Spanish, English, and have learned some language from your father."

Canosa watched emotions play in the young man's face.

Zephan started out in halting Spanish, then English, finally pouring out his whole story in his native tongue.

The Canosas had planned a festive dinner to celebrate the newcomers' arrival. Seated at a table with the family was an old, old man. He was bald, except for silvery hair around the back of his head. If creases in his face could measure years, then surely this man was not a day younger than one hundred years. He was even more ancient than Grandpa Amoz.

Ben ached for his grandfather.

But the man's eyes were young, even behind his glasses. When he smiled, recognition lighted his eyes, as if he already knew Ben. Perhaps he had known Amoz. Perhaps the old man saw in Ben a trace of his grandfather.

Before taking his place, Canosa stood beside the old man. "*Familia* Benamoz, I present to you Brother Joseba Bianco. He is an Apostle and prophet of the Lord."

With amazing agility, Brother Joseba sprang to his feet and embraced Zephan. "Zephan, God remembers you in your afflictions. Allow His Spirit to comfort you, my son."

Zephan's eyes filled.

"Well, now. Your father would soon have taken his place with the elders here. On the Sabbath the brethren will ordain you also, for your worthiness is known to the Lord."

Zephan nodded humbly.

"Now, my son, and all your loved ones, eat with us, and feel our welcome in this choice land."

Canosa finished his chicken *paella* and glanced at his wife, who inclined her head. "Is it settled, then? In these few short hours, Aurelia and I feel as though we have always known you. We know it is impossible to fill Amoz and Marta's place, but we would be honored if you would stay on with us. You can live in freedom here."

Zephan nodded. "I understand. Father would have wanted it that way. We are grateful."

"Your position in my metallurgy business here is assured," Canosa continued, beaming. "And our quiet home will now be alive with children's voices. Brother Joseba, here, is presiding elder, but he also schools the children."

"Ugh! School!" Haman and Leb chorused.

"Boys!" Sarita shushed them.

"In fact," Canosa went on, "Brother Joseba does just about anything!"

"Well, now. Tomorrow I will show the children around our little city," Brother Joseba said.

"Count me out." Though Haman mumbled through gums puffed from dental work, his voice blasted a hole into the conversation. "I'm not a child. I'm going to sleep till noon, then Leb and I are going to the beach."

"Haman, your rudeness is inexcusable," Zephan said.

"No matter," Brother Joseba said mildly. "There will be other times."

11

Next afternoon Brother Joseba picked up Ben and Abiram. His wooden station wagon looked old enough to be a senator.

The boys said nothing and clambered into the car, but gawked at the driver with eyes like fried eggs.

Brother Joseba laughed. "Well, now. You boys are too polite to say it, but you think I'm too young to drive, don't you?"

Abiram giggled.

"Not I, but this car is immature and undependable. I told your father we have only one way to make this car perform her duty and get you home safely."

"Yes?"

"You see, the old girl has a tendency to get overheated." He winked. "Especially when she's carrying two warm-blooded adolescents. So you two boys will just have to do your part."

"So what is it, already? Get out and push?"

Brother Joseba's grin was boyish. "Well, now. We will simply have to make one stop, or maybe more, at the *heladeria*, and you boys will just have to eat ice cream as cold as you can stand it, so we can keep her temperature cool."

Their first stop was at the pyramids. The boys raced each other to the top of a very large one. Though he came on more slowly, Brother Joseba climbed steadily, and was not winded when he reached the summit. Ben, ever the observant one, noted this and marveled, for he and his brother were both panting, despite their youthful vigor.

Ben thought he could feel the warm sky's blueness with his fingertips. His gaze flew to a far horizon, lighting on tops of ruined buildings poking up from endless jungle. He spotted wildlife, but not another human soul was to be seen anywhere.

"Well, now. We begin your first history lesson," Brother Joseba said. "Perhaps typology is a better word. Do you mind if I use a big word now and then?"

"We are used to it," Ben said. "Mama insists upon daily vocabulary study. She doesn't want us babbling like ignoramuses."

The old man chuckled. "Good. Then I needn't worry about talking down to you, which I refuse to do, anyway."

"Typology. So what is it already?"

"Typology is unique to us as a people, and to our brethren in the house of Israel. It is like curtains on the windows of time. We may only see an occasional motif on today's curtain. But when we get outside, truth, like sunlight, transcends all boundaries, and we can see eternal patterns which weren't visible within our narrow personal experience. Types from our past foreshadow our future. Do you understand?"

"Not exactly."

"For example, I will tell you a story about Lehi and his family. Lehi's exodus from the old world and his life here is a type of obedience to God and following the path to eternal life. Lehi had a compass, called a *liahona*, which served to guide his family when they were faithful and obedient. The *liahona* is a type and shadow of the word of Christ."

The boys stared at him with intense concentration. "I understand," Ben said, "I think."

"Do not worry if you don't comprehend everything at first. It is good for you to ponder serious questions in life and stretch your minds. If you never think deeply, then you will be deceived by appearances and enticements from men's philosophies. Now, if you ask questions, and hold on to my words, you will understand before this day is over, I assure you."

"Who built these pyramids? Were the people advanced?"

"Earlier people were exceedingly advanced. They were a temple-building people, who built structures modeled after Solomon's temple. The people did not build fancy pyramids. Instead, simple and functional temples were built, which were used to worship the Lord. Though later inhabitants built exquisite and artistic buildings, they were in reality a savage and cruel people. Their buildings served no holy purpose, except as a monument to their pride. When pride brought them down, the jungle grew over everything and buried their city, just as the web of false precepts they embraced came to strangle their souls. But I am getting ahead of myself. We must begin with this city's predecessors, for whom we have a stronger bond."

"How can that be?"

"Simple. We picked up where they left off. Today we have their records, and all the same blessings those ancients enjoyed: prophets, seers, and revelators, miracles, even temples, and power to act in God's name. We have come full circle, and everything is like it was long ago."

"But aren't things really quite different now? Those people lived even before invention of the wheel."

Brother Joseba smiled. "Well, now. We do have many marvelous inventions in our day which were inspired by the Spirit of Christ. However, it is foolish to think these discoveries and inventions have come to light because men are more intelligent today than in former times. Remember these particular people about which I am telling you were quite advanced, because they were righteous. And their attitudes were quite similar to people today, even down to some astonishing details."

"You mean, we think like those people did?"

"More than we are willing to admit. Ah, today men flatter each other as if they know more than the ancients, but some day we moderns might be embarrassed to learn how ignorant we really are. Remember how we said types are windows to the future? Today many people can't see through those windows because they are too busy looking at themselves in the mirror."

Abiram laughed. "Leb spends hours before the mirror, already."

"For him, a lifetime would not be long enough," Ben added.

A breeze stirred Brother Joseba's thin silver hair. "But for God, a day is as a thousand years, and time is one eternal round."

Ben studied his teacher. Perhaps those words explained why this man seemed so. . . ageless.

"Remember, God and the Atonement transcend time. In eternal covenants, time is only measured by men. But prophets can speak of future events as though they had already come. Now imagine you are in the time of our fathers. And I must get on with my story about the legendary fiery serpent."

12

Long ago, about six hundred years before Christ, a prophet named Lehi, descended from Joseph of Egypt, was led by the hand of God to bring his family out from Jerusalem to this land. This is a choice land, and the Lord made a covenant with Lehi that his descendants would possess it forever. In a wonderful vision, Lehi saw a tree of life. In that same dream, the Lord showed him a great and spacious building, and warned him to avoid pride.

Lehi possessed cherished records of his family, with writings from Isaiah and Zenos. Also, being a successful merchant, he brought with him many skills and great understanding. His young son Nephi had knowledge about farming, animal husbandry, building, and working with steel. And the Lord even taught Nephi how to build a ship in which to traverse the great waters. Coming from Jerusalem, this family was familiar with chariots and other wheeled vehicles. Lehi was well educated and taught his family to read and write. He also taught them the astronomy and herbal healing which God had imparted to Abraham. And thus we see that not all civilizations in the new world were primitive and ignorant, as some learned men would have you believe.

Upon arriving in the new world, Lehi and his family found horses, for a post flood people came to this land and brought animals. Modern anthropologists call these post

28

flood people giants, and the book of Joseph identifies them as Jaredites.

Lehi had six sons and some daughters, who loved and honored him. But the two oldest sons, Laman and Lemuel, did not love their father. Because these two men had very hard hearts, they understood not the dealings of the Lord. Not believing their father's visions and prophecies, Laman and Lemuel resented their family's journey to the new world. These two oldest sons were so angry with their father that they often sought to kill him.

After arriving in the new land, more contention arose. Soon a major political issue divided the family.

"You mean, they had politics, even way back then?"

"Oh, yes, Ben. In fact, from the very beginning, God's family has been divided over the same opposing policies. Should man go to heaven by his own free will and choice?"

"Mama said that is God's plan."

"She's right.

And now, my sons, I speak unto you these things for your profit and learning; for there is a God, and He has created all things, both the heavens and the earth, and all things that in them are, both things to act and things to be acted upon.

And to bring about His eternal purposes, after He had created our first parents, and the beasts of the field and the fowls of the air, and all things which are created, there had to be an opposition. So the forbidden fruit was in opposition to the tree of life; the one being sweet and the other bitter.

Wherefore, the Lord God gave unto man that he should act for himself. Wherefore, man could not act for himself except he was enticed by the one or the other.

And after Adam and Eve had partaken of the forbidden fruit they were driven from the presence of God.

"Now, the only way back to our Father is to become like Him.", Brother Joseba said.

"Why?"

"Because no unclean thing can be with Him, you know. Besides, why not?"

"But how can it be possible?"

"To shape godly character takes daily toil, delayed gratification, and moral courage. But One offered to rescue all who could not make it alone, if those who desired would but follow Him on the path He would tread. Of course that Way would be very narrow, and fraught with thorns, pain, and sacrifice. It would not be easy, but all can get there who really want to. You see, all things were done in the wisdom of Him who knows all things. Adam fell that men might be; and men are, that they might have joy. The Anointed One came to redeem the children of men from that fallen existence.

"But then the Other came forward. He wanted a short cut. The Father's way looked too hard, and certainly he saw no one worth rescuing. The Other insisted everything would be so much easier and faster if he just took charge. If he could just have the power to choose for everybody, then he could *make* everyone get to heaven."

"So they both wanted to reach the kingdom of heaven?"

"Yes," Brother Joesba replied. " God just wants everyone to come home to Him. Where Love is, there God is also. That would be heaven. No tricks. No gimmicks. At home with God we are free forever, knowing good from evil, to act for ourselves and not be acted upon, except by God's just law. We are free to choose liberty and eternal life, or to choose captivity and death.

"Now, the Other's plan is enticing, too. But the Other is not totally honest about his version of heaven. He didn't tell anyone that heaven for him is rather dark, and it is more like a cage than a home. It is quite small, too. You see, in his domain, nobody goes very far — at least, not forward. Oh, according to him, it would be *the* perfect world, all right. He does tell everyone it would be heaven on earth, here and now, immediately. None of this waiting around for some future date. No one would have problems, the Other tells us, because he already has a solution for everything. None would be happier than anyone else because everyone would be the same. No one would need to help anyone else, and no one would have to pay for his mistakes. Now, my young friends, as I told you, the Other is not totally honest."

"You mean he doesn't tell us about some things?"

"Yes. He boasts about his heaven on earth, in which no mistakes are made. But no one can make choices — a detail which he fails to mention. For everyone in the Other's kingdom, one important thing

30

would be missing: free will. And this principle has been the source of disagreement, even wars, since the beginning of time."

"So, Brother Joseba, did Lehi's family fight over freedom, too?"

"Yes, that's it. Even though people confuse us with different words and meanings, you could say freedom has always been at the heart of all human conflict. Here, let me continue with my story."

Now, Laman was Lehi's first child. Because he was the oldest son, he thought he should be king, and rule over the people. But Nephi, the younger son, believed that God's appointed steward, or prophet, should teach the people eternal principles, and the people should rule themselves. As it turned out, God did appoint Nephi to be his prophet, and Nephi governed his people in righteousness, under God's direction. Laman believed he was deprived of his right to rule over the people, and for this, he hated his younger brother. Laman tried to kill both his father and his brother Nephi. Finally, the family was permanently divided, and Laman, an exceedingly prideful man, led many away after his traditions. The people multiplied and became two great nations: the Nephites, who kept the commandments of God, and followed God's prophets, and the Lamanites, who rebelled against God.

For hundreds of years, Nephites continued to prophesy about the coming of the Messiah, and the Lamanites continued to murder and plunder, and many wars and contentions embroiled both peoples.

"So Nephites were good, and Lamanites were evil?" Benjamin asked.

"Not that simple. The Nephites continually sought to teach the gospel to their brethren the Lamanites, and some Lamanites saw error in their ways, repented, and joined with the Nephites. Fortunately, God, who is Father of us all, does not judge us by our race."

"But what is good, and what is evil?"

"Whatsoever is good comes from God. That is a vital question, Benjamin, because the reason we are here on earth is to distinguish good from evil."

"If it is so important, then how can we know the difference?"

"Remember this. There are opposites in all things: good and evil, light and darkness, truth and error."

31

"It sounds simple."

"But these days, some will tell you a little evil is not so bad, but if you are too good, then you are evil."

"Now I am confused."

"God is not the author of confusion."

"Truth comes from God, so it is good," Ben said. " Of course, lies would confuse people. Is truth the opposite of confusion and lies, like light and darkness?"

"You are catching on. Now, here is an eternal verity. Good and evil are opposite. "

"That seems obvious."

"But sometimes good and evil appear the same. Some men will believe so strongly in an error that they will use their power to establish it as true. This is called enforced priestcraft. In such cases, anyone who opposes their philosophy is often labeled as evil, and is sometimes killed."

"What do you mean?"

"For example, a man named Galileo discovered the earth revolved around the sun. This was contrary to political conformity during his day, so even though he could prove it was true, he was put to death. Galileo was not a prophet, but throughout the ages, prophets and many good men and women believing strongly in the word of God have been killed, not because their teachings were false, but because others believed in error just as strongly. And those in error had more power."

"But how could someone believe a falsehood so strongly as to call truth evil?"

"Frequency and density. Let me give you an example which is not so severe. If you had lived long ago, you might have been told a theory that the world was flat, even though God revealed to Abraham it was round. Suppose you were the only one who believed Abraham's principles of astronomy. Every day, a hundred times a day, you were told the earth was flat. Would that make it flat?"

"No, sir."

"But everyone else in the world believed it was flat."

"Still not true."

"Now, let's test another theory, with the same frequency and density of acceptance. Suppose you were taught your grandfather was a chimpanzee."

"I get it."

"Now, I will continue with my story, and you can apply this principle."

Centuries passed, and the Meridian of Time drew near. Nephi and Lehi, two Nephite prophets, went among the Lamanites and converted many to the gospel. Abroad in the land was a powerful band led by a man named Gadianton. And this band began to rob and plunder, and to commit secret murders.

The Lamanites hunted down the Gadiantons, and preached the word of God among the more wicked part of them, until this band of robbers was utterly destroyed from among the Lamanites.

But the Nephites supported Gadiantons, and voted for them, until they had spread all over the land. Now, Gadiantons were not only burglars, but also had political power, which they used to plunder and murder in the name of law. Gadiantons took control of government, trampled the law of prophets, and made it legal to plunder, take people's property, and destroy their liberty. Thus they seduced people until even the more part of the righteous had come down to believe in and vote for Gadianton works, and partake of their spoils, and to join with them in their secret murders and combinations. Gadiantons filled the judgment seats, and usurped power and authority of the land by laying aside the commandments of God. They condemned the righteous for their good works, and let the guilty go unpunished because of their money.

And it came to pass that it was five years before the birth of the Son of God. Many Nephites had become lifted up in pride, and were more wicked than the Lamanites. And one faithful Lamanite, a prophet named Samuel, stood on the city walls, and told people that in five years the Messiah would be born, and a great sign would be manifest. He told them there would be a day, a night, and a day with no darkness, and a new star would shine in the skies. Many believed him, but many more did not. When dissenters tried to kill the prophet as he stood upon the wall, their arrows could not hit him, for he was protected by the Spirit of God. Seeing this, many were converted to his message. Samuel said when the Redeemer would shed his blood in the old world, a great and dreadful disaster would devastate this land – a destruction more terrible than had ever been seen before. After three days of total darkness, the Holy One would come to this land. Samuel completed his message and left, never to be seen or heard from again.

Those who believed the prophecies looked forward to the great sign, but unbelievers began to talk and contend with people of faith.

"There is no such thing as the Son of God," unbelievers said. "And why would Christ not come to us as well as in Jerusalem? How can we be expected to believe such a thing, if it happens in a far away land, and we cannot see it for ourselves? As for a day, a night, and a day without darkness, that is scientifically impossible! These are fantasies from religious fanatics."

Samuel the Lamanite had told people to repent of their plundering and adulterous ways, their secret murders and combinations. This made the doubters look bad, so they saw this prediction of uninterrupted light as a way to discredit Samuel for giving them bad press. The doubters came up with their own dogma.

"Samuel was a false prophet," said the doubters. "See? He spoke his lies and then he left. Of course! Do you think he would stay around to face our wrath when we found out he was lying? Everyone knows his bizarre predictions could not possibly occur, because they are scientifically unsound. This man was a threat to society, and he slipped out of our hands. We must teach his followers a lesson. Those who are tempted by this nonsense must be stopped."

A prophet among the Nephites, whose name was also Nephi, was moved upon by the Holy Spirit. Said he, "If this counsel or this work be of men, it will come to naught. But if it be of God, you cannot overthrow it, or you will be found even to fight against God."

"We cannot take any chances," said the doubters. "Society must be protected from these dangerous ideas."

"But Samuel said we are free to act for ourselves, because God has given us power to know good from evil," the believers said. "Let us think for ourselves!"

"You obviously aren't intelligent enough to think for yourselves if you believe a crazy fanatic like Samuel," the doubters scoffed. "It is unfortunate, but there is a rise in this sort of fanaticism all over the world. If we don't stop it now, we may have to confront it again. If you don't renounce these ridiculous ideas, you shall have to be punished."

The time drew nigh, and persecution was intense. The unbelievers set apart a day on which, if the sign spoken of by Samuel did not come to pass, all believers would be put to death. When the prophet Nephi saw his people's wickedness, he bowed himself to the earth and cried mightily to his God in behalf of those who were about to be put to death for their faith. And it came to pass that he cried mightily all the day long, and behold, the voice of the Lord came unto him, saying:

"Lift up your head and be of good cheer; for behold, the time is at hand, and on this night shall the sign be given, and on the morrow come I into the world, to show unto the world that I will fulfil all which I have caused to be spoken by the mouth of my holy prophets."

And it came to pass that the words which came unto Nephi were fulfilled, just as Samuel had spoken, for at sundown no darkness came. Everyone was astonished because night held no darkness.

The unbelievers fell to the earth, because they knew their plan to destroy the faithful had been frustrated. The manifestation of the sign could no longer be denied, and the unbelievers began to fear because of their iniquity and unbelief.

And it came to pass, in all that night, no darkness fell, but it was light as midday. And it came to pass that the sun rose in the morning again, according to its proper order. The people knew it was the day the Lord should be born, because of the sign which had been given. And it had come to pass in all things, every whit, according to the words of the prophets.

In four or five years, people began to forget the signs and wonders which they had seen and heard. Public opinion molders began to persuade people that the phenomenon had been a vain thing wrought by men to deceive people. For some people it was easier to believe men, not God, had caused the miracle of light. People began to believe that teachings about Christ were a foolish and vain thing, and they were told there were no more miracles or revelations.

Nevertheless, people began to reckon their time from the miracle of light, and years passed. After the Lamanites and Nephites joined together and defeated the Gadiantons, peace was in the land for a score of years. People remembered the Lord, and he prospered them, for He blesses those who put their trust in Him. They grew rich in flocks and herds, horses and cattle, grain of every kind, gold and silver, and many precious things. They lived in peace in all the land, from the land northward to the land southward. Many old cities were repaired, and new cities built. Highways were cast up, and many roads were made which led from city to city, and from land to land, and from place to place. And many merchants were in the land, and many lawyers, and many officers.

But in only the twenty and ninth year since the miracle of light, pride and boastings came among the people because of their exceedingly great riches. Some were ignorant because of their poverty, and others received great learning because of their riches. Soon the very rich set their hearts upon the things of the world, were lifted up in pride, and were tempted to seek for power and authority. The people divided themselves into classes, and persecution began against the followers of God. Some returned railing for railing, and others endured all manner of afflictions and remained humble.

Thus we see, in the very moment when God prospers his people, doing all things for their welfare and happiness; then is the time they harden their hearts, forget the Lord their God, and trample under their feet the Holy One. And this because of their ease and exceedingly great prosperity.

The people were deeply divided, and many holy men stood among them in all the land, calling upon them to repent, and teaching them about the Holy One.

Among the people were chief judges, and they who had been high priests and lawyers, who began to exercise unrighteous dominion, and they left off following the Lord. These apostates were exceedingly angry with the holy men for exposing their iniquity. But these judges, lawyers, and high priests could condemn no one to death without the signature of the governor in the land. Without the governor's knowledge, judges secretly put to death many prophets of the Lord.

And people raised a great complaint against this grave injustice.

Now it came to pass that those judges had many friends and kin, who all united together and made a pact with one another, like those secret oaths given anciently by the father of lies. The judges pledged to combine against all righteousness, and combined against the Lord's people to destroy them. The judges and their friends pledged to cover up their secret murders and deliver those who were guilty of murder from the grasp of justice. This group set at defiance the law and rights of their country and pledged to destroy the governor and establish a king, that the land should no more be at liberty. This the wicked did to get gain, and for glory from the world. Thus they destroyed the government of the land, and the people were divided into tribes.

The people formed themselves into a league of tribes. The tribes did not war with one another, but had turned their hearts from the Lord their God, and stoned the prophets and cast them out from their midst.

By the thirty and first year, the more part of people were doing evil. However, a great prophet named Nephi had been visited by angels, had seen by revelation the ministry of Christ, and had begun to go forth among people and minister to them. So great was his faith that, in the name of Jesus, he even raised his brother from the dead after people had stoned him to death.

The thirty and third year passed away, and people began to look for the sign which had been given by the prophet Samuel the Lamanite — the sign of darkness for the space of three days over the face of the land.

And it came to pass in the thirty and fourth year, in the first month on the fourth day of the month, such a great storm arose as had never before been known in the land. A great and terrible tempest began, and thunder, and an earthquake which shook the whole earth as to divide it asunder. Lightning rent the sky with a fury hitherto unknown, the city took fire. Another city sank into the depths of the sea, and its inhabitants were drowned. Another city was buried beneath a mountain. Great and terrible was the destruction in the land northward, for the face of the land was changed. Highways were broken up, level roads spoiled, and many smooth places became rough. Many great and notable cities were sunk, and many were burned, and many were shaken till the buildings thereof had fallen to the earth, and the inhabitants thereof were slain. Some cities remained, but the damage was so great that many in them were slain. Some people were carried away in the whirlwind; where they went no one knows.

Thus the face of the whole land became deformed because of the tempests, thunder and lightning, and earthquakes. The rocks were rent in twain and broken fragments, with seams and cracks upon all the face of the land.

And it came to pass that after about the space of three hours, the thunder, lightning, storm and tempest, and earthquakes ceased. Behold, darkness was upon the face of the land.

The darkness was so thick that those inhabitants who had not fallen could feel the vapor of darkness. No light could shine because of the darkness; neither candles, nor torches, nor could fire be kindled with their fine and exceedingly dry wood, so no light could shine at all. No light was seen, neither fire, nor glimmer, neither sun, nor moon, nor stars, for so great were the mists of darkness which were upon the face of the land. And it came to pass that it lasted for the space of three days; no light was seen; and great was the mourning and howling and weeping among all the people continually.

And in one place people were heard to cry: O that we had repented before this great and terrible day, then our brethren would have been spared.

And in another place people were heard to mourn: O that we had not killed and stoned the prophets, and cast them out; then would our mothers and fair daughters and our children have been spared and not buried beneath the earth. And thus were the howlings of the people great and terrible.

And it came to pass that silence was in the land for the space of many hours.

And a voice was heard among all the inhabitants upon the face of this land:

"Behold, I am Jesus Christ the Son of God. I created the heavens and earth. I am Alpha and Omega, the beginning and the end. And you shall offer no more sacrifices by the shedding of blood; they are done away. And ye shall offer for a sacrifice unto me a broken heart and a contrite spirit. Will you not now return unto me, that I may heal you?"

When people heard this, they began to weep again, because of the loss of their kindred and friends. And thus did three days pass away. It was morning, and the darkness dispersed from off the face of the land, and the earth ceased to tremble, and rocks ceased to rend, and the dreadful groanings ceased, and all the tumultuous noises passed away. And the people's mourning turned to joy, praise and thanksgiving. They were also conversing about this Jesus Christ, of whom the sign had been given concerning his death.

While they were conversing, a voice seemed to come out of heaven, and everyone looked round about, for they understood not the voice; it was not a harsh voice, neither was it a loud voice; nevertheless, and notwithstanding it being a small voice it did pierce them that heard it to the center; and their frames quaked; it pierced them to the very soul.

The second time they heard the voice and understood it not.

And again the third time the people heard the voice and opened their ears to hear it and looked steadfastly towards heaven, whence the sound came. Behold the third time the people understood the voice which they heard, and it said unto them:

"Behold my Beloved Son, in whom I am well-pleased — hear ye him."

And it came to pass, the people understood, and looked again towards heaven; and behold, they saw a Man descending from heaven, clothed in a white robe; and he came down and stood in the midst of them.

And now, whosoever can read, let him understand; he who hath the scriptures, let him search them. For many testified of these things and were slain because of it.

And it came to pass that He stretched forth his hand and spoke unto the people, saying:

"Behold, I am Jesus Christ of whom the prophets testified. I have drunk out of that bitter cup which the Father gave me. Whoso repents and comes unto me as a little child, him will I receive. Behold, for such I have laid down my life, and have taken it up again; therefore repent, and come unto me."

And the multitude remembered the prophecy that Christ would show Himself unto them after His ascension into heaven.

"Arise and come forth," He said, "that ye may thrust your hands into my side, and also that ye may feel the prints of the nails in my hands and in my feet, that ye may know I am the God of Israel, and the God of the whole earth, and have been slain for the sins of the world."

And it came to pass that the multitude went forth, and obeyed Him, and this they did, going forth one by one until all went forth, and saw with their eyes and felt with their hands, and knew of a surety and did bear record it was He, of whom it was written by the prophets, who should come.

And He was with them for three days, and healed them, and taught them, saying:

"Verily I say unto you, except you shall keep my commandments, you shall in no case enter into the kingdom of heaven.

"Therefore, all things whatsoever you would that men should do to you, do ye even so to them, for this is the law and the prophets," He said, and He showed them by example.

"Beware of false prophets, who come to you in sheep's clothing," He continued, "but inwardly they are ravening wolves.

"Ask, and it shall be given unto you. . ." He paused.

"How can the people know if a false prophet is among them?" Nephi asked.

"By their fruits ye shall know them," He replied.

"A good tree cannot bring forth evil fruit, neither a corrupt tree bring forth good fruit. Whosoever hears my sayings and does them, I will liken him unto a wise man who built his house upon a rock.

"If any man would do the will of my Father," He said, "he shall know of the doctrine, whether it be of God. A man who speaks of himself seeks his own glory; but he who seeks the glory of God, the same is true, and no unrighteousness is in him.

"Now," He said, "prepare your minds for the morrow, and I come unto you again. But now I go unto the Father and

40

also to show myself unto the lost tribes of Israel, for they are not lost unto the Father, for he knows whither he has taken them."

And it came to pass that when Jesus looked at the multitude, He beheld they were in tears, and did look steadfastly upon Him as if they would ask Him to tarry a little longer with them.

And He said to them, "Behold I am filled with compassion toward you. Have you any who are sick among you? Bring hither the lame, or blind, or halt, or maimed, or leprous, or are withered, or deaf, or are afflicted in any manner. Bring them hither and I will heal them, for I am filled with compassion and mercy. I perceive you want me to show you what I did in Jerusalem, and I see your faith is sufficient that I should heal you."

And the multitude brought forth all the afflicted, and He healed them, every one. He bade them bring Him their children, which they did, and all knelt upon the ground.

Jesus groaned within himself, and said: "Father, I am troubled because of the wickedness of the people in the house of Israel." Then he knelt and prayed to the Father, saying things too sacred to be written.

And He bade them arise, and He said to them, "Blessed are ye because of your faith. And now behold, my joy is full." And when He had said these words, He wept.

"Behold your little ones," He said. And angels descended from heaven as if in the midst of fire, and all were encircled about by the fire of the Spirit, and angels ministered to them.

Neither the disciples nor the multitude had brought bread, or wine. But He gave them all bread to eat and wine to drink. When they had all eaten and were filled, He continued teaching them.

"You remember I told you the words of Isaiah would be fulfilled. They are written and you have them before you. Therefore search them. In fact I command you to search these things diligently, for great are the words of Isaiah. For surely he spoke as touching all things concerning my people which are of the house of Israel; therefore it must needs be that he must speak also to the Gentiles. Now write these things, for the time will come when they shall go forth unto the Gentiles.

"Now I finish the commandment which the Father has commanded me concerning you," He said to the people. "You are a remnant of the house of Joseph.

"If the Gentiles will repent and listen to my words, and harden not their hearts, I will establish my church of the Lamb among them, and they shall be numbered among this the remnant of Jacob. My Father will begin among the dispersed of my people, even the tribes which have been lost."

He told them He was their Shepherd, saying:

"Verily I say unto you, ye are they of whom I said: Other sheep I have which are not of this fold; them also I must bring, and they shall hear my voice; and there shall be one fold, and one shepherd. And verily, I have yet other sheep, which are not of this land, neither of the land of Jerusalem, nor anywhere else I have been to minister. My Father commands me to go unto them, therefore I go to show myself unto them, also.

"I will establish this people in this land, and the powers of heaven will be in the midst of this people; yes, even I will be in the midst of you." He gazed out over the vast assemblage of people, and all worshiped Him. "Behold," He continued, "I am he of whom Moses spake, saying: A prophet shall the Lord your God raise up unto you of your brethren, like unto me; him shall ye hear in all things whatsoever he shall say unto you. And it shall come to pass that every soul who will not hear that prophet shall be cut off from among the people.

"Behold," He said, "this is my gospel — I came into the world to do the will of my Father, because my Father sent me. And my Father sent me that I might be lifted up upon the cross; that even as I have been lifted up by men, even so should men be lifted up by the Father, to stand before me, to be judged, whether for good or evil. And for this cause have I been lifted up; therefore, according to the power of the Father I will draw all men unto me.

"Now ponder upon the things which I have said. And I command you to write these sayings after I am gone. If it so be my people in Jerusalem do not ask the Father in my name for a knowledge concerning you, then this book shall be kept and shown to the Gentiles. And through the Gentiles, those who are scattered shall be brought to a knowledge of me, their Redeemer. And I give unto you a sign, that I will gather them in from the four quarters of the earth, and I will fulfil my Father's covenant with the house of Israel. These scriptures the Father commanded I should give unto you, for it was wisdom in him that they should be given unto future generations.

"In that day the Father shall do a great and marvelous work. By this they will know the great work of the Father has commenced. And when that day shall come, it shall come to pass that kings shall shut their mouths; for that which had not been told them shall they see; and that which they had not heard shall they consider. And this shall be a sign unto you."

And the multitude saw, heard, and did bear record; and they know their record is true for all of them did see and hear, every man for himself; and they were in number about two thousand and five hundred souls; including men, women, and children.

And after He left them, they lived in peace and harmony for two hundred years. And thus we see that hundreds of men, women, and children on both continents became special witnesses of the world's greatest miracle, the resurrection of Christ.

13

"What is the sign, Brother Joseba?" Ben asked. "I don't quite understand."

"It is the book which has come forth among the Gentiles, the story of Christ's ministry in this land."

"You mean, the story of the remnant?"

"Yes."

"You mean, the same book we brought from —"

"The same. And the book contains the secret to lasting liberty and prosperity."

"What is that, Brother Joseba?"

"When the people obeyed God, they enjoyed liberty and prosperity. When the people rebelled against Him, they suffered bondage. It is that simple. And it really was no secret. Everyone knew it, but just would not live it."

The boys were silent for a long time, pondering the old prophet's words.

Ben stared out over the valley. From the depths of tangled greenery, rippling columns of heat emerged and mounted to their vanishing points. Perhaps it was a curtain of steam which appeared like a mirage. He felt lonely, as if the multitudes of people who had once inhabited this place had moved to another valley of time and left him behind.

"So," Ben said at last. "This story is very familiar. I have seen and heard it before."

"It is a type and shadow of our day," said the old man.

"Then you are not finished yet, are you?"

"No, and I'm afraid the ending is not a happy one." He looked into his listeners' pensive faces. "This ground once sustained mighty nations. All are gone, now. Destroyed. Hundreds of thousands of people mingled their blood with this very soil our people today plow, plant and harvest for their daily bread. Nothing is left. But their voices cry out from the dust. Listen! If you would only listen, they say."

Ben and Abiram listened.

"Great nations, destroyed. Not for lack of military prowess, for the people fought fearlessly. Not for an excess of weapons, nor for the lack thereof. Without weapons, they would have clubbed each other to death. Not for lack of lands and wealth, for the people had a whole continent, but could not live in peace. They did not die from old age. Yet all are swept from the earth without a trace."

"Why?"

"Pride. Two hundred years after the presence of the Holy One, the people were again divided into classes, which warred against each other. Envy became a political art. The people killed the prophets and fought against the Lamanites, who had become totally degenerate. When the Lamanites conquered a faction of Nephites, they would sacrifice Nephite women and children to their gods. This made the Nephites so furious that they tortured, violated, and sacrificed Lamanite women and children."

The boys gasped in horror.

"It grieves me to expose your tender hearts to such barbarism," Brother Joseba said, "but you will see why it is important for you to know. By four hundred A.D.," he continued, "the Lamanites, who are still exceedingly numerous today, wiped out every last Nephite. The Nephites abandoned God and perished. Only a lone prophet and his son remained. Soon the grief-stricken prophet died in battle, also, and his son had to flee for his life, for if the Lamanites found him, they would murder him."

"Do you know what happened to him?"

"Yes. You see, that prophet was very special. He had collected and compiled all the records of God's dealings with His people on this land. The records covered more than a thousand years. The dying prophet gave those records to his son and commanded him to hide them; otherwise, the Lamanites would destroy them. This lone survivor wandered for thirty years, far from here, away up north into the Land of Goyim.

"Oh, how the young prophet mourned the fall of his people. Before he hid up the record, he added a final message from his father to us:

> Behold, I write unto all the ends of the earth; yea, unto you, twelve tribes of Israel, who shall be judged by the twelve whom Jesus chose to be his disciples in the land of Jerusalem. And I write also unto the remnant of this people, who shall be judged by the twelve whom Jesus chose in this land. And you must all stand to be judged, whether you be good or evil.

"Long ago, Isaiah told us what would become of the remnant: 'And thou shalt be brought down, and shall speak out of the ground, and your speech shall be low out of the dust, and your voice shall be familiar, and you shall whisper out of the dust.'

"And it came to pass that the last surviving prophet in this land made a mighty prophecy about the day in which the great sign would come forth."

> For the eternal purposes of the Lord shall roll on, (he wrote), until all His promises are fulfilled. I say unto you that those who have gone on before me, who have possessed this land, shall cry out from the dust unto the Lord. And He knows their prayers were in behalf of their brethren. And He knows their faith, for in His name could they remove mountains; and in His name could they cause the earth to shake; and by the power of His word did they cause prisons to tumble; and even the fiery furnace could not harm them, neither wild beasts nor poisonous serpents, because of the

power of His word. And also their prayers were in behalf of him who the Lord should suffer to bring this work forth.

Now, you need not say it shall not come. For as the Lord hath spoken, it surely shall, and out of the earth it shall come, by the hand of the Lord, and none can stay it.

And it shall come in a day when it shall be said that miracles are done away; and it shall come even as if one shall speak from the dead. And it shall come in a day when the blood of saints shall cry unto the Lord, because of secret combinations and the works of darkness.

Yea, it shall come in a day when the power of God shall be denied.

"In his mournful exile, the last prophet completed his mission and sealed up the testament of his people in the earth. There the records lay hidden through a long, dark night of apostasy, until the Gentiles found them some fourteen hundred years later. So, just as the Holy One promised, the scriptures given to the remnant of Jacob were saved up for our day. And the sign has come forth by the hand of God into an unbelieving world, just as the lonely prophet said it would."

"And what about the fiery serpent?" Abiram asked. "Do Christians around here worship such a thing?"

"No, *joven*. It is a corrupted image, as I shall explain. But first, we shall go down to more modern ruins."

14

The present government seat centered in a huge shaded plaza. Slightly northward were more pyramids, to which Brother Joseba next conducted his little tour. "Here are the famous pyramids of Montezuma. By 400 A.D., the people had thoroughly forgotten the Lord their God, but they did not forget how to practice human sacrifice. The people had become a ruthless and bloodthirsty people when Cortés found them in 1519. But surprisingly, they did not at first see him as a new kind of delicacy for their gods."

"You mean, they liked him?"

"Yes, because he had a beard."

"Excuse me?"

"If I am not mistaken, you can observe the descendants of Laman did not grow beards. One mannerism Lehi and his people brought from Jerusalem was the custom of wearing a beard. In those days, all the Elders who honored the priesthood wore a beard, like their Jewish brethren. It was a sign of respect. When the Lamanites rebelled against God, they were cursed and lost the privilege of bearing the priesthood. They also stopped wearing beards. Among various Hebrew characteristics found on artifacts in these parts are figures with beards."

"Ha!" Abiram said. "So Cortés was saved by the hair on his chinny-chin —"

Brother Joseba laughed. "More than that. You see, indelibly impressed upon the people's barbarous consciousness was a vestige of that wondrous peace and beauty which the Holy One had brought to earth. Without understanding why, their souls longed for the return of that golden age of love and harmony. Through the dark mist of depravity which clouded their minds, they still remembered the breathtaking sight of a glorious and ultimately mysterious Being appearing from heaven. Down through the generations, the people tried in their way to describe that unforgettable experience. The ascension of the Pale Bearded God was like the flight of the quetzal bird. They compared the appearance of the Holy Being in burning white light to the fiery serpent of bronze which Moses raised up in the wilderness."

"That human sacrifice is disgusting," Abiram said. "I'm glad Cortés conquered them."

"So the people believed Cortés was the returned Redeemer," Ben observed. "That's why he conquered them so easily."

"It is a supreme irony that perhaps only the sovereign Lord of Life could fully appreciate," Brother Joseba said. "It was also a fulfillment of prophecy. And a type."

"A foreshadowing?"

"Yes. A type of modern antichrists who deceive the people. In fact, this entire history of the remnant of Joseph is a foreshadowing of our day. Pay close attention to what I have told you, my sons — even ponder it deeply — for you will see that the story of the remnant holds prophetic parallels to these last days before the second coming of Christ."

Finally Brother Joseba and the boys came to Parliamentary Square. "At least here we have freedom to worship God as we choose!" Ben said.

Brother Joseba sighed. "Yes, our faith is growing here. But every man walks after the image of his own god. We don't lack for religions in this land. Here in the square you will find the many idols of man, some with their own priests, even others with their own savior."

At the westernmost point in the plaza, classic architecture of old government buildings remained, almost apologetic reminders of glories past. Ben walked gingerly over crumbling steps, inspected bullet-pitted Greek columns, and stooped to pull a weed which had forced its way into sunlight through a crack in the sidewalk.

Parliament's sagging posture was dwarfed by a neighboring building whose outline shot into the clouds. An acre of white-washed cement blocks bore Roman letters as big as trees: "Cumorah Times: Clarion Voice of World Opinion".

"The people's building looks pathetic next to that one," Abiram said.

"The Times is financed by that religion over there." Brother Joseba pointed to a massive corporate office building attached to a towering bank.

"It does not look like a church," Ben said.

"They do not call themselves a church, but their treasure is their god."

"I understand," Ben said slowly. "So what do they worship in this great spacious building before us?"

"Graven images."

Abiram gaped at the giant structure, looking for a golden calf.

"Those who seek power over the flesh have become popular in the eyes of the world and are heroes of the electronic screens. Their images are transmitted through the universe by a satellite and projected on a device called television," Brother Joseba said. "This god gains money from millions of people who bow at its feet for hours every day, seeking lusts of the flesh and things of the world. According to the prophet of whom Moses spoke, the time will come when these gods will be brought low in the dust."

The boys enjoyed their ice cream, and then the old station wagon limped home by way of the seashore. Ben pointed to a distant spherical structure rising from a forest of multi-colored flags.

"That one sits upon the many waters which divide West from East," Brother Joseba explained. "It is over the border in Zarahemla."

"Is it a religion, too?"

"It is the mother of idolatry. They believe in, and practice, human sacrifice."

Again, the boys gasped. "Today?"

"Too many people on the earth, these idolaters say. Members of their religion meet every year to figure out how to kill off people to make more room on the planet for animals and trees. And for themselves. This is done by promoting slaughter of any humans who are too old, or sick, or too inconvenient, or have too many children, or are the wrong gender, or have the wrong parents, or the wrong environment, or the wrong beliefs, or born too soon, or born too late, or not born at all. Wars are also a very efficient way to reduce population."

"Who. . .who worships there, Brother Joseba?"

"Some politicians. Kings from many nations. The powerful, the elite, and lovers of war. Merchants of the earth who deceive nations by their sorceries. Their merchandise is gold, and silver, and precious stones. Wheat, and beasts. Chariots, and slaves, and souls of men."

"The merchants do not love liberty?"

"Perhaps, but they love money more. But you are right, Benjamin. This is a free country, and although the press does not like it, I am free to express my opinions. At least I am better off than Abinadi, a prophet of an earlier era. He dared to speak against a political leader, and he was burned at the stake."

Ben brooded on the way home. Even free people sometimes chose the dark side.

And he was afraid.

The Book Of
Oliver

THE BOOK OF OLIVER

1

Isles of the Caribbean
May

F ragrant breezes, a tranquil sea, a starry, tropical sky ——— all
an unlikely setting for works of darkness.   Jack Mecha
pulled his van up next to the ditch and turned off his parking
lights. He scanned trees and highway while his partner
dumped the body into a pit already heaped with other corpses bagged
in plastic. Headlight beams appeared at the bend ahead.

"Hurry up!" Mecha whispered.   After the passenger door
slammed, Mecha settled back in his seat. "I can drive this route with
my eyes closed. And by noon tomorrow we'll be a few clams richer."
Mecha kept his headlights doused and rolled away into blackness.

Just before noon Orton Beck left a side door of the
International Banking Complex (IBC), Caribbean Branch building.
That old pickle-face, who ran the operation's finances, was the
meanest bugger this side of the Atlantic, but when it came to
laundering money, he was a wizard.

From a street vender Beck purchased a tasteless sandwich, gulped some, and crossed the parkway to Golden Triangle Casino. He stuffed the other half of his food into his mouth and wiped greasy hands on ample white trousers. He nodded to two men seated at a side table and cut a direct path through game tables to a back-room office.

Beck closed the door, locked it, and faced Mecha.

"One more needle-snatcher is put away," Mecha said.

Beck belched.

Mecha turned slightly away from the stench.

"Proof?"

Mecha tossed an ID onto the desk.

Beck recognized the statistics of a drug enforcement agent.

"Nice work, gents. But this is just one of the stupid ones. You still didn't find Jaime Canosa, eh?" With his silken sleeve, Beck dabbed mustard off his satchel. He extracted two fat stacks of currency and handed them to Mecha and his companion.

"You'll have to up the ante, Beck," said Mecha. "Canosa is well known in the whole land of Cumorah. It'd be like an assassination."

"Shall I tell the boss you can't deliver? Maybe I should tell Immigration Control? Vladimir pays you to run the band here, not give me excuses. You punks are getting too expensive. Ha! There are plenty more where you came from!"

The two men swore vehemently and left the casino.

Muttering to himself, Beck rifled through the victim's personal effects, pocketing what he wanted and discarding the rest. One had to know how to deal with these thugs, or they wouldn't get anything done. Then there would be hell to pay with the boss.

2

"Hurry up, son! This Banberg Conference is a very important meeting. These are the richest men in the world. They buy armies, and navies, kings, and whole nations!"

Oliver David Beck scrambled alongside his father into a tall building with tinted windows. He followed his father up carpeted stairs and entered a long room with a big table and big dark pictures of stuffy old men.

"Don't talk!" His father whispered as he leaned down to his ten-year-old son. "Just listen and learn. You will be doing business with these men some day."

Oliver's little nose wrinkled at the garlic and whiskey on his father's breath.

Oliver David Beck was already bored. He wanted to play soccer. He drew soccer heroes on a notebook brought from home.

Papa would ask him who was at this meeting. How would he ever remember their names? He decided to sketch them. The tall skinny one who seemed to be in charge —— Banberg. His eyes bulged, his mouth was square and toothy, like the grill of a '53 Buick. Buick Banberg.

That fat smiling man who was talking. Kept talking about peace. Looked friendly, like a teddy bear. What was his name? Der Mukluk or mukk-something. Oliver drew a teddy bear wearing mukluks.

Then there was the one they called King Man, or something like that. Many people seemed to bow to him, like you would a king. But under that pile of black hair he had a narrow, pointed face, with small, beady eyes — like a rat. A large rat with a king's crown on its head.

That bald man who crashed down on a seat by the bar. His name was Cornelius. What a name. Corny's face was red, with bloodshot eyes. Like Papa when he was drunk. He jerked when he moved. There. Strings on Corny, like a puppet at a show in the park.

The men were still arguing. . .

Oliver yawned.

3

Finally the smiling man turned to the others. "What do you think, gentlemen? We must support a man for Chief Judge. Solano keeps railing against our campaign donations. He is trying to discredit my generosity. Can I help it if I have friends in Tartarus who are laying their money on Cabrios? Solano can't be bought. So, then, Solano is out. Cabrios, on the other hand, is too radical. "

"We already own Botina. He is the safe choice."

"Then that is settled."

Oliver watched his papa stand up to speak, spreading a large map out on the conference table.

"The Caribbean connection is developing nicely," he said.

Oliver noticed his father's whiskey glass had left a round wet mark on the map, on the middle of Cumorah.

"Through Cumorah, Fomentio Cabrios is building a natural conduit into the most fabulous source of wealth in the entire market, namely Zarahemla. Our only obstacle to smooth operations at present is the man Canosa, but my men claim it is impossible to nab him."

Oliver looked up. *Canosa. I've heard that name before.*

". . .need someone to infiltrate the Canosa family," Papa was saying.

"That would be easy," King Man said.

"But you are so young!" Mukluk said.

"I can do anything you old geezers can do, only better," King Man said.

"You better have a code name, for all our sakes," Banberg mused. He flipped pages in a small book. "How about Raul. . . Raul Marcados."

"Consider it done," King Man said.

"Your first assignment, young man!" Mukluk said proudly.

"Let's get back to business," Buick-face Banberg said. "Speaking of profits, we have just cut a lucrative deal with Tartarus. Zarahemla will now lease one of her key harbors to Tartarus, so now her citizens will have more jobs. The Tartarus Empire will also have access to the anchor ports at the narrow neck of land!"

"Does this mean the order of Voltaire will have Zarahemla by the throat?" King Man asked. He was smiling.

Not a nice smile.

Everyone looked at King Man with a kind of awe. King Man was young, but the older men seemed to bow to him. Oliver stared at the King Man, seeing a rat attached to someone's throat. Oliver did not like the rat-faced King Man.

A soldier spoke next, waving a big cigar around. "I wouldn't put it that way, Arch," he said. "We should just get used to Tartarus as a mega economic power. It is simply smart business practice."

Oliver's father nodded, and his chins bounced to the rhythm of the words.

The boy felt faint from smoke in the room.

"Nothing like a nice little war. It is the most efficient way to accomplish our goals and still make a lot of money," the man with the cigar said, using very big words. "Cocaine traffic opens a path of invasion into Zarahemla by way of Cumorah, Cumeni, and Jershon," the soldier went on.

I remember Jershon. I've been there with Papa.

"I like your idea of a war," said Buick-face, "but who would be the enemy? We are already making good money shipping surplus military hardware to Tartarus."

"We don't want to look bad," Mukluk said. "If you insist on a war, then we must be clearly seen as the ones who brought peace to the world."

"War or no, we must show a profit," Buick-face said. "The Empire wants to pipe drugs from Cumeni into the teenagers of Zarahemla." He shrugged and looked around the table at everyone. "They have their reasons. I do know the Empire is a good trading partner, because of the broad tax base. World trade brings world peace. After all, this is our larger goal. When you have global armies to finance in order to keep the peace, you can't be quibbling about old-fashioned moral issues, you know. . . . ." Banberg stopped talking.

Oliver looked up. Buick-face was staring at him. The room grew quiet.

4

"Beck! You know the rules. No children are allowed here."

"Aw, Banberg. It's just a business meeting." Beck shot a glance at King Man. "After all, a certain financier from the land northward (I won't mention any names) had the impudence to send his son to represent him. This son of You-know-who is just a kid, too. And to boot, he's an illegitimate —" His words trailed off with a derogatory term.

"I believe 'love child' is the correct term these days," Banberg interjected mildly. "Really, Beck. We will not have you insulting anyone here."

Oliver stared at the Buick-faced man. Banberg began to scold, like Mama sometimes did.

"If you had any sense, Beck, you would certainly show more respect. This boy's father is worth trillions," Banberg continued.

"Doesn't that mean anything to you? He can call his kid Raul Marcados, or Arch Kingerman, or the Prince of Egypt, or anything he pleases, for all I care. When you have that kind of money, you can do anything you want. But *you* better watch what you say."

Oliver did not understand why Buick-face was scolding Papa.

"Isn't that right, Mr. Kingerman?" Banberg finished scolding.

"I don't know what this has to do with anything. It's stupid," King Man said. "And I want Cabrios for Chief Judge. Things are moving too slow under Botina."

Oliver did not understand what King Man was talking about, but it looked as if he was pouting. Oliver had never seen a grownup pout. Mama would say he was acting spoiled.

"I just didn't want you to be offended, my boy." Banberg was talking fast, and his face was red, like he was embarrassed.

"Well, you're being stupid. And you shut up, Beck," King Man said.

How rude. Oliver felt angry. *Mama would never let me talk that way to Papa.* But Papa didn't say anything. No one scolded King Man for being so rude. Everyone just bowed to King Man anyway. Mama called it kowtowing.

But Oliver did not believe King Man was really a king. He was just mean.

Beck peered at his son's cartoons, and he wiped sweat from his forehead.

But Mukluk laughed aloud. "Relax, Banberg! Why, the boy's an artist! Take a look at these caricatures!"

Oliver felt rat-face and Buick-face looking over his shoulder. They were not laughing.

"Uh, not too complimentary, perhaps," Beck said.

Mukluk put a chubby hand gently on Oliver's shoulder. "Aw, no harm done. You take yourself much too seriously, Banberg."

Oliver liked the jolly Mukluk man.

"All the same, the child makes me nervous," Buick-face said. "Destroy that material at once and send the boy out!"

Beck pressed some bills into Oliver's hand. "Here, kid. Go to the casino across the parkway. Get somethin' to eat, and play some games if you like. Tell Maude I sent you. Now beat it!"

58

The Book Of
Canosa

*"The Liahona is a shadow or type
of the word of Christ"*

THE BOOK OF CANOSA

1

June, 2069

Over his third cup of hot chocolate, Jaime Canosa glanced across the breakfast table at Aurelia. She was so much a part of his mind and heart. What should he decide?

"Well, Jaime, are you going to do it? The position Solano offered you if he's elected Chief Judge, I mean."

There, it was out. Thank you, dear Aurelia. "You know what it would mean. A threat to our peace and safety."

"What's to guarantee peace and safety if you don't? Zephan can run the company without you, and young Abiram is a tremendous help. You have worked at drug enforcement for years now, and you are effective. The citizens want and need it, they trust you, and are willing to pay you for it. Everyone wants safe homes and streets as much as I do. "

He nodded. "You're right, as usual. I will do my duty, but I almost take consolation in evidence that Solano has little chance of being elected. We will be making a statement for moral uprightness. Botina, scoundrel that he is, has at least left alone people of faith. But Cabrios has not disguised his hatred of God and traditional families."

"Do you think he's part of that cabal promoting the order of Voltaire?"

"He denies it," Jaime said. "My sources say Cabrios plans to take over the entire western hemisphere with military power. Botina is more subtle and less violent with his methods. Still, with his Western Economic League, he is playing into the hands of other global political combinations linked with Voltairism. As the incumbent, he has another advantage."

Aurelia groaned. "Zephan and Sarita Benamoz, with four soldier-age sons, have much to lose if Cabrios wins this election." She tightened her lips and lifted her chin. "It's settled, then. What happens next?"

"Zephan has arranged a forum at the Yeshurun Academy tonight, where Solano is to speak. It's a good beginning."

2

Solano arrived at the Yeshurun Academy in the afternoon for a complimentary tour of the school. Dotting the enormous campus were large alabaster buildings, nestled on startling green lawns and among towering ceiba, cypress, and palm trees. Here and there a tall modern building sprang above red tile roofs to pierce a fleeting cloud. But far more fascinating to Solano than exquisite architecture were the students themselves. As he watched them, he sensed something special he could not quite identify. He felt an air of concentrated purity; these were a beautiful and delightsome people. But the most remarkable feature was found in their eyes: a look of peace that was other-worldly.

His guide was a nymph-like, blue-eyed redhead named Alison Russell, who had that same look. Was it a certain wisdom unknown to the world at large, or was it simple naivete? After all, these students were quite sheltered here: iron-clad curfew, no co-ed dormitories or rest rooms, entrance requirements which were incredibly high, and a record of academic standards and achievements which were the envy of the world.

Alison took him to the fine arts building where, after two hours of pure awe, he purchased several Friberg reproductions for his private gallery before he could finally tear himself away.

The next point on the tour was a lookout on the mountain. In a vast open expanse in the valley below, students over the years had placed white-washed rocks to create a massive figure-drawing of a quetzal bird. It was so immense that it was best seen from a summit. The peak itself, mirrored in windows of a tall modern building, created a dazzling effect. Solano stopped to gaze at his surroundings and take a few photos.

A young man, probably in his early twenties, trotted up to them. He was skinny, and his face had an unhealthy pallor. "Sorry I'm late."

"I'm not." Alison's innocence had a blunt edge. "Mr. Solano, meet Strobe Fenley. He is our political officer," she added, her lips making a wry twist that did not quite pass for a smile.

"Only those who are guilty, as your actions demonstrate, are as defensive as you are! " Fenley said to Alison.

"Guilty of what?" Solano asked.

"Discrimination. Fraud. Contempt. Hate." Fenley clipped out his words like a ticket machine. "Could be anything. I am a representative of the Anti-Hate Committee, and I am here to ensure your freedom of speech."

Solano smiled. "A little young to be a bureaucrat, aren't you?"

"Let there be no mistake, error, or misconception. Administrators are a very important and necessary part of society," Fenley replied. "I have a degree in law and I aim to see the law is enforced down to every last word, letter, and comma, *period*."

"That should be easy," Alison snapped. "The list of correct words is so short, even a beetle-brain like you can keep track of it."

"I take offense at that remark. How dare you insult the quality of my brain?" Fenley checked his watch. "Only one minute past and you are already using hate-words, pressure, prejudice, and bias."

"Does your jurisdiction extend to this school?" Solano asked.

"A school to which Fenley was denied admittance because of poor academic performance," Alison said. "The only reason he is here is by government decree."

"I take offense at that remark. How dare you question my intelligence? Your people discriminated against me because I don't believe in your old scriptures, commandments, doctrines, and prophets," Fenley protested.

"That's because God's prophets always say, 'If you don't work, you don't eat!'" she said.

Solano suppressed a smile.

Fenley scribbled in a notebook. "You are proselyting! It is against the law for you to proselyte, persuade, imply, or talk about your religious prophets with a public official."

"This is a private school," Solano said. "I think you are a little out of line."

"National law transcends privacy, both individual and group privacy. Especially when a public official is in danger of being influenced by a private party, or individual, or group of two or more, which I can see is already beginning to happen."

"Good grief!" Alison said. "I know it is hard for you to understand, but give it a try. Mr. Solano can make up his own mind, Fenley. Do you get that?" She turned her back on him and directed her words to her guest. "Now, Mr. Solano, if Fenley can refrain from interfering, we will take a short walk up to the lookout on the mountain, and you can take some photos of the valley."

The remaining tour passed pleasantly, despite devastating insults exchanged by the two young people. Alison Russell was definitely not naive, Solano decided with amusement. She was also a law student, and the fiery redness of her hair seemed to signal her brilliance of mind. At sixteen, she was youngest in the school, but she invariably outwitted Fenley.

Uncomfortable under the stage lights, Anastasio Solano shifted in his metal folding chair. He straightened his back and braced himself for the meeting which lay ahead. Arranging a pleasant expression on his face, he looked out over the growing crowd. A nearby flag bore the blue and white school emblem: a quetzal bird in flight, its wings superimposed over the wing-shaped western hemisphere. The motto was "Truth abides forever." All at once Solano's nervousness left him. Impressions from his afternoon campus tour remained with him. Trustees of this academy were the house of Yeshurun, a peculiar people for sure — a people who from the day of their ancient genesis had traversed a wilderness of time with honesty for a compass. This school had steadfastly refused state grants and had forbidden its students to depend on grants. Everyone in attendance was here due to support from himself, his family, or school employment, in that order. This was a fiercely independent institution, reflecting the standards of its people, and true to the rugged heritage of Cumorah.

At least the large auditorium was nearly filled to capacity with people who evidently wanted to hear him.

Many, but perhaps not all. A small contingent of students filed in — no, they were not students of this academy, for their slovenly appearance was in stark violation of the strict Yeshurun dress code. The men wore clothing so shabby it looked like it had been retrieved from the rag hamper — dirty, used rags. Their trousers had great gashes in the knees, and hung precariously on their hips as if to drop to the ankles at any moment. Perhaps these people were too poor to afford anything else. Perhaps Botina's policies had taken their jobs. One man, his face mostly hidden in a conspicuous bush of whiskers and a matted, leonine mane, appeared to be their leader. The young women with them had long, straight, dull hair, and their eyes were outlined with hard, dark paint. The girls wore faded, baggy shirts in nauseating hues which could only be compared to dried monkey vomit splattered with paint. It seemed strange for young women, who normally made great effort to appear attractive. There was no other word for it but ugly, and these women seemed almost proud of it. Yet these people must be grossly underprivileged. Their skirts fit like snake skin, even looked like snake skin, and were so short, anyone could see their underwear. Solano looked away quickly, his face burning. What were those men doing here with women of the streets? These girls, though but children, looked unusually wanton, even alien. Solano had heard of such looseness in the Land of Goyim. Surely these children had left mothers and fathers, and innocence, far behind. Who had brought them here? Hecklers, perhaps?

"Canosa!" he whispered. "Who are they?"

"Cabrios supporters from the Land of Goyim. Can you believe the goyim pay top dollar for those rags? It is the fashion where they come from . . . Solano, you've been announced. You're on."

Solano welcomed his listeners, and then he said, "I will speak sparingly, for every man running for office talks excessively and says nothing. My record speaks for itself. You all know where I stand. My beliefs are no secret, and I stand by them. I promise you nothing. In fact I will do nothing for you that you can do for yourself. Besides limited functions of government which are truly legitimate, I pledge only to stay out of your way."

The audience nodded agreement.

65

His voice dropped to a low pitch, and the vast room was saturated with silence. "William Blackstone said, 'We look forward to a time when the power of love will replace the love of power.'"

Scattered chuckles broke the tension. "It is Cumorah tradition to trust no man, including myself, to rule over you. Choose only honest, wise, and good men who honor God more than themselves. Then be vigilant. That is all. Thank you. "

After the enthusiastic applause died down, questions began.

"What would you do in case of a crisis?" came the first question.

"First of all I would pray to God."

The Big Beard group laughed raucously, and continued their laughter for several minutes until the majority stared them into silence.

"Then I would stick to Cumorah law, which is based on the Ten Commandments," Solano continued with quiet dignity. "I will remain answerable to Parliament, the legislative body chosen by the people."

"What will you do for those who depend on the community, village, and neighbors to survive? You have to do something!" came a plaintive voice out of the darkness.

"Ask your father to help you," Solano replied. "The taxpayers are not your family, young man."

"I have no other family. Government largesse, charity, and benevolence are all I have to turn to."

"Let me ask you something . . . " Solano said. "Oh, hello, Strobe Fenley. I see you decided to join us. Tell me, Fenley, how did you get here?"

"I drove an automobile skillfully and deftly."

"How did you enter this building?"

"I walked briskly, healthfully, and effectively."

"Can you read?"

"Yes, very well. My comprehension is excellent."

"Do you have a television?"

"Of course. Hey, what is this, anyway?"

"Just getting to know you, Fenley. You have demonstrated to me that you can see, hear, walk, and even drive. You can read, and have all the capabilities you need to get a job. I know people who are much worse off than you are — deaf, paralyzed, even blind — who earn a living for themselves, or maybe are helped by their churches. I have seen handicapped people do everything from get college degrees to coach soccer teams. They don't come whining to the chief judge. It all depends on your attitude. The churches handle the welfare of the poor more effectively, with much less red tape than the government."

"That is discrimination. I do not attend a church."

"Cabrios' plan is much more efficient than churches," Big Beard spoke up. "The churches require people to work for their food and pay for their schooling, and someone always gets left out. Under Cabrios, everyone will be required by law to support the needy, give community service, and have free schools. That way, those outside the church are provided for."

Solano looked intently at Big Beard. "Do you find people of faith using government to take goods and services from you without paying for it?"

"Hey! I guess I hadn't thought of it that way," Fenley said. "But if national government does not provide for the needy, who will?"

Solano pressed his point. "My province is leading the way in reforming the poverty programs. We have outreach groups who work personally with the poor to help them enhance their skills and improve their employment. Volunteers are teaching them how to get out of debt. Even many of the more wealthy people are not debt-free. Church teachings of individual responsibility and spiritual priorities have done much to decrease illegitimacy. Every quarter, governors meet in my hometown as an inter-Province council to help each other. Our plan includes tax-reduction. Botina's excessive taxes sap our incentive to help voluntary humanitarian groups."

"Oh."

"A lawyer humble enough to concede a point?" Solano said. "Remarkable. Perhaps I misjudged you, *joven.*"

"Likewise," Fenley said affably. "But you talk about church involvement. I personally don't believe in God."

"Church involvement is strictly voluntary. Would you, in the name of government, force others to do for you what you refuse to do for yourself, just because you don't agree with them? Isn't your Anti-Hate Committee supposed to arbitrate disagreements?"

"You're right."

"The best way to combat both hate and poverty," Solano said, "is with the Ten Commandments and the Golden Rule."

"That is against our guidelines," Fenley said. "The Anti-Hate Committee has other ways of achieving the same objective and keep God out of it."

Solano shrugged. "Suit yourself. But when you are totally on your own, Fenley, that is when you will need most to pray." He smiled. "Especially if you are a lawyer."

He turned to Big Beard. "As for Cabrios, who does he think he is? A light unto the world? His program is the politics of envy and grinding in the faces of the poor. It is called legalized plunder, and I refuse to be a part of it. Have we learned nothing from history? Only a few decades ago, the Land of Goyim disintegrated because of such immoral policies."

"You insult the Land of Goyim because it is a Gentile nation!" Big Beard shouted.

"Why do you always bring up the question of race? You miss the point entirely. In Cumeni, which you favor so highly, judges and lawyers have exploited racism to gain millions in taxes, then turn it to their own corrupt purposes. Some people are puffed up with pride, a desire to be different, an obsession for public notice, and are forever coveting what others have earned. A few people demand recognition and rights, but don't even take the opportunity to earn what they want. The rest of us simply want to be left alone to live our lives in peace. We care not one jot nor tittle what race you are, as long as you do your share. But no, some people must do things their own way, and force everyone else to do things their way also, even if it is wrong. Cumorah law protects life, liberty, and property. This system tolerates every race and creed. It is our common language and history, not a specific religion or race, which binds us together as a nation."

"Ha! You sound just like all those reactionary friars, monks, and religious fanatics," Big Beard tried to shout down the loud cheers from the audience. "No one else would ever vote for you."

"Yes, sir. In this country, even religious people have the right to vote. And people have to vote for someone, don't they?"

Laughter.

"Are you running for Chief Judge, or preacher?"

"Cumorah has roots in the law and God's prophets. I intend to respect those roots. That is where I stand, but no one is compelling you to vote for me."

"But you seem to be against most everything. Are you for anything?"

From his position, Solano could see clearly the faces of Big Beard's group. He looked into each young girl's eyes, but he saw only nothingness. "Absolutely. I am for the principle of work. And

68

I believe a man should enjoy what he earns. I also believe Botina's busybody bureaucrats should work for a living and stop eating the bread of the taxpayers!"

This brought a standing ovation.

3

It was nearly midnight when Canosa stopped by his office at the Metalworks for some files needed in Solano's campaign. He longed for the hot meal he knew Aurelia had waiting for him and hoped it would take care of his crashing headache. His nerves were frazzled. He had second thoughts about his clandestine other job. With the executive position in Canosa Metalworks now safely in Zephan's capable hands, Jaime had become increasingly involved in investigating the illegal narcotics trade. Now he needed time to devote to the political campaign.

Canosa turned onto Gaviota Street and passed by other buildings already darkened. His office at the metals plant offered the low profile he needed.

Why had he chosen this stressful and demoralizing kind of work when it was so much easier to simply go into administrative work? Or perhaps the militia, where the enemy was forthright and visible, instead of these slippery drug cartels who were at once evasive and pervasive? No denying the answer to that. "Know your enemy" was drummed into his head at the military academy he attended as a youth. The real enemy was not an external military threat, but moral corruption from within, of which the drug market was most visible.

Canosa noted a van parked on the street in front of a neighboring building.

Strange. For security reasons a city ordinance required vehicles off the street after dark.

Canosa sat still in the dark, studying the building. There. A light flickered in his office window. A flashlight. No money was on the premises. The neighboring middle-class homes would be much more profitable. The intruder had to be looking for specific information instead of loot.

Canosa switched off the dome light so it would not come on automatically when he opened his door and quietly shut it. At his office, the screen door had been slashed, and the inside door was ajar. He did not have long to wait. When a figure crept from the door,

Canosa dove for the feet. The man pitched over Canosa's shoulder and hit his head on the step.

This one would be out cold for a while.

After police had picked up the burglar, Canosa took inventory. Except for the door, all else was untouched, but the files in his office were a mess.

A few days later he received a visit from Clarence Rook, Director of Cumorah Bureau of Investigation.

"Good job, Canosa!" Rook congratulated him. "What on earth did you do to this fellow? I'll wager nothing like that ever entered his head before." Rook chuckled. "Anyway, he revealed more in his delirium than he would have if awake. We have identified him as Jack Mecha, one of Cabrios' drug agents. He muttered a lot in Spanish. Something about 'the plague'. Probably a code name for a drug network."

Rook inspected Canosa's office. "Sir, do you realize Mr. Solano is in danger?"

Canosa turned. "Even now?"

"If he is elected, he will expose the Cabrios network."

4

"The onions must be weeded by hand," Mama had said, "because they are still young and tender. We don't want them to be discarded by mistake when you use a hoe. The east quarter of our vegetable garden you may hoe, but water it first, as that soil has much clay. You had better fertilize it. The south terrace must be irrigated today without fail. Try to get as much done as possible before school, so you can beat the heat."

Haman glared at a stubborn weed he had just broken off. Sure. She wanted him to get all this stupid work done before it got hot.

He felt fierce sunshine already.

Why did he have to do this? Why not Leb? Or better yet, that brat, Benjamin. Ben claimed he hurt his leg on the tractor, but he was lying so he could get out of his work. He was supposed to be doing this. Haman was too grown up for this. Mama spoiled Ben, and she treated her eldest son like a field worker. His own parents ——

treating him like a slave. Already it was hot. The rows were as long as a tennis court. He'd rather be playing tennis. Or swimming. Those old weeds kept breaking off. And they'd all be back next week. Well, he wouldn't do this again. He'd get out of it somehow.

He tried to brush the dirt off his hands, but moist soil clung to his skin.

I hate dirt. I hate onions. The smell makes me sick.

He pulled up two immature onion bulbs.

Now why couldn't weeds be as easy to pull as those bulbs? It wasn't fair!

I know what I'll do.

For every one of those weeds that broke off, he'd just pull out an onion.

The work went faster then. He managed to finish one row.

He couldn't wait till school was over, so he could go swimming . . .

"*Hermano!*"

It was Leb, who came racing through the garden, trampling everything in his path. Haman didn't care.

"Look who's coming," Leb said in a hushed voice.

Brother Joseba Bianco emerged from the fields, headed for the large Benamoz courtyard where he taught the Benamoz children and workers' families. This man must be much older even than Grandpa Canosa. He was there when the Benamoz family moved to Cumorah, and he seemed older than the land itself. He even looked like some pictures in history books, except he wore workers' overalls instead of ancient robes. He was so old. Haman looked down at Brother Joseba as the slight little man wiped his glasses and mopped his face with his arm. His bald head glistened with sweat. "Let's have some fun," Haman said. "Hey, Baldy! Where are you going?"

"Good morning, boys!" Brother Joseba said good-naturedly. "Didn't you know baldness is a sign of intelligence? Shows I use my brain a lot. Come with me to class and you'll become wiser."

"Not if all that thinking makes me bald like you!" Leb called.

Brother Joseba laughed.

"First one to plant a dirt clod on that shiny dome of his gets to go swimming," Haman said to his brother. He threw a glob of sticky soil, but missed.

Leb threw a stone, and didn't miss.

Brother Joseba cried out in pain. His head was bleeding. "That's going too far," he said.

The boys laughed.

"Hey," Leb said, "we better skip school today. He's mad."

"Nah," Haman replied. "What can he do? Let's see what he does. We're much bigger than he is. If he gets nasty, we can leave, and he won't be able to stop us."

The boys slipped into their seats, in back. Bianco stood by the blackboard, a bandage on his head. As usual, Ben was already at the front desk. He got good grades on all his papers, just because he was teacher's pet. And he was always asking questions, but it didn't get Brother Bianco to skip anything. It just seemed to make class longer.

"Brother Bianco?"

There he goes again.

"Question, Benjamin?"

"It is concerning an incident in the Bible in which dozens of children mocked the prophet Elisha, and he cursed them. Forty-two of them were brutally killed by she-bears shortly thereafter. I do not understand. It seems cruel."

Haman glanced in surprise at his young brother. Did Ben know what had just happened? Nah, it was just coincidence. Even so, Ben seemed to be siding with his brothers for a change. And Papa kept saying this Bianco was a prophet of God. This could get interesting.

"To the King James translators 'little children' meant *young* as compared to old. *Child* could also refer to a young man."

"So these were young men?"

"About the age of Haman and Leb."

Haman avoided Brother Bianco's look.

"In that era," he continued, "those boys would have been young men, considered old enough to be soldiers. It does not seem likely a mob of very small children would be roaming the woods unprotected by their parents. These young men were old enough to be responsible for what they were doing. With that age comes a tendency to enjoy daring adventures. Perhaps those youth thought it would be great sport to kill whelps of she-bears."

"Don't try this at home," Abiram said. Everyone laughed.

"You're right," Brother Bianco said. "Nothing is more fierce than a she-bear protecting her young. In this case, it is quite likely the whelps may have been injured or destroyed earlier, either by these youth or something else. So the bears were already intent on revenge."

"So this was just a coincidence?" Haman said. "Elisha had no way to tell those bears to do anything."

"You are partially correct, Haman. Elisha would do nothing unless it was the will of God. He could have commanded the beasts, but I do not think he did in this instance. He did pronounce a curse, but did not specify. It was God who provided the timing."

"I still think it was cruel," Haman said. "Those young men merely made fun of the old man because he was bald. Their words didn't hurt anybody. Why would God punish someone so violently just for words?"

"These were not empty words, Haman, but a manifestation of these young men's entire attitude. By their previous actions, the youth possibly had already shown a blatant disregard for life and for God's creations. They were old enough to understand that a prophet of God is worthy of respect, but chose to mock him. Someone in the mob probably started the mockery, and by his *words*, goaded his peers into joining him."

"Those young men would have been cursed anyway," Ben said, "even if the prophet Elisha had not pronounced a curse."

"Why?"

"Because anyone who reviles God's prophets without remorse ends up paying serious consequences."

"You mean, in the past. Those were old prophets in the Bible, and God did big, noisy things back then," Leb said. "It's not the same today. There are no prophets today."

"Why not?" Ben said. "We need a prophet, too."

Haman watched Brother Bianco closely. "That is impossible. No one around here is perfect enough to be a prophet."

"Only One was perfect," Brother Bianco said. "For example, Peter was only a man, and made mistakes, but after the Lord left mortality, Peter was a prophet and leader of the Lord's people. Moses, too, made mistakes. But through the atonement of Christ we can be made perfect. Nevertheless, remember this. We, the Lord's servants, are not perfect, but the doctrine which comes to you through us, directly from the mouth of the Lord, is perfect."

"We are the only people in modern times who claim to have a prophet," Leb complained. "For crying out loud, this is the twenty-first century. Only old Bible people had prophets. Why can't we be modern like everyone else? But no, we have to have senile old prophets and be the laughing stock of the world."

"Yeah," Haman said. "The rest of the world is getting along fine without prophets. Why do we have to have some old prophet telling us what to do?"

"They are not our prophets, Haman. They are the Lord's prophets," Brother Joseba said. "Earlier in this dispensation, a prophet held up all the written scriptures and said, 'There is the written word, concerning God's work from the beginning of the world almost to our day. I would rather have the living oracles than all the writing in the books.'"

"More important than the written word? How could he say that?"

"Don't misunderstand. The holy scriptures are to be reverenced, cherished, and studied daily. The words of the prophets are always consistent with scripture. But to us, the living prophet is more important than a dead prophet."

"Why?"

On the chalkboard, Brother Joseba made a drawing of a boat filled with people, on a river, headed for a great unseen waterfall. On the bank he drew a man waving his arms at them. "A prophet can see things that others can't, and his warnings can keep us from disaster. The living prophet is like Today's News Today. God's revelations to Adam did not instruct Noah how to build the ark. Therefore, the most important prophet is the one living in our day and age to whom the Lord is currently revealing His will for us."

"Why were prophets so unpopular?" Ben asked.

"People in ancient times did not have the Bible as we do today. They had only the prophets who were living at the time. Prophets are not just a crystal ball, you know. Future events, based on the past, are only revealed from time to time, for the welfare of the people. The rest of the time is spent in teaching people about eternal life."

"That sounds like fun."

"But for our people, idolatry and the ways of the world are much more fun." Brother Bianco pointed to the drawing. "You see, the life of a prophet is not as dramatic as this drawing. Our course on the river is determined by the many small and simple things we do ——— the unreported events which require us to make moral decisions every day. This is why we don't see that waterfall, which is really the consequence of disobedience."

"Still," Haman argued. "I can think for myself. I don't need a prophet telling me what to do."

"If you choose to get on a boat or an airplane, and you depend on the pilot to guide the ship safely to its destination, does that mean you are no longer free to think for yourself?"

"No."

"You still can make choices. You can follow the pilot's guidelines and arrive safely, or you can jump off the ship and try to get there on your own.

"The prophet is only a mouthpiece for God, who tells us the truth. Let's face it," Brother Joseba continued. "The truth is not always fun to hear. So the trouble is, people see the prophet is a man just like any other man, and they forget his words are from God."

"So when people didn't like what the prophets said, they would kill the prophets," Ben observed.

"Like shooting the messenger?" Abiram said.

"You might say that. Babylon, or the world, is not known to be kind in her treatment of the prophets, but people without knowledge are not accountable like we are. God has given us a prophet to guide us, and that is what makes us different as a people. And a prophet is not without honor except in his own country. Nations who despise and kill God's prophets will perish."

"Oh. Then as long as the nation is doing what it is supposed to do, it does not matter what I do," Haman said.

"This ancient story of Elisha was preserved all these years for a reason," Brother Joseba said. "What was true then is true today. Anyone who reviles a prophet of God imperils his soul. Thus saith the Lord:

What I the Lord have spoken, I have spoken, and I excuse not myself; and though the heavens and the earth pass away, my word shall not pass away, but shall all be fulfilled, whether by mine own voice or by the voice of my servants, it is the same."

The old man gave Haman an enigmatic look, and the young man turned away.

"I want to finish one thing in Isaiah before we go on to mathematics today," Brother Bianco said.

Maybe Bianco forgot about the incident. It was no big deal, anyway. Haman let his mind wander. "Great are the words of Isaiah!" Bianco kept saying. Yeah. One great, intolerable bore. And everyone had to read hundreds of pages, and write a three-page essay every week. The topic was always hard. Something from the textbook or the newspaper. It was a lot of work. It was too hard. Once when Haman had asked Bianco how to answer an essay question, Bianco had simply said, "You have to think, Haman." That was all he said. And that was only history. Math was impossible, and science was just a bunch of difficult projects. Boring. Boring!

Haman squirmed and defaced his book with a pen. Fifteen pages to read! Shakespeare didn't make any sense. How could Mama love it so much? And Ben over there, reading it as if he actually understood it, or even liked it! Disgusting.

Haman listened to the surf instead.

Leb is bored, too. Don't look at him. He'll talk, and get you into trouble. Then we'll have to stay after school.

At last school was over. Sweltering hot. That water would feel great.

Haman suddenly felt Bianco's hand heavy on his shoulder.

"Wait here," he said. "Your mother will take you and your brother to the nursing home to help with the patients every afternoon this week. I hope you will learn more respect and compassion for those who are older and more infirm than you are."

Haman smirked. "You act as if we committed a crime. It was just an accident."

"You must take responsibility for your actions. Then when you get back, Haman," Brother Bianco continued, "you will finish what you started in the garden. Then get the water started on the south terrace."

The youth paused. The weed and onion count were about even. He would skip that. But he would have to drag those irrigation pipes over to the south terrace, and it would already be late. He would miss swimming. His thoughts darkened. Why did the old man have to go and tell Mama? She would make life miserable for him.

"Your father is working long hours these days, and your mother does a man's share, despite her handicap," Bianco said.

Terrific. The old codger was pulling the sympathy trick. Haman scowled. "And why not? They're my parents. They owe it to me." There. That would shock the old geezer.

Brother Bianco's frown dissolved into a smile. "Then I will go with you, and we can get it done quickly."

Bianco always smiled. And that kindness of his, even when he was down and someone was kicking him. Didn't he ever get hopping mad? It was sickening. And he had been staring through everyone all day, especially Haman and Leb. Now he was demanding overtime. "Never mind," Haman said sullenly. "I'll take care of it."

"Very well, *joven.* Remember, work and service are gifts from God. When you are at the nursing home, think of repentance. It is also a gift."

5

Haman cast a baleful glance toward the descending sun and yanked out the last obstinate weeds. Mama had made him come out here, and she had watched him like a hawk at the nursing home. He and Leb only saw many old, senile people. Some of them couldn't even walk or talk. Those people were used up and good for nothing. Of what use were they to anyone, except to waste people's time and money, and eat everybody else's food? The world would be better off without them.

And what did all this have to do with him? He was just having some fun. These grownups took everything so seriously and were always ordering him around, as if he had to obey, like some little kid. Like Ben. Well, he would show Mama. He would leave the terrace for tomorrow. This just wasn't fair.

"*¡Hola, chico!*"

Haman looked up, startled.

A boy, maybe nineteen or twenty, in old but clean clothes and sandals, appeared quickly from the grove. "Hot, isn't it?" the boy said, smiling. His eyes were small and set close together, always moving. He handed Haman a bottle of soda.

Haman's eyes shone. Mama never bought that stuff. She said it was a waste of money. "Where did you come from?"

The boy nodded toward the road. "I've got my own wheels over there."

"Aw, you're lucky. I wish I had a car."

"What's your name, *chico?*"

"Haman Benamoz. And you?"

"Raul Marcados. I live in the village."

Haman stuck out his hand. "Pleased to meet you."

Raul grinned. "My, we talk pretty. Your father must be rich. You go to some fancy school?"

Haman wrinkled his nose. "Wish I could. Last year we moved out here to the plantation, because Papa said it was quieter. Trouble is, we are tutored at home with some farmers' children because we are too far from the city schools. I miss the city, and Grandpa Canosa's big house. I am bored here in the country."

Raul's narrow eyes got narrower. "Did you say Canosa?"

"Yes. My father's parents died and Grandpa Canosa unofficially adopted him. Grandpa is pretty nice. He always brings us chocolates. I think he's an important man in town, too." Haman drained his pop bottle with a manly flourish.

"Yes, I know." Raul opened a can of beer for Haman and took a long draft on his own. "This heat sure makes me thirsty."

The can was cold to Haman's touch. He held it up and sniffed it, and cool droplets of evaporation trickled down his arm. He had never even held a can of beer before, and least of all, tasted any. A song of his childhood sprang unwelcome to his mind:

That the children may live long,
And be beautiful and strong,
Tea and coffee and tobacco they despise,
Drink no liquor and they eat
But a very little meat;
They are seeking to be great and good and wise.

Haman scowled. He was not a child anymore. The time had come to prove it to himself. But Mama would be furious if she found out, and she had a way of discovering everything . . .

"What's the matter?" Raul asked. "Don't you like that brand?"

"No! I mean yes. It's fine. It's just that I, uh . . . "

"You mean, you've never had beer before?"

Haman's face burned with embarrassment. "It's against my religion!" he blurted out. His mortification intensified.

Raul gave a short laugh. "How amusing! It's quite funny, actually. I've never heard of anything so *weird*—" He stopped. "I'm sorry, *amigo.* I didn't mean to hurt your feelings. Look, why don't you just take a little sip? That can't hurt anything. Trust me."

"My parents are very strict. If they ever found out . . . "

"Your parents don't have to know, do they?"

"Of course not." Haman felt better. Raul wasn't laughing at him after all. He was showing sympathy, and kindness, like a good friend. He was right. What harm was there in trying one little sip?

Those old rules made no sense, anyway. Mama and Papa were no fun . . .

Raul was watching him.

Haman took a sip. It wasn't so bad. In fact, it tasted rather good. It was cold and warm at the same time . . . *mellow.* He took another swallow. Not as sweet as root beer. "Hey! That's it!" he said aloud. "I'm drinking root beer without the root!" Haman laughed. It was fun.

They talked for a while. Raul politely asked about Haman's family. Haman was too ashamed to talk about his parents. He talked a lot about Grandpa Canosa.

After a time, Raul glanced at the house many yards away, nestled in the shade of avocado trees. "Haman, I have to go now. Let's meet here again tomorrow afternoon."

"I would like that. Here, take this with you. If my father found this, you and I would be — " He crushed his empty can and handed it to Raul.

Raul grabbed the boy's arm and looked directly into his eyes. "Don't tell anyone about our meetings," he whispered.

Haman felt his neck tingle. "Hey! Do you really think I would tell anybody what I did today?"

Together they laughed.

He watched Raul slip through the trees and drive away.

6

Canosa Metalworks was working around the clock now, filling huge orders of strong sheet metal and steel for armored vehicles for the nation of Zarahemla, an ally. Despite long work hours, Zephan was usually home for dinner with the family.

But Haman was late for dinner, again.

"You missed the blessing on the food," Zephan said to him.

Papa had a strange habit of praying over everything. Every time anyone sat down to the table, even for a snack or dessert separate from the meal, Papa would bow his head and say thanks to the air. What difference would it make to skip one prayer, more or less? "I don't care," Haman mumbled.

With his recuperating leg resting on a stool, Ben took up a whole side of the table. As he reached for the bowl of piping hot *polenta* Leb snatched it from his grasp.

"Why doesn't he eat separately from us, Mama, so he doesn't hog all the space, and especially the food?"

Sarita ignored his question, poured a glass of milk and passed it to Zephan. "At least he's safe. He'll soon be back to normal."

"He'd better be," Haman said.

"We could sure use your help at the shop right now, Haman," Zephan said.

"Papa, how many times do I have to tell you? I will not work there. I don't like that kind of work."

"How about some bookkeeping?"

"I hate math. I'm going to get a real job."

No use discussing what a "real job" was. No way to reason with Haman. "Then," Zephan said, "I need someone to help clean out the stables. If I don't, Brother Joseba will do it. Brother Joseba must be as old as Hill Cumorah, but he never stops working. He refuses to accept pay for teaching the children, and he already earns his keep with all the other work he does. How about it, Haman?"

Haman considered. He was getting paid a modest sum for doing Ben's work, and it gave him a chance to get away with Raul. Besides, Ben's work was already beneath him. The stable was unthinkable. "Nah. I have plenty to do with all Ben's work. Leb can do it."

Leb's mouth took an exaggerated downturn.

"Your lips look like an ear," Abiram said.

"Ha! That'd be good," Haman said, "the day Leb listens as much as he talks."

"At least I make sense when I talk," Leb retorted. "Every time you open your mouth we get a clodstorm of the very things I have to clean from the stable tomorrow, only piled higher and deeper —"

"Leb!" Sarita glared at her son.

"Thanks for your help, Haman," Ben said quietly.

"Never mind, *tonto*. Just hurry up and get well. I won't do this much longer. Then I'll expect you to return the favor."

7

"Somebody smart like you has more important things to do than gardening." Haman remembered Raul's words as he moved along on his knees picking green bush beans. So many to pick. Mama would be angry when she found out how big he had let them grow.

A whistle came from the direction of a grove by the south terrace. No point in picking beans now. They were too big, anyway. Haman took off at a run.

"Mm." Haman savored the last of a chocolate bar and licked his fingers. "How can you buy all this, Raul?"

"I don't buy it."

Haman's eyebrows shot up.

The older boy leaned over and whispered, "Can you keep a secret?"

"Of course!"

"Come with me."

Without hesitation, Haman climbed into Raul's jeep. It was fun to be with Raul; it made him feel important.

Raul parked his jeep in the garage of a small, rather dingy house in the village. He took two cans of beer out of the refrigerator and tossed one to Haman. "Here. Compliments of Cercado Mercantile."

Haman had graduated from soda to beer and was proud of it. He had not tried hard liquor yet. Raul said it must be done gradually, so he could learn how to hold his liquor. Raul never got drunk. Raul was always in control.

Raul took a bottle of whiskey off a shelf, then walked out to a porch and sat on the step.

The older boy pulled a package of cigarettes and several candy bars from inside his shirt. "Look, Haman. I can't spend so much time with you anymore."

Haman said nothing, but drained his can of beer.

Raul took a long pull on a cigarette and tapped the ashes into a geranium pot beside him.

Haman looked with longing at that cigarette. He couldn't wait to try one. Raul was so smart, and he made Haman feel grown up. Haman was tired of the way his parents treated him like a baby. He wasn't allowed to do anything. Well, he was going to put all that behind him.

"You look like you're going to cry. Hey, don't worry. I told you the beer was free. You can get it just like I do. Merchants, especially at Cercado's, have so much money they don't notice if you pay or not."

"You don't. . .pay for it?"

Raul swung his head, lifting thick black hair from his brow. "I take what belongs to me. My father says everything belongs to the people."

"What is your father's name?"

Raul laughed. "That is classified, because my father never married my mother. But I handle the accounts of Fomentio Cabrios, who works for my father."

Haman considered that for a moment. "Well, if Cabrios works for your father, then he must not be the same thieving, lowdown crook some people talk about."

Raul turned, his eyes two points of anger glaring from a darkened countenance. "Who said that?"

"Brother Bianco, for one," Haman heard himself blurt aloud.

"Joe Bianco!" Raul barked out the name with a derisive laugh.

Haman shrank, wishing back his words.

"Haman, you are not a child anymore, and it's time you grow out of certain childish superstitions. There is no God, Haman, and Joe Bianco is a fraud."

Haman opened his mouth, but no words came.

Raul idly fingered white velvet petals on the geranium, then began stripping off its leaves, one by one.

Haman's emotions tumbled about as if taking an exhilarating ride. His heart fell into a pit of confusion. In his mind, Haman could see Brother Bianco opening the Bible, talking about God, time and again. Like a chant he could hear Brother Bianco drilling the Ten Commandments. *Thou shalt . . . Thou shalt not . . .* Haman spoke his fears in a very small voice. "You do not like . . . Brother Bianco?"

"The man is a fanatic. His ideas are dangerous. People like him are enemies of society." Raul swung his foot back and forth.

"Why?"

"Priests and pastors are selfish and greedy."

"Greedy? Really?"

"Sure. Clergymen protect the rich. For example, everyone knows how rich the merchants are, right? And we are poor. Therefore, we have a right to take what we need. Merchants don't need all that money. We do. From each according to his ability, to each according to his need."

"Sounds right."

"Sure it's right."

"Hey!" Haman said. "I think that's in Cumorah's constitution, isn't it?"

"Sure!" Raul replied. "And I took those things from Cercado's because I had a right to them. I need them. But the merchants are selfish and don't want to share. If the merchants found me out, they would throw me in jail."

"How cruel!"

"The merchants should be more generous to the needy, but they refuse. So we must force them to give things they have to people who have not."

"But how can you make the merchants be generous?"

"You see, that is why we must change the laws. One person alone can't make people change, but the power of government can take from the selfish and give to the needy."

"I'm surprised we don't already have laws like that. It's only right. It's right out of the Bible."

"You would think so, but people like your Brother Bianco are fighting it the hardest."

"Brother Bianco? No! I don't think Brother Bianco is selfish. In fact, he is always so kind and good he makes me sick."

"I told you he is a fraud. He really sides with the merchants, and if he found out what I did today, he would throw me in jail."

"How terrible! I just don't understand. He is always telling us to be kind, but he would do such a thing to you, my friend?"

"Yes, because the merchants have more money than I do, and they pay Bianco to help them. That's why you always hear churches screaming we should have private property. But the only people who have private property are the rich." Abruptly Raul stood up and overturned the potted plant with a furious kick. The clay pot toppled off the step and split open with a dull crack, its contents spilling onto the concrete.

"So all this time Bianco has been lying to me. I never did like him anyway. But now I hate him."

"I don't blame you."

"And my father! He is a merchant, and I know he is making a lot of money, but he never gives a bit of it to me. He never gives to anybody. If he does anything at all to help the poor, I never hear about it . . . "

"Yes? Go on."

"Brother Bianco is always hanging around our house, and Mama feeds him. When he leaves, he fills his car with food . . . our food! He says he takes it to the poor, but I'm sure he doesn't. I'm sure he eats it all himself." Haman's body tensed. "Of course! Now I understand it all. Papa gives Bianco all that money and food in exchange for throwing poor people in jail. How cruel! I feel awful about my parents, Raul. I had no idea."

Raul nodded sadly. "Doesn't it say in your Bible that sometimes we have to leave our family behind for the sake of world peace and justice?"

"Huh? Yeah, something like that, I think."

"You're the one who knows all about it. After all, Brother Bianco has been teaching you."

"Obviously he knows nothing about peace and justice."

"Some people talk about peace and justice all the time, but no one cares, otherwise we wouldn't have all this inequality in the world. We need somebody to do something about it, and not just talk."

"Hey, you're right. But who?"

"Cabrios is running for Chief Judge. He wants to enforce generosity, and make the merchants give the people what is rightfully theirs. The churches are in league with the rich. That's why churches are against Cabrios. One thing Cabrios will do is put these religious fanatics and hypocrites where they belong. I intend to help him get elected."

"So that's why you won't be around so much any more?" Haman asked, deflated.

"Well, maybe you can do something to help me."

"Anything. Just don't leave me alone in this boring place."

Raul raised a hand in warning. "Remember, Haman. These things I have told you are secret. Let's make a pact." Out of a pouch he took something which looked like a dried weed of some sort. He broke it in little bits and rolled it in a piece of white paper. He put it between his lips and lit it and cast a sidelong glance at the boy. "You have to be twenty-one years old to do marijuana like this."

"I. . .just turned twenty-one," Haman lied.

"Here." Raul held the smoldering white tube to Haman's mouth. "Don't inhale! Just puff a little."

Haman took a breath and cautiously let out a small amount of air. So far, so good. He held the cigarette between his two fingers and sucked in a tiny bit. The fumes made him cough violently.

Chuckling, Raul thumped him on the back and held the whisky bottle to the boy's lips. "Here, put the fire out!"

The substance Haman swallowed was not cool and soothing. It felt like the hot smoke had turned to blazing liquid. The fire rushed down his throat, burning into his stomach with a searing pain.

"That was easy, wasn't it? Now our secret is sealed, and you are a man!"

With a hand over his mouth, Haman fought back a wave of nausea. His eyes stung, his head ached and he wanted to throw up. But it didn't matter. He had a friend forever.

8

November

On election eve, two guards at Canosa Metalworks discovered a bomb planted in the plant's research wing. Canosa had the Cumorah Bureau of Investigation on site within minutes. An emergency bulletin to all industries saved nineteen out of twenty-five factories from disaster.

On election day, people in middle-income neighborhoods were attacked at the polls; many were beaten and mugged; others were frightened away by armed gangs. Zephan's sugar and pineapple crops were burnt to stubble, as were crops from dozens of other farms all over the nation's production belt.

But voter turnout was the highest in history. Anastasio Solano was elected by a landslide.

Two days after the election, Cabrios supporters claimed responsibility for the terrorism.

9

The first year of Solano's five-year term had passed uneventfully for Zephan and his family. A letter from Canosa, though welcome, brought disappointing news. Zephan's old friend would be detained for one or more years. Canosa's investigations in Zarahemla and Cumeni revealed the proportions of international cartels, and revealed connections uncomfortably close to home —

A screech from automobile tires broke into Zephan's reverie. Must be Haman, home from another party. *Stay calm.* Zephan's oldest son banged the door and clattered into the house. *Don't raise your voice.*

"How was school today, Haman?"

"Boring. I hate the teachers. And all the homework." Haman snatched the letter from his father's fingers. "A letter from Canosa? Is he still trying to bring down Cabrios? Why doesn't he give it up? What is it with these old men? Grandpa Amoz kept talking about captivity in the old country. He didn't know what he was talking about. He made it up, because he was old. I don't know what his problem was."

"Do not dishonor my father. You do not know the sacrifices he made for all of us. You owe him respect."

"I owe him nothing."

Zephan winced as if he had been struck.

Haman rushed on. "Really, Papa. It was your fault. You had money. And you left it all there! We came here without anything! We never should have left. And we came here with nothing. Nothing! Now we've been here for three years in this shabby old farm house. It's not fair!"

"Stop your whining!" Zephan said. "You weren't happy in the old country, either. You complained when we lived at Grandpa Canosa's house. I felt bad that day you disappeared when we needed your help, when the crops were burned. I need your cooperation. It upsets me when you complain so much."

"You are so negative!" Haman complained. "You are too strict and never let me do anything. Now you're rich again, but you won't give me any money. All my friends get more money than I do!"

Zephan sighed. "I can't give you money. What else can you suggest? Many times I have offered you a job at the Metalworks, but you refuse! "

"I hate your work! Only a fool would work that hard."

"Then go to work somewhere else. You don't even help your mother at home."

"You make me work all the time. It's not fair!" Haman shouted. "I never have time for any fun."

Zephan smiled. "You're not afraid of work, are you? You can sleep right next to the toughest jobs."

"I'm not going to stand here and take your insults." The young man stomped out of the room.

"Good night, Haman."

Sarita emerged from the library, set her mending on the table and crossed the room to her husband. "I can see you are trying to be patient, *corazón*."

Zephan shook his head. "In the old country, children would never so dishonor their parents."

"I pray every day he will have a change of heart. And Leb follows him around like a hungry puppy."

"I know. They pick on the younger ones, too."

"Abiram, and especially Benjamin." She held up a ragged shirt. "Ben never says anything, but from the looks of his dirty and torn clothing, he takes the brunt of it. Of course Ben does the heaviest work, but he is careful with his clothes."

Zephan frowned. "I worry about their safety, too. Haman and Leb scare me — they are as volatile as the Sidon River after a heavy rain."

"Abiram and Benjamin, on the other hand, are as steady and dependable as their father," she replied softly.

"Benjamin is mature far beyond his years." Zephan patted his wife's arm. "Don't worry. The boy will be all right."

10

Something was special about being fifteen.

Benjamin Benamoz shuffled through avocado leaves and stopped on an upper terrace of the grove. After laying down an irrigation pipe and lining it up with another, he glanced around to make sure no one would see him, then flexed his muscles.

Yup. He could beat Haman in arm-wrestling now. Well, Haman had just reached nineteen, and bragged about his strength. Still, he was now a head shorter than Ben. Haman never did any work, though. Oh well, if Ben didn't triumph over him now, the time would come. And soon.

But something else was special besides growing tall and getting muscles. Something stirring in his mind. He wasn't sure what it was. Questions. *Who am I, really?*

"You are a child of God," Mama had said.

If I lived in heaven before, why am I here?

"This life is the time for men to prepare to meet God," Mama had said.

But how do I prepare? How do I know what to do?

"Humble yourselves, and continue in prayer unto him," Mama had read out of the little book with no cover. "Cry unto him in your fields, in your households, in your wilderness, both morning, midday, and evening."

Mama and Papa would kneel in their bedroom, clasp hands, and pray together. Ben had seen Mama on her knees, praying. Many times.

Maybe I'll try that.

Bright green avocado leaves filled the sky, filtering the sunlight. He couldn't see the house. Ben was surrounded by a family of trees — silent, except for warm air breathing a mild licorice aroma from avocado blossoms. And the crunch of dry leaves under his knees.

"There he is!"

Instantly two figures dropped from a tree and landed upon him like fiends, knocking him forward to the ground, pressing his face into the soil, clawing and tearing at his shirt, yanking on his trousers. If they pulled off his pants, it would not be the first time. But he was determined it would be the last.

Throbbing in the boy's ears were not the derisive jeers of his brothers, but quiet words from Mama's book. *Cry unto him against the power of your enemies.* Ben didn't cry. He roared. His arms pinned beneath him were suddenly an advantage. Pushing himself up with all his might, he rolled over and grabbed an arm. Leb's. Ben pressed his teeth into the skin until he heard a howl of pain. Lying on his back, he thrashed his feet against Haman's midsection. With a grunt of surprise, Haman released his young brother.

Benjamin was on his feet, racing from tree to tree, searching for a place to hide. Crops in the fields were too short to shield him. Climbing a tree would be a trap. He could hear their footsteps nearing, their voices shouting insults.

"Sissy!"

Ben's toe bumped something. A metal rod. An irrigation pipe.

"What were you doing, Ben? Hmm? Praying?"

"God doesn't help sissies!"

Ben's face went hot. If only he had seen them in that tree!

"What God?" Haman laughed in a high-pitched shriek.

Let them babble. At least I know where they are. Must not let anger cloud my thinking.

Quickly he reached down and unscrewed a four-foot segment of the pipe. Seizing the length of metal, he stepped into a crook in a low branch and waited.

"Little Benjamin will never be a man. He's a Mama's boy." The brothers came closer, then stopped. "Where did the little worm go?"

Ben said nothing, but poised the rod like a club. He hoped his brothers couldn't hear his heart pounding.

Leb's clumsy attempt at stealth gave him away. From his perch, Ben could see down on his brother's head. Leb had not yet spotted him. Peeking around the tree, Ben let out a battle cry, "War Eagle!" and brandished the pipe.

Leb jumped. Ben was towering over him, holding a. . . sword? Where did the kid get that? With a scream Leb lit out for the house.

"What's the matter with you?" Haman appeared, calling after the fleeing Leb.

Haman's head was within easy striking distance. "Don't make me do it, Haman." Ben's voice was calm.

Haman looked up, startled. "You can't get away with that. I'll—"

"Maybe, but whatever you try, I can smash your face first."

"You wouldn't!" Haman took a step forward.

Ben was suddenly afraid. He could seriously injure his brother. But if Haman caught him bluffing, there would be no end to the torment. He prayed for help. "Don't make me do it, Haman," he repeated.

Haman backed away, out of reach, then whirled and bolted for the house.

11

A tiny breeze played chimes on the patio, and Sarita let the mending fall in her lap. Zephan bought those chimes for her three years ago, when the family first came to Cumorah.

Absently Sarita picked up a fresh green bean from a kettle of vegetables Abiram had brought from the garden earlier.

A shout came from the grove. She winced. The boys were fighting again.

Sarita turned to her mending. Anxiety clutched at her stomach, twisting her insides with fear for Benjamin's safety. "Merciful Father in Heaven," she whispered, "please protect my boy."

Leb whipped suddenly by her, upsetting the kettle. Horror bulged his eyes.

Haman soon followed, his passage marked by the slamming of doors.

Minutes passed. Silence.

"Where is Benjamin? What have you done?" Sarita jumped to her feet but could not move forward. "Ben!" Her voice choked in her throat. She must go to him. No, she could not bear to go. But she must know. Why would her feet not move? Benjamin. What if he's . . .

What was that sound? A sprinkler turned on in the grove. Music! Benjamin emerged from the grove, walking toward her. She sat down, trembling, allowing herself to look at him. No blood on him. He was walking swiftly, with exuberance.

My, he has grown tall lately. Tanned. Blue eyes, like his father. And such an innocent face! Why would anyone want to hurt this boy?

He leaned down and planted a kiss on her cheek. "Thanks, Mama."

Tears sprang unbidden to her eyes. "Why, son?" She managed an uncertain smile.

Ben took a raw green bean from the pile remaining inside the container. He bit into the bean, savoring its crunch. "I remembered what you taught me." He grinned. "Those two bullies won't be ambushing me anymore. I found for myself a power greater than they will ever know."

The Book Of
Abíram

*"And I, Nephi, did take the sword of Laban,
and after the manner of it did make many swords."*

THE BOOK OF ABIRAM

1

Failing to rise to power in Cumorah, Fomentio Cabrios took his followers to a small island nation named Cumeni. There he took control of an already unstable government and ruled for several years with unbridled hostility. At first he proclaimed The Year of Education, but the watching world called it The Year of Execution. "To the firing wall" was heard everywhere among the unruly mobs; scores of young dissidents were shot down in cold blood. To silence their cries of faith in God, Cabrios had the victims gagged before execution.

Guajiros — the peasants — tried to fight back, adding acid to the sugar at the mills. The peasants were motivated, determined, and organized, but lacked political power. Cabrios nationalized the farms, fired public servants and replaced them with his cronies. During Cabrios' first year, any professionals and artisans who were not killed fled to Cumorah and Zarahemla. Having emptied the island of all educated and civilizing influence, Cabrios began to release hardened criminals to make room in the prisons for political foes.

But a contingent of Cabrios sympathizers in Cumorah, supplied with modern weaponry from the Tartarus Empire, were spilling blood in an increasing radius on the land. In the village of Ammonihah, one notorious terrorist, Horacio Mortera, entered the prosperous Cercado Mercantile with his henchmen. When the gang began to loot the store, the owner politely showed them where to pay for their purchases. "We don't have to pay for what is already ours!" Mortera declared, and immediately he gunned down Cercado and his family. Cumorah recoiled from this gross violation of domestic tranquility. Alarmed over this encroaching terrorism, Chief Judge Solano summoned state consul Archibald Kingerman to the executive office in Granada.

"Over the years I have been watching Cabrios' growing factions of terrorists tearing down our government. Everyone knows he is getting outside help for this insurrection." Anastasio Solano paced the floor in his spacious office. "This recent massacre in Ammonihah, in our own land, is unforgivable. Mortera was an illegal alien. And then he fled to Cumeni. He literally got away with murder." Solano studied a Cercado family photo in the newspaper. "I am very sorry for the people of Cumeni, whom Cabrios thoroughly deceived until they were ripe for takeover. We cannot let that happen here."

"We should put a ban on all weapons until the crisis is over," Kingerman said. "Then it can't happen here."

"Of course it can. And if it does happen, how would the citizens defend themselves against these crimes if we take away their weapons? We have to stop Cabrios and everyone like him. Stop the criminals from even entering the country. Genuine refugees from tyranny — these we can take — but not all these drug agents and common criminals. We must keep out those parasites who creep in and live off Botina's remaining welfare state. Mortera is a terrorist, plain and simple, and he brings with him tyranny. Cabrios is exporting revolution, and we are paying for his products with blood. Cumorah needs to start screening immigration much more closely and stop Cabrios from bringing drugs into this country. Sensible laws are already in place. All we have to do is enforce our laws to secure our borders and stop the narco-terrorists before they even cross the border."

"That will be difficult. The Anti-Hate Committee will brand you a racist, and you will fail."

"CBI informs me the Anti-Hate Committee is a front for narco-terrorism."

Kingerman raised his head slowly, his small eyes hooded. "Hmm. Which agent fed you this information?"

"Canosa."

"I see. You appointed Canosa, as I recall."

"Various other sources confirm Canosa's report."

Kingerman put an arm about Solano's shoulders. "You're right. Actually, Stasio, you should make an alliance with Zarahemla, and we could band together against Cabrios."

"I don't quite trust Zarahemla. Their Dermucker Foundation and other coteries have supported the Empire and Cabrios for years, and recently they began pouring money into illegal immigration. Zarahemla claims humanitarianism, but in reality Dermucker wants votes for his programs."

Kingerman frowned. "Canosa, again?"

"Not just Canosa. More especially, an independent investigative committee in Parliament."

"See here. A popular move would be to send the military into Cumeni, depose Cabrios, mop up, and establish a democracy."

Solano stared at his aide. "Send our sons into harm's way for imperialist purposes?"

"Not so. Cumeni is very close to our shores. Cabrios is piping drugs into our society, and he is a puppet of Tartarus Empire —"

"I have many friends who have fled the Tartarus Empire," Solano interrupted. "I want no part of foreign entanglements. The Black Sea Democracies are far away. Let's leave them and their politics alone."

"But my dear friend, we can no longer afford to isolate ourselves. Strength is in the collective. Cabrios has been bought by the Tartarus Empire; he is the hand of tyranny in our back pocket. We have already been given a taste of Cabrios' brutality right within our own boundaries."

"You have a point there," Solano replied. "But I prefer a nonmilitary solution. Ours is an internal problem . . . "

"You're right about that!" Kingerman rubbed his soft hands slowly. "CBI is infiltrated. Stasio, we have a mole in the bureau!"

"Your source is —"

"Not Canosa, I'll tell you that much."

"Kingerman! Are you implying that Canosa —"

"I have said nothing about Canosa. The suspect could be anyone, but we do know it's someone from Cabrios' camp. Cabrios already has too much power. He must be eliminated. The only way to do it is through a military liberation effort."

"No! I won't endanger our men for the sake of a tinpot dictator."

"That's why we have Pax Universalis. Just a battalion of men from each nation. We cannot bring peace all alone. It must be a collective effort."

"And start a world war over it? Arch, what are you thinking?"

"Now Stasio, you are over-reacting again. Pax Universalis is our ally against terrorism. But if you would feel better about it, you could stage a small, covert operation, with volunteers only, and clean out Cabrios before he causes any more trouble."

"I might consider that."

"Why not have Canosa head the operation? That way, you could be certain it would be done the way you want it."

"I will consult him."

"What if Canosa balks?"

Solano drew back. "What if he does?"

Kingerman smiled. "Trust me, Solano. He won't."

2

Abiram had finished at tech school and had gone to work at Canosa Metalworks. He worked many hours a day, but sometimes Benjamin would lure him away from work to ride the Canosa horses or swim at the beach. Abiram cherished those times.

In his last school year, Ben took honors at the academy and received awards for rescue work with the navy Coast Guard.

Zephan built a new home for his family in the Granada province, but Ben still spent many pleasant hours at the Canosa plantation. He loved the horses and the land. Summers he worked the fields at the plantation, trained the horses and helped with the harvests. Ben worked hard at the metalworks and played hard, spending his leisure hours boating, riding, and swimming with his friends, or just as frequently, alone. He would return to school tanned and vibrant. That Ben seldom dated, Abiram decided with a twinge of envy, was surely a disappointment to many young ladies.

Ben told Abiram he felt awkward at dancing, though he was surprisingly light on his feet for his large stature. On the rare occasions of a military ball, he had no trouble getting a date. Abiram suspected an occasional broken heart when Ben singled out a girl for these occasions.

One June evening, Abiram returned home from work to find his younger brother seated at the kitchen table behind a mountain of books, studying for final examinations.

"Ben," Abiram said, "I know you read extensively, but that cannot be the only reason you retain everything."

"Grandpa Amoz once told me to read to remember for the rest of my life. But everything is so fascinating — that's why it's easy for me. I want to understand everything. Even if we could figure out how everything works, it would be a gray and puzzling world. One must know *why*. History and literature show us the reason we learn everything else." Ben opened Zephan's copy of Macbeth. "For example, Shakespeare."

Abiram wrinkled his nose. "I don't know what Papa sees in that stuff."

"It was Mama who got him interested in it. They met at a Shakespearean play."

"I see. Only a woman could get a man to waste his time on such nonsense. On second thought, maybe you have something there. Girls are always attracted to you."

"I don't know why. I definitely don't have Leb's looks."

"You are more interested in others than Leb is in himself, and that is a lot. Face it. You have a soft heart, Ben. Perhaps I should take a cue from you and develop interest in literature. Women seem to like all that arty stuff. But can you make sense of that crazy language? It's beyond English, already. In fact, it's all Greek to me."

Ben laughed. "You just quoted a line from Shakespeare's Julius Caesar!"

3

That summer, Canosa returned at last from Zarahemla and visited Zephan's new home in Granada. He lounged in a burgundy overstuffed chair opposite Zephan's oak desk. Zephan Benamoz, now president of the Granada branch of Canosa Metalworks, was still dressed in old work clothes and a protective hard-hat. Canosa loved him as a son.

Sarita definitely had good taste. Canosa loved the spacious atrium with its high ceilings and rich furnishings, especially the chandelier. It was smaller than the one at the Canosa villa, perhaps, but exquisite, nonetheless.

Large windows lit every corner and welcomed fresh breezes on warm summer days. A well-worn recording played Zephan's favorite concerto. Zephan's home here was a bit of heaven. And he had much to lose.

Ben was graduating, so this was a celebration dinner. Canosa recalled that first dinner over ten years ago. Ben, the frightened young boy, had become a man, serving courageous rescue missions when called to duty. Abiram was a success in his own right at the company. Leb had left home to join the armed forces of Pax Universalis. Haman, at twenty-six years old, was still at home, and he never seemed to work much. But he dressed in elegant clothes that subtly bespoke wealth. Canosa was thoroughly familiar with the wellspring of Haman's lucre.

Upon his return, Canosa had been given ecclesiastical responsibilities by the brethren, and his first assignment was not a pleasant one.

Canosa wished he could pretend that all was well on this jubilant family occasion, and avoid a dreaded confrontation with someone he loved. But at the first opportunity after dinner he must get on with it. The matter could wait no longer.

After dessert Abiram left the table briefly and returned with a long, narrow box. With obvious excitement, he stood before Ben with his graduation present. "I am honored to present to you, from the Canosa Metalworks employees, and especially from myself, this replica of the sword of Laban."

Ben gently turned the enormous sword over in his hands. The workmanship on the hilt was exceedingly fine, like none he had ever seen before. On the broad blade were engraved these words: *The word of God is quick and powerful, and sharper than any two-edged sword. Hebrews 4:12.*

"How barbaric!" Haman said. "Why don't you just give him a machine gun? A sword is just as lethal as a gun. It should be banned."

"According to the book of Joseph," Ben said, "the sword in ancient times was used two ways. Nehor used a sword to enforce his own ideas. Today Voltaire represents the sword of the state. Otherwise, the ancient Nephites in this land needed the sword to defend their families, their religion, and their liberty against their enemies. The sword of Laban was one symbol and type that remained constant. It still reminds us that the Lord will help deliver us, as individuals or nations, from our enemies."

"Meaning no disrespect," Abiram said, "but these days that sword works great for slashing through the jungles and clearing land for building homes. It's a symbol of peace and security to me."

"Wrong! It's a symbol of violence!" Haman flared.

"Calm yourself, Haman," Ben said softly. "Why do you always have to spoil our dinner conversation with your political hyperbole? This sword is only a symbol of the word of God."   "I still say all lethal weapons should be restricted to the hands of Pax Universalis peace-keeping forces!" Haman grumbled. "Especially not within reach of someone as deluded as you are!" He stood up, as to address a large audience. "Get a load of this, everyone. The other day when Ben was in the library, and he thought no one was around, I heard him say he could tell the water to be earth, and it would be done! He actually said that! Really, Abiram, should you be giving this dangerous weapon to a crazy man?"

"Sit down, Haman," Ben said. "It says in the scriptures that by the power of His word He can do anything. You must have heard me reading that the other day. I *do* read out loud sometimes." Ben winked at Canosa. "Of course, Haman left out the part I read about him."

"And what was that?" Haman asked.

"The part that says 'thy neck is an iron sinew, and thy brow brass.'"

Everyone laughed.

Haman said to Canosa, "He's been teacher's pet all these years, and it has gone to his head." He leaned very close to his mother. "Listen to this braggart, Mama. Look what you raised."

"Don't speak to your mother like that, Haman." Zephan's voice was quiet, but he gave Haman *the look*, and the young man shrank back into his seat as if he had been slapped.

"Now Ben thinks he's favored of God, or something," he mumbled.

Ben could not resist the bait. "How do you know what I think?"

"Well, you don't deny it. You do think you're better than everybody."

"Haman is so anxious to control what everyone else thinks," Ben said, "and he can't even control his own thoughts. Did you hear anyone say I was better than you?"

"Huh? You implied it."

"Some people worry too much about what everyone else thinks and start imagining things. You have no idea what I'm thinking, and that bothers you, doesn't it?"

"I know all about — "

"You just told us all you know."

"I think —"

"Everybody knows what you think," Ben said. "What I think is my own concern."

"See? That proves I'm right." With a pointed look at Ben's formal military attire, Haman changed the subject. "Well, Benito, or maybe I should say, Señor Pomposo, you are getting to be quite mercenary, aren't you?" he said.

"You are confusing me with Leb," Ben said mildly. "I'm only a volunteer with the Coast Guard. Leb has a global commander ordering him around all the time. He seems to thrive on it, but I couldn't tolerate it."

"Correction. PAX wouldn't tolerate you. You move heaven and earth to get that stupid Solano into office, and now, after he was reelected, he is finally turning from isolation to make a move for peace. So you insult him with that article of yours in the newspaper."

Sarita turned wondering eyes to her son. "Is this true, Ben?"

"I simply stated my disapproval of Cumorah becoming entangled in the Pax Universalis alliances."

"He is an embarrassment to our family, Mama!" Haman complained. "He said Pax Universalis was no better than a league of tribes and compared it to the Tower of Babel!"

Canosa chuckled. "I enjoyed your article, young man! It has drawn the attention of Chief Solano himself. He has requested to see you Wednesday afternoon, if you can."

"I'll be there."

Sarita seized the moment to steer the family away from further bickering and used her old standby. "Let's play ball." After two broken windows at the old house, Sarita was grateful that Zephan had built a *cancha*, or court, for jai alai, the game he loved.

Zephan and Sarita formed one team, with Abiram and Ben on the other side. Zephan served, and a long volley ensued.

Haman sat behind the wire fence and watched Zephan's skillful playing. Then Ben missed.

"Why do you bother?" Haman shouted to Ben. "You always miss the ball."

"I know," Ben called back with a grin. "This isn't my best sport. Too bad Leb isn't here. Why don't you play?"

"No, thanks." Restless, Haman studied his parents. Nations were at war, people were starving, and his family isolated themselves, playing their little games. They refused to see outside their rigid traditions or accept reforms made by others who were acclaimed world experts. How could this family be so ridiculously happy? Did these people feel no obligation to the outside world? Arch Kingerman had told him the answer to that question. Haman's parents, like most parents, were stupid little people living out their selfish little lives, with no concern for the unfairness and inequality surrounding them. And surely Zephan Benamoz was the worst. "Be *in* the world, but not *of* it," he would say. Whatever that meant. "You worry too much about fixing the world," he would say. "God will do that. You just keep his commandments, and you will be happy. The world will take care of itself."

Father had a very naive view of the world: everything had its opposites —— light and dark, good and evil. Poor old Father had no idea of that complicated gray area which everyone except him seemed to understand very well. Zephan oversimplified everything. He still believed in angels and visions, prophets, miracles, and the like.

Haman shook his head. He had long since put those superstitions behind him. But Father was so sure he was right, and everyone who disagreed with him was wrong. Things just were not that simple. The visionary ways of Zephan Benamoz didn't work, and never had. Someday Papa would be forced to face reality and listen to other men's ideas. . .

Canosa tapped him on the shoulder.

4

Canosa met with Haman in Zephan's office, alone.

"What is this, Canosa?" Haman did not try to hide his annoyance. "Why are you looking at me like that? Are you laughing at me?"

"Not at all, *hijo*. Would you rather have me frown? I have been gone so long, and it is always good to be home."

"Oh, is that all?" Haman started to leave.

"Not quite. As your bishop I am here to give you counsel."

"What happened to Grandpa Canosa, who always used to be so nice to us?"

"Are you still the boy who used to listen to his Grandpa? I'm asking you to listen, carefully, one more time. To begin with, the proverb: 'wealth maketh many friends.' What about your friends, Haman?"

"Are you trying to tell me how to choose my friends? My father put you up to this, didn't he? He doesn't like my friends, because he doesn't agree with their politics. "

"This is not a political matter, Haman. It is spiritual."

"Don't preach to me."

Canosa held up his hands in a mildly defensive gesture, as if to deflect verbal darts headed his way. "I will try not to. I will ask you some of the same questions I ask in every interview, and perhaps you will gain some important information. Haman, do you belong to any organization which stands in opposition to the gospel?"

"Sounds political to me."

Canosa smirked with impatience. "People make everything political these days. So answer my question."

"The answer is No. And my friends are not of our faith so you have no control over them. Besides, do you discriminate against others who are not of our faith?"

"Slow down, *joven*. Many fine people do not share all our beliefs, nevertheless they honor our God. But others worship Babylon, or the world, and are steeped in idolatry —"

"Babylon? Idolatry? In our day? Really, Canosa. This is quite absurd. Nobody worships idols these days."

"Think about it, Haman. 'Thou shalt have no other gods before me.'"

A small sigh of relief escaped Haman. "Well, then you needn't worry. My friends are very sincere, and all their beliefs can be found in the Bible."

"Our prophets warn us continually about those who mix scriptures with the doctrines of men."

"Nobody believes in prophets any more, Canosa. And I think we should be ashamed of the way we force our religion on others."

"To force any religion, secular or otherwise, is not the Lord's way, Haman. You think we do this?"

"Well, Arch is always worried about opposition from churches, because all my friends are very sincere, but some people misunderstand them."

"Do you agree with your friends' beliefs?"

"Very much," Haman said with enthusiasm. "Harvey Dermucker owns the biggest bank in the world, but he is the kindest, most generous man you could hope to meet. He is devoted to the poor. He works tirelessly to pass legislation to give the poor what is rightfully theirs! Arch Kingerman is a world class diplomat. He is working so hard for world peace that he hardly ever sleeps. Rupert Banberg . . . these are all citizens above suspicion, Canosa. World peace, helping the poor. These are noble ideals, straight from the Bible."

"I know this is important to you, Haman. But often the light of the past can increase our understanding."

"History." Haman rolled his eyes.

"But this history involves your own family."

"Oh."

Canosa stared out the window for such a long time that Haman began to wonder if the old man had forgotten him. Finally Canosa spoke as if he plucked a moment from his past and held it up to examine more closely.

5

My grandfather, Sein Canosa, lived most of his days in the Land of Goyim, during the Empire wars. His years in college were to change his life forever.

He attended the most prestigious university in the land, and his best friends became so powerful that they influenced the entire course of history. Since he and his friends made a brotherly agreement that would ultimately lead to my grandfather's ruin, I will tell you about three men who had a lasting effect on his life.

Sein Canosa was very intelligent, and he excelled at the university, but he was not as brilliant as Mervin Dermucker and Adolph Banberg, his fellow students. Of the three, Sein was the only member of the house of Yeshurun, and the others did not always agree with his beliefs. Nevertheless, they were the best of friends and did everything together in those days.

Sein was an exceptional student in architecture, and his professors and colleagues greatly respected him. A promising career lay ahead of him.

Mervin Dermucker was destined to become top world financier. Adolph Banberg was unsure about his career choice at first, but he loved to study and learn. He was the most intellectual of the three. Dermucker and Banberg received stupendous awards and praise throughout the world for their achievements. Although he was happy for his friends and knew they deserved these accolades, Sein felt a twinge of envy that his success was not as sensational as theirs. "I hope these young men do not become prideful," Sein's mother said. "Remember this, my son," she said. "Seek first the kingdom of God, and place no other gods before Him."

And it came to pass that at graduation time, the friends made a pact in which they would be as brothers forever. As they went out into the world to make a livelihood, each would help the other, in case one was ever down on his fortune.

Dermucker invested in oil and became a billionaire. He never missed an opportunity to make money. The more money he made, the more he loved it, and the more possessions he acquired.

Banberg liked to argue, so he decided to go into law. He swept through the course in record time. But with all his intellectual prowess, he was superseded by two other students, who, incidentally, both happened to be Jewish. Banberg developed a vague suspicion of Jewish people.

The Land of Goyim plunged into a devastating economic crisis, but Dermucker, with his superior knowledge of the market, not only lost nothing, but doubled his fortune. Banberg, on the other hand, had acquired great wealth with his law firm, but lost heavily in the market. "Why didn't you warn me?" he complained to Dermucker.

"You didn't ask," Dermucker replied.

Banberg asked Dermucker for financial help in suing his three stockbrokers, two of whom were Jewish.

Dermucker refused to be involved in the suit, but he gave Banberg a wildly generous grant to get him back on his feet.

The crisis shut down the construction business, but Sein Canosa got by, doing household and auto repairs, until he was called into a great war. Sein was upset because his friends did not fight for their country. Dermucker and Banberg paid large sums of money to be excused. Nevertheless, Sein shrugged; they must have had their reasons. He returned to society as a decorated soldier, and virtually penniless. Dermucker offered him a tempting financial gift to get a business started, but my grandfather was determined to make his own way.

Now, this was at a time called "The Great Anarchy" in one of the Atlantic Democracies. The king of one land had fomented terrorism among extreme outlaws in that region, and the violence reached such a crisis as to precipitate the Great War in which my grandfather fought. Now, the aforementioned king had a baron who orchestrated the loss of freedom in that region, and the name of that baron was Alger Rotcraft. And it came to pass that the king fell from power, and Rotcraft lost everything. Destitute, he came to the Land of Goyim. Being from an aristocratic family, however, when he arrived in the new world, he gravitated toward the very rich. He met Mervin Dermucker, and was introduced to my grandfather. Rotcraft was exceedingly humble because of his poverty, and Sein Canosa was very understanding. Rotcraft was quite young, only slightly older than my brother, so my father took him in like a son. But Alger became the closest friend of my grandfather, Sein. And it came to pass that Sein Canosa taught Rotcraft the gospel of Christ, and Rotcraft was baptized into the house of Yeshurun. My grandfather was a bishop at that time, and in due time, Alger Rotcraft advanced in the priesthood and became a member of the bishopric. Rotcraft was charming, and he was a beloved leader in the church.

By this time another war loomed on the horizon, and Sein Canosa had added a great skill in metals to his other talents. He decided to make strong military vehicles.

"How can you make a living off military equipment when people are destroying each other?" my grandmother asked him.

"We didn't ask for this war," he said. "Since we must fight it, I intend to make certain our men are as well protected as possible."

Canosa offered Rotcraft a partnership in the business, but Rotcraft had other ideas. Friends from the old world had contacted him about forming a new firm called I.G. Uben, to manufacture lethal chemical weapons. When my grandfather heard about this investment, he protested, saying he would not support the killing of defenseless civilians.

Dermucker had discovered tremendous moneymaking opportunities in war, so he did not pay much attention to which side he was supporting, as long as everyone paid the interest on bills due. He also trusted Rotcraft's recommendation, so without further research, he sent twenty million goyim dollars in aviation fuel to the firm called I.G. Uben.

Banberg, too, seeing Dermucker was making more money than he, and not to be outdone, invested heavily in the firm, and both made a fabulous profit. Dermucker either did not know, or did not care, that the Uben Company believed in and practiced human sacrifice.

"What?" Haman exclaimed. "You can't mean that."
"Call it what you like. The Uben firm manufactured the deadly Solution F gas, used to exterminate millions of Jews."

And it came to pass that Canosa quit making vehicles when the war ended and returned to architecture and construction. He did not move in the same circles as his elite friends, but he was highly respected in his community as a man who understood the working class. So Canosa was elected Senator, and he was determined to represent the people honestly.

After the war, Rotcraft brought Dermucker one astonishingly profitable deal after another, and Dermucker loved him, and he loved his wealth. On the other hand, Rotcraft and Canosa had a serious rift.

"What happened to the deep humility you had when I first met you?" Canosa asked.

"That was when I was poor," Rotcraft snapped. "I will never be poor again."

"But on ill-gotten gains your tithe will not be accepted. You have promoted the practice of human sacrifice, Rotcraft, which is an abomination in the sight of God."

"Spare me your moralizing. Your church is a narcotic for the poor. I don't need it."

Alger Rotcraft made oceans of money, though not as much as Dermucker. He longed for the days in his homeland when he had great political power, so he bought some armies and navies in distant parts of the world. Rotcraft financed some rulers in various kingdoms, but still was not satisfied. He thought the Land of Goyim should be ruled by an aristocracy instead of the people. Rotcraft did not like or trust the common people, whom he thought were too foolish to govern themselves. So he wanted to establish a king to rule the Land of Goyim. Moreover, that king in the old country had made many mistakes. Rotcraft decided, if he were king, he would not make such mistakes. In fact, he began to devise a plan to rule the world, because he knew many kings who were doing a poor job, and Rotcraft knew he could do much better. Everything would be so much easier and faster if only Rotcraft were in charge. And peace would spread throughout the world. He was sure of it. What the world needed was the benevolent rule of an enlightened few, who had the wisdom to bring a lasting peace. Rotcraft wanted to revive and strengthen the order of Voltaire, by which his ancestors had ruled many Atlantic nations for decades, and which even had roots in ancient civilizations.

So Rotcraft contacted Stanislaus, his former associate in the old world. Now, Stanislaus kept experimenting with one economic policy after another, but nothing worked. He even owned all the tillable land, but he couldn't get the peasants to produce enough food for their countrymen. The more he cracked down on them, the worse it got. People were starving to death in the tens of millions. By the time Rotcraft called, Stanislaus was beside himself.

"What am I doing wrong?" Stanislaus wailed.

"You are doing nothing wrong," Rotcraft assured him patiently. "The key is organization." Then Rotcraft advised him how to keep the peasants from rising in revolt.

"Could you send me something to keep myself and my men alive until I get this straightened out?" he begged.

After he hung up the phone, Stanislaus felt much better, and he proceeded immediately to carry out Rotcraft's instructions. Since crime was a way of life in his country, Stanislaus decided to organize it and use it to gain money for his coffers and enforce his programs. At the same time, he started a new policy. Since food was scarce, it was essential to weed out the weak so he would have enough food to go around. So anyone not meeting the quota was charged with a crime against society punishable by death. He also made it a crime to criticize the new policy.

After Rotcraft hung up the phone, he immediately wired his friend a few million dollars and made a visit to Dermucker. He wanted to present his ideas on world peace, and now he had a hard case with which to prove his point. Stanislaus was a good friend, but he was a lousy ruler; this increased the urgency of creating a benevolent oligarchy. Unfortunately, he would have to keep propping up Stanislaus until the global governance was in place. That was where Dermucker's billions would come in handy. Rotcraft made a quick list of other rulers he knew who were his friends — there were Asubad, Ahab, Gerhard, Ding Po . . . and also Omar, Ivanov, and Xavier. And there were many more whom, like Stanislaus, he had advised over the years, and sent them money when he could. They all owed him something. Once he and Dermucker sent them the desired money, his plan would get their support. He just knew they would love it.

Rotcraft began to discuss his ideas with Dermucker, who began to see his money would buy not only pleasure for himself but could also bring about world peace. He, Dermucker, could influence the leaders of entire nations to establish peace, and nations would revere him. Rotcraft told him if he was going to pacify the world, then he would have to forget national boundaries and become a world citizen. They agreed Dermucker would create a world bank to loan money to the international community, and Rotcraft would negotiate with the nations of the earth to resolve their differences and merge them together to live in peace under one flag.

Together Dermucker and Rotcraft planned to create an instrument of Voltaire, called Pax Universalis, to bring about universal peace. The first concern was to establish a system of laws to enforce on a world scale. So they sought out Adolph Banberg.

And it came to pass that Banberg had become bored with common murder trials, for in such cases neither murderer nor victim could afford to pay his fees. Banberg began to work for organizations which paid well. He became well known as a prosecutor for the national government. Political crimes were ever so much more interesting than petty crimes. Banberg, with his vast intellectual acuity, was proud of his talent for comprehending obscure legal terms which were utterly mystifying to most people. He was so skillful that kings, princes, and rulers from all over the world began to call on him to serve as their legal advisor. So when his old friend Dermucker approached him, he was well prepared and zealous about the idea.

"You definitely need someone who is an expert in international law," he said.

"I knew we came to the right man," Dermucker gushed.

"I have learned from years of experience that this will work on one condition."

"Which is . . . "

"We must disabuse ourselves of the notion that Western culture is superior to other cultures. What some people might call a crime, others may not. Citizens of our nation tend to be prejudiced against other rulers, saying they punish the innocent and let the guilty go free. But for all people to be judged equally, we must detach ourselves from the moorings of old-fashioned morality. For example, to expect the entire world to abide by the Golden Rule is pathetically provincial and naive."

"I agree with you," Dermucker said, "but how will we ever convince Canosa?"

"Easy," Banberg replied. "We simply have to make sure he is outnumbered."

Subsequently Banberg met with his clients from all over the world and formed the Egalitarian association, for the purpose of subverting national governments and pressuring them to adopt certain political programs.

And it came to pass that when the treaty for Pax Universalis came before the Senate, Canosa was skeptical, because he trusted not the doctrines of men. He especially did not trust Alger Rotcraft any longer. All his colleagues were exceedingly enthusiastic, but Canosa wanted to know all about anything he was expected to vote on.

The more research Senator Canosa did, the worse he felt. It was bad enough that Rotcraft had financed the gassing of millions of people, but he had also convinced Dermucker and Banberg to be involved with it. The more he searched and researched, the more the devastating truth was confirmed. It was even a matter of public record.

Senator Canosa spent many sleepless nights. How could he speak against his friends? But how could they participate in such horrors? Dermucker and Rotcraft were determined to pass their treaty because they believed it would bring peace. But this treaty would cost his nation's sovereignty. And would it bring these atrocities to the shores of his country? Canosa made up his mind. His silence would compromise all he believed in. He would inform the public.

Senator Canosa worked tirelessly to expose the truth. He taught the people what he had learned from his study of history, which was that the constant Empire wars in the old world were caused by the doctrines of Voltaire. The Pax treaty was designed to bring those same doctrines to the new world. Senator Canosa warned that many rulers, though strong allies of Rotcraft, had caused mass murders in their own nations. And he warned that those who were building up alliances with the order of Voltaire were studying to overthrow the liberty of the Land of Goyim ——— even to overthrow the liberty of all nations. In those days, the order of Voltaire was not accepted as widely as it is now. When people learned about the Pax treaty's connection to Voltairism and the hated Empire, they were angry. And people distrusted Rotcraft, because he was a foreigner.

Rotcraft fought back. He decided the best way to get Canosa was to destroy that which was most important to him. He began to revile openly against the people of Yeshurun, and he began to lead others away after him. Shortly thereafter, he was excommunicated from Yeshurun for teaching false doctrine, deceiving others, and exercising unrighteous dominion.

But even people of other faiths began to feel threatened. When the people learned of Rotcraft's complicity in genocide, they condemned him as a traitor and drove him from the land in disgrace. The Pax Universalis treaty was voted down by a large majority.

Frustrated but undaunted, Dermucker and Banberg pressed for passage of the treaty. The Senate wrangled for years, and the national memory of Rotcraft began to grow dim.

Canosa was depressed and disillusioned because his friends could not see the ultimate bitter fruits of their works. He could no longer avoid it; he must confront Dermucker with the truth, and give him one more chance to explain. The next day he appeared at Dermucker's office.

"It will never restore the lives which were lost, but you could double the sum you invested in the Uben Company, and pay it to the surviving families, to show your true repentance," Sein Canosa suggested.

"Repentance? What do I have to repent of? I am helping people. If I send these nations enough money, the day will come when they will be free."

"You think despots will relinquish their power if you throw money at them? Can it be possible you are so naive that you will sell tyrants the rope to hang you with? You can't bribe tyrants to liberate captive nations, Mervin."

"Looks like we have a difference of opinion, Canosa. This is strictly business. I engage in trade for its own sake. Money is a universal language, and it's all you need. I can't be going around preaching to my trading partners. I can't afford to ignore a good business deal just because the other party doesn't think the way I do."

"You can't afford it?" Canosa was incredulous.

"Well, if I don't, some other nation will. And yes, I would get edged out by the competition."

"You are one of the richest men in the world, Dermucker. You could afford to come out against this great evil."

"And offend my world trading partners? I wouldn't even consider it. My public image would be ruined. Besides, it's all in the past now. Let's just forget it."

Canosa just looked at his friend.

"Tell you what," Dermucker said. "I hate to offend an old friend like you, either." He pulled out his checkbook. "What was the amount you mentioned? I believe that would be forty million. I'll round it off to fifty. Why don't I just pay it to you instead of making a public spectacle? You'll be set for life, and we can leave the whole thing behind us . . . How do you want it? Actually, I can just set it aside for you in the Dermucker Foundation, and you can live off the interest. Easy as can be. How's that?"

Canosa sucked in his breath. "You would pay me millions to wash the blood off your hands and cover up this evil?"

"Calm down, Canosa. You're getting too dramatic. I thought we were friends. What happened to the agreement we made, years ago, to help each other?"

"Good grief, Dermucker," Canosa said in disgust. "With all your education did no one teach you the difference between right and wrong?"

"I don't know where you've been through the years, pal," Dermucker retorted, "but these days everyone has a different idea. There is really no right and no wrong. It is up to the individual."

"Murder is still a sin, and mass murder is an abomination in the sight of God."

"Ha! You went to the same school I did, and you are the one who is still narrow-minded, nursing those outdated ideas." Dermucker's tone was heating up. "With you, everything is either good or evil."

"There is no neutral area between good and evil. You are on the devil's turf, Dermucker, and you had better get off it as fast as you can."

Dermucker snorted. "I outgrew those superstitions a long time ago."

"God is not a superstition."

"I believe in God, too, Canosa. But my church is global, not provincial like yours. Besides, it is foolish to let religion interfere with politics and business. Rotcraft did that, and I don't plan to make the same mistake."

"You don't believe in God, Dermucker. Your god is money."

"I can see I cannot reason with you." Dermucker sighed. "But you can do nothing about any of this."

"You give me no choice. I must be honest about the treaty, but I will not try to punish you. That is in God's hands."

"Blast it! Stop talking like this."

"If the whole truth comes out, Dermucker, so be it."

Dermucker swore. "You are going to betray me, just like you did Rotcraft, you lowdown snake!"

"To sacrifice my country's freedom to an oppressive treaty would be a greater betrayal."

"Well, I'm not going to betray my world class citizenship. That is more important. I will deny your story to the end, and no one will believe you."

"No matter the frequency or density of your denials, the truth is the same."

"Get out! You will regret this, you fool!" he screamed at Canosa's back.

Immediately Dermucker purchased every newspaper in the country. To this day, Dermucker owns controlling shares in most major newspapers in the Land of Goyim, and his philosophy is the established line for reporters.

Canosa tried to publish the complete story of the Pax Universalis treaty and the murderous policies of most nations who would be members of Pax. But when he tried to warn of the dangerous threat to Goy culture and sovereignty, he was censored.

On the other hand, Dermucker's presses rolled continually. He had enlisted Banberg's help in leveling charges against Canosa, and it showed: Canosa was an enemy of the people, he had tried to bribe public officials, he couldn't be trusted in business, he had breached vital business contracts and was not reliable, his family possessed illegal drugs, he was selfish and isolationist, and he was paranoid; he had lied about Rotcraft for reasons of personal vengeance, he had been personally responsible for kicking Rotcraft out of his church, he ruled the senate like a tyrant; but worst of all, he was smearing innocent people like the Dermucker and Banberg families, reviling their past, and making false accusations. How could he lie about such great benefactors to society, just because he disagreed with the glorious Pax treaty? Did his opinions justify such tactics?

The frequency and density of coverage finally took its toll. Sports and theater celebrities publicly condemned Canosa; the senate threw him out; the people laughed him to scorn; death threats were made against him.

Fearing for his family, my grandfather fled to Cumorah and we all went with him: Grandma, my parents, my sister, brother, and myself, and my uncle and family. Everyone bearing the Canosa name was banished from the Land of Goyim.

The Dermucker Foundation presses reshaped Goy opinion so thoroughly that the people forgot their concerns about Rotcraft. The people welcomed him back with open arms. But they never forgave Sein Canosa.

Our days in exile were peaceful. Grandfather made his peace with God, but he never got over his sorrow.

We all tried to forget about those people who had caused us so much pain, but after I grew up, I heard a few things about them, especially since many people migrated from the Land of Goyim. Several decades ago, the Land of Goyim suffered a major technological breakdown, and it declined into barbarism. Therefore many left, seeking a better life in other lands.

By the time he died, Adolph Banberg had established the famous Banberg Scholarships, and he drafted many legal documents for Pax, which members of his Egalitarian association are currently laboring to pass in nations of the world. A Dermucker girl married Banberg's son. She must have inherited her father's financial genius, because their son Rupert is now a renowned financier, and resides in Zarahemla.

Dermucker's son, Mervin, Jr., married Rotcraft's daughter Elidor and had Harvey, who also lives in Zarahemla.

Rotcraft has been out of sight for several years now. He is at least ten years older than I. I don't know if the old buzzard is still alive. But his legacy of idolatry still causes death, slavery, and suffering to untold numbers of people.

6

The hour was exceedingly late, but Haman was wide awake, stunned to silence by what he had heard. At last he said, "But what does this have to do with my family?"

"It grieves me deeply to tell you this, *joven*. All the while my family was trying to forget Rotcraft and get on with their lives, Rotcraft forgot nothing. He tracked my grandfather and all of us very closely, especially my brother, who lived and worked in España for many years. There his daughter was born, and her name was Sarita."

"My mother?" Haman asked in amazement.

"The same."

"Then you are my great-uncle."

"And your mother is a Canosa."

"Why did no one tell us?"

"You were too young to be burdened with such dangerous knowledge. Even so, it afforded little protection."

"What do you mean?"

"Alger Rotcraft knew of Sarita's marriage to your father, and that Amoz ben Gideon tried to smuggle out vital information concerning the Tartarus underground, including the extensive persecution of Christians in the Tartarus Empire. So Rotcraft placed a call to his friend Vladimir, who captured Amoz ben Gideon. Because of Rotcraft's betrayal, your grandpa was wrenched from the arms of his family."

Haman showed no emotion. "I find it difficult to believe you actually know someone connected with the MVD, or the FSB, or whatever that gestapo is called. Those police always seemed without names or faces."

Canosa groaned. "But your grandpa is real, Haman — your own flesh and blood. And you may never see him again."

"My grandfather was harsh and impatient."

"For that, did he deserve to be thrown in the Gulag?"

Haman was still in denial. "This is impossible. The Gulag no longer exists. The terms you keep using — Gulag, idolatry, human sacrifice — those are relics of the ancient past. Nobody does those things any more."

"Every now and then, evil gets a face lift, but truth never changes."

"Still, I have few memories of my grandfather. He frightened me, and I tried to stay out of his way. I didn't like him much."

"It is better to be trusted than to be loved."

They sat quietly for a few moments, and Canosa wondered what more he could do to soften this young man's heart. "Oh, I forgot to tell you the rest of the story about Rotcraft. While he was in exile, he begat an unknown number of illegitimate children. I think the youngest one is just a few years older than you are. Of course, Rotcraft changed the name of all his offspring, so they wouldn't bear the stigma of his disgrace and arouse suspicion. But he took up the work of Voltairism on two fronts: the Tartarus underground robber bands, who plunder, murder, and terrorize all nations, and —"

"Why aren't those robbers arrested?" Haman asked.

"Because Tartarus has agents of influence deep within the Cumorah Bureau of Investigation and Zarahemla Republic Intelligence organizations. Although good men are involved in both CBI and ZRI, the agencies as a whole are often neutralized by the pervasive influence of Tartarus sympathizers, called Egalitarians. Now, let me finish what I started to explain.

"And it came to pass that, over the years, the leadership of Egalitarians came to rest in the Rotcraft branch of this dynasty. Membership of this association is public knowledge, but traditionally the identity of their leader is kept secret. In fact, speaking of ancient things, a relatively small number of hard core Tartarus leaders use oaths of secrecy which are as old as the tower of Babel. They vow to protect each other in whatsoever difficult circumstances they should be placed, so their members won't suffer for their murders, plundering, and stealing done both in the criminal underworld and with approval from governments. Of course, this is not generally known, because agents of Tartarus promote Egalitarian ideas, which on the surface appear to be benevolent. These days Egalitarians have an air of respectability, and are represented in the government. Gradually, they are taking over many elements of our society."

"How could such a group ever be respectable?"

"It's called semantics. Egalitarians and their followers twist the meanings of words . . . Remember we just spoke of new names for old evils? For example, let me read a portion of their manifesto, and I quote: 'By international standards of law, and for the good of mankind, killing is sometimes justified. The following exceptions to the judgment of murder are made out of respect for other cultures who revere such justification as: population control, mercy killing, gender selection, expediency, abnormalities, undesirable characteristics, ethnic cleansing, rebellion against the dictates of society's leaders, complicity of family, or any and all political reasons or pagan rites not covered in the above —"

"Stop!" Haman covered his ears. "This can't be true. Why doesn't someone arrest these people?"

"Because in this land we have freedom of conscience. The law can have no hold upon them, because there is no law against a man's belief. The Egalitarians have a great influence on our lawmakers. We now have laws which legalize some forms of murder. Some people sincerely believe these things, so to arrest them would be tantamount to taking political prisoners."

"How confusing."

"Some things which are legal in the society of man are against the laws of God. Do you see now why I asked you about lending your support to some organizations, Haman?"

"I think so. Still, just because Harvey's grandfather did all those awful things, doesn't mean Harvey will, too."

"You are right about that."

"Maybe Harvey feels bad about his father's actions. That must be the reason he is so anxious to help the poor. Yes, I'm sure that's it. Besides, nobody is perfect."

"You don't have to be perfect to be a good person, Haman. One who is true and faithful to eternal principles is a just man in the sight of God. It is called integrity."

"I call it prejudice. Harvey is a good man, with worthy goals for all mankind."

"But remember how powerful these men are, Haman. An old maxim says power corrupts. We have learned by sad experience how men who start out with the best of intentions can end up exercising unrighteous dominion. And it is easier for a good man's seed to go bad than it is for children to turn around the wicked traditions of their fathers. This evil can go on as far as the third and fourth generation."

"But you said Rupert Banberg is no longer involved in the Egalitarians."

"I did not say that. Rupert and Harvey are members."

Haman gasped.

"Remember, Haman, many, very many people sympathize with the beliefs of Egalitarians. Many government officials belong to that organization, and most members are highly respected in society. Many people join just for the prestige, and may or may not endorse every core belief. I have not begun to explain all their doctrines, some of which sound quite appealing on the surface. Nevertheless, Egalitarians violate the commandments of God, and Yeshurun stands unalterably opposed to their goals. Of course," Canosa added with a wry smile, "we are not nearly so popular as Egalitarians."

"So they are popular?"

"Quite. And Haman, Alger Rotcraft is probably dead by now and has passed control of the Egalitarians on to one of his many offspring. So the Egalitarian leader's name is unknown. Whoever he is, his father will have carefully taught him to despise the Canosa family. And he will have learned a deep and violent hatred for Yeshurun and all we stand for. There is no enemy quite so venomous as an apostate —— one who once united with the believers but has left the faith and turned against it. Be careful."

"It looks pretty obvious."

"Trouble is, it's not. Unlike Dermucker, Adolph Banberg had a heightened sense of good and evil. Only his definitions were often the opposite of Grandfather's, and he was exceedingly zealous about them. For example, if Banberg thought you could help him achieve his goals, he would treat you like you were his friend forever. But once he decided you were his enemy, watch out! He had no mercy."

"Who would be his enemy?"

"Anyone who interfered with his global plans."

"Terrific. So I am related to the mortal enemies of the world's most powerful leaders."

"It's not all bad. Babylon will fall, anyway."

"Babylon?"

"The world, I mean. To be on the Lord's side, we must keep ourselves unspotted from the world."

Haman wrinkled his nose. "Now you sound like my father. This is the modern world we live in, Canosa. Living in the past is not the answer. You must stop this visionary nonsense and raise your awareness to your obligations to the world."

Canosa chuckled. "Now who's preaching?"

Haman was not amused. "This is not religion, but rather every man's duty."

"The religion of Babylon is secular, Haman, but a religion, nonetheless."

Haman stiffened in his chair. "The scriptures say a time comes when every man must leave his family and pursue world peace. Without world peace, nothing else matters, Canosa!"

"Is it so important that it justifies any means to achieve it, Haman? Even abandoning your true family, the God of Abraham, or your Father in Heaven, to worship at the altars of Babylon? And all this for such peace as the world gives, and not as God gives us? Is it worth it?"

"Now you are using semantics."

"Truth is eternal, Haman. The prophet warned us not to turn unto fables."

Haman laughed without mirth. "I can endure this no longer! It is you who speak fables. Prophets. Babylon. Indeed! You expect me to believe the words of one obscure prophet when the whole world is telling me he is wrong?"

"Sometimes those who trust in God are few and unpopular."

"It seems to me, prophets are always against the whole world."

"That is the general idea."

"I still find it very difficult to believe the most respected leaders in the world are as bad as you say."

"Throughout your life you will be enticed by the sweet or the bitter. It is given you to decide for yourself."

"I don't think you really care what I do. You just want to keep the numbers of your flocks looking good."

Canosa sighed. "The kingdom of God will roll on, with or without you, Haman. But I do care about you. Very much. I pray for your happiness, and wickedness never was happiness."

"Good grief."

"Look. Don't take my word for it. For the sake of the fairness you champion so eloquently, investigate it all on your own. If you can prove me wrong, then we can all rejoice. If not, then you have been warned in time. Will you?"

"Well, I guess I can do that much."

Canosa stood to show the interview was over. Then he surprised Haman, and swept him into a great hug. "I may only be a distant uncle, but I have always loved you as a grandson, Haman."

"I. . .love you, too . . . Grandpa."

7

Wednesday Jaime Canosa visited the home of Chief Judge Solano. His old friend had said the meeting was of grave importance.

"Canosa," Solano turned to a tall young man standing beside his chair. "Meet Archibald Kingerman, State Consul, who will head intelligence for the Cumeni liberation effort."

Canosa regarded the suave complexion, the stylish suit and silk tie. Very young to hold such a high post. He nodded and shook hands. The young man did not look him in the eye.

"To the point." The Chief was brisk. "With the help of *apparatchik* agents and massive arms shipments from the Empire, Cabrios has created a police state. He has nationalized the market, placed spies on every block, and wiped out any opposition. He has murdered thousands, and holds more as political prisoners."

The Chief slammed his fist on the desk. "This tyrant is at our door, and we must rid the hemisphere of this cancer before it spreads any further!"

"Sir." Kingerman thumbed a stack of papers. "Intelligence sources have informed us Cabrios' forces are still not well organized. If we organize and train opposition forces, including the underground freedom fighters and the various groups in exile, the oppressed in Cumeni can successfully liberate themselves and install a neutral caretaker government until free elections can be held."

"Here you come in, Canosa," the Chief said, "with your experience and fluency in their dialect. I want you to organize the Freedom Fighters into a tight, well-disciplined unit."

Solano leaned forward, stroking his balding head. "Then, if we provide massive air cover, Cabrios will never get off the ground, and we will rid ourselves of this menace. With adequate air cover, the invasion cannot fail. Canosa, we must not fail!"

8

The afternoon sun glowed in the summer sky, hurling golden lights down on Lake Tantagua. Ben drove northwest from Granada to the federal district and the vast Solano plantation. Immense, well-tended fields and modern equipment were evidence of education, industry, and enterprise. Ben parked at the gate to admire the lake. The Chief Judge of Cumorah lived on an island, with the vast lake forming a moat and resembling the layout of a medieval realm. It was surrounded by floating gardens, restored by the state to much of their previous grandeur.

"Mr. Solano is expecting you." After the customary weapons check, the guard let down the drawbridge for Ben to pass through on foot.

Ben walked over the long bridge, wound his way up the drive and around the curve. Hard to believe that behind these banks spangled with blue blossoms and neat terraces thick with roses were high fences and hidden armed guards. Solano managed to maintain the balance between gracious living and tight security without losing touch with the people. Every precaution had been taken against external threats. But Solano had the magnanimity of a King Arthur.

Curse the day when any man should undertake to ruin the nation from within.

Ben could taste a scent of honeysuckle, and the same air which breathed rose perfume across his face brought melancholy strains of Tchaikovsky's "None but the Lonely Heart". Imperfectly but well, somebody was playing a piano.

Ben made a mental note to find someone special to whom he could spirit away one of those red roses.

A man, probably a government official, came out and closed the front door quietly, looking back at the house as he walked away. Ben entered the courtyard and waited. The man strode toward him, head down, deep in thought. His tie tack bore some manner of insignia: an outline of the world with a large money sign imposed upon it. In his preoccupation, the stranger almost collided with Ben. "Oh! I didn't hear you drive up."

The music stopped. "Of course not," Ben replied. "I parked at the road."

"Are you cleared?"

"Yes."

The man smiled apologetically. "Sorry, young man. I guess in a perfect world I wouldn't have to ask such questions." The stranger hurried away without another word.

The official disappeared around the bend. No doubt, this was one more nice man, just trying to do his job. Ben chided himself for his inclination to lump all bureaucrats and politicians into one negative category. It was probably the muckraking blood charging around in his sarcastic veins. Unlike most of the news industry who had a tendency to fawn over their favorite politicians, Ben distrusted all persons with political power, including Solano.

Constant lionizing or vilifying was done far too much in the press these days —— to the extent it had almost become a Pavlovian response. Reader and journalist alike would leap into the judgmental fray, salivating falsehoods and slinging all facts to the ensuing dust-filled winds. All too often this could result in glorification of the most despicable persons, while the just were vilified, denounced, ruined, and driven out. An innocent person could be destroyed. If he was going to be a journalist with integrity, Ben reminded himself, he must not participate in this confusion. He resolved from that moment to give every man the benefit of the doubt, first impressions notwithstanding. After all, as the proverb said: "As a man thinketh in his heart, so is he."

"You may wait here." A young woman showed Ben to the patio. He selected a wrought-iron chair by a small table near the veranda, partly shaded by citrus, banana, and poinciana trees. Surrounding a fountain centered in the garden were fragrant gardenias, plumeria, white and purple orchids, and other flowers. But Ben was not looking at the flowers.

Ben stretched out his long legs and leaned back casually, staring at the girl. He watched the sun heap gold upon her long dark hair. She walked like a royal princess from another world. Color rushed to her face; she smiled, and then she was gone.

Anastasio Solano soon appeared and shook hands. His manner was cordial. "I know your father, Benjamin, and I respect him. I invited you here to honor you as valedictorian of Yeshurun Academy, a school I found to be unique. Also, your newspaper article intrigued me. Now, young man, before we begin this interview, did you have a particular question?"

"Uh, yes, sir . . . uh . . . What is that girl's name?"

Solano laughed. "That is a particular question, all right."

Ben stammered. "Forgive me, sir. I don't know what came over me. Actually, I am always interested in improving our public relations with community leaders . .uh . . . " He spread his arms in despair. "Could I leave and start over?"

Solano's laughter burst out anew. "Oh, wait till I tell the Señora this one!" He stopped suddenly. "I'm sorry, *joven*," he said gently, wiping the tears from his eyes. "I really needed a good laugh but didn't mean to do it at your expense." He coughed to regain his composure.

"Canosa speaks highly of you. At my request, he gave me a copy of your senior paper which the dean read to the Cumorah Historical Society."

Ben nodded.

The General settled in his patio chair and closed his eyes for a moment in the sun's warmth. "In it," he continued, "you quoted the Spanish philosopher and writer, Juan Donoso-Cortés, who said something like this. When religious influence, or internal self-control, declines, then external political control, or tyranny, rises. Donoso-Cortés called this relationship between morality and liberty 'the law

122

of history.' The school is justifiably proud. Your treatment of this profound subject is brilliant."

"Thank you, sir. Actually, the idea does not originate with Donoso-Cortés, but is as old as God's dealings with man. It was a covenant discovered among writings from a distant branch of Israel."

"And what is this covenant?"

"Serve God and prosper, or forsake God and be swept from the land."

"So tell me, Benamoz. Do you think I am serving God by inviting a Pax Universalis Peace Force to help me rid the land of terrorism?"

"I admire your goal, sir, but you are making a big mistake to ally yourself with PAX."

Solano leaned back, amused at this young man's boldness. "So what is my mistake?"

"The Hebrew prophet Samuel warned about tyrants such as this. He spoke about one man as a king, but PAX is a committee of such men. If you yield Cumorah sovereignty to PAX, you will be one of them. Do you have a son?"

"Yes."

"'He will take your sons for his chariots', Samuel said, 'and he will take your daughters. He will take your fields, and the best of your vineyards and olive yards, and give them to his minions. He will take your best young men . . . '"

Solano drew back as if he had been jabbed. "You drive home well your point, *joven*. Still, you are trained for the military. Why are you not in the thick of battle, for example, like your brother Leb?"

"We need to be prepared at all times to defend our families, our lands, liberty, and religion. But war is not justified in an attempt to enforce a new order of government, or even to impel others to a particular form of worship, however better the government or eternally true the principles of the enforced religion may be. But it is more than a military conflict, sir. It is about ideas. Every man walks in his own way, and after the image of his own god."

"How so?"

"The battle for a soul takes place in the minds of men. Pax Universalis is like a league of tribes which developed anciently in this land. That league did not live by the law and the prophets, but rather according to the minds of men who were their leaders. They enforced a strict obedience upon member tribes, thus achieving a

123

degree of peace among themselves. But their hearts were turned to idolatry, and they stoned the prophets of God and cast them out from among them."

Solano rose from his chair, greatly agitated. "But young man, how can you say this? Supporters of PAX have suggested their alliance represents the consummation of Christian teachings. Here, let me show you something."

The two men walked across the courtyard to a far wing which harbored Solano's art gallery. "I have a few originals," he said modestly, "but mostly I content myself with reproductions. To my good fortune, Monet would sometimes do several studies of one subject, so here's a small original of this water scene. The Renoirs and my one Rembrandt, though reproductions, are excellent. Some originals are being smuggled out from the Land of Goyim now, because the people don't care about great art — their tastes are degenerating."

"This is the one I wanted you to see." Solano indicated a large painting of a destroyed ancient city, with a crowd of its inhabitants looking heavenward toward a figure robed in white, descending into their midst.

Ben gulped back his astonishment. "An original Friberg?"

"Oh, no. I was lucky to get this one. These Fribergs were at your school, Ben. They were expensive, but worth it. This one depicts a visit of the Messiah to this land in the early first century. That visit has been said to originate a legend of the fiery serpent . . . " Solano looked at Ben's face. "You know this artist?"

"Yes, his work corresponds to the history of ancient nations in this land."

"Then, do you believe, as do I, that this fiery serpent represents the Christ, at least figuratively?" Solano's face softened. "And that He will return?"

"Yes." Ben's voice took on a harsh tone. "And when He does return, He will find, as did the Spanish conquerors, rampant human sacrifice."

Solano stared at the young man. "You have a most vivid way of expressing your opinions, Benjamin. Come to think of it, though, these last two centuries *have* seen the rise of ghastly ways to destroy human life. How I long for the return of the Holy One, that this evil might be ended. Which brings me back to my dilemma."

Stroking his chin, Solano led the way back to the patio. He handed Ben the day's newspaper. "Every day, terrorism threatens the lives of my people. What am I to do? Is not this PAX well intentioned? Is it not the world's answer to peace?"

"Is that what you want? The world's answer? Have you ever heard of a well-intentioned dictator on a world scale?"

Solano studied his young visitor. "How do you do it?"

"Do what, sir?"

"Confound me repeatedly with your insights."

"Brother Bianco is my mentor."

"Brother Bianco?"

"He is a prophet of God."

"Wait a minute! You're telling me there is again a living prophet of God among us?"

"Yes."

"Hmm, and you are of Yeshurun. I suppose it's possible," he mused.

"You should talk to him, Mr. Solano. Brother Bianco has seen this before. He knows."

"He knows what?"

"If you must ask, then you will not understand. You must find out for yourself."

"I will consider it. But for now, give me your response to this puzzle. On the right, we have Cabrios' terrorism, and on the left we have PAX, which seems benevolent but is potentially a world tyranny. And where would you place Yeshurun's position, Benjamin . . . on the right or the left?"

"Neither right nor left. We are centered on Christ. 'Look to God and live!' our prophets always tell us. God does not walk in crooked paths, neither does he turn to the right hand nor to the left. His paths are straight . . . "

"Of course. I should have known. Religion has no part with this political jargon."

"Your idea of the political spectrum comes from the seating arrangement in France's legislative body during the French Revolution," Ben said. "We think of the left as more government control, with the extreme left being total government. On the right are found those who favor less government, with the extreme right being anarchy, or no government. Anyone who does not agree with the media is labeled as an extremist."

"You have to admit Cabrios is pretty extreme."

"Definitely. Cabrios' philosophy comes from the eastern countries, where the order of Voltaire exploded into being."

"Yeshurun seems to be strongly opposed to the order of Voltaire. Isn't that a political position?"

"Our history holds a pattern that prefigures the order of Voltaire. An ancient type among the tribe of Joseph was a man named Nehor. Nehor killed a man who disagreed with him. After the murder, the judgment upon Nehor was that he tried to enforce his philosophy with the sword. Thereafter, those who forced their doctrines upon others by criminal means or by the sword of the state were said to be after the order of Nehor. The order of Voltaire closely parallels Nehor. For this reason, Yeshurun opposes Voltairism and other doctrines of men."

"That is a different view. My children's school books characterize Voltaire as generous, enthusiastic, and sentimental," Solano said. "The world esteems him as a defender of tolerance. How could the man's philosophy have brought forth so much evil?"

"As always, court historians are very selective," Ben replied. "Voltaire harbored a deep and abiding hatred for all religions, monarchs, and religious moral standards."

"Why this extreme animosity toward religion?"

"He considered religion to be the cause of all of society's ills," Ben said. "His obsession to 'crush' Jesus Christ and His Church is a matter of record. According to Voltaire, in the war against Christianity, it was necessary to lie ——— 'not timidly and for a time, but boldly and always.'"

"So in his mind, the end definitely justified the means," Solano said.

"Voltaire's ideas ultimately influenced the French Revolution."

"And now," Solano said, "these factions still exist. Revolutionaries continue to be the obvious enemy."

Ben chuckled. "If you can be found swaggering around in the forests, bellowing about a forceful overthrow of governments, you are as obvious as a wolf baying in the night, and become but a pawn for the order of Voltaire. By contrast, the left column *evolved* here in the west. Here, the Egalitarian approach is more subtle . . . "

"In fact, insidious. Egalitarians work the inside track. They are doing more to demoralize this nation than Cabrios could ever hope to accomplish. Yet the Egalitarians are forever yapping about doing good and helping others —"

"Much as a wolf might pose as a sheep dog. Whatever the approach, the result is the same."

Solano nodded. "Tyranny."

126

"Egalitarians come to us in warm and fuzzy clothing, but inwardly they are poisonous serpents."

"Have you considered going into teaching, Benjamin?"

"I see myself as a teacher, but my two older brothers always accuse me of trying to run their lives." Ben took a pen from his shirt pocket. "My brothers figure somebody must always rule over everyone else. They have no confidence in a people's ability to govern itself."

On the newspaper margin he drew a circle with small openings at top and bottom of the sphere. He wrote "obedience to God" at the top. "Here we are," he continued. "At the top, just right of center, is the peak of a civilization, or golden age. Here you have minimum external government, with discipline coming from within the individual. Each of several persons in governing positions answers to the electorate. Each citizen is accountable to God, the source of all liberties. This system generates maximum freedom, peace and prosperity."

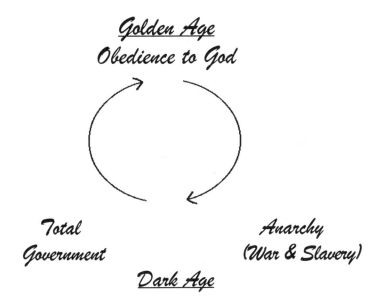

Golden Age
Obedience to God

Total
Government

Anarchy
(War & Slavery)

Dark Age

Solano leaned over and peered at the diagram, fascinated.

Ben traced down the right leg of the circle with his pen. "As people distance themselves from God through pride, covetousness, and immorality, they descend to turmoil and contention, then anarchy. In reality you can see the two supposed extremes of anarchy and total government are close together. Terrorists bridge the narrow gap of anarchy only to impose their choice of tyranny. So here at the lowest point in the cycle, or the dark age of a civilization, you have war and slavery." He traced his pen up the left side and skipped over a gap at the top. "Once you lose true liberty, you can only get it back by spilling blood and returning accountability to God. But most nations never recover from the falling away period."

"How exquisitely simple." Solano marveled. "Who taught you this?"

"No one. It is a historical pattern. Such simplicity and plainness come from the book of Joseph. It is the word of the living God, and will convince the world of the Bible's truthfulness."

"This book is true? You have it on good authority?"

Ben smiled. "I have it on the highest authority, and it is self-evident."

"Quite a claim."

"It is not a claim. It is a quote. The Lord himself said it is true." A gull called in the distance, and Ben scanned the far line where pale sky met the sea. "It was brought forth in our era by the power of God."

"If this is true, it explains why tyrants frequently resort to book burnings." Solano's tone was heavy, but he smiled. "This is the most scintillating conversation I've had in years. You have definitely influenced my thinking. You say war is not justified to change another nation's form of government. How could I ever hope to cure terrorism with aggression or tyrannical laws? Why, I wasn't thinking at all! It is all clear to me now. We will work for principled arbitration, defend our own, and not be drawn into war. Let me make a brief phone call, then you must stay and eat with us, *hijo*."

Solano withdrew to his private phone. "Arch? Solano here. Listen carefully. I have deliberated extensively on the Cumeni matter, and it must be stopped before it is too late. I have decided to abort the mission immediately. Canosa is to be recalled. All covert operations are to be canceled, effective from this moment."

There was a long pause. "Are you sure about this?"

"Absolutely. We shall deal with this matter without resorting to war, and thus save lives. My decision is final and irrevocable."

"I hear you, sir. Consider it done."

The sun settled down, turning the indigo sea to shimmering copper. Ben was invited to the library to browse until dinner. Ceiling to floor shelves held: Aristotle, Homer, Cicero, John Locke, William Blackstone, Frederic Bastiat, many volumes of history, complete writings of the founders of the great and fallen civilization in the north — the Land of Goyim — and every other published work which was a hallmark of western civilization. The historical works especially showed heavy use.

Attracted by the grand piano in the family room, Ben went in and looked over the family pictures on the mantel. General Solano was riding with a younger man, the oldest of five children. Wedding pictures, grandparents, friends and babies. This Chief Judge was real. He was human, and he was humble. A rare quality in a political leader.

On a wall behind the piano bench hung a large Renoir painting of a young woman playing a piano; her serene face, and her white dress done in frothy brush strokes, had a quiet, dreamlike quality. A color photo with gilded frame sat on the piano. In it was a family, including the girl who had greeted him. He had never seen her before today, but the family looked somehow familiar. Ben had seen that mother and father and two young children somewhere before, but could not remember where. No matter. He gazed at the girl. She was here, she was entrancing, and he would see her again.

· A good dinner and warm hospitality renewed his nerve. Solano and his wife Flora were not only good hosts, they were friends.

"General, forgive me, sir, but I am still interested in that young lady. Would she be your secretary?"

"Ah, yes, our bookkeeper, staff manager, and tutor for the children. She is a very valuable employee." Solano smiled. "If you are entertaining plans which would remove her from our employ, then her name is classified."

Benjamin grinned. "As far as I know, it is still a free country, so it is legal for me to call on her. As for her employment, that is her choice!"

Solano chuckled. "You win!" He gave an exaggerated sigh. "I have this feeling that a major sacrifice will soon be required from me, and I shall have to find a new domestic manager! Her name is Anahí Cercado."

"Cercado? The family that —"

"The same."

The young man excused himself from the table and returned to the music room. Solano followed him. Ben held the photo and looked from it to Solano and back again, speechless.

"The poor child was away at the university in Sheffa when the massacre took place. She heard it on the news. The incident so incensed me that I immediately visited Ammonihah myself and was there when she arrived. She has no one. I took her in."

"Anahí," Ben said softly.

"You must be careful, Ben. If she detects pity, she will run from you. But perhaps you will be good for her. She is with the children. I will call her and you may see her now."

"About that sacrifice, sir." Ben's smile was a trifle sheepish. "Not major, though."

"Mercy!" Solano nursed a mock pain in his heart. "However much is enough?"

"A red rose for the lady."

"Oh. A dozen is enough, then. Maybe."

9

"My name is Benjamin Benamoz," he said.

"I know."

She accepted the rose, her face unreadable. "How thoughtful," she said. "This is from the center bush on the terrace with the most southern exposure, isn't it?"

"How did you know?"

"How did you know it was my favorite? I walk in the gardens every day, and I know that bush receives the most sunlight, so it has perfect blooms."

To hide his immense pleasure, Ben turned to the Renoir. "It was you playing the piano earlier, wasn't it?"

"I teach the children in the morning, but sometimes I get a chance to play in the afternoon."

"No doubt all the visitors are a frequent interruption. I met one on my way up here. An admirer of yours, perhaps?"

She stiffened. "Arch Kingerman. He is here every day. We argue often about politics. Something about him . . . I know you are a historian," she said abruptly. "But are you familiar with literature?"

"Hmm. I enjoy Shakespeare."

"Ah, yes. Well, Arch Kingerman reminds me of Macbeth."

Whoa. Methinks the lady scorns the knave. "I have no spur to prick the sides of my intent, but only vaulting ambition, which o'erleaps itself," Ben quoted.

She giggled. It was a delicious sound. "That says it all. I do not understand why Arch Kingerman is in Mr. Solano's administration."

"Mr. Solano is kind to everyone. He is a great soldier, but he does not always recognize the more subtle adversary."

"Mr. Solano has been like a father to me, and I love him very much. I hope he doesn't get hurt. Forgive me." She hung her head. "I have become cynical, and I forget my manners." Above a hesitant smile, her eyes were flashing with bitterness.

"Nothing to forgive," Ben said gently. "Here we stand, and I have not even offered you a chair." He ushered her to the dining table, where she sat facing him, and began to twist and untwist a fresh white linen napkin. Ben looked past her to the Renoir in the adjacent family room. Unlike the woman in the painting, Anahí's face showed suffering and turmoil and gave him no peaceful illusion. There before him in a river of moonlight, she looked very alone, but he resisted an urge to take her hand and comfort her. "So who taught you to play the piano?" he said at last.

"My mother . . . " Her face softened. "My mother taught me all she knew, and urged me to continue at the university."

"If music be the food of love, play on."

"From the Twelfth Night," she returned, a smile playing about the corners of her mouth.

"You must meet my brother. He wants to learn more about Shakespeare. But now, Anahí, would you play for me?"

She played "Claire de Lune". Music flowed at her fingertips, rippling over the milk-white keys, filling the room. The light which now filled her face was not from the moon; for the moment, she was at peace.

"Tell me, Anahí, is the moon still blue now?"

"Oh, yes," she said. "Tonight happens to be a rare time, you know, when we have a second full moon in the calendar month."

He laughed softly. "Did you learn that from your mother, too?"

Her eyes misted. "Yes. She taught me so much about beauty —— music, art, literature, nature. But now . . . " she stopped herself, then continued bravely. "When I was home from the university, we would go for walks. Once she saw a quetzal bird. You know, that rare and exquisite creature native to this land. Its breast is red as this rose, and its sweeping tail is green as the ferns in the floating gardens. Have you seen it, Ben?"

"No, I've not had the pleasure. I should make the time."

"Me, too. I spent so much time at the university, and now I wonder what good came from it." Visibly, her anger returned.

He waited.

"I graduated from a fine university, Ben. My professors taught me how things work, what happened and when, and all about those who are great in the sight of men, and yet . . . " She paused and turned to the window. "For example, the professors refused to teach history. They said it was all clichéd and dull."

"Of course. All life is boring to dullards. Those who don't do their homework always repeat the worst mistakes from history, since they refuse to learn from it."

"Not only that, those professors were allowed to write their own history!" she continued with dismay. "I think Professor Cromwell made it up as he went along, as if it were a fable. The narrative is, not facts, but only what the teachers think it should be. I wouldn't mind so much if they would only be honest and admit it was all their opinion."

"Hmm. You think like I do."

"Then you are the first. Look out there," she said. Pale white stood in stark contrast to black shadows and the surrounding sky. "It reminds me of Nils Cromwell, my history professor who taught fables." Moonlight had transformed the house, patio, courtyard wall, and the lake beyond into an ethereal white. "Now, you and I know the grass in the yard is not really white, and the trees and their leaves are not really gray. But Cromwell changed the rules. He redefined the words. We were discussing the history of Cumorah — something which I know very well. When the Gentiles came, they brought both good and evil. Good men taught the Ten Commandments and the Golden Rule. But Gentile soldiers did many evil things to my people."

"It was prophesied."

"Yes, my mother spoke about ancient prophets who foretold the conquest of my people because of their wickedness. I am not proud of many things my ancestors did, Ben. But I am grateful for my colonial-era ancestor who was wiser than his peers. My ancestor believed in the ways of peace. But Professor Cromwell said, 'The so-called holy men of the Gentiles were actually all greedy, egotistical monsters because they conquered the Lamanite culture.'

"'Idolatry was wicked,' I told him.

"'The words *idolatry* and *wicked* are condemned in your social studies book on page sixty-six, because those are hate-words used by an obscure culture not recognized by our official histories,' he replied.

"'Well, my ancestors were glad to accept the Golden Rule instead, because they saw it would lead to a more peaceful and prosperous culture,' I told him.

"'To imply one culture is better than another is an insult!' Cromwell shouted. 'Your ancestors were traitors to your culture!'

"'But human sacrifice was evil!' I protested.

"'Who knows what is good, and what is evil? You only think that because your mother told you so,' he said, and everyone laughed.

"'Killing is wrong, no matter who does it!' I insisted.

"'Killing is sometimes justified,' he said. Then he described the darkest and most evil things — things which I would call sin — and Ben, he had every person in that class convinced those evil things were good, that light is evil, and darkness is good. When I disagreed, he ridiculed me, and he got the whole class to embarrass me. I was so humiliated."

"Nils Cromwell. I know about him."

"You do?"

"He was fired from Yeshurun Academy, because he loved darkness rather than light."

"Hmm." She tilted her head. "I have heard that expression before. Well, the state university hired him, and he brought his darkness into the classroom. Cromwell was the worst, but he organized the remaining educators, and now all of them grope around, pretending to see by the artificial light of their bias. It seems the school pays them to teach lies."

"This is called enforced priestcraft, and it's what got Cromwell fired from Yeshurun Academy. He set himself up as some kind of light unto the world, but his light dimmed to mere pinhole illumination by the time it escaped the conceit-choked tunnels of his constricted mind."

She gave him a surprised look, then smiled. "I didn't expect such words from you."

"Oh, I'm full of such things. My enemies — "

"*You* have enemies?"

"I'm the one who wrote the article in the school paper exposing Cromwell's priestcraft, and it got him fired. Oh, he hates my guts, and others, too —"

"It's hard to believe you would have enemies, Ben. Somehow, you look so. . .so. . ."

"I know. Beneath this jolly countenance of mine lurks a sarcastic ogre."

"Oh, my."

"Sometimes the ogre gets downright obnoxious. I really have to fight it." He feigned a slap on each side of his face, cringing from each exaggerated blow, and simulating the sounds of a fist fight.

She laughed.

"It's very hard to control." He grinned. "I need a refining influence, like you."

"Thank you, Ben, for making me laugh. And for not laughing at me . . ." she stopped. "I am rather old-fashioned, and still believe in right and wrong, good and evil."

"You are not alone. I understand, Anahí."

"You do?" Her eyes searched his face. "Yes, you do."

"That which does not edify is not of God, and is darkness. That which is of God is light."

"Somehow, this sounds very familiar."

He nodded.

"Long ago my mother told me the key to my past is that grotesque fiery serpent. Isn't it strange? She, who so loved beauty. She refused to tell me more. Only that I must search out the answers for myself, and when I found the truth, I would know."   "Your mother was more honest than your educators."

Anahí frowned in concentration. "Her words are like a riddle. It haunts my yesterdays —"

"— and casts a shadow on your tomorrows. You are onto something. It is a type."

"What do you mean?"

"I think I have a clue."

She clapped her hands together. "Really? Oh, do tell me."

"It is best explained in the sunshine." He stole a sly glance at her. "Can you wait till tomorrow?"

She flushed a delicate pink which started at her collar and rode to the top of her forehead. "I am caught," she shot back with a radiant smile. "Tomorrow it is."

10

The next day the younger Benamoz men lingered over a late lunch at home, sparring over Shakespeare.

"I feel sorry for you, having to study all that Shakespeare. What good is it?" Abiram turned to his brother with a knowing look. "Unless you want to be some flatulent, greasy-tongued politician!"

"Ouch!" Ben hung his head. "Never. Julius Caesar and Macbeth were politicians. They taught me about the weaknesses of human nature."

"You studied military science and Shakespeare. Quite a combination."

"Okay — military science teaches you something about the way the enemy thinks, which can be logical. Politics are never logical. This is how Shakespeare helps, because he shows you human nature. But don't forget history. It is the story of God's dealings with man. Remember Brother Joseba said you see the future through windows of the past."

"You have a mind for such things. I've forgotten most of it."

"But you have to start with ancient history, in order to see the patterns."

"Like Rome?"

"Even earlier. The book of Joseph speaks about old civilizations on this continent, who were blessed with prosperity as long as they honored God. Now look at the Goyim civilization in the north. Beginning in the eighteenth century, A.D., the Land of Goyim reached its apex of liberty, enjoyed splendid wealth, then went on to dazzle the world with its technology."

"So where did they go wrong?"

"By the twenty-first century, Goyim had altered historical records and corrupted their language. Many Goyim forgot about the Bible, or book of Judah, and they denied the idea of a Creator. The technology in which they took so much pride collapsed because of a pervasive flaw. This is why that nation has sunk into an abyss of barbarism."

"They abandoned their heritage?"

Ben nodded. "And freedom was handed to the Goyim of last century. What we obtain too cheap, we esteem too lightly."

Abiram felt a sting of guilt. He had been totally involved in his work. He never again wanted to think about oppression in the old

135

country. It could never happen here, he had told himself. Not a wise course for a businessman —— complacency could be deadly. Worse, he knew better. "But Solano is doing a good job," he said. "Looks like our future is bright."

"One hears things on the campuses, you know. So-called new ideas which are somehow very familiar. Students are zealous about politics but don't know anything. Trouble is brewing, I can feel it."

A soft knock came on the heavy door in the atrium.

Must be a friend of Ben's. Abiram headed for the shop. "Time to get back to work."

"You can't run away yet!" Ben smiled and backed toward the front door to open it. "Here is someone I want you to meet." He returned with a beautiful young woman on his arm. "Señorita Anahí Cercado, this is Abiram, the man who hates Shakespeare."

Abiram frowned at his brother. "I didn't mean . . . " His eyes took in this girl framed in the open doorway. The sun at her back rested on her hair like welding arcs on black steel. He felt a sudden ache of loneliness. Ben could have all those other women. This one was special. "*Encantado.*" He stammered, and hated his accent. He was making a fool of himself. Abiram lost his voice, so he took her hand and lifted it to his lips. All of a sudden, life was bright and promising, after all. "Please sit down. To what do we owe this delightful occasion, Señorita?"

Ben grinned. "This man says he pities me for studying literature," he said, his eyes gleaming with mischief. "Can you see how barbaric he is? We must needs infuse some culture into him, Señorita!"

Abiram raised one eyebrow. "I? Barbaric? I am only being honest. Ben doesn't care about your fine poetry, Señorita. Behind that cherubic face and dimpled smile lurks a dangerous man." He chuckled.

Ben lunged for his brother, but was a half-second too slow.

Abiram skirted the corner of the table, placing its length between him and his brother. "Come on, *hermano!* If she knew the truth —— that you are really a tomcat on the prowl —— she never would have come here, would she?"

"Why, you . . . " This time Ben's face reddened.

Abiram pressed his advantage. "And I, by my brother's own admission, am at least capable of pity."

"It is not I, but Abiram, who will need pity!"

136

Abiram danced away from Ben's playful fisticuffs. This woman was worth fighting for. But he turned to Anahí in mock fright. "Now who is the barbarian?"

She stifled a giggle.

Then Ben laughed. His mirth filled the room.

Abiram laughed, too. It felt good. "What can I do with a brother like him?"

She shook her head. "This is going to be difficult. I won't be able to say until I get to know this family better," she said.

"Where do we start?" Ben pulled up a chair beside her, edging out his brother.

"Just call me Ani," she said, a trifle breathless.

Señorita Cercado was subtle, but Abiram knew she was sizing up Ben's stature, his striking features, his countenance. It was as though Abiram was not even there. His heart sank. He left for work.

"He can't stay?" she said. "I brought a book of brief Shakespeare quotes which I think he would like."

"He had to leave. If you can trap the moonbeams as well as you did last night, you might succeed in pinning him down at another time." Ben tried to feel guilty, but failed. "You're not in a hurry, are you?"

She looked around the room, apparently disappointed. "I really can't stay."

Ben tried not to show his surprise. She did prefer Abiram, then. How presumptuous he had been. "But you can't leave till I tell you what I promised," he said, feeling like a chump.

"I, uh . . . "

Ben panicked. What had he done to frighten her? She looked confused, embarrassed; as if she wanted to run away.

"Ben! Why don't you offer the Señorita some refreshment?" Sarita emerged from the kitchen, carrying a tray with two glasses of piña colada.

"Anahí. My mother," Ben said quickly.

"*Perdón*, Señorita. Ay, it is difficult to raise four boys. They never remember their *manners,*" she said with exaggerated emphasis, and gave Ben a customary family gesture for little children: *I will take you over my knee and paddle you.*

With Anahí's relieved laughter, understanding came to Ben. In this Land, young people from respectable families were to be accompanied by a chaperon at all times. It was a charming old custom which made the lifestyle of students he had known look a bit forward in comparison, almost coarse. Anahí was a proper young woman who would have brought her own mother if she could. Sarita had gracefully rescued her son from his own thickheadedness. Ben cast his mother a look of gratitude. It would almost be worth a spanking. "Perhaps you can persuade the lady to stay, Mama. She was in a terrible rush."

"I, too, am remiss, Señora. I almost forgot Ben had something important to show me."

He guided her to the giant picture window, where warm gold light cascaded into the room. "Look, the sun is casting shadows upon the wall, now. Just what we need."

"I wish it would enlighten my mind."

"Not only that, it will fill your soul with joy."

"Really?" Anahí clapped her hands together in delight, a small gesture which would always endear her to him.

"Count on it. No more artificial lights of academia for you. This is the authentic light which shines in darkness, but the darkness comprehends it not."

"Somehow, your words often prick my memory. Perhaps my riddle will not remain a mystery forever."

"Pretend for a moment that the sun is the most glorious personage you know. Hold your hand up by the wall. See? Your hand is like a template. It casts a shadow, projecting the shape of your hand. Now move your hand back, closer to the light." This time he took her hand, moving it toward the sun. "The shape is the same, but it covers a larger scale."

"I think I understand."

"It's the same in our lives; the closer we move to the Light, the more encompassing is the pattern. It can go deeper than the nights, and broader than the days."

"I see."

He held her hand in both of his for a long time, and the pattern he saw took on another dimension.

11

Abiram returned to his routine at work, but a new awareness penetrated his former isolation. Solitude had begun to distress him. He wanted what Ben had, but he didn't want to admit it. "So,

138

hermanito," he said with reluctant humility, "you seem to have a gift for women. Tell me, how do you do it?"

"I love them." Ben grinned, but became serious. "That is, I love a certain one who is not vain, who is real. Perhaps it's because I make her think. Women are a practical lot, but they love to talk about ideas, too."

"But why bother her with ideas?"

"Not just any ideas, Abiram. I mean things of the spirit."

"Surely that can't help her bake better bread or raise a better garden."

"Actually, it can. In the garden of a woman's heart are found the blossoms of children's souls."

"Oh. Tell me in plain words, Ben."

"Never underestimate a woman's mind, Abiram. If she is filled with truth, the fruits of her influence will be peace and liberty. But if she's in error, she can ruin the world."

Ben left, whistling.

Abiram gulped back his disappointment and whistled, too — a wedding song.

Abiram did marry before his brother, however, because that night Ben was called into service with the Coast Guard, a mission igniting events which would change his life.

Abiram fell in love with a college acquaintance of Ben's named Alison Russell. One day Abiram asked his mother to explain his helpless adoration for the girl.

"How can it be that I, a practical and simple man, can feel such an attraction to a woman so erudite as Alison?" he had asked.

"There must be opposites in all things," Sarita had replied with a knowing smile. "You will be good for each other. The balance makes a strong marriage."

"I hope so," he said. "But Mama, please teach her how to cook. Her cooking is more terrifying than her intellect."

12

Puerto Cristobal
15 April

Canosa assembled his forces for a briefing session.

"Intelligence says the beaches are sandy," Officer Rook said, "with only a few civilians nearby."

"What about those shadows on the aerial photographs?" came a question.

"Just seaweed," Rook replied. "Military Assistant Archibald Kingerman will now present the Chief Judge's instructions."

Kingerman waited until all eyes were upon him. "It is a difficult flight over the mountains to Cumeni from here, so in order to carry enough fuel, we will have to remove the tail gun turrets from the B-4's."

"Tail guns? What are you thinking, Kingerman?" Canosa demanded. "For our stealth bombers, those mountains are no challenge!"

"Oh, of course. I only want to be sure our men are not put at risk, you know. You see, in the first air strike, we will use ten B-4's, instead of the twenty, originally planned."

The troops broke into agitated consternation. Canosa signaled for silence. "This will leave us extremely vulnerable to Cabrios' Vultures and jets!"

"Trust me. We will be making a powerful first strike to make up for it," Kingerman went on. "Besides, our pilots and an aircraft carrier with modern fighters will be on hand."

Everyone gasped. "But sir, Cabrios has a puny air force, and if we use all our bombers, we can use surprise to wipe them out!"

"Sorry, captain." Kingerman's voice was neutral. "We'll be using eight . . . I mean, ten. And that's final. Those are orders from the Commander-in-Chief."

Eaten up by misgivings, the troops sped off on their mission. Two pilots were killed in the first strike, but the squadron continued with the planned air strikes.

13

On the night of the ground troop invasion, Del Vente took the first troops in fiberglass boats in to shore at the Bay of Zafada. Eighty yards from shore, the silence was broken by a grinding noise, then another, and another.

"Hey!" someone shouted. "That's not seaweed! It's coral reefs, and they're razor-sharp!"

"Retreat!" Del Vente gave the command. As water gushed into the hull, a soldier frantically tried to start the outboard engine. Nothing. No sound of engines starting anywhere.

Slowly, the boats began their withdrawal, rowing. Daylight found them desperately trying to consolidate troops into undamaged boats. The boats not ripped open by the coral were strafed to powder by machine-guns on Cabrios' low-flying Vultures.

With assurances of all-out assistance from Cumorah, Canosa urged on his forces.

Canosa took 150 prisoners at Girón. Fifty of them joined his forces. A radio message from Rook soon diminished even that small victory.

"Cabrios' Vultures took out the CRS Neapolis, Canosa." This raid destroyed a ten-days' supply of food, ammunition, gasoline, and communication.

"What about the other seven ships?" Canosa shot back.

"They headed out to sea without unloading their ammunition."

Aboard the Coast Guard flagship, Ben radioed Cumorah, seeking either low jet cover or a navy destroyer to escort the ships back to shore at night to unload their ammunition.

Cumorah refused air cover and kept the ships sixty miles offshore.

Despite this lack of support, Canosa's brigade landed at Playa Larga, overpowered two thousand of Cabrios' men and captured a dozen enemy tanks.

That day, the Cumeni Freedom Fighters brigades were encouraged by their success. They had less then twenty dead and some fifty wounded. But Cabrios' forces, undisciplined and untrained, totaled five hundred dead and a thousand wounded, with many troops surrendering and deserting.

Victory looked possible, after all! Canosa and his men braced themselves to hold the beachhead until additional ammunition and the promised air cover arrived.

In a short and furious battle the next afternoon, Captain Jaime Canosa managed to scatter Cabrios' forces. Many surrendered. It was clear the enemy was weak, but Canosa's men were forced to retreat because they were running out of ammunition.

The surviving pilots at Puerto Cristobal were totally exhausted. Because radios were inexplicably jammed, the air squadron flew more than twenty missions in two days before it was discovered that the B-4 stealth bombers were armed only with practice bombs. Fourteen pilots were killed. Four men from neighboring Zarahemla, having volunteered to fly with their friends, also lost their lives.

Pilots radioed the CRS Hellenis repeatedly for air cover. "MAY DAY! MAY DAY! Mad Dog four! A MIG-32's attacking us!"

The Hellenis steamed by swiftly. Silence. The call was either unheard or unheeded.

One brigade plane plunged into the sea and another crashed near a sugar mill off the Bay of Zafada.

14

The promised six-day victory threatened to drag on to inconclusive weeks. Casualties were on the rise, and only the Cumorah turn in fortune was decisive. Spent, Canosa and his troops withdrew into the wilderness to regroup.

Canosa surveyed the wasteland of broken bodies while his men buried sons, fathers, and brothers. What man who risked his nation's blood and treasure did not first sit down and count the cost? This was not even a price. It was waste. The once-clear objective was now muddier than an oil slick. The very murk they breathed seemed to stifle all purpose. Kingerman had abandoned them. What could Solano be thinking? A leaden fog obscured communication from the Commander-in-chief, and it was not to be broken.

Ammunition was nearly gone. Evening routine set in. Those who were not wounded cleaned up the gore. Canosa had already made his rounds through the gunpowder haze and closed all the dead eyes, lowering the fragile curtain between mortality and eternity, and beseeching God to comfort the families of those who were gone.

Even day's end did not bring peace. Screaming bullets were replaced by the whine of mosquitoes from hell, rising into the yellow night to search and destroy, and relenting only to carry their cargo of human flesh back to a slimy swamp.

In this setting, Canosa wrote a letter.

15

Down to two rounds of ammunition, the brigade retreated while Canosa insistently radioed for jet cover.

"You could evacuate your men, sir." From his end of the line, Ben's urgent voice pleaded with Canosa.

"We need . . . "

"Jets are coming!" Ben exclaimed.

Canosa cheered. The jets flew over, never firing a shot.

By afternoon when the battered brigade had withdrawn to Girón, Ben's report came over the air, explaining the air force's negligence.

"The pilots were only authorized to take pictures!" Ben nearly shouted in his anger.

16

Two a.m. Flora slipped into her husband's study where he sat at his desk, nodding over a stack of papers. She gazed at him with affection, noting how his term as Chief Judge had aged him. These days he was very distraught. At times she saw fear in his eyes.

She picked her way through empty liquor glasses, over-full ashtrays, strewn papers and books on a stained carpet. Even the smallest bureaucracies had their built-in habits, she supposed. She stumbled over someone's shoe.

Solano woke up with a start. "Oh, it's you. Shut the door!"

"You know how late it is?"

He sighed. "Too late, and too little time. Something's very wrong, Flora."

"What, Stasio?"

"Canosa is not to be found. Since yesterday, Kingerman cannot be reached. My key advisors are out of touch. "Not only that." He turned and glanced over his shoulder. "Yesterday Arch said a growing faction wants to overthrow the republic and install a dictator."

"No, Stasio!" She placed her hand on his.

He nodded. "And now I get this cryptic message purportedly from Canosa. I'm not even sure he wrote it. I'm not sure about

143

anything any more. I feel like everyone knows what is going on except me." He held up a letter. "Since Canosa is also your personal friend, I want you to take a look. Does it make any sense to you?"

She held it to the light and read it.

Honorable Sir:

Can you sit upon your throne in a state of thoughtless stupor, while your enemies are spreading the work of death around you? Have you neglected us because you are in the heart of your country and are surrounded by security?

Many have fallen, and it is to your condemnation because of those who seek for power and authority, even those king-men. They seek to overthrow the freedom of all lands. We do not know if you are also traitors to your country.

You ought to stir yourselves more diligently for the freedom of this people. These things should be shown you.

Awake to a sense of your awful situation. The time soon comes that God will avenge the blood of those who have been slain, for he will no longer suffer their cries from the dust.

I write on behalf of my fellow soldiers.

Captain Jaime Canosa

"Stasio!" she said, stunned. "You do not deserve this!"

He shook his head. "This is why I don't think Jaime wrote it. Soldiers? The covert operation was canceled. He might be referring to that revolutionary faction Arch was talking about. And this archaic language, like it was lifted out of an ancient scroll or something. Whoever wrote this seems to be in serious trouble, but it is like some hidden world which I cannot reach. This writer seems no longer to trust anyone." Solano stood wearily. "And neither do I." He now turned to his steadfast companion a face etched with lines of worry, eyes filled with dread. "In desperation, I have summoned one trusted friend of Canosa, a pastor or patriarch of some sort, whom everyone calls Brother Bianco." The light on his desk flashed. "There he is now."

"Stasio! At this ghastly hour?"

"I told you, Canosa may be in danger. This minister has been living at the Canosa villa. I sent my escort for him, although it is a bit far from here. Given the location of Canosa's estate, can you imagine the controversy if I met with him in broad daylight? We are ready," he said to his intercom.

The man who entered the office wearing a plain business suit brought with him an air of peace which Flora envied. Maybe once you got as old as he appeared, you could have peace. She hoped so.

"This is indeed from my friend and brother, Jaime Canosa," Brother Bianco said, after reading the letter.

"Do you know what it means?"

"It is a coded message, paraphrased from an ancient document, intended to warn you. He is in the midst of a battle, either physical or spiritual, or both. Perhaps he is involved in a drug raid connected with his work. Of course you don't need to answer that, because I know it's all classified, and I am not a political agent."

"That can't be, sir. I canceled all operations weeks ago." Beneath the old patriarch's gaze, Solano felt nothing was unknown to this man, that in his quiet way, he held a power far greater than the greatest earthly king.

"Then your problem is more serious than it would first appear," Brother Bianco said. "Your enemy is within."

Solano grimaced. "Arch did say a mole is in the bureau. Maybe Canosa found him out! But Canosa himself is missing, and my other advisor is unavailable! I am in a terrible quandary, sir. My best and bravest man may be in danger, and my hands are tied!"

"Jaime selected this type of message because it holds a pattern which he knows you alone will understand. I believe with further study you will discover the name or location he is trying to convey to you."

"You said something about a pattern?"

"It is this. Who among you is humble, seeks not his own, and obeys the commandments of God? But he who is overcome with pride and envy, and loves himself more than God, is not to be trusted. You will know them by their fruits.

"God be with you, *hijo*." The little man embraced Solano and his wife, and went away.

"What an unusual man," Flora said. "He seemed to speak from the distant past and transport us into the future all in the same instant."

Solano was wide awake. "I need an answer *now*. Bianco said this letter is authentic. I will act on that."

"When was the last time you saw Canosa?"

"Three weeks ago Wednesday." Solano chewed his lip. "But he can be gone for months, and he reports to Rook. Arch said Canosa was on a routine foreign assignment, so I didn't expect to hear from

145

him.   Kingerman was in Zarahemla all last week, negotiating an international law enforcement pact to stem terrorism. Kingerman also said both CBI and the military were highly suspect for subversion, and he is conducting his own investigation, screening all communications himself. Maybe this explains why Rook was absent for his last weekly CBI report; he sent word through Kingerman . . ."

"The ubiquitous Mr. Kingerman is a busy man," Flora said. She snatched up the letter and together they read it slowly. *Many have fallen, . . .because of those who seek for power and authority, even those king-men. They seek to overthrow the freedom of all lands.* "I don't know about you, Stasio, but I'm beginning to see a pattern —"

Solano stared at his wife. "I respect your hunch, Flora. But this is not proof."

Four a.m., at the CBI office, Solano pushed by a confused security guard to the one room with a light on, where he found Dalton Mortfield, a director of operations.

"What is keeping you here so late, Mortfield?" Solano asked.

"Carrying out your orders, sir."

"Which are. . .?"

"Checking Rook's trail. He is suspected, you know."

"Where is Rook?" Solano demanded.

"In the field," Mortfield replied, unruffled. "You wanted him out of the office, sir. So it was cleared with you."

"Get me Rook."

Mortfield reached for the phone. "Kingerman is the only one who knows —"

"Just a minute." Solano's hand flew out to block the call. "Did Rook leave any notes or messages, or say anything before he left?"

"He said only that it was a typical maneuver. . ." Mortfield paused. "You are familiar with Rook's bizarre humor, sir? He said the egg had fallen off the wall, and he was joining the king's horses and the king's men to put it back together."

Zafada
5:00 a.m.

Jaime Canosa's disheartened radio messages came through to the flagship.

5:09 a.m. Situation desperate. No support. Send low jet air cover. Enemy has support. Our survival in doubt. . .

6:13 a.m. Under attack. Cabrios is using our planes! Where is promised air cover? Canosa.

8:15 a.m. Left flank highly vulnerable. Air support now. Urgent. Canosa.

9:14 a.m. Two MIGs and artillery attacking now. Where in blazes is jet cover? Canosa.

9:25 a.m. Two thousand troops closing in. Air support vital. Canosa.

9:55 a.m. Are you reading me? Situation desperate. Send help. Anything. Just let jet pilots loose. Canosa.

Toward the end his messages carried the signals of despair:
"In water. Out of ammo. Enemy nearly upon us. May last one hour."
"Fighting on beach. Send help now."

"Keep fighting!" Ben urged Canosa from the flagship. Still hoping to receive the green light from Cumorah, he told Canosa: "Hold on, we're coming with everything."

But the situation at the beachhead became impossible. By mid-afternoon, Canosa radioed his last message: "Am destroying all equipment. Tanks everywhere. Nothing left. Fleeing to the woods. Can wait no longer."

Waiting in the flagship, Ben and his companions heard Canosa's heartrending farewell and wept.

The troops scrambled into the Zafada swamps to await the promised support, which never came. The brigade's last redoubts collapsed. The Zafada liberation operation was over. More than a thousand men were captured by Cabrios; over a hundred died in combat or captivity, and sixty were seriously wounded.

The enraged Solano fired Archibald Kingerman, who immediately fled to Zarahemla. Solano began an investigation but could find no compelling evidence. Promising leads were somehow blocked, potential witnesses either disappeared or maintained stubborn silence. At last Solano was told Kingerman held immunity due to his connection with Pax Universalis, and that any legal action would mean swift punitive measures against the entire nation of Cumorah by the Pax peace forces.

Six months later, the Cumorah administration negotiated the release of Cabrios' prisoners. Jaime Canosa was not among them.

The First Book Of
Zephan

THE FIRST BOOK OF ZEPHAN

1

Peninsula, Gulf of Marah

Horace Verman surveyed the serene shoreline with binoculars and laughed. "We've lost him," he said.

Skadden Wilkes spat over the yacht's edge into the bay. "Zarahemla Republic Intelligence! Ha! They're not intelligent. They're dumb. And they're gettin' too nosy!"

"Shut up, Wilkes!" Verman paused, listening to sounds of revelry on the ship, then relaxed. Speaking of noses, Verman had just bought this massive yacht from Mesopotamia, and was partying full tilt, right under the beaks of the ZRI. "Let's go some place where we can talk."

Verman picked his way through reclining swimmers and party debris and signaled to Haman and several other men to follow him to the captain's suite. There Senator Penlock was with a young woman. Lines of cocaine sat on the table.

"Get out!" Verman said.

Penlock paused to snort a line of cocaine before retreating with his wench.

151

Dalton Mortfield, Pax intelligence operative, secured the cabin. Tidily groomed as for a business meeting, Mortfield felt out of place in these bawdy surroundings.

Mortfield's dedication to global politics bordered on fanaticism, robbing his patience for this undisciplined, unprofessional lot. Proceeds from drug traffic were stabilizing life support for fringe regimes wavering in their commitments to Pax Universalis. Only unshakable conviction favoring the larger good of Pax enabled Mortfield to suppress his distaste into forced tolerance for these sleazy underlings.

Try as he might to loosen up, it just took too blasted much concentration to keep this thug Verman out of the slam. But Verman was a darling of the Egalitarians, Mortfield's own brotherhood, which he was duty-bound to support. Moreover, the wealthy Verman poured funds into the Anti-Hate Committee, another worthy cause.

And Skadden Wilkes, lawyer for the Anti-Hate Committee, was on the payroll of narco-terrorists. This was another uncomfortable inconsistency which Mortfield forced himself to ignore. No denying it. He detested Wilkes, who oozed depravity.

Then there was this new kid, Haman Benamoz, with hair disheveled, and shirt smudged with lipstick. Though awestruck by the opulence around him, the boy tried to appear blasé. But he looked more like a dazed puppy, kicked off the porch to run with the big dogs. These diplomats and their proteges were all the same. Slow to produce but quick to demand, and forever consuming. Illogical but true, this kind were the most powerful controllers. You never could tell who was manipulating whom. And Rameses had this Haman kid pegged for an important assignment. "One down, one to go," Rameses had said. Dalton Mortfield shook his head. The things one had to do to infiltrate the opposition.

"Welcome to my party!" Verman was a trifle giddy. "This proboscis called Zarahemla is sniffing narcotics from Cumeni by the ton, and we are inhaling the profits! And I own Cabrios. Don't I have reason to celebrate?"

Skadden Wilkes laughed the loudest.

"Perhaps," Mortfield said quietly. "I've been working overtime, Verman, to keep the lid on all your embezzlement in face of the Senate investigation."

"Ridiculous!" Verman snorted and spat on the floor, narrowly missing Mortfield's immaculately polished shoes.

"One more foul up, and you can be replaced," Mortfield said. "Your Cabrios is too messy." He turned to Karl Devon, media king, who preened shirtless before the mirror. "Passage of the Pax Universalis treaty is stalled in Parliament," he said. "Egalitarian agents of influence are running into some sticky opposition."

Skadden Wilkes licked his lips. "Who?"

"The house of Yeshurun. One of their bishops published the complete Egalitarian manifesto. How he got access to that information, we can only speculate."

"Who?" Skadden said again.

"Shut up, Wilkes!" Mortfield's voice held unmistakable warning. "It doesn't matter now," he went on quickly, with a furtive glance at Haman Benamoz. "That person is gone. The important thing is, the Yeshurun religion itself opposes the principles of Voltaire. Those people might start a tax revolt or—"

"No worry there," Haman spoke up. "Yeshurun people pay their taxes. They may yell a lot, but Yeshurun is taught to obey the law, no matter how much it is hated."

"Well, that helps. But until we are certain this opposition is neutralized, the treaty will go nowhere."

"Where is this house of Yeshurun?" Verman asked. "It's simple to arrange to have it ransacked or burned."

Devon guffawed.

"We could always accuse this group of racism," Skadden Wilkes said. "Works every time."

"*Yeshurun? Racist?*" Devon made a gesture of mock despair. "You idiots!"

"Well, what is it?" Verman asked, intrigued. "A church?"

Devon shrugged. "More than that. Like a family, or something. Yeshurun claims to be the family of an old biblical prophet, Abraham. Rather peculiar. You know how most families are. Not very well organized. But these people are numerous, and they have influence."

"Your, uh, father, Zephan Benamoz, has been the most outspoken, Haman," Mortfield said carefully. "And he seems to have considerable influence."

"Aw, he's an old windbag who lives in the past," Haman said. "He can't do anything."

"The boy's right," Devon said. "Besides, if we openly target a religious body, it will get us in big trouble. *Voi là!* Politics to the rescue. What we need to do is go after the Chief Judge, who was elected with their support. Bring him down, and their political power is eliminated."

"But how? We found no dirt on Solano. Dermucker already tried to buy him before."

"Think, Mortfield. It was Yeshurun influence which caused Solano to change his mind about Pax Universalis. Whoever heard of a religion that teaches specifically against the order of Voltaire? and against peace? This tells you those people are mighty strange. Besides, I heard they still believe in prophets, angels, miracles, and such. Can you imagine, in our day, believing in such things? Is this true, Haman?"

"Unfortunately, yes."

"So Yeshurun is a political liability," Devon said. "No sensible politician would be caught associating with them."

"Solano has done things we don't agree with, but he seems to be popular in spite of it," Mortfield said.

"But this is one mistake the voters won't forgive. Religious moralizers are scary, and once people know what this Yeshurun crowd is really like, everyone will stampede like frightened cattle and trample Solano's career right into the ground. And we will plant the Pax Universalis flag triumphantly on the fresh mound over Solano's remains."

"Skip the theatrics, Devon," Mortfield grumbled. "You're getting carried away."

"Sorry, Mortfield," Devon said cheerfully. "Just a figure of speech. We journalists do have a way with words. Nothing personal against Solano." With a meaningful look at Mortfield, he philosophized, "Sometimes one has to sacrifice friendships or careers for the greater good, you know."

"Yes, yes. So what shall we do?"

"You? Nothing. Let us handle it. It's quite simple, really. We lionize Kemen Ponte. Then, everything bad in the world, all evil, all that is darkness, is Solano."

"And people will believe you?"

"Of course. When MBS speaks, people listen. Tell them the world is flat. Tell them day is night and darkness is light, and people will believe you." Devon laughed. "But we need all the bizarre human interest we can muster. We need an inside man."

Mortfield put an arm around Haman's shoulder. "Haman, son of Zephan Benamoz, our boss needs some very important work done, and he has chosen you to do the job."

154

Despite the stale taste of loud laughter and lewd jokes left by the departing men, Mortfield felt better. At least he thought he did. Why was he, Dalton Mortfield, having second thoughts? Things had not gone as planned. He was to have engineered the removal of Zephan Benamoz, and he had every reason to do so. Benamoz was a nasty opponent of Pax Universalis, a know-it-all religious hothead, and kinsman to the hated Jaime Canosa.

But not Solano. Mortfield had fought beside General Solano in previous campaigns. Maybe the man's politics were different, but Solano was an able general and a decent man.

So now ideologies had placed him opposite Solano on the battlefield. He could accept that. He and Solano were both military men. Mortfield looked at war like a game of chess. Defend the realm against invaders. Keep the peace. Fight with honor. Respect the opponent. Nothing simpler.

Not so with Devon. Karl Devon's style of warfare was far more devious. His victories were not measured in terms of bullet wounds and body bags. Devon could inflict pain which wiped out entire families, affecting generations, and whole nations. All with the power of his words. To him, lying was an art. But Devon could make things happen. Devon always won. After all, only winning mattered.

And now Haman Benamoz. If Zephan was anything like his son, it would be good riddance. Mortfield did not like Haman, although he was not sure why. Haman reminded him very strongly of someone. Ah, the young and petty bureaucrat who betrayed the great Thomas More to his death, then went on to achieve major political power. Actually Haman was much like Rameses, only the boy was very immature. Selfish. He would never amount to much. But he was a favorite of Rameses, which could take him far. He might even be giving orders to Mortfield some day.

Though Dalton Mortfield ground his teeth, he did not rub out a spark of resentment which suddenly flared within him. War these days wasn't really like chess, was it? It wasn't so easy any more. Dalton Mortfield saw himself as the valiant knight in the game of life. He would fight to the death to defend what he thought was right. Yet, somehow courage wasn't enough now. However brave, a knight was little better than the pawns. Each was advanced or removed by a force greater than them all. But did this capricious power truly benefit the majority? Surely, he could endure it for the good of the cause. But the cause belonged to the one who played the game. And the player was Rameses.

2

The Cumorah Chief Judge, a big man of broad shoulder and wide girth, moved swiftly across the huge courtyard in Zephan Benamoz' home in Granada.

Solano walked ahead, with his body guards at a discreet distance, and it made Zephan nervous. True enough, Cumorah had reached unprecedented prosperity under Solano's leadership. Unemployment and crime were low. Technological advances were frequent, national exports were rising. Cultural arts were flourishing, and church attendance was high. Provincial governments were busy. But national Parliament, having drastically reduced national regulatory laws, had virtually voted themselves out of a job. With so little to do, Parliament only met half a year, and with reduced salaries, most were compelled to join the industrial work force to support themselves. In short, the people were governing themselves, and God was prospering them. In fact, the people were growing exceedingly rich.

Solano had simply delivered on his campaign promises. He and Parliament drastically reduced the income tax to a flat five per cent. Additional revenue was acquired from moderate tariffs on imports, and modest sales taxes (since the change in tax policy had increased purchasing power). This kept the nation in the black, but no money was left over to subsidize the bureaucrats and their spending programs. Of course, this required firing the entrenched bureaucracy, who unfortunately were forming alliances with revolutionary factions from Cumeni. Besides these administrative changes, Solano had done little except return most of the power to the provinces and the people, respectively. His determination to maintain adequate defense and protect the national borders occupied his time. Zephan knew it was about these issues which Solano now approached him.

It seemed the mainstream, having become deeply involved in their personal lives, had virtually forgotten about Solano, who was satisfied with his low profile. Zephan hoped Solano's popularity with the mainstream would not lead to fatal apathy. For Solano had enemies. The relative few but volatile malcontents had mouths disproportionate in size, and they were bolstered by the media, who from the start had been opposed to Solano.

"History is the patter of silken slippers descending the stairs and the thunder of hobnailed boots coming up." Solano joined Zephan at the outdoor breakfast table.

Zephan looked up from his newspaper. "Something must be wrong." Maybe Solano was more alert than he had supposed. "So the thunder comes from the south?"

Solano nodded. "Cumeni. Cabrios is trying to cut off the southernmost Cumorah province and make a new republic from it. Border incidents are increasing. Thanks to your able endeavors in Canosa's absence, Zephan, at least the flood of Cabrios' drug traffic appears to be receding. And Haman?"

"Claims he's out of the business. We find no traces of his activity at this time. I'm afraid he has only learned to cover his tracks more skillfully. Sarita and I are very concerned about his dependence on his peers, Solano."

"Oh, he's just a boy, Zephan. He probably just had to grow out of a phase. With this settled, I must devote my time to helping the national guard protect citizens from terrorist attacks on our borders."

"Don't forget the coming election," Zephan said. "A man named Kemen Ponte is organizing an opposing faction called *Partido Universal*. My sources say he has a collectivist mentality, with a tendency to stir up contention and envy, and get people to do unseemly things as a crowd which are illegal for individuals."

"*No importa.* The election is over a year away, and Ponte seems harmless enough. He appears to have but one word in his vocabulary: Peace! Well, we already have peace within our borders, and I have my record to stand on. I must keep our peace and freedom by maintaining a strong defense." Solano drained his coffee cup and wiped his black mustache with the back of his hand. "With Kingerman gone, our security is tight once again, and my CBI director Clarence Rook can be trusted to keep out any further moles. I cannot be everywhere at once, Zephan. I need you to keep things calm on the occasions when I must leave town. I'm asking you to be my secretary of defense."

"Aw, Solano, you know I'm no politician."

Solano grinned. "All the better. Then perhaps you can be trusted." He took up a pencil and paper. "Look, you're the businessman. We have two men coming in from Zarahemla who could supply us with much-needed arms. We are prepared to make a deal. But if it smacks of Central Committee interference, I want no part of it. We will handle our problems without help from the Community of Nations." Solano leveled his gaze on his friend. "How about it, Zephan?"

Zephan squared his shoulders. "I'll do my best."

"Remember you cannot be paid; unelected appointees are barred from receiving taxpayer support. But I assure you, at this time your work should only require part-time involvement."

Zephan nodded. "And you understand I will continue to earn a living." With a chuckle, he added, "With politics limited to my spare time, I will have little opportunity to cause trouble."

"Zephan, when you see Brother Bianco, tell him we are still doing everything possible to find Canosa. Convey to him my gratitude. He warned me about the inside threat to our government."

"He has seen this before. He knows."

Solano tilted his head. "Benjamin said the same thing. By the way, your son is seeing Anahí Cercado frequently, with her full consent."

"How is she?"

"Still struggling. Searching for something. The poor girl is determined to get a live sighting of the quetzal bird."

"Extinct, isn't it?"

"Probably, but I have not the heart to tell her, and crush her hopes. Especially now, with Benjamin, she seems happier. When is he going to marry her?"

"He does not want to rush her."

Solano became serious. "Well, he had better hurry. He may be called into active duty at any time."

The chief shook hands warmly and left.

Haman heard it all. He saw his father approaching him, and thought he knew what was coming.

"Haman, I will forget all your past debts so you can have a clean start to live on your own."

Haman drew back slightly at this unexpected generosity. Papa was more of a pushover than he thought. But aloud he said, "I know. I know, Papa. You want me to leave because I oppose Solano."

"You are entitled to your own opinions, Haman," Zephan said in an even tone. "Although I disagree with your politics, I do care about you and want what is best for you, my son. But you are responsible for your own choices. No one can fix everything for you. You are a grown and able-bodied man, and my subsidizing you does not help you. My company has offered you work over and over again."

"I have a job."

"The Anti-Hate Committee? I don't trust those people. They are an instrument of Voltairism."

Haman stiffened. He had been sent to gather specific information. "So. Politics aside, Papa. Why this religious crusade against a purely secular entity like the order of Voltaire?"

"Its roots are religious, Haman."

"Then it's true. Our religion really does teach against Voltaire. No one ever told me why."

"The order of Voltaire resembles an ancient pattern from our scriptures, Haman."

"What do you mean, Father?"

"Anciently in this land, a man named Nehor went about among the people, bearing down against the church, mixing his own doctrines with scripture, and calling it the word of God. Nehor flattered the people, saying they could lift up their heads in pride. If people sought any pleasure, it was of no consequence, he said, for Nehor's plan was the easy way; it promised security for all. Now, if they would only let him be in charge, he told them, in the end he would see everyone had all the money, power, and glory their hearts desired. People began to believe him and give him money, and he established a following. And it came to pass that he met an old man named Gideon, who belonged to the church of God. Nehor began to contend with him, but Gideon withstood Nehor with the words of God. Angered, Nehor drew his sword and began to strike him, but Gideon, being old, could not withstand his blows. So Nehor killed Gideon with the sword. Nehor was a type of antichrist, and the order of Voltaire, which also enforces its doctrines, is diametrically opposed to the gospel."

"How dare you say such a thing?" Haman flared. "My friends believe that Voltaire was a kind and peace-loving man. And my friends are far more Christlike than you are!"

Zephan shrugged. "Why do you take offense? This is history straight from the record of Joseph, of the house of Israel. Am I to alter sacred writings because you don't agree with them?"

Remembering his objective, Haman calmed himself. "So what became of this Nehor?"

"Nehor was brought before Alma, the prophet and Chief Judge, where he pleaded boldly for himself," Zephan continued.

"But Alma said, 'This is the first time that priestcraft has been introduced among this people.' And he said to Nehor, 'Behold, you are not only guilty of priestcraft, but you have tried to enforce it with the sword. If priestcraft is enforced among this people, it will cause their entire destruction.'

"Unfortunately, Haman, enforced priestcraft did cause the destruction of that people."

"At least this has nothing to do with the Anti-Hate Committee. First, it's not a religion, although its goals of world peace and the elimination of hate are biblical. It is more like, um, a universal ethic, perhaps."

"Babylon may or may not call them churches, Haman, but it has all kinds of religions, with or without the Bible. Even terrorists have faith in their holy mission to destroy all who do not share their beliefs. The nations of Babylon are united by the guiding minds of Pax Universalis, so the members have some degree of peace among them, but the people's hearts are turned from God, and they oppose His prophets."

"Sometimes we have to help those who are different from us, in order to achieve the greater good."

Zephan stared at his son. "The terrorists get tax money from their victims."

"Good grief, Papa. The Committee men are here to stop such things. They dedicate their lives to world peace, and somebody has to pay them for all their time and work."

"Ministers of Yeshurun, who teach the word of God, take money from no one. They support themselves with the labor of their own hands. We do not force anyone to pay for the teaching of our ideas."

"Yeshurun serves nobody."

"Just our God."

"But these men serve the whole world, Papa. So they get tax money. That makes it legitimate. Certainly it's not enforced with a sword."

"Ultimately, tax money is paid by force, and it is only legitimate for a few reasons —— "

"I know, I know!" Haman cut in. He rocked his head back and forth. "The protection of life, liberty, and private property. How could I forget? You drummed that into our heads so much it made me sick. But this is different. This is for the welfare of people all over the world, not just ourselves. But of course, you wouldn't understand. For you, there is only one true way, and you won't listen to anyone else's way of achieving the same end."

"I? Not listen?" Zephan frowned. "The Egalitarian way is broadcast full blast hourly, daily, and weekly. What choice have I? But regardless of frequency and density, a lie is still a lie."

"Good intentions mean nothing to you."

"Your friends use the sword of state to promote their intentions, good or not. You can give it any fancy name you like, but it is still enforced priestcraft."

"So what does it matter? These days people don't care about such things."

"It matters to the Eternal One, because often the worst censorship, stealing, and murder are done in the name of good intentions. It is still an abomination in His sight."

"You are cursedly bullheaded." Haman began to shout. "Rigid! Uncaring!"

Zephan sank into his chair and rested his head in his hands. "Let us not debate. This is not about Solano, Haman. I am concerned about your character. You have changed since you began associating with those Egalitarians from the Anti-Hate Committee. Are you stripped of pride? If so, why do you mock your brother Benjamin, and heap persecution upon the brethren of our faith? Are you stripped of envy? If so, what about your idleness? An idle mind is the devil's workshop."

"My God." Haman made a gesture of disgust.

"Don't take the Lord's name in vain."

"Well, I am a grown man, and I don't have to endure your platitudes."

"Then stop whining, Haman, and be a man. I will allow no son of mine to live off the fruits of other people's labors. It's just plain dishonest."

"You throw me into the street with nothing."

"Don't blame others for the laws of life, son. Just work hard and you won't starve."

"All you can think about at a time like this is money! You are cruel."

"How can I help you understand? Can you not let God's justice, mercy, and longsuffering make a change in your heart? Try a little humility."

"You and your justice. You have always wanted to throw all my friends into jail. And mercy? You don't know the meaning of it."

"I'm sorry you feel that way, Haman. But I must warn you. Egalitarians are deceitful and are not worthy to be your friends, my son."

"How can you say such things? My friends are kind and generous. They will do anything to help me, and each other! My friends are the most Christlike people I know, and not cruel and mean like you."

"I understand you like these people, but Egalitarians are not what they seem, Haman. I beg you to seek more information before you decide to join with them. Are Egalitarians truly disciples of Christ, or perhaps are their motives political? Egalitarians will use any means to justify their goals, but talk about mercy! Do not cross them, for their enemies receive no mercy. Egalitarians will use you, and then when you no longer serve their purpose, they will destroy you. You can choose your actions, but you cannot choose the consequences."

"Good grief, father. You have always been paranoid about the Egalitarian philosophy. But you refuse to admit all the good they do."

Zephan shook his head. "*Good*? We are in the throes of a great struggle between good and evil, Haman. Egalitarians are not like Christ, as they have persuaded you to believe. Their theme-songs of compassion and mercy are but a thin veneer for their ark-adjusting arrogance. Their ways are not God's way. Like Nehor, they think they are better than God."

"Father! You are obsessed with this silly notion of good and evil. You look for the devil in every corner."

"I warn you, Haman. An Egalitarian is not to be trusted. To save his own skin, an Egalitarian would murder his own mother and then rob the body."

"How dare you say such things? I hate you."

"This must be upsetting for you. It is hard to hear the truth about people you thought you could trust and admire. But I don't hate you, my son. I love you and am concerned about your welfare. Please, let me help you. You don't need to depend on the Anti-Hate Committee."

Haman stepped back warily. "You are on the Committee's black list. The Committee is designed to destroy people like you."

"Haman, Haman. Look at their fruits. The Committee itself is showing hatred ——— the very thing they are sworn to eliminate. Is this what you want? To blacklist your family? To destroy those who love you?"

"You are not my family. Kemen Ponte is my family." Haman started toward his room. He was supposed to contrive a way to stay at home and keep his superiors informed, but Mortfield did not know how impossible it was to live with Zephan Benamoz. Haman had to get out. He could not bear another minute with his father.

"Haman, I love you," Zephan called after him.

In twenty minutes Haman was gone, and within the hour he arrived at the huge, sparkling Anti-Hate Committee office building. In the immense lobby, small tables clustered around tropical trees and fragrant flowers. Sounds of fountains, clinking glasses, and laughter were like a dream. At one end of the glistening marble floor he found an acre of food: fancy sandwiches in tall stacks, heaps of fine meats and cheeses, sliced paper-thin, platters of colorful fruits and vegetables, snowy mounds of bread, tureens of soups and exotic foods with rich sauces. Great frosted-glass vats held bright red, pink, and green punch. Two fountains held champagne. Haman helped himself. At least this would take care of dinner.

Haman did not see anyone he knew, but everyone greeted him with a warm smile. Then Kemen Ponte came to his side.

"Haman! So glad to see you!" Ponte greeted him. "You can work for my campaign now?"

"Sure."

"All our supporters have to be members of the Egalitarian association, you know. Otherwise, we don't get our funds. Whether you are selling cookies or causes, you have to run it like a business." He laughed. "My little joke. Money works the same, no matter where you get it. But once you have it, you can have anything in the world."

"How do you become an Egalitarian?"

"You just have to be invited. . ."

How did one arrange to get invited? Haman knew the requirements for members of good standing in Yeshurun: the Ten Commandments, the Golden Rule, the health code; pay tithes and fast offerings; study, prayer, weekly worship meetings; lifetime service without pay; the list went on and on, strict and demanding. . .

"Hey!" Ponte stopped his pleasant chatter and put his arm around the younger man. "Don't look so serious. I thought you were already an Egalitarian. Otherwise, I would have invited you a long time ago."

"Is that all there is to it?"

"Sure. I'll bet you thought it was hard, didn't you?"

Kemen Ponte, rich, powerful, charming, a future world leader, was extending his hand to Haman Benamoz, offering a personal invitation into the most prestigious society in the world. "I have never met so many nice people in my whole life," Haman murmured.

"Oh, you must remember one small thing. Sometimes, to move our cause forward, we have to do a few things different from what your mama taught you." Ponte laughed in a rich, mellow baritone. "But now and then, we all have to ignore our personal preferences to bring about the greater good, don't we?"

"Of course." Haman laughed, too. "I'm in. Sign me up."

"Actually, it is quite popular. In fact, everybody in the whole world is doing it, except Yeshurun. Some silly superstition they have about it." Ponte glanced at Haman. "You don't have anything to do with them, do you?"

"Oh, not at all. Wouldn't dream of it. I mean, I don't buy into their silly superstitions," he added quickly. "I do have contacts which are valuable to some very big men in the Committee, though."

Ponte nodded, impressed.

Haman drained his champagne glass and stood to refill his plate. "And by the way, tell Devon that Zephan Benamoz threw out his own son, destitute in the street. He hates me because I will not support Solano."

3

Benjamin and Anahí visited a secluded part of beautiful Lake Tantagua. Anciently, he explained to her, this was called the Waters of More Good, where the prophet Alma had led his people, numbering about two hundred, to escape the oppressive regime of

164

King Noah. Here Alma taught them concerning the things pertaining to the kingdom of God. He taught nothing but repentance and faith, and he commanded them to have no contention one with another; that their hearts should be knit together in unity and in love one towards another. And it came to pass that all this was done near these waters, and in the forest near the Waters of More Good. And Alma's people were baptized in these waters. How beautiful this place was to the eyes of those who there came to know their Redeemer.

The young people frequented the more remote beaches of Sea North. And Sarita accompanied them, insisting it was no imposition on her time —— she brought her sewing, letter-writing, and books to read while the couple walked the shores.

"I feel like one of those bubbles, thrashed about in the tumbling surf," Anahí said as they outlined the tide with their barefoot steps. "It is so frightening, Ben."

"I understand."

"The world is in such turmoil, yet you seem so steady, so confident."

"It has come over time, Ani."

"How do you do it?"

"Faith gives you hope for a better world. It makes an anchor to your soul."

"What do you hold onto?"

"An iron rod."

"This is figurative?"

Ben nodded. "It's what an ancient prophet in this land called the word of God." From inside his shirt, Ben pulled a small book with the front cover missing, and offered it to her.

Taking the book from him, Anahí settled onto the sand and arranged her long full skirt in a half circle around her. She read for a long time, pausing now and then to gaze seaward and listen to water lapping the shore.

Ben stretched out on the beach and watched her. A breeze playing with her hair, slender fingers turning pages, her lovely brow furrowed in concentration —— he stored this picture of her in his heart.

Anahí studied patterns in the sand etched by the sea. Ebbing, flowing. Again and again. She felt strangely drawn to the Creator of this cosmic vastness before her. Surf buffeted distant boulders, resounding like great drumbeats.

Echoes from the past. Swirls of truth, circling, drifting back to her.

She read on.

And it came to pass that the whole multitude fell to the earth; for they remembered the prophecies that Christ would show himself unto them after his ascension into heaven. And it came to pass that the Lord spake unto them saying: Arise and come unto me, and thrust your hands into my side, and so also ye may feel the prints of the nails in my hands and in my feet, that ye may know I am the God of Israel, and God of the whole earth, and have been slain for the sins of the world.

Anahí looked up. Shadows of yesterday reached for eternity. Again, the drumbeats. Echoes from the past. Voices from the ancient dust. She looked at Ben, her eyes glistening with a joy of newfound truth. "Yes. This record of the family of Joseph ——— these are my people."

In a warm blue sky, plump clouds sailed by, white as the pearls of foam rolling down the rocks offshore. The sun, overflowing with its own vitality, spilled excess energy into crimson, butter-yellow, and pink hibiscus cups for the day's nectar. Anahí loved the jolly tangle of vegetation playing out onto the beach, and poinciana trees, everywhere, with their graceful foliage. This was a wild and lonely place, but she and Ben were not alone.

Again she turned to the pages open in her hands. "Somehow, I have seen this before. I know it is true."

There, in the far poinciana, a burst of flame leaped heavenward. With a heart-shaped breast of fiery red, a magnificent bird ascended from the earth, trailing iridescent plumage like a long banner of green lace.

"Ben!" she whispered. "Did you see him?"

"No, Ani. What is it?"

"The quetzal bird."

4

Parliamentary Square, Cumorah

Like most Cumorah government offices, the conference room
was pleasant, but not elaborate. Chief Judge Solano's lifestyle lent
dignity to the office while diligently avoiding excesses.

Zephan reflected on his last discussion with Haman. What was
happening to his family? Leb was leading an idolatrous life as a
mercenary soldier, having willingly cut himself off from the family
faith and turned his allegiance instead to war gods, and his affections
to camp followers. Haman now worked for Kemen Ponte.
Something about Ponte was very unsettling. . .

With a sigh Zephan pushed aside his personal thoughts and
turned to the business at hand, emissaries from the Zarahemla
Republic.

He studied a stack of information before him. First, dossiers on
expected visitors. For help in assembling these files, Zephan had
consulted Mitchell Hunt, director of Zarahemla Republic Intelligence
and friend of Canosa.

Horace Verman, assistant ZR State Consul. Reputation
in Zarahemla of deceit, flattery. Allegations of blackmail and
murder on record. Enriched by suspect international
connections, has amassed a sizeable fortune. Currently holding
responsible position in International Banking Complex, a
scandal-ridden institution supporting fraud and plunder in
dictatorships around the world.

A handwritten note from Clarence Rook:

Verman, though under investigation himself for drug
peddling, has powerful financial support and important friends
in the international media. Cronies in the media could smear
any innocent person or even a whole nation Verman dislikes.

Verman was the only representative from ZR. Zephan was
given no other files. And he was supposed to do business with this
sleazeball? The Zarahemla government, though an ally, did not
inspire much confidence these days.

Next. Verman was seeking Cumorah support for two proposed Treaties: Pax Universalis Peace Force, and Community of Nations (CON) Code of Human Rights. What was the meaning of those Treaties?

Intensive study revealed no reservation of Cumorah's sovereign rights. Zephan struggled with the obscure bureaucratic language in the two documents, but one thing he did understand. Both treaties were alliances with other nations who served, not the God of Israel, but the order of Voltaire, or doctrines of men.

Zephan perfunctorily handled the necessary protocol, then turned to the issue at hand. "Mr. Verman, the present threat to our national security exceeds our domestic arms reserves. The Tartarean Empire and the drug underworld have heavily armed the insurgent terrorists in this country. I'm sure you see the strategic advantage for Zarahemla if you provide weapons to Cumorah."

"Possibly," Verman replied, "with one contingency. Have you examined the two documents?"

"Quite thoroughly. Those treaties have nothing to do with us here in Cumorah."

"To the contrary," Verman said. "A Global Peace Force will protect you."

Zephan shook his head firmly. "We have no desire to invite foreign troops onto our soil. Simply augment our arms and munitions, and we will care for ourselves."

Verman shrugged with exaggerated indifference. "If you do not support the treaties, we cannot help you."

Zephan stood, indicating dismissal. "So be it," he said.

That's the last we'll see of him.

5

But three months later Verman came back, and he brought someone with him.

Scheduled to attend a meeting of the Defense Committee, Zephan grimly made his way through a sizeable crowd of Ponte supporters picketing the Parliament Building.

The mob had been there all week. What did they do for a living?

He saw Haman waving an anti-Solano placard and winced, averting his eyes.

A small stir at the crowd's edge drew his attention. Verman again. And Kingerman! They were shaking hands with the Ponistas.

"Haman!" Kingerman's voice rose above the crowd. "After all these years, my friend!" he said, embracing Haman.

Zephan ducked through the door and hurried up the stairs to his meeting.

"Our most recent delegation to Zarahemla has again been unable to obtain the munitions we need," he reported.

"Yet the terrorists seem to have unlimited supplies," a committeeman complained.

"A reliable source shows at least half the support is coming from Zarahemla," said another.

"Two emissaries from the ZR government are due to arrive any moment, " the chairman said.

Verman spoke first. "The Congress of Zarahemla withholds aid unless Cumorah complies with all terms of Pax Universalis."

"Pax Universalis? You mean 'P.U.', for short?" someone quipped.   Laughter crackled across the room, resounding a joviality of men optimistic about their future, secure in the sovereignty and goodness of their land.

A senator spoke up with firm voice. "How about humanitarian aid? Cumorah has been Zarahemla's strong ally for most of the century!"

Verman grimaced, impatient. "Evidently the senator has not heard, but our administration's policy is not to interfere in affairs of other countries. The fact is, we're against Solano. Not only does he stubbornly resist our Pax Universalis Peace Force, but for some mysterious reason he opposes the Code of Human Rights."

"Who would you have instead of Solano?" Zephan asked. "The terrorists? Do you think terrorists are more civilized?"

"This is beside the point!" Verman snapped.

"Oh, is it?" Zephan said. "Then tell me, sir, just what is the point of this *doublespeak* of yours?"

Everyone laughed.

"You're being irrelevant," Verman said in a small voice. "Look. Don't make me tired. We have no problem with the Cumorah people. In fact, for their own benefit, your people had better not resist the Community of Nations. Increasing interdependence will force you to accept our management. Solano stands in the way of world peace. Therefore, he must go."

"But the Cumorah people elected him!" the parliament members chorused.

"The Central Committee will supervise a new election," Kingerman cut in smoothly. His words shot through a wall of stunned faces, searing the edges of their understanding.

As images from a far land welled up in his memory, Zephan eyed his compatriots.

"You mean. . .no, you can't mean. . ." someone muttered.

"That we will make an end run around national sovereignty?" Kingerman finished for him. "Trust me. We mean exactly that. Solano, without help from global government, cannot bring you the peace and shared prosperity you deserve."

"Tell me, gentlemen," Zephan said quietly. "Where do you get authority to depose an obvious ally, when the only alternative is terrorism?"

"That is the beauty of it!" Verman exclaimed. "Our Global Peace Force is the only alternative to terrorism."

"Everyone knows majority control in this Global Police Force of yours will be held by aggressor nations, chiefly Fomentio Cabrios, narco-terrorist!" Zephan struggled to conquer his rising anger.

"Not *Police* force. *Peace* force!" Verman threw in quickly.

"What difference does it make?" Zephan said. "What peace does Cabrios bring us, hmm? The peace of a mass graveyard."

"You are wrong, Benamoz," Verman said. "The Pax Universalis Peace Force is doing the work of the Lord."

"I tell you it is mockery."

"Look, Benamoz. Be reasonable. Cumeni is Zarahemla's most preferred trading partner," Kingerman argued. "Our Chief Judge has made promises to the merchants in our nation. We can't have the prestige of Chief Ashley damaged before the whole world, can we?"

"I can see the political cartoons now," Zephan retorted. "'See Ashley, the proud little Emperor with his new clothes'! "

The room reverberated with discussion rising in pitch.

"Silence!" the chairman bellowed.

"Mr. Verman," Zephan said, "we can win this campaign to rout these Empire-supported narco-terrorists. We shall proceed, with or without your help, if you will only refrain from interfering."

"Solano goes!" Verman bellowed. "That's final!"

After a futile attempt to restore order to the furious uproar, the chairman shouted, "This meeting adjourned. . .until further notice!"

Zephan left abruptly.

The next day, the entire parliament voted down Pax Universalis.

A week later, the Central Committee imposed an arms embargo against Solano's *Guardia Nacionál*. Shortly thereafter, Pax Universalis imposed a world-wide economic embargo against Cumorah.

6

City of Zarahemla

Alerted by Zarahemla's Rupert Banberg, Central Committee officer Archibald Kingerman called an urgent meeting at the Dermucker business offices. Kingerman conducted the agenda, which detailed specialists selected from an international pool experienced in political assassination. Clad in business suits, carrying briefcases, a line of silent participants filed into a tightly secured conference room, where all were duly sworn to secrecy.

Kingerman surveyed the gathering. Drug lords from the lands of Manasseh and Tartarus would fill the need for necessary cash. Representatives from the International Banking Complex, all members of CON alliance, especially Zarahemla, would launder the money. Sharp shooters came from the Tartarean Empire, Mesopotamia, and nihilist leftovers from the Empire wars. All these, trained in political assassinations using high-powered rifles at 1,000 yards, would make up the final "kill unit" which would actually carry out the plan. CON agents from the Atlantic Democracies and Empire intelligence, having long ago infiltrated the ZRI, would be responsible for covering up the action for the press.

The sheer numbers of the seed of Abraham alarmed central planners, who ordered international anarchists to infiltrate world religious organizations. Kingerman noted with satisfaction many believers, who trusted anything and anybody, would be a useful front for the operation. Perfect cover for arms transports. Weapons masquerading as "humanitarian aid" could easily skirt customs hurdles in many nations. An ultimate advantage was to blame orthodox religious elements for expressing any political opinions, and for making extreme political moves.

"Mortfield, you know what you have to do," Kingerman instructed. "Kemen, the code name for this operation will be Amalickiah."

"Where did you get *that* name?"

"Straight from Yeshurun history. Amalickiah is the name of a politician who successfully overthrew a king."

"Sounds appropriate," Ponte said. "But why Yeshurun history?"

Kingerman laughed. "Don't you see? Then if the press gets too nosy for details, we can always blame it on Yeshurun."

"Hmm. I never would have thought of that."

"Which is why I'm your leader," Kingerman replied. "Trust me. I know what I'm doing."

The different factions having met for several days previously, Kingerman's job was to organize the data and coordinate the entire operation. Kingerman heard the various reports, then dismissed them all to their assignments with a terse comment.

"Gentlemen, the Chief Judge of Cumorah Republic has become an intolerable nuisance. We cannot trust the people to vote in our man. Unless we take matters into our own hands, our entire mission of world peace is seriously jeopardized."

7

Summer, 2079

The embargo extended to importation of ore and all other essential raw materials for arms and munitions production. Canosa Metalworks lay idle, and virtually every other industry languished under the pall of a world economic blockade. Unemployment caused internal strife, making the land vulnerable to Cabrios' terrorist attacks on the southwest border. Food shortages developed due to random pillaging and burning on farms and ranches, destruction of small businesses, and highway looting in the trucking industry.

Abiram became indispensable in repairing old equipment, various items which people could not afford to discard and replace.

Benjamin was called to active duty in the National Guard. Zephan devoted increasing time to military intelligence and dreaded the moment when his two sons Leb and Ben would face each other in combat.

Sarita worried about Aurelia Canosa and suggested to her husband that they take Abiram and go to Ammonihah for a visit. Zephan took advantage of the opportunity to move some Canosa equipment to his company's other branch. Perhaps Abiram could stay there with Aurelia and at least put the farm equipment division to some use.

Granada looked increasingly like a war zone, and Solano began to evacuate the domestic staff at his residence, leaving the grounds heavily guarded. He would soon depart to lead his troops in pushing back Cabrios' invading terrorist guerrillas. Anahí made her rounds on the entire estate, viewing with a feeling of sad finality the piano, gardens, library, kitchen, and the bedroom which she had grown to cherish. She ended her tour in the art gallery, where Solano had requested to meet her by a painting entitled *The Farewell*.

The colossal Friberg painting held tension and gloom, but it filled her with awe. It portrayed the sunset of an ancient civilization. Two colors dominated the scene. Red, everywhere, tinted the corpse-strewn ground, the bloodied soil. Scarlet shame and defeat drenched capes, shields, and feathered helmets of a mighty nation once proud, now dead. Against a sky blazing fiery orange from the setting sun and flames of war, circled an army of gray vultures, swooping to devour grisly spoils from their gruesome victory. A lone arrow-studded tree drooped in weary gray shadows that bespoke an end to a brief but glorious era, and the beginning of a long night. Mortally wounded, an aged prophet lay in his son's arms and added his noble blood to the ravaged earth. Father and son were large of stature, each with massive chest for a heart of unparalleled courage, shoulders of heroic proportion, and well-muscled arms that rippled with strength. But not strong enough.

Nevertheless, the prophet's strength was in his vision, with which he saw far beyond that short and carnage-littered horizon of his day to a bright dawn in a future time. From the picture's focal point a singular symbol of hope glowed in living gold among morbid grays of death. Voices of truth, engraved upon invincible gold plates, illuminated time's corridors, muted only by the dust of senseless

173

human conflict. Throughout the ages, a remnant of Jacob would endure martyrdom, persecutions, and long dangerous journeys for the sake of that cherished record . . .

This will only be temporary, the Chief Judge told himself over and over as he walked the grounds of the Solano estate in all its sprawling magnificence. There, across the water, a fleck of light, and another —— dozens of them, like serpentine fireworks on Independence Day. Lights snaked along all over the ground, and the field caught fire. From a storehouse of equipment used for tourists, he grabbed a pair of high-powered binoculars, and his curiosity grew to astonishment. Tails ablaze, frantic rats raced about like drunken pyromaniacs, igniting everything on their trail. Solano continued on his way, shaking his head at this peculiar protest statement from the *guajiros*. Kerosene-soaked rags, tied to rats' tails, were set afire and thrown into the fields. Perhaps it was an appropriate farewell. . .

"No! No! Don't take them!" A scream hung on the damp night air.

Anahí! He had forgotten he was expected to meet her. Solano sprinted across the field, vaulted a low courtyard wall, and raced for the far wing and art gallery.

Beneath the enormous Friberg painting, Anahí had sunk to the luxurious carpet and crumpled in uneasy slumber.

Solano knelt and cradled her head in his arms.

"Papa, is that you?"

He thought his heart would break. If only he could be there for her until she was safely married. "It is Solano, dear child."

She sat up, blinking away her confusion. "Same old dreams about. . . "

"*Mi hijita.*" Solano held her close, stroking her dark silken hair, but could draw no comfort from the dry hollows of his own aching heart.

She stood resolutely. "I'm all right." Her voice lacked conviction. "Really."

He attempted nonchalance. "It is about this art that I have summoned you, Anahí."

She nodded toward the painting. "I hope this is not a pattern."

"Nonsense. The people freely elected me, and I have their support. We will have these thugs cleaned out in no time."

174

She smiled, and some of the old fire returned to her eyes. "I surely hope so, sir. Goons have no appreciation for fine art."

"I am sending my Flora to Zarahemla until this crisis is over, and she will take as much of the art as possible with her — just as a precaution," he added quickly. "You may accompany her, or go to Sheffa. Take whatever you can manage." He made a sweeping gesture toward his collection. "But do not take unnecessary risks. Family is the life stream of our culture. Everything else we can rebuild."

8

Within weeks of the embargo, the entire Granada province buckled under heavily armed and superior numbers of Cabrios terrorists combined with Pax Universalis Peace forces. Adding irony to bitterness, the capital city fell on the traditional Independence Day in July. Commander-in-Chief Solano moved his headquarters to León, on the shores of the Sea North.

That evening at Canosa's old plantation, Zephan received a distressing phone call from Haman. He replaced the receiver and sat still for a long moment, his head bowed.

"Tomorrow morning at dawn," he said, his voice shaking, "all male adults, including the local militia, are to meet at the central square and bring their weapons for registration. Haman informs me that a so-called neutral international committee has volunteered to help us get our factories running again. To do this the committee will internationalize all industries, including my factory and all my patents. The committee will even sell the Canosa Metalworks farm machinery, and my profits supposedly will be divided with the public. My life's work is taken from me."

Sarita took his hand in both hers and knelt beside his chair. Her face mirrored his anxiety.

Zephan drew his mouth into a determined line. "Sarita, you must go to the Canosa villa in town and bring Aurelia back here, where it is safer. Bring back as much food and supplies as you can. I have no choice but to report to the village."

9

On the Canosa plantation, the workers' children knew Doña Aurelia Canosa as "Grandma", and the Benamoz boys, though they were grown, so addressed her as well. When she arrived in early morning from town after a lengthy absence, the children gave her a noisy welcome. Immediately she began stocking the shelves with extra food. "I can't eat all this anyway."

Abiram helped unload various crates and boxes.

"Take these loaves of bread," Aurelia said. "Store them in the cellar with the corn, potatoes, bedding, and camping equipment. You'll know what to do with those things, Abiram." She gave him a meaningful look.

Down in the storage room, Abiram began unloading the supplies. Concealed beneath a dozen loaves of bread were eight pistols. Ammunition was stashed in pillowcases.

Sarita was out in the orchard helping Manuel Fernandez pick fruit. Aurelia wondered how they were doing. She stepped around the children's rollicking circle game to look out the window, and stopped. A loud knock at the door silenced the children.

Haman, in a gray Pax Universalis uniform, stood on the patio with pale blue cap in hand. "*Buenos días*, Grandma."

Be calm. Deliberately she wiped her hands on her apron.

"Don't worry, Grandma. I have orders to fetch Brother Bianco."

Aurelia felt herself go rigid with alarm. "He is not. . ."

"Now, Grandma, don't lie to me. I know he's here." Haman pushed past her and walked briskly down the hall to the guest room.

Aurelia stood still and said nothing. What could she do? She no longer could understand Haman. Poor Sarita, outside in the orchard, was unaware of this ominous development. Just as well. What could she do with such a son? Aurelia bit back angry words as Haman ushered the old prophet into the entrance hall.

"Why do you need him?" Abiram asked. "He has no weapons to declare."

"Precisely why he must come with me." Haman's voice was cold, as if talking to a total stranger. "When the people hear him speak, their fears will be calmed, and we will have no trouble."

Aurelia saw how old and frail Brother Joseba looked, even though she knew he worked as long and vigorously as plantation hands half his age.

"I will go with you, Brother Joseba." Abiram's eyes, dark with anger, met the pools of calm in Brother Bianco's face.

"Who will protect the women and children? No, Abiram, you must stay."

Fear crept over the children's faces. Aurelia gripped the back of a chair.

Only Brother Bianco stood unruffled, his face tranquil. He slipped an arm around Aurelia's thick waist. "It will be all right," he said, looking at each of them. "The power of God is greater than all the soldiers of Babylon."

10

At the square, people did not simply sign papers. They stacked their weapons and walked away unarmed. Pax troops supervised the process. Zephan gave them nothing. After all, the committee was taking his entire factory.

While in line, Zephan brooded over recent events. Numerous merchants had fled to Zarahemla. In their absence, Cabrios troops occupied their homes. But he, Zephan, had been unable to bring himself to face the truth. Cumorah was at the same stage as the old country was ten years ago. The inexorable pattern was depressing. Where would it end?

A pall of uncertainty hung over the crowd. Seeing a few women milling around heightened Zephan's apprehension. At least for the moment his women and children were safe in the country with Abiram and Brother Joseba.

A crude wooden platform had been hastily built in the central square for visitors to address the people, and tightly sewn security meant attendance at this event was mandatory. The Cumorah flag had been taken down, and in its place was the PAX flag with its insignia of Voltaire: a world map surrounded by traditional branches of peace. Superimposed upon the globe was an ambiguous symbol. At first glance it appeared to be a money sign, but closer examination revealed the sign was a serpent coiled about a sword.

Zephan was certain Cabrios agents were present. A winter of subversion had spawned terrorists who swarmed the countryside like locusts at an Independence Day picnic. Agents scurried everywhere under scorching heat of political treachery, eating the hearts from the fruits of liberty. Long after the day was spent and hosts returned home to prepare for another day's work, demagogues would drone on. Hot air from their hollow minds would bleach and leech the last vitality from picked bones and scraped peelings of human endeavor.

Someone touched him, and Zephan turned, wrenched from his thoughts. "Anahí! Whatever are you doing here?"

"I'm passing through on my way to Sheffa, and I wanted to see Brother Joseba one more time before I leave."

"I will take you to him as soon as we can get away from this place."

Applause rumbled, signaling the arrival of. . .Kemen Ponte? The man was resplendent in his Pax uniform, with a blue cap topping waves of light brown hair touched with gray. His charming smile immediately captivated the audience.

"A handsome devil, isn't he?" Zephan said to Anahí.

She frowned. "That he is."

"Citizens of Ammonihah, welcome in the name of peace!" His mellow voice carried over the square. "We are here to discuss our economic crisis. Mr. Verman has asked me to speak. We all know you have had no jobs for months, and Mr. Verman, from the international mediating committee, is here to help you. Once we restore peace, you can have your jobs back.

"You have just completed the first step to peace by surrendering your weapons. Everyone knows weapons are the cause of war," Ponte said. "Now the time has come for *Partido Universal*. We will beat our swords into plowshares, like it says in the Bible."

People jostled each other in uneasy expectation.

"As a gesture of tolerance for the Bible, I have invited Mr. Bianco, prophet from Yeshurun, to say a few words."

Zephan gasped. What had happened to Sarita, Aurelia, and Abiram? Had the prophet been harmed in any way before coming here to speak?

Anahí grabbed his arm, and Zephan felt her fear pulse through him.

Brother Joseba's voice was deep and strong, but calm. "Well now, we must render unto Caesar that which is Caesar's." He gave a wry smile and gestured toward the stacks of weapons. "Caesar's peace is not without a price!"

Laughter.

Brother Joseba began singing a hymn, and all joined in.

Keep the commandments; keep the commandments!
In this there is safety; in this there is peace.
He will send blessings; He will send blessings.
Words of a prophet: Keep the commandments.
In this there is safety and peace.

"Now, my brethren, sisters, and friends," Brother Joseba began. "These are days when men preach all manner of false doctrine and set themselves up for a light unto the world, that they might get gain and praise from the world, but they seek not the welfare of Zion.

"Behold, the Lord has forbidden this thing. The Lord has commanded that all men should have charity. For if we would have charity, we would not suffer the laborer in Zion to perish. My people, I remind you that, in addressing humanitarian needs, our God-given individual liberty is far superior to the doctrines and systems of men and their committees.

"Thus saith the Lord: I, the Lord, justify you, and your brethren of my church, in befriending the constitutional law of this land. As pertaining to law of man, whatsoever is more or less than this, cometh of evil. I, the Lord God, make you free indeed, and the law also maketh you free. Nevertheless, when the wicked rule, the people mourn. We believe that rulers, states, and governments have a right, and are bound to enact laws for the protection of all citizens in the free exercise of their religious belief."

Brother Joseba looked out over the crowd. "My people, our Chief Judge has honored the law of the land, and the Cumorah Republic has been exceedingly prosperous. Did we fail in vigilance? Did pride and apathy cause us to tolerate idolatry, then embrace it? Are we guilty of covetousness and ingratitude? If so, let us repent of our pride, envy, and ingratitude. For in nothing does man offend God, save in those who confess not His hand in all things, and obey not His commandments."

His message was heard. People looked at each other.

"We sought long and diligently for an honest man like Mr. Solano, and now we should observe to uphold good and wise men in our government. Wise laws protect the innocent and punish the guilty. Such laws are best calculated to secure the public interest; at the same time, however, holding sacred the freedom of conscience, never to suppress the freedom of the soul. To wise and just laws all

179

men should show respect and deference, as without them peace and harmony would be supplanted by anarchy and terror. Otherwise, anything more or less than these cometh of evil."

"Thus saith the Lord through his prophets," Brother Joseba continued:

> The laws and constitution of the people, which I have suffered to be established, should be maintained for the rights and protection of all flesh, according to just and holy principles;
>
> That every man may act in principle, according to the moral agency which I have given unto him, that every man may be accountable for his own sins in the day of judgment.

The prophet spoke softly, and all leaned forward, straining to hear.

> Beware of secular humanism. For some will deny the power of God, saying the Lord has given His power to men. And there shall be many who will make a man an offender for a word, and lay a snare for him who speaks uprightly, and turn aside the just for a thing of naught.
>
> There shall also be many who will justify a little sin, and they will teach after this manner: Go ahead, lie a little, take advantage of one because of his words, dig a pit for your neighbor. There is no harm in this, they will say. Therefore, beware lest ye are deceived.

"People, remember, obedience to God is the habit of a free man. If you would lift this nation, trust in Him who gave you liberty. Let this be our motto, as it is engraved on our coinage. In God we trust. Let us preserve our representative self-government under God. Look to God and live."

Into the stunned silence, Brother Joseba again began to sing, this time a song that his people had known from childhood.

> As I have loved you, Love one another.
> This new commandment: Love one another.
> By this shall men know ye are my disciples,
> If ye have love one to another.

Again the crowd was drawn into his song. When the song was finished, the people looked at him expectantly.

"Now," Brother Joseba said, "I will pray for this nation."

At this moment, Ponte jumped to his feet, crowding Brother Bianco from the microphone, so the older man returned to his seat.

11

Ponte's sonorous baritone resonated into the residual hush that enveloped the crowd. "I congratulate Joe Bianco for his fine speech. By law, he was given equal time. But for his own good, I cannot allow him to continue. We all know it is against international law to pray in a public place. We don't want to offend Mr. Verman, now, do we?

"Now to the business at hand. Why have you no jobs? Because your Chief Judge, Mr. Solano, refuses to sign an alliance with Pax Universalis. Solano sees enemies left and right, but he will not make an alliance for peace.

"Where are your jobs? Why do you not have what is rightfully yours?"

Anahí shuddered.

"And whom can we blame for Mr. Solano's misguided position? Our friend Mr. Solano has been mixing church with state. The church has trumpeted certain values through the centuries. We have all paid a terrible price for those values. The centuries have been fraught with wars, misery, poverty, cruelty and injustice.

"In the past we have had the nation-state," Ponte continued. "And what did we get? Wars.

"'Money is the root of all evil', the church told us. So what did we get? Poverty.

"Poverty brings us crime. So what does the church tell us to do? Repent!" Ponte laughed. "Can you imagine using such a silly old hate-word? We need a new value system. The church's intolerance does not work. We need a new, universal ethic.

"Citizens! We fear for our very future, and Bianco says all you have to do is trust in God. But let us say no more about Bianco's God. I speak of a new heaven, earth, and Ammonihah. We are creating a new culture. What is heaven, if not peace? Why not heaven, *now*? Peace, today."

The crowd mumbled in confusion.

"Joe Bianco claims to speak the will of God. But the issue is jobs, jobs, jobs!"

"Give us back our jobs!" was a garbled message from the crowd.

"Mr. Solano's ideas have failed to mend this national ruin."

The July heat already bore down in earnest, and sweaty bodies pressed around Anahí. Zephan watched dozens of armed troops guard the multitude. So much for escape. And would Brother Joseba escape from here alive?

"Who stands between you and humanitarian aid?" Ponte asked. "Mr. Solano."

"How could he do this to us?" someone shouted.

"Solano's bad luck!"

"But Mr. Solano is not alone to blame," Ponte said. "As Joe Bianco has clearly shown, Mr. Solano is your Chief Judge because of the wealthy and prosperous house of Yeshurun."

Tongues clattered and arms waved, but no words were distinguishable.

"Cumorah law keeps state and church separate. But Mr. Solano listens to the voice of Yeshurun, and the poor man is confused," Ponte continued. "You can't blame him for cracking under such pressure. On the one hand, Yeshurun urges support for the established government, separate from religion. On the other, Yeshurun pushes its rigid, intolerant value system. But I ask you, whose side is Yeshurun on? The left, or the right?"

A disgruntled din rose from the crowd, growing in intensity like an approaching swarm of angry insects.

" Man cannot live by mythology alone."

Everyone began to yell at once. "We need jobs!"

"We'll starve!"

"Who can save us?"

Ponte leaned forward and lowered his voice. "Now, Joe Bianco is a nice man. Personally, I like him. But even a so-called prophet of God is powerless to solve our problems. Cumorah's policies of rigid absolutism have kept her out of Pax Universalis, but the time has come for a world body to step in and help us."

Heat pushed the mercury to dizzying heights, forcing emotions to hazardous peaks. It made some people pant for breath; others fainted. Fear or anger energized others. All eyes were fastened on the speaker.

"I believe that together we can achieve a perfect world. Together we will forge a new, universal ethic. We will build a Tower of Understanding." Ponte smiled into the astonished eyes of the crowd, but no one said a word.

"Ladies and gentlemen," Ponte said, "humanitarian aid is within our grasp. Would you be interested?"

"Yes! Tell us!"

"Very well, then. If you insist. On the stand is Mr. Horace Verman, from the Egalitarian Foundation, who is waiting to give us humanitarian aid."

"It's about time!" someone shouted.

"Listen carefully," Ponte said. "The Cumorah Republic is dying, because it is chained down by traditions. Mr. Solano has stolen your jobs and Mr. Bianco has tyrannized us all with moral absolutism. The only thing that keeps these men from destroying us is Cumorah law."

"But we elected Solano!" came a small voice.

"Exactly!" Ponte said. "Cumorah made her choice. Solano is Cumorah's only hope for deliverance. I know how scary it is, but it cannot be helped." Ponte shook his head sadly. "The law is the law. . ."

"But what about the humanitarian aid?" a woman called out.

"Yes, of course. The only way we can get humanitarian aid is to break off and become a new republic, so that Solano's parliament cannot keep us out of Pax Universalis. Ladies and Gentlemen, I propose we create the People's Republic of Amalicki—" Ponte coughed.

"Excuse me?" Brother Joseba interrupted.

"*Ammonihah!*" Ponte said. "The People's Republic of Ammonihah." He coughed again. "This is a great day in history. At last our government is free from the restraints of a fundamental God . Look for god within you! Now our new nation can make new laws compatible with Pax Universalis. From there it is but a trivial matter to get humanitarian aid.

"Citizens of Ammonihah, can we show our gratitude to the Egalitarian Foundation for guaranteeing Pax protection and humanitarian aid?"

A ringing cheer exploded from the crowd. "Yes to Egalitarians! Egalitarian, yes! Egalitarian, yes!" The chant oscillated through the crowd, blowing from a mild conjecture into an overbearing assertion.

After a brief consultation with Horace Verman, Ponte returned to the podium. "Mr. Verman says your message clearly supports aid from the foundation. But we must make it official. Even religion must have public support. *Vox populi, vox Dei!* The voice of the people is the voice of God. Right, Mr. Bianco?"

"No, Mr. Ponte. It is not right." Brother Joseba suddenly appeared at the podium, with Ponte towering beside him. "It is not right if a time comes that the voice of the people chooses iniquity. Political leaders have set themselves up as a light unto the world, and are forever creating new crises. The adversary will not save you, but seizes upon your fears to persuade you to accept tyranny and oppression. Thus he flatters you away and leads you carefully down, not to heaven, but to hell.

"My people, we find ourselves in a war of ideas. Do we believe in separation of church and state? Of course we do. We do not believe that a state religion of any kind is just, whether that religion be Godly faith or Godless secularism. This is enforced priestcraft and is an abomination in God's sight. However, governments have a responsibility to all citizens to preserve freedom of conscience and worship.

"We of Yeshurun do not agree with Mr. Ponte's ideas of sedition and conquest. And we do not believe that human law, be it national or global, has a right to interfere in prescribing rules of worship to bind the conscience of men, nor dictate forms of public or private devotion. Over the years, we have not interfered with others' beliefs. Men are free to choose truth or error. We believe that God governs with love; He never forces the human mind. Why would anyone censor another's beliefs, or compel a people to accept a prescribed doctrine, be it false or true? Is it fear of honest inquiry?"

Ponte opened his mouth, but said nothing. Something about the old man forbade interruption. In fact, for some reason Ponte felt silly standing there, mute, so he sat down.

"Now, behold," Brother Joseba continued, "God loved our fathers, even Abraham, Isaac, and Jacob; and He remembered His covenants with them; and He brought them out from Egypt.

"And He straitened them in the wilderness with his rod, because of their iniquity, for they hardened their hearts. He sent fiery flying serpents among them; and after the people were bitten He prepared a way to heal them; and the people had to look neither right nor left, nor to trust in the doctrines of any man. Only look to Christ. Look to God and live! But many refused because the way was simple. In vain the people looked everywhere but to that divine center, and Christ. They despised and rejected Him, and reviled against His prophet. And many there were who perished.

"And as the Lord God liveth, that brought Israel out from the land of Egypt, and gave Moses power to heal the nations. . ."

A collective intake of breath was heard from the audience.

Brother Joseba's voice rose and filled the air with a power marvelous for one so slight and small of stature. ". . . that he should heal the nations after they had been bitten by the poisonous serpents . . ."

Zephan and Anahí looked at the PAX flag, and then at each other.

". . .if the nations would but look to the type raised up in the wilderness, that whosoever would look upon it might live. Now this was a type of the Son of God, even He who visited this choice land in the first century; yea, even the Christ. And behold, whatsoever nation shall possess this land shall be free from bondage, if they will but serve God.

"Many did look and live, but few understood. Because of the hardness of their hearts, the people would not look to God, therefore they perished. Now, the people would not look because they did not believe it would heal them. Behold, not only did Moses testify on these things, but also all the holy prophets, from his days even to now.

"Now I give you the words of a prophet of this, the dispensation of the fullness of times:

There are some in this land, among whom I count myself, whose faith it is that this land is reserved only for a righteous people, and we remain here as tenants only as we remain in the favor of the Lord, for He is the landlord as far as this earth is concerned. If we are to remain under heaven's benign protection and care, we must return to those principles which have brought us our peace, liberty, and prosperity. Our problems today are essentially problems of the Spirit.

The solution is not more wealth, more food, more technology, more government, or instruments of destruction — the solution is personal and national reformation. In short, it is to bring our national character ahead of our technological and material advances. Repentance is the sovereign remedy to our problems.

185

"My children, doubt not, but be believing. Doubt not, fear not. Look unto Christ in every thought. Look to God and live! And now I say unto you, as the Lord God liveth, these things are true. . ."

Silence rained upon simmering tempers. Heated strife grew placid, if only for a moment. No one even whispered. Some tried to return Brother Joseba's thorough gaze. Others looked away.

Whoa! Zephan peered at the rapt faces of those next to him. Once again, Brother Joseba had used the Word to communicate to his people, and none could mistake his message. Every man and woman of Yeshurun within hearing of the prophet knew full well what he meant, but would they have the courage to turn to God at this critical moment? And what would Ponte do with this?

Ponte soon shattered the calm. "We are tired of the old church's rigid principles and consequent failures. According to the Pax universal ethic, truth is relative, not rigid and absolute as in biblical faiths like Yeshurun. We are tolerant of all beliefs, but by sheer force of world opinion, no repressive religion ——— whether Christian, Islamic, Jewish, or whatever ——— has a long-term future. The best way to solve this issue is to vote on it. After all, Pax is a global democracy, and we are expected to vote on everything. Mr. Bianco claims democracy is not always right. But we all know that the majority is always right.

"But before you decide, think carefully. No one will force you to vote for one program or the other. But if you reject the Egalitarian Foundation, we do not get the funding we need. This should be an easy choice. It's time to face reality. We can't resolve this crisis without more money. This is our last chance for a perfect world, ladies and gentlemen.

"Each of us has a brain. So rather than follow blindly, why not choose for ourselves? The time has come to make your choice. Your future hangs on the decision you make this moment," Ponte said softly.

The audience stirred with uneasiness.

"Do you think Kemen Ponte is right?" a young lady asked her neighbor.

"Bianco is getting awfully old. And look at the mess he got our nation into. Maybe he should retire before he gets too senile and embarrasses himself further. These days, world leadership taxes the strength even of a younger man."

"Ponte seems humble, and not ambitious for power," the young lady continued. "He seems to care very much about us and wants to improve the quality of our lives. Peace, now! After all the hardship we have suffered, it sounds heavenly. Maybe it is time for a change."

"Both men believe in heaven," a man said with a shrug. "It's just a difference in definitions."

"But only one of them speaks the truth," said the person with the small voice. "The other must be false — a wolf in sheep's clothing."

The young lady groaned. "But how can we know who is a true prophet?"

"By their fruits ye shall know them," the small voice replied. "Jesus said, I am the Good Shepherd. My sheep know my voice, and they follow me."

"We will do this in an orderly fashion," Ponte said. "Any who think the dying Republic of Cumorah can still be saved, stand over here, next to Joe Bianco."

Zephan and Anahí, with eyes riveted on their old friend's peaceful face, slowly made their way to Brother Joseba's side. A handful of others followed.

"Mr. Verman, clearly the new People's Republic of Ammonihah has a mandate. You are authorized to go ahead with the plan." Ponte laughed. "I trust Mr. Bianco and his impotent church will step aside gracefully. It's obvious that society has chosen a new, universal ethic, which will allow a world body to resolve this crisis. You will cooperate, won't you?" he said in a loud and jovial tone to Brother Joseba. "You would not want to stand in the way of reform and bring persecution upon your church, would you?"

Separated from the others, Brother Joseba's flock stood taciturn in its tiny solidarity. Zephan watched the crowd back away.

Ponte held his hands up high in a theatrical gesture. "Citizens! Solano cannot help you. You must help yourselves. . . to what is rightfully yours!"

"Yours, mine, and ours!" someone shouted. Many laughed, resembling an audience at a lascivious movie.

187

"Lift up your heads in pride. Now is the moment we have all been waiting for. The dawn of your destiny! From this moment on, everything will be easier.

"Now that we are a new republic, however, we have certain obligations. The humanitarian funds will be paid out in the new global currency just as fast as you surrender your old Cumorah money which, as of this moment, is no longer valid. If you voluntarily surrender the old money, we will grant you a six month exemption from the global tax. Hoarding of Cumorah coinage for its intrinsic value, or even for souvenirs, is punishable by law, in the form of heavy fines and imprisonment.

"The old nation of Cumorah is now defunct, forever barred from membership in Pax Universalis. But New Ammonihah will have a vote in the Pax Select Council!"

Ponte's voice rose above the restless crowd. "A perfect world has no room for the old hatreds, does it? We will have peace. In order to qualify for the money, we must purge our society of all hatred. We shall have no more demonstrations. After all, demonstrations are hateful, aren't they? Think of anyone who might disrupt our society. Do you have a neighbor who flies the flag from any old nation-state, especially Cumorah? This might cause unrest. Who exhibits a cross or a six-pointed star, or displays any documents pertaining to a specific religion?"

"Religion?" someone asked.

"Oh, we can all have religion," Ponte replied hastily. "We will simply *redefine* religion. Everyone here can witness that Yeshurun was rejected by the will of the people, because its views, which are based on the house of Israel, are too narrow. We have long seen that this always offends someone. But at last this religious hatred has come to an end. Under a universal ethic, we will all have a broader, more tolerant religion."

"A state religion?" asked a very quiet, but piercing voice.

"Of course not!" Ponte said. "How dare you imply such a thing? I find the very suggestion of a state religion extremely offensive. From now on, whoever offends anyone in the name of religion will be subject to full prosecution under the laws of our new republic."

Into the strained silence, Ponte read from a lengthy document in front of him. "We must not permit any songs which portray any type of intolerance," he continued. "Maybe you know someone who wears a shirt bearing an appalling hate-word. Stickers on automobiles also identify dangerous people. We must be extremely careful in every word and action. After all that Pax is doing for us, we wouldn't want to offend the new order, would we?"

No one spoke.

"Anyone still in possession of the old Cumorah gold coinage will of course be suspect," Ponte said. "Most obvious, however, are firearms. After all, we don't want anyone hurting him or herself, do we? Or worse, hurting someone else. Peace Forces will ensure those weapons stay in the proper hands, but Pax can't do it alone. Do you know anyone who failed to come to this meeting? What would this mean? Someone might be thinking dangerous thoughts. This means someone out there could hurt somebody. That somebody could be you."

Ponte lowered his voice. "I know you all want a perfect world, and would do nothing to disrupt order. But it only takes one person to upset our earthly balance. That person could be your neighbor. But don't worry. The solution is easy. If everyone will just check up on one neighbor, we will soon have everything under control. Sound easy enough?"

"YESSS-S-S!" hissed forth from the crowd.

"Then what are you waiting for?"

A roar erupted, sounding somehow inhuman. The crowd, too, seemed to lose all individual sensibility. Fused into a monstrous, flowing mass with thousands of eyes, screaming mouths, running feet, and busy hands, the mob raged down the streets, crushing bystanders, bashing automobiles, shattering windows, looting shops, vandalizing homes.

Zephan put his arm protectively about Anahí, then felt a hand on his shoulder. Brother Joseba.

"Best to wait, *hermano*. You'll only get killed out there."

Ponte approached, and Zephan's heart plummeted. "Will we ever see our families again, Brother Joseba?"

"Yes, but as soon as this violence subsides, you must leave. You must flee Babylon, Zephan," the prophet spoke quickly. He looked upon his friend. "Zephan Benamoz, my fellow Apostle of Jesus Christ, please keep the Brethren appraised.

"Whatever happens, I cannot leave this people now," Brother Joseba said. "My life is spent, now to be used in God's hands. Go, my friends, and live for freedom. And remember, the power of God is greater than all the soldiers of Babylon."

"No, Brother Joseba, nothing must happen to you!" Tearfully, Anahí threw her arms around the old prophet.

A strong forearm slipped around her waist and separated her from Brother Joseba. Anahí could feel Ponte's breath upon her ear as he said softly, "Don't nail your dreams into a coffin, my dear. I can give you the world at your feet. Don't let it pass you by."

In a single, swift motion, Anahí swung from Ponte's grasp. Her fist flew into his face like a guided missile, leaving his lip split and bleeding. "I know your kind, you adulterous babbler of semantic drivel! You double-minded, fork-tongued, father of lies! Get away from me!"

Zephan laughed.

Ponte touched his mouth gingerly with his starched new sleeve, but his eyes ravaged her. "Spirited little thing, aren't you? Ah, how I love a challenge! But we will have time for that. No one will get very far from here. For now, Bianco, it's you we want. You, my good friend, will come for questioning. Guards!"

Anahí watched in horror as chains were fastened upon Brother Joseba's wrist and ankle. "Why are you doing this?" she said to Ponte. "Is it really necessary to put chains on a frail old man?"

"There's no telling what he might do, señorita. He's being stripped of all his political power, you know. He could be dangerous."

"His power to act in God's name is endless. You cannot take it from him."

Ponte started to smile, and winced. "You are wrong, señorita. The people have already done so. I only act on their behalf. It is their will."

"Is it, now?"

"Don't blame me for Bianco's defeat, señorita. After all, the people did choose me."

Anahí stared at the old prophet in chains, then directed her disdain upon her adversary. Ponte looked so. . . small, but beads of sweat gathered upon his smooth face. "The people could have kept God as their king," she said, "and they chose. . .*you.*" He became yet smaller beneath her gaze.

Ponte stepped backward, as if this young village girl had a power greater than his.

Her eyes telegraphed her revulsion. She had read the dark spirit behind his proud words, and was not deceived.

Ponte turned from her, signaled to the guards, and led Brother Joseba away.

12

Zephan escorted the young woman to her car, a beat-up old station wagon with wooden sides. His eyebrows sprang upward. "That looks like —"

"Brother Joseba's old car. Solano gave him a newer car in payment for extensive horticultural work in his gardens. So he said I could have this one." She patted the dented beige hood affectionately. "The old girl gets me where I want to go. That's all I need."

"But will you make it over the mountain pass into Sheffa?"

"No challenge. If this car was good enough for the prophet, it's good enough for me."

"All the same, you keep your doors locked. This land is crawling with lunatics."

"I'll be careful. I promise I won't do anything to attract attention."

Zephan was doubtful. Most men could not keep their eyes off her. That alone would attract too much attention.

Anahí reached into the pocket in her long calico skirt and pulled out a .45, handling it with astonishing ease. "Besides," she said with a mischievous lilt, "the old Cumorah law is still in effect. If somebody forces me to, I'm prepared to defend myself."

"Are you sure you can —"

"I was busy at the Chief's place, you know. Solano let me learn self-defense under his best instructors. My teachers complimented me on my speed and accuracy, and with this old skirt, I don't even have to draw."

Zephan gave a low whistle. "All right then, *hijita*. Best to put this corner of hell in your rear view mirror, right now while these crazies are occupied here in town. I radioed ahead for you, and you'll have an escort waiting at the border."

Her face became grave. "Last night in my old house, my father appeared to me in a dream, Zephan. He told me to live on for our people, and not let Cabrios' murderous combinations get above us. I will press forward with a steadfastness in the Messiah ——"

"Having a perfect brightness of hope, a love of God, and endure to the end," he finished for her. "You are the daughter I never had, Ani. Go with God."

He gathered her in his arms and held her for a long time, and then they parted.

Anahí reached the top of a ridge and stopped for a last look at her homeland. Eastward was the road to Sheffa and the rugged Hermounts in Jershon, but peace. Behind her lay her childhood village, in ruins. Like a simmering volcano, the rumble of destruction reached her ears. A vast grievous picture loomed before her, painted in stark colors of desolation.

Raging on the horizon, the work of arson enmeshed with that giant ball of flame which daily lit the earth for both prodigal and faithful. Wooden frames of modest homes and community buildings leaned momentarily against the encroaching darkness like flimsy red neon baskets over laden with brimstone. Blazing light flooded the streets like a river of blood. Smoky night swallowed up all that remained alive, banishing any hopeful daylight under threat of death.

Anahí mourned all war victims and beseeched the Lord not to suffer the blood of her loved ones to cry out from the dust, unavenged. Remembering the words of Brother Joseba, she prayed that anger be lifted from her heart.

Where did it begin? Ammonihah was an innocent village, with *guajiro* farmers minding their own business. Then Cabrios' agents perforated the confidence of the unwary. With those of weaker character stirred up to contention, the land was prepared for a demagogue. Then came the liar, Ponte, who flattered the proud and reviled God's prophet. He trampled people's freedom as a thing of naught, as if people who obeyed the law, kept the faith, and prospered were something evil, as if the law and the prophets were not good enough.

The law and the prophets. . .

Something about this scene was terrifyingly familiar. She had seen it before. Her mind plunged into a well of memories within her. She floated on a red sea of trial, past a black wilderness of affliction, through joy and pain, light and darkness, good and evil, and came to rest before the painting of *The Farewell*.

No, she was *in* the painting, standing in the place of those who wrote the word of God. She gazed into the eyes of the prophet and transcended boundaries of time. Today she breathed the air of ancient Eden, but her fingers touched the gate to paradise. Today the prophet was Brother Joseba and in his hands he held words of the living God. Eternity was compressed into those golden engravings, and the lamplight of ageless hope shone beyond a world drooping in sin, to a radiant dawn over the promised land.

A siren in the distant town pierced her consciousness, and she leaned against the tailgate to regain her bearings. Night had fallen, but to Anahí it was no longer dark. She had packed many paintings into the car, but not enough. Somehow she must make room for them all, for she felt in her heart she would never return. She must go back to Solano's mansion to retrieve every last painting. Turning the wagon around, she headed for Granada.

13

The next morning Aurelia and the Benamoz family returned to the city to assess the damage.

The Canosa villa rose like a battered island above the expanse of charred debris. The storage room and other outbuildings were burned and gutted, but the inferno, failing to consume the cement block structure, had somehow raged past the house, leaving only blackened walls and an acrid odor of hot metal and melted plastic in its wake.

Inside, Aurelia Canosa made her way to the couch, replaced a slashed cushion and sank down upon it. Zephan and Sarita stood amid the wreckage, surveying the room in stunned silence. Every cupboard and drawer had been ransacked. Chairs had been thrown across the room. Fine vases had been hurled against the wall.

Like a beacon on a lonely night, morning sun filtered through a shattered, soot-blackened window, casting a delicate web of light into the semi-darkness. Through the smog Aurelia could see the wreck of the chandelier. Cut from its moorings by an enemy hand, the splendid fixture had come to rest on a splintered mahogany shore, where it lay half submerged in a sea of ashen dust.

Aurelia uttered a cry, and her hand flew to her mouth. A large kitchen knife protruded from an oil-painted shepherd scene hanging on the wall above the couch. Pages from the family album had been brutishly ripped out and lay partially burned in the fireplace. Jaime's new record player, the speakers kicked in, was pitched forward. Recordings had been randomly thrown on the floor and trampled.

"The tires are slashed on the car, and the windshield has a bullet hole in it," Abiram reported. "How's that for lip service to the weapons ban? And the tools are gone, but the car is repairable."

Zephan laughed without mirth. "With all the destruction the mob didn't find those few weapons we were able to conceal. Fortunately Anahí was able to escape safely."

"And no one here was hurt . . ." Aurelia began.

"Except maybe Brother Joseba," Abiram said.

Sarita turned to her husband. "What do you think they'll do to him, Zephan?"

Zephan stared at the floor. "I don't know." He turned pain-filled eyes to her face. "It was so awful, Sarita, the way Ponte manipulated that mob. Poor Brother Joseba didn't have a chance."

"Only one person could help him," Abiram said. "Haman. He's very close to Ponte. Do you think he would intervene for the sake of his family, Papa?"

"I don't know, Abiram. I don't even know Haman any more. My own son is like a stranger to me. And we have another problem, too. Who would have thought Granada would fall during the few days we were here visiting our friends?"

"Zephan, all our family heirlooms are back in the house at Granada," Sarita said.

"It is much too dangerous to go back to Granada now. But somehow I must. Our greatest treasure is left there. The book of Joseph! It would be so easy for Haman to get into Granada and retrieve our few things."

"I don't trust him," Abiram said.

"But what could he lose by doing a favor for his own family? Politicians in power always make exceptions for their own families, or whoever pleases their imperial whims," Zephan said, his voice hard.

A slam of the heavy entry door echoed through the house.

"Must be Haman," Abiram said. "You can ask him yourself."

Haman stopped short, framed in the same archway he had entered as a wonder-eyed, youthful immigrant years ago. Now he stood straight as a post, unyielding in his impeccable uniform, eyes hard, his head so high that his neck looked stiff. "Well, if it isn't Bianco's little flock. The remains, anyway."

"Can you do something for Brother Joseba, Haman?" Zephan kept his voice calm. He already knew the answer, and he would not kowtow to this implacable young man.

"Why should I? Joe Bianco is a fraud."

"He has done nothing illegal. You can't hurt him just because you don't agree with him."

"Oh, he will not be hurt. He will be questioned and released. But he will be watched. The people must be protected from him."

"Whatever for?"

"His ideas are rigid and extreme. He is very close-minded. But the danger is his extensive influence. He misleads too many people."

"What is Ponte afraid of?" Zephan asked softly.

"Nothing!" Haman wore his prized how-can-you-be-so-stupid expression. "Don't you see? Ponte is trying to save the nation from Solano before it is too late. We are on the brink of economic disaster, and Ponte's plan is our only hope. And if you know what's good for you, you will stay out of his way."

"I hear you."

"This is your last warning. Get out while you can. We cannot guarantee the safety of Solano supporters. I can do no more for you." He turned on his heel and walked out, slamming the door.

14

Abiram patched slashed tires on the old Canosa Thunderbird, and they returned to the plantation.

Zephan drove ahead alone in Abiram's pickup. He found the gate chained, however, and an unmarked car blocking the entrance. The driver, wearing an ill-fitting Pax uniform, and although a young man, had prematurely gray hair, a sagging face with an unhealthy pallor, and a paunch hung over his belt, which carried his revolver.

"Well, hello, young man," Zephan said. "Do I know you? What is your name?"

"Strobe Fenley."

"You're not from around here, are you, Fenley?"

Fenley gritted his teeth. "I am from the capital, here on special assignment, to enforce Pax Universalis in this region."

"How long have you been here?"

"Two years and five and one half months."

"I mean, at my gate."

"Oh. Three hours."

"This is out in the country, away from the comforts of the city. You don't like it here, do you, Fenley?"

"I'm here to do my duty." Fenley rearranged a tall stack of manuals and papers on the passenger seat. "I am a lawyer for the Anti-Hate Committee, I am a Egalitarian, I helped pass Pax Universalis, and I am a fully trained and qualified administrator."

"Bureaucrats pack pistols these days?"

"Only in case of trouble."

"But why are you here?"

"Unregistered weapons found on these premises is the first violation. Hey!"

Zephan's hand shot forward, and suddenly he held Fenley's pistol. He fired at the gate, splintering the lock, then hurled the weapon far into the thicket.

"You can't do that!"

"And you have trespassed," Zephan said quietly.

Fenley's mouth opened and closed, his eyes bugged. "Who are you?"

"Zephan Benamoz. I own a share in this property." Somewhere a tractor sputtered, then roared. "What did you do with everyone else who lives here?"

Fenley ducked into his car and grabbed a sheet off the pile. "This property owner is guilty of crimes against Pax. It is documented here under article 90613 of the treaty."

"Just like that, young man? Guilty, without due process?" Zephan raised his voice over the noise of the approaching machinery.

"This is an emergency. Until we restore law and order. You are under arrest, Benamoz!" Fenley had to shout over the din.

The old red tractor loomed into view. It was Manuel, he was grinning, and he was coming fast.

"Look out!" Zephan yelled.

Manuel rolled into the iron gate, which swung wide. Despite screaming gears and thumping floor pedals, the machine's brakes were not nearly as effective as Fenley's car, which, unfortunately, would not perform that function a second time.

A geyser of oil soaked Fenley's papers on the passenger seat, then the engine finally stilled. Manuel jumped out, his grin even wider than Zephan thought possible. "So sorry, Señor. I must get those brakes fixed. I hear gunshots, so I hurry."

Fenley gaped. "How in the world did you ——"

Manuel lifted his wrists, showing broken handcuffs. "Paquito, my leetle *hijo*, he break them, with *un* adz. Adz not classified as weapon!"

Zephan laughed, then turned to Fenley. "What have you done to these people?"

"He refuse to speak Spanish," Manuel said. "My English very bad. But something about ownership of property, I think." He fished a tattered document from his shirt pocket. "I bring the deed, in the case it is *necesario*."

"What are your charges, Fenley?" Zephan demanded.

Fenley resumed a stern demeanor in effort to hide his confusion. "I have specific orders to bring you in, Benamoz. You are a threat, a danger, a menace to society."

"What are your charges, Fenley?" Zephan repeated.

"Possession of illegal weapons and failure to pay taxes."

"Why me?"

"You own this farm."

"I don't own this place. Show him the deed, Manuel."

Fenley snatched the paper and stared at it.

"Several years ago I sold it to the workers; they work it, manage it, and own controlling shares in this business. I only possess a few small shares."

"We are legal, Señor Benamoz. We show him the tax records, but he cannot read Spanish. We try to tell him. He would not listen."

"I thought those people, in their ignorance, were trying to cover up for you ——"

"You thought wrong, Fenley."

"But under the Pax Universalis treaty ——"

"There is no Pax treaty, Fenley. Parliament defeated it. Didn't you know that?"

"But I thought Ponte ——"

"You thought — correction. A robot doesn't know how to think, Fenley. You are the one guilty ——— of breaking and entering and violating these good people's civil rights. How are you going to explain that to them?"

"I don't think ——"

"You don't think! That's the first truth you've spoken all afternoon, Fenley!" Zephan laughed uproariously.

"I don't have to take this." Head thrown back, eyes narrowed, Fenley walked stiffly toward his car.

"What? A lawyer for the Anti-Hate Committee, speechless, walking off with no explanation to these poor people?"

Abiram arrived with his mother; Aurelia stayed in the car. Sarita moved to her husband's side and slipped her arm through his. "Zephan," she said.

He patted her hand. "Don't worry, Mama. I'm doing the boy a favor. Maybe I'll persuade him to take up an honest career. Good grief, *muchacho*, two and a half years in this mountain region and you still don't even speak their language. What *have* you been doing? Perhaps you're not cut out for this career."

Abiram was tinkering with Fenley's car. He started the engine and gunned it. "Still runs," he said. "Question is, will it run fast enough?"

Everyone laughed.

"For what?" Fenley asked.

More laughter.

Zephan wiped tears from his eyes. "Are you going to get that wreck of yours off our property, or do I have to call the police?"

Abiram held the door for the bureaucrat. "You look uncomfortable. Don't you like it here in the country?"

"I hate it. I hate you all. You are all criminals! Ruffians! Gangsters!"

"Are you a religious man, Fenley?"

"Of course not!" he snapped.

"Oh, that's right. You're from the Anti-*Hate* Committee." Laughter. "If I were you, I'd start praying. . . for a transfer!"

The still, hot afternoon at last yielded a whispered breeze, carrying with it fragrance of pineapple and sugar cane from the valley. On the mountains, Zephan saw a vast, uneven latticework of green, gold, and brown on miniature terraces against nearly vertical highland cliffs.

So steep was the terrain that plants themselves seemed to hug the escarpment to avoid sliding to the valley. A common joke was that peasants in the highlands planted crops on hillsides because they had one leg shorter than the other. The patchwork had no logical pattern discernible to the observer. But each farmer carried out his own plan, driven to produce food, and no one wasted a single square foot.

The peasants were poor, but food was on their tables, and their children laughed and sang all day long. Let government only protect life, liberty, and private property, and people would care for themselves.

But to Fenley, who never left his office, and for whom reality was a stack of papers black with verbiage, and for whom people were mere instruments of theory, the mountain people posed a threat. A public administrator could not bear to look upon nature without suffering nervous tension. Nature was chaotic, and needed an administrator's hand.

One look at those mountain people, walking along the roads and up and downhill, was enough to inspire terror in a public administrator. Where were all those mountain people going? How could they be going in different directions? Everyone knows traffic is supposed to flow into town in the morning and out at night. Correction. Traffic was not to flow, but rush. These mountain people did not hurry enough. Had they no idea of time? No common purpose? What were they thinking? An administrator must know what everyone thinks. Too many private thoughts disturb the collective mind, then the people become ungovernable.

All administrators considered an assignment to any mountain provinces to be the worst form of punishment, a blight on his career, a banishment that could only lead to ruin. This extreme terror of all wilderness was due to abnormal anatomy in the bureaucrat.

A source of this anomaly lay in the glands. A normal glandular system is designed to regulate and balance the individual human body. But a bureaucrat's glands suffered from a nearly incurable reversal; the glands functioned only to regulate other human beings. This, of course, resulted in great stress on the bureaucrat's own body, because his extreme desire to control other people dominated him completely, causing a systematic shutdown of all other normal functions. This condition in the blood was an ancient malady, found among the Romans. Benjamin, ever the student of human nature, had quoted some historian named Fuller: prolonged lust for "gold had curdled the Roman blood: it was no longer red, but thin and yellow." No wonder Fenley looked so peaked.

The first organ in a bureaucrat to suffer from this chronic constipation was the heart, which became excessively hard, due to built up impurities. The neck, too, was stiff, the sinews having reached a brassy consistency to support his brain, which was almost dead weight, since three fourths of it was defunct.

The remaining quadrant — which performed functions such as categorizing, organizing, filing, compartmentalizing, number-crunching, statistical analysis, management, and public regulation — was vastly overstimulated. With plain linguistic capability lost, a person so stricken could only communicate in a combination of legal terminology and bureaucratic jargon, which resulted in an unintelligible babble. Devastating brain damage also occurred in the spiritual quadrant, often first to reach clinical death. This explained a bureaucrat's unreasoned fear of, and sometimes violent hatred of, anything or anyone religious.

Regulators could not tolerate mountain folk who did not fit the complexities requisite to a new order in the world. Daily, bureaucrats wrung their hands because these people did not have a television in every house, carpeted floors, and convenience foods. Despite eloquent good intentions, Botina's welfare state never reached the mountain folk. Now this regime had taken a turn for the worse, yet peasants would go on, as they had for generations, close to the land, perhaps a little closer to God than their harried counterparts in noisy big cities. Maybe these folk would survive as well as anyone, for they still lived off the land, and had never learned to depend on empty political words for their sustenance.

Even on plantations in the valleys, farmers had managed sizeable crops despite political upheaval. It was a tribute to their character. Through the years, while tyrants sowed seeds of death, farmers toiled steadily on, harvesting fruit and grain to sustain life. But Ponte's regime, ignorant of natural laws for prosperity, would be bent on managing everything and everyone, and would surely upset any balance in the market. Perhaps as many famines had been caused by senseless theories and policies as by nature.

Abiram had managed to repair Jaime's record player, and salvaged Zephan's favorite, a Chopin piano concerto. Perhaps Zephan so cherished it because in the Black Sea Democracies it had been condemned, as were the works of other great European composers who were from the "wrong race and the wrong culture."

The sweet melody briefly assuaged his pain, and for a moment he traversed time to those early days of their arrival in the promised land, when the Benamoz children had grown up on this plantation. Those were days when each man's life was his own, unmolested by distant strangers who deemed the human family naught but another species of living matter with which to experiment. Those were days a man could raise his family in the nurture and admonition of God, accountable only to Him. Those were simpler days indeed. . .

Zephan gave himself a mental slap back to reality. Had life ever been so easy, really? No, only a brief and pleasant interlude in the great war of life. There had always been opposition in all things, rumors of wars, and men making war. Human nature, forever resistant to change of heart, drove men to excel at predatory skills, justifying any means to gain power over their fellows.

So it had come to this — reduced to primitive instinct of fight and flight. Poor Canosa was gone. Better days were gone, perhaps for good. And no amount of wishing would bring them back. One reality now loomed large: Chief Solano's life was in jeopardy.

While Sarita helped Aurelia pack a few things for her trip to Sheffa with Abiram, Zephan updated his files, then placed a call to Zarahemla Republic Intelligence headquarters.

"Good evening. Mitchell Hunt speaking."

"Is this line clean?"

"Yes, Zephan, I have been expecting your call."

"CBI is defunct. Clarence Rook has fled. Since he opposes the new regime, his life would be forfeit here."

"Roger. He is safe with us. And Solano?"

"He's not a quitter, sir. Even with their backs to the wall in León, he still has Parliament on his side. He is an excellent General, and he would have our enemy on the run, if it weren't for this cursed embargo."

"I know, Zephan. Our Chief Ashley is a puppet of Pax, so our hands are tied until the election next November when we hope to throw him out and get you some help. To boot, we ourselves have Pax officials in here daily, and they are forever snooping around. But hang on and keep fighting."

Hang on. The words rang in Zephan's ears. Was this the ghost of Canosa's so-called allies? Was this to be a repeat performance of the betrayal in Cumeni?

"Benamoz? Are you there?"

"Yes, sir."

"Very well. You know the code word in an extreme emergency. Above all, Solano is guaranteed asylum here. . . Uh, Zephan, one more thing."

"Yes, sir?"

"Our man Mortfield here says to beware of someone named Amalickiah."

15

Tantagua, Land of Cumorah

Cicero Boulevard was a river of people and automobiles flowing unevenly through Tantagua, one last stronghold remaining in Cumorah.

Benjamin gazed at the large red cross on the city's hospital as his plane circled to settle on the airfield. The days following Ammonihah's destruction had seen quick escalation in the conflict, and now his beloved Cumorah bowed herself beneath the bludgeoning scourge of war.

At Zephan's message that he and Sarita would depart from Cumorah through the border town of Tantagua, Benjamin obtained leave and flew on the next plane to meet them.

Ben's father waited near a wire fence surrounding the hospital compound. Strain during the last months had aged Zephan Benamoz, whose hair was a shock of white. His face was gray with dejection.

"I couldn't reach you," Zephan said without preamble. "It's over, son. Parliament voted to accept Pax Universalis, and Solano resigned."

Father and son held each other for a long moment. "Our countrymen couldn't help it, Ben. They had no choice."

"I know, Papa."

"Come, your mother is anxious to see you. Everything is happening fast," Zephan explained as they walked to the compound. "While we were visiting Aurelia, the terrorists took the capital, and we could not get back. I sent Abiram to Sheffa, and we depart for Zarahemla at dawn, abandoning everything, but. . ." his voice was barely audible. ". . .Ponte has ordered his troops to shoot on sight if Solano or I return home."

The words struck terror in Ben's heart. He stopped as his father walked on. *Why are you still here?* he wanted to cry out. *Don't you remember what happened to Grandpa Amoz and Grandpa Canosa? They tried to oppose the regime, and now they are gone. Gone, Papa! Let us get away from this place! Please, Papa, before it's too late.*

But Ben said nothing. He only stared at his father's broad back. He had never seen Papa's shoulders droop. Zephan never complained. Ben stood a little straighter.

Zephan held the door open for his son and several medics bearing stretchers. "Sarita wanted to get one more day in at the hospital. You know how she works."

They found Sarita changing dressings on the wounded. She paused to embrace her son. "Look, Ben." She sighed. Five more stretchers, bearing a man, woman, and three children, were brought in and wedged into the overcrowded ward. "Not only soldiers, but whole families, partial families, orphans, widows. It's an unending stream."

Ben saw dark circles under eyes drooping with weariness. "Please rest a moment, Mama."

"No place to sit down. Nearly all the chairs have been used to make cots. No time, anyway. Look at these people, poor souls. I'll see you later."

Outside, Zephan busied himself constructing stretchers and cots, and Ben had an idea. "Mama won't be much help if she collapses from exhaustion," he said.

"I know, son. I can't get her to stop."

With trembling hands, Sarita set a pitcher of water on a tray next to a newcomer. She knelt down, steadying herself on the edge of a cot. At her gentle touch, a little girl quieted her piteous cries.

"There you are!" Benjamin plopped down a small stool made from canvas and wood. "This little girl needs you."

Sarita turned grateful eyes to her son.

"Sit with her a moment, Mama. Long enough to explain to me how I can help."

16

Pulling his jeep in behind a loaded ambulance, Solano jumped out and strode into the compound.

"Zephan." His voice was hoarse. "My son was killed last night on the battlefront at Chinandiga."

"Solano!" Zephan reached out for his friend.

The leader raised a hand in protest. "Don't, Zephan. Do you realize how many mothers have lost their sons to this instrument of hell called the order of Voltaire? My grief is no greater than theirs. I must be strong, Zephan, and comfort my people."

Slowly the two men walked through the building, preceded by whispers of "*El Jefe! El Jefe* is here!" Solano paused frequently to offer kind words.

"Nothing heals like encouragement from their leader!" a nurse said gratefully as she hurried by. Then, remembering, she turned to Zephan. "You can be proud of your son, too, Señor Benamoz. He repaired two washing machines and has done more than his share of the dirty work." She nodded toward a door down the hall.

Clad in a smock and surgical mask, Ben removed blood-drenched sheets from soaking and placed them in the machines. He plunged the emptied bedpans into hot soapy water, washed them thoroughly, and sprayed them with disinfectant. Mopping his way out the door, he backed into the Chief Judge and turned with surprise.

Solano embraced the young man and wept.

17

Past midnight. Solano and the Benamoz family retired to a group of huts several hundred yards from the hospital, where medical personnel tried to sleep in shifts, despite an unrelenting rumble of artillery.

"Ponte never sleeps!" Solano grumbled. "We have little time left."

Sarita yawned. "If only we had a few more days to —"

"*Señor Jefe!*" An orderly poked his head through the door and beckoned to Solano. "Excuse me, sir! A message. The radio is across the way."

Zephan followed the two men out.

Between sounds of war and the crackle of static, Solano strained to hear the voice on the other end.

". . . the CON commander speaking," the voice said. "Mr. Solano, Pax troops are now arriving and engaged. . . negotiating with Ponte. . . demand your departure. . ."

Solano stared blankly at his companions.

". . .within twenty-four hours or we begin killing hostages . . . Zarahemla offers asylum."

"Ponte is a madman, sir," said the orderly. "His own mother, who has tried to reason with him, is now among the hostages."

Zephan turned to Solano in amazement. "I warned Haman the Egalitarians would do this very thing, but I was being facetious to make a point!"

"I have not wanted to abandon my people," Solano shouted over the racket as they hurried back to the hut, "but perhaps it will spare them."

"You have no choice. . ." A deafening explosion drowned out Zephan's words.

Sarita felt Ben yank her away from the bursting window and throw her on the floor beside him.

The brief silence soon filled with the scream of sirens. She looked up to see yellow tongues of flame licking the hospital roof. "Run!"

At the doors, Sarita and her son struggled against throngs of terrified people staggering, crawling, pushing or dragging cots for those who could not walk. Those patients were free from the fire. Medics and nurses raced frantically back and forth, hauling stretchers, hastily placing broken bodies on the grass beyond the east wing and going back for more.

"The west end can't be saved," someone said.

"We will take the most serious cases to the huts," Sarita said. "Oh, Ben, where do we start?"

Moving quickly from patient to patient, Ben and his mother decided on a very pregnant mother with a severe chest wound. As gently as possible, they moved her to a less damaged hut.

"*Señora!* I've been searching for you." Wild-eyed, Solano's orderly grabbed Sarita's arm. "It's your husband. He's been hurt."

"Flying shrapnel ripped away some tissue in his shoulder," Solano explained. "By the time we could get a doctor he had passed out."

Sarita stared, aghast at the figure lying so still on the cot. Zephan, *mi vida.*

He moaned softly.

"You are lucky, *Señora*," Doctor Escudo said kindly. "His heart is fine. He has lost some blood and with my limited equipment I can't be sure all the metal is extracted, but he is strong and can travel. You are leaving. . ." He glanced at his watch. "Today?"

"I. . ." Sarita stopped, bewildered.

"The border is sealed off," the orderly blurted out. "Tanks and soldiers everywhere."

"I have a plane in León," Solano said. "We must travel now, while it is yet dark."

Escudo nodded. "A wise decision. If I can be of further help, sir, I am at your service. I wish you Godspeed."

18

North Shore, Land of Cumorah

Rhythmically, foaming waves pounded the shore, throbbing with Solano's heavy heart. Had freedom, lifeblood of Cumorah, ebbed away beyond return?

Would he, the freely elected but banished *Jefe*, return to Cumorah, or remain forever in exile, alone with poignant memories from his homeland? Would he even escape here alive?

Scattered shots sounded in the distance and Solano moved to the hotel window to peer out, watching the road for activity. Red sky in the morning, sailor's warning. The weather was going to be beastly today. Red sky. For an instant he was transported to his art gallery in Granada and that unhappy night with Anahí by Friberg's *Farewell*. . .

"*I hope this is not a pattern,*" she had said. All those paintings. Flora had taken as many as she could, but it was impossible to take them all. Now sadistic brutes would destroy them, along with what remained of Cumorah's culture.

He turned to Zephan. "The plane leaves shortly, and you must be on it," Solano said.

"What about you, sir?"

"My men are holding a private jet for me in Puerto Cristobal. If I board the same plane with you, Zephan, I will endanger your family and all the other passengers. You know those murderers wouldn't think twice about blowing up the whole plane just to get me."

"How about your body guards? Can they be trusted?" Zephan asked.

Solano sighed heavily. "It is getting difficult to trust anyone, but I know them well. All my men are good, I think. They have all been briefed by ZRI, which has the best handle on international gangster activities. Besides, I am always well-armed, myself. My guards know it would be foolish to try anything."

Zephan remembered Anahí and prayed she had made it through.

"We have taken every precaution," Solano continued. "The State limousine is being driven as a decoy, but I will go in the accompanying unmarked car, which is more heavily armored. At least that is Plan A. Sometimes we change it at the last minute to throw the enemy off guard."

Satisfied, Zephan walked unsteadily to the desk and turned on a small tape recorder. "*Jefe*, let us record your final testimony, in hopes we can get it published in Zarahemla."

Zephan, face rigid with pain, forced himself to keep moving around.

"You can rest on the plane, Papa," Ben said. "Soon in Zarahemla you can be treated with highly advanced medicine. At least something for the pain. Why this self-inflicted torture?"

Zephan sat down at the desk and held his face up with his good hand. "If I don't retrieve it and it is lost. . ."

"If what is lost?"

Not seeming to hear, he mumbled on. "I must go back."

"What is it, Papa?"

"The book of Joseph."

"You can hardly travel like that," Solano cut in. "Besides, you are a marked man. Return to the capital means certain death."

"He's right, Papa," Ben said. "I will go and do it."

Zephan paused. Of his four sons, only the youngest remained in peril. Upon Benjamin, the most faithful and courageous, fell the dangerous task of retrieving this precious record from a land now fettered by unreasoned hatred for the past. Recollections of public book burnings in the empire seared Zephan's memory.

Benjamin will make it. A sudden assurance flooded the anxious father's heart.

"I believe the boy could make it," Solano said. "No one knows him. And troops guarding the city are minimal. Most are fighting in Chinandiga."

Zephan nodded slowly. "Very well. Ben, get the book and any other letters or documents from our home vault in Granada. Go to the Sheffa border, on Bahia Verde's east shore, where I will have Mike Clayton meet you."

Ben nodded, sketching a map in his notebook.

"Clayton can usually be found in Bahia Verde, gathering intelligence and helping organize the resistance."

Arranging his notes and sketches into a neat package, Ben inserted them into his backpack.

"Now, Benjamin, do not join the resistance forces. You must get to Zarahemla."

"One of my pilots is not going to return and is leaving a vehicle behind." Solano handed Ben a set of keys. "By coincidence, he was just asking me a few minutes ago if I knew anyone who could use it. It's parked behind the hangar. You're welcome to it."

19

Ben found the '59 pickup and decided to watch the Chief Judge's departure before setting out himself. Thunder sounded in the west, heralding a stormy day, but it was hardly distinguishable from the incessant artillery fire. He studied each rooftop of the surrounding buildings carefully, and examined every window. There, across the street, on the second story, a curtain moved. Someone could easily pick off a target from such a height. How could he alert Solano?

Sprinting toward the hotel, he reached the corner as guards hustled along a man who kept his face downward. They crowded him into the limo. It was a dummy in a business suit. It was plan A.

He checked that window. Nothing moved.

Rushing through the door, he pushed back two of four more guards who followed, heading toward the other car. He managed to convey his warning and convinced them to go out the east door. Returning to the hangar, he stationed himself, with weapon ready, where he could see both exits and any possible points of ambush.

Where was Solano? There, among the guards, dressed as one of them, and with a helmet. Brilliant. Car doors were closed, the two vehicles pulled away from the curb, and Ben let out his breath slowly. They made it.

Now he could say goodbye to his mother and be on his way. Unable to shake his uneasiness, he again glanced at the same window, but still nothing moved, and no one came out. He did not rule himself out as a target and determined to see his parents safely onto the plane.

In an instant he was thrown to the ground by a massive explosion. And another. He remained face down on the ground for several seconds, his arms braced over his head and ears, before he ventured to look up. The hotel was still standing. To the west, angry thunderclouds scowled on the horizon. To the east, black smoke billowed up into a fiery red sky where the two automobiles had exploded. Ben trembled with grief and rage. Those hellish fiends could not risk using mere firearms, and the possibility of missing their prey. They had to be sure.

Screams, shouts, sirens announced the cowardly deed. Police, panic, terror. Everywhere.

Within minutes it was confirmed. There, beneath a scarlet and gray dawn, the Chief Judge of Cumorah was dead. It was the end of a free nation, the end of an era.

Ben rocked on his feet, his mind reeling from trauma and exhaustion.

An eagle ascended on a thermal in the distance, rising with wisps of lingering smoke, and the sun began its daily climb into the sky. The light was the same today as it would be forever. The same sun had shone thousands of years ago upon another lone survivor who hid up a record for his people, to preserve for this day eternal keys to liberty. Wars past were long forgotten, but the legacy yet lived.

The day ahead promised to be grueling and fraught with peril, but hope stirred within him, not to be quenched. He must not let that sacred book be lost. Prophets of old, seeing a future day, had pressed forward with a steadfastness in Christ. He could do no less. Somehow he would go on.

20

The small aircraft began to lurch violently, but Sarita Benamoz forced herself to stay calm. What luck to have to head out right during a late storm in the rainy season. Now it seemed the very elements were against them. As if confirming her thoughts, the turbulence grew in fury. Sarita feared the little plane would be wrenched in two.

"*Amigos*," the pilot said, "the weather system has grown more severe than anticipated. We are forced to make a brief landing in Frontera until the storm passes. Do not expect the delay to be great."

In the torrential rain, the pilot managed to spot the town of Frontera sprawling by the River Sidon and landed skillfully at the tiny airport.

No one disembarked. With the hour well past noon, only the pilot left to seek more weather information. Shortly the pilot returned and spoke to Zephan.

"Señor Benamoz, your son Haman is in the hangar, saying he has an urgent phone call for you from Abiram in Sheffa."

"What could it be?" Sarita's voice trembled with anxiety. "Haman is involved in this —"

"Sarita, if Abiram is in trouble, I must see to it." Zephan lowered his voice. "No matter what happens, you stay on this plane!"

Her eyes widened. "But Zephan. . ."

Zephan set his jaw. "You and these others must not be endangered any further."

"Do be careful, *mi vida*. Take someone with you. You cannot serve Cumorah if. . ." She fought back the tears.

"Nonsense!" He laid a gentle finger across her lips. "I didn't mean to frighten you." He smiled. "Be brave, my love. Have faith." Then he was gone.

The rain slowly abated, and small talk among the ten other passengers soon lapsed into silence.

Sarita's tension grew as the afternoon wore on. What could be keeping him? A siren burst the taut stillness.

Finally, Sarita saw the pilot walking toward the plane with Haman, who was speaking with wild gestures.

Haman hurried up the ramp to throw his arms around his mother.

"*Mamacita*, I am so sorry! We cannot find Papa!"

"What was the call about?"

"I don't know!" Haman blinked rapidly. "I only know he, uh, we went for a short walk to look out over Cumorah for the last time. Though this area is close to dense rain forest, Papa still insisted on walking outside. Before I knew it, he slipped and fell into the quick sand near the river! I tried to reach him through the overgrowth, but couldn't. Papa just disappeared!"

As Sarita stared, speechless, Haman rushed on, his words tumbling out in torrents.

"It all happened so fast. Couldn't reach him! I went for help. Everything happened so fast. . ." Haman's voice increased in speed and pitch. "The paramedics dragged the pit, but they couldn't find his body! I just don't know what else to do!"

Sarita was silent for a long time. Zephan, in his condition, take a walk? Haman was lying. Not enough time to drag the pit, either.

Haman began to fidget with his fine silk tie.

"I'm sure you did all you could." She sighed. "Pray for us . . . you will do that?"

For an instant, anger flickered across Haman's smooth, handsome face. High cheek bones, dark brown eyes, straight hair black as night.

Why did this hellish child have to look so much like his mother? But Sarita knew her son. She could see into his soul.

Haman's features now wore concern like one of many masks. "Yes, Mama. Of course. You'd better go on. You mustn't stay here where it's so dangerous. . . " Haman smoothed Sarita's traveling blanket. "Where's Benjamin?" he asked with forced nonchalance.

"He left, " Sarita said. "Why?"

Haman lowered his voice. "You already know anyone connected with Solano had better leave.

"Solano is dead!" she said brokenly.

Haman shrugged. "But Solanistas are still rampant, and they are dangerous. Especially the son of Solano's personal advisor!" He looked past his mother.

"And you?" she shot back. "You are not his son?" It was more of a statement than a question. "Goodbye, Haman. Zephan lives. I know it. God will protect him. I am leaving here, but I will see him again." Sarita glared at him, willing her eyes to peel back the layer of pretense from his mind.

Haman avoided her burning gaze.

"Go, Haman. We must depart."

"It is best," he said. Turning abruptly, he left without a backward glance.

The fugitives boarded a dimly lit jet in Gibeah as evening settled in. Zarahemla in an hour. Sarita drew a shawl about her shoulders and huddled in the gloom, wishing the darkness would swallow her.

Sarita did not want to believe the events of this summer. Everything had to be a dream, an evil dream.

What had happened to the Benamoz family? Haman, caught up in various Egalitarian causes. Leb, always the bully, leading the life of a revolutionary. Or rather, following. Would he shrink from violence, immorality, or even murder?

Abiram, ever the practical one. Surely he had made it safely to Sheffa, where he would meet Alison, and soon be married. But why did Abiram call Zephan? Or was the purported call Haman's ruse to trap his father? Haman never did get along with his father. Heaven knew how hard Zephan had tried. In fact, he had been too easy on the boy. Zephan was tough against unscrupulous politicians, but Haman would walk all over him. It hurt to see Haman's treatment of his father.

Zephan, my husband! Her heart cried out for him. What had she said to Haman? That Zephan lives? How could this be true? But. . . somehow, she had a distinct impression that Zephan was alive. Sarita felt he had a work yet to do. Could it be? She must cling to this hope.

And Benjamin, her youngest child, risking his life to return to the war zone. She pleaded with the Lord to protect her husband and son.

On solid ground in Zarahemla, Sarita's resolve also became firm. Mitchell Hunt. That was the name of the intelligence man Zephan knew here. She would contact this Mr. Hunt, and he would help her find her husband.

The First Book Of

Benjamin

THE FIRST BOOK OF BENJAMIN

1

Ben's twenty-year-old truck struggled to negotiate jagged chunks of pavement, charred tree limbs and fragments from exploded automobiles. Columbus Highway, once pulsing with community life, lay torn and bleeding under a sightless vigil of shattered windows in ghostly buildings.

Leaving city limits, Ben recoiled from the grisly sight —— corpses strewing the roadside. Many were civilians, all apparently unarmed. He spotted several military trucks bearing the Pax insignia, all loaded with small domestic weapons. Had the citizens been disarmed before the attack or after their deaths? Ben did not want to know the answer.

He traversed the land on back roads, making a wide berth around the few tanks in sight. He saw no moving civilians. All were either hiding or dead. No children. Only a dog or two, looking lost and forlorn.

Granada. Formerly a growing industrial center, now most factories were trashed and gutted. Once flourishing coffee and sugar plantations were now depressed from neglect.

By late afternoon Ben arrived at his parents' large home on the outskirts of Granada. Doors were kicked in, furniture upended. In the kitchen, cupboard doors hung open on broken hinges, revealing empty shelves.

In the atrium he found the gun case emptied of its contents and its glass door shattered. On dust-laden rays from a broken window, sunlight flashed on metal, the hilt of an enormous sword. From the floor, Ben picked it up; it was Abiram's gift.

Ben hefted it. The thing's unwieldiness had spared it from theft. Soldiers preferred to shoot from a distance rather than to fight close with a sword.

Ben unsheathed the weapon from its soft leather case and admired its glow in the afternoon light. Unlike the thin and flexible dueling rapiers from eastern countries, this sword's long blade was firm, of a high-grade steel, with two razor-sharp edges.

At a sound in the music room, Ben took the sword, crept to the archway and peered into the adjoining room. The piano was tipped over, caved in on one side.

Vandalizing pigs.

Propped against the wall next to the piano, a soldier, shirtless, chest wet with liquor, an upset whisky bottle beside him, slept with rag-doll oblivion. The soldier was a revolutionary commander of fifty. No mistaking that face. Ben recognized Horacio Mortera, the murderer of Anahí Cercado's family.

The man lay in a drunken stupor before him, armed only with a knife and a small .45 stuffed in his belt. Astounding. Ben looked around for evidence of other intruders who might have stolen the man's assault weapon.

Ben's own semiautomatic was too noisy. He fingered the knife in his belt. This would not be murder, he argued with himself. Simply a well-deserved execution.

But Mortera opened his bloodshot eyes, peered at Ben, and with surprising speed, hurled his knife. Liquor had impaired the man's faculties, however, and Ben easily dodged the flying dagger. As the knife glanced off the opposite wall and clattered to the floor, Mortera grabbed for his pistol, and Ben lunged with the sword. The blade pierced the man's naked shoulder, incapacitating the shooting arm. A swift blow to Mortera's head, and the old drunk was out cold.

Ben continued to look around for others and quickly donned Mortera's military garb, placing his own *Guardia Nacionál* shirt upon the wounded man. In seconds, he bound the man's hands and feet.

The quiet was unnerving. That the commander was alone did not make sense. Starting for the patio, Ben heard behind him an unmistakable click. He whirled to face the muzzle of an AK-47 looming out from shadows in the hall.

"Drop your weapons or I'll shoot!" asserted a female voice, low and menacing.

2

She would, too. The law of survival demanded it. He dropped the sword, then the handgun.

"*And* your knife!" she said.

Dropping the knife, he kept his face in the shadows, dreading recognition.

The voice's owner slowly emerged. Dark hair piled high on her head made her appear tall and regal, even though she was clad in a faded blouse and a long calico skirt. Only one person in the world could look like that . . .

"Anahí!" he whispered.

"Ben? It *is* you!" Carefully she disengaged the heavy weapon and laid it aside.

Ben picked up his knife and replaced it in his belt, then took her in his arms.

A shot rang out, and a bullet pierced the unconscious Mortera's head.

"Why, Anahí! I'm surprised at you!" A familiar voice came from the kitchen. "Wait till I tell Ben you've been cheating on him, and with a revolutionary soldier!"

Ben instinctively released the girl and reached for his knife. He turned to face the intruder. Leb!

"Well, well, what an unpleasant little surprise!" Leb sneered. This young man's good looks, long admired by his peers, were now marred by his fierce anger. Taking in with a glance his careless and fatal mistake, he turned with even more fury upon his brother. "You lowdown sneak! You'll pay for this!"

"Take me." Ben spoke evenly. "Only leave her alone."

"My, aren't we gallant!" Leb kept his weapon leveled on his brother and stared, gloating at Anahí. "Keep your hands off that knife, boy, or I'll finish what Mortera didn't. Of course, I'll have my fun, first."

Ben winced.

Leb spat out the words. "You are nothing to me! You and your high and mighty airs, like you were trying to rule our lives, or something! Well, this time you won't get the better of me."

"I don't want to believe you are really one of them," Ben lamented.

Anahí spoke loudly. "If you were half the man you think you are, you would . . . "

"Shut up, *mujer*!" Leb swung his rifle around like a wild man, then paused. "Killing you won't be necessary." He glanced at Mortera's body. "I'll simply render you helpless. When my fellow troops find you and blame you for this murder, they'll bring you to justice." His smile twisted with malice. "Pax troops include men from all over the world, you know. You should see what the Arabs and Turks do to those they don't like. Oh, and there are the Tartareans . . . "

Anahí saw a movement behind Ben. "Ben!" she screamed hoarsely. But it was too late.

Ben felt a crushing blow to his head.

3

Anahí grabbed the AK-47 and leveled it at Leb, but positioned square in front of the man was a mere boy.

"Stay there, *chico*," Leb commanded. With a swift motion from much experience, he yanked forward on Ben's leg at the knee. The snap of the bone made a sickening sound.

"You are a coward!" Anahí shrieked.

Leb held a .45 to Ben's head. "Put down that weapon, *mujer*, or I will finish him!"

"I'll do anything you say, Leb," she cried, laying down the heavy piece. "Don't touch him, I beg you!"

Leb smiled nastily. "That's better. Tie her hands, Pedro, and let's get out of here."

Furious, Anahí insisted on riding in the back of Ben's pickup so she didn't have to be near Leb, who stopped at empty domiciles along the street to help himself to abundantly stocked pantries. When evening settled in, the three entered outskirts of a city southward. In a deserted villa Leb discovered a plentiful wine cellar and announced plans to tarry the night.

"Tomorrow in León I will report on Ben's location," he told Pedro. "Wait till they see what we've scouted out!"

Anahí's mind raced. Leb must be kept from reaching his companions. "This is excellent liquor." Anahí kept her voice nonchalant and gazed at rows of elegant bottles at the bar.

Leb grinned. "I'd like to see you get really drunk, you little *bruja.*" He nodded to Pedro to unfasten her bonds, as he poured two glasses of whisky.

Anahí snatched the bottle and began to pour the liquor back. "Let's save it for the others, too."

"You are afraid!" Leb thrust a glass into Anahí's hands while downing his own.

Pretending to sip the amber liquid, she made a great show of choking.

Anahí watched Leb laughingly drink another portion with voracious greed. So, he glories in his manhood, does he? How about a third glassful? She fixed a cheerful smile on her face and poured him another, and another.

Pedro stared wide-eyed at Anahí's untouched glass. "You have not . . . "

"Want some?" Anahí quickly tossed its contents in the boy's face. "You say a word, and he'll kill me!" She put the words to a little tune, ending with uproarious laughter. "Pedro, *querido,* get us another bottle, *por favor!* This tastes better than I thought!" she lied. She refilled her glass with a trembling hand and spilled with convincing sloppiness.

"You're too drunk to know the difference!" Leb punctuated his slurred words with an occasional hiccup.

Anahí reached for a third whisky bottle and continued laughing. Pouring the liquor into a large decanter, she said, "Only two bottles of whisky, Leb? I have yet to see you drink like the big boys!"

She let Leb grab the bottle from her hand and pour the whiskey down his throat. Senseless, the man collapsed on the floor. Anahí turned to Pedro.

"Why didn't you kill me, back there?" the boy asked.

"And be a murderous coward like the Ponistas?" She glared in Leb's direction. "*Joven*, you are in with evil company, not to be trusted. When you are no longer useful to them, these men will kill you, just as Leb would have done to Ben, his brother."

"His brother?"

She nodded. "You're not a killer like them, Pedro. Will you help me escape?"

Pedro returned from the pantry with the harsh herbal laxative Anahí had requested. She made the herbal tea so strong it looked like coffee and poured it all into the man. Then, with Pedro's help, she dragged Leb's drunken body to the truck.

Anahí drove him to a tiny hospital with few facilities, and as remote from the battle front as possible. She dropped off Leb in a nurse's care and left instructions: he was not to be moved for several weeks. She did not delude herself that her ruse would work. Leb's cronies would return for him soon.

Chinandiga was an armed camp; thousands of world troops had poured in overnight. And return to Granada alone would be suicide. How could she reach Ben? Anahí turned northeast toward the mountains, determined to get help.

4

Strains of a piano concerto permeated his being, like the balm of Gilead to his physical pain. Scratchy old recording, but Papa's favorite piece. *Did I die and go to heaven?* Ben sniffed an aroma of chicken soup.

He forced his eyes open and focused on a fly on the kitchen ceiling. He was lying on a thin mattress on the kitchen floor, near the small heater. Upon trying to move, Ben realized most decidedly he was not in heaven. He groaned.

A plump little woman in a pale blue cotton dress appeared and knelt beside him. "Señor Benjamin."

"Who . . . are you?"

"Maria Mundo, your neighbor since you were a little *gauchito*."

"Of course, Maria. I'm sorry." Ben smiled weakly. "I'm just so . . . disoriented."

"And no wonder. You've been delirious for two days. All you ever said was 'Ani', over and over."

"Oh, Ani!" Ben lamented. "He kidnaped my girl . . . my *novia*. That hated Leb. . . . my own brother . . . if he harms her, so help me, I'll . . . " He clutched at his skull, gasping with anguish.

"Easy, *muchacho*. I came, just like always, to keep an eye on things. Day before yesterday, I found you lying yonder with a broken leg, and beat up pretty bad. *Mucho!* No one else was around. I did not see the *chica*, your little lady. We were afraid to get a doctor, so I set your leg myself." She beamed with pride.

"You set my leg? However did you do it?"

"I tell you the truth, Señor Benjamin, I heard your mother's voice, clearly, telling me simply, how to do everything, step by step, including what herbs to use to dress your wounds. It was in my mind, exactly how your leg was supposed to look, and exactly how to create the splint. The bone was jutting out. Mercy that you were unconscious. The pain would have been excruciating when we set your leg."

"You are an angel of mercy, Maria. If the guerrillas had found me . . . " He shuddered. Suddenly his face clouded. "Did you see the body? I mean, Leb killed a man. . . . "

"Mortera! And good riddance, I say. He is in a plastic bag in a ditch, at the park. Don't worry. You left no finger prints, and *we* certainly weren't going to leave any!"

"We? Someone else knows about this?"

She nodded. "Enrique. He is my friend."

"You trust him, then?"

For a second she looked hurt, then nodded again. "He helped me set your leg, and he's been bringing us food."

"I didn't mean to question your judgment, Maria. My own brother beat me up and must have broken my leg on purpose, and by now he may have ravished the girl I love. It's hard to know who to trust."

"Don't worry, *joven*. When my own son Francisco became an intellectual at the university, he changed. He betrayed everything I taught him." She sighed. "This war has divided many families. I understand how you feel."

Maria took Ben's large hand in her two small ones. "Lucky you are as big and strong as you are, or you might not have survived so well. We found out just how big you are when we tried to move you.

221

You are a big boy! Almighty muscular, though, even for a young buck."

Ben grinned. "Have you heard from your sons in Zarahemla?"

"Few letters have gotten through lately. My sons wanted to come home and fight the invaders, but they would be fighting against their own brother!" Maria exclaimed. "Here the university students have been dancing in the streets since Solano's fall." Her eyes were still lively in a face worn by years of affliction. "Once the hand of tyranny closes about their throats, those students will leave in droves, if they survive the terrorist slaughter."

"And now I have put you in great danger!" A series of rhythmic taps sounded on the kitchen porch door. Ben groped for a weapon.

Maria cocked her own pistol and peered through a peephole in the heavy door. "It's Enri," she said.

From his place in the far corner of the big kitchen, Ben had a bizarre view. Protruding through the narrowly opened door was a hand, held high, grasping the yellow legs of a chicken. The bird's head, still attached, dangled downward, but the carcass was cleaned and plucked.

Don Quixote's fearless sidekick. Our safety is assured. Ben suppressed a smile.

Enrique flopped the chicken on the kitchen counter, wiped his hand on his trousers, and proffered it to the boy on the mat. "Enrique Cordero. Finally we are formally introduced!"

"How can I thank you for all your help?" Ben said.

"No need, *joven.*" Enri placed some vegetables in the refrigerator. "Your parents were good friends. I only hope they are safe."

"My parents flew out several days ago. I was hoping to meet my father's friend at Bahia Verde by this time. Now, this!" Ben grimaced.

"Cabrios' thugs teach'em how to break legs, among other things, at his terrorist training camps," Enri said, bitterness edging his voice.

"I'm further endangering your lives!"

Enrique smiled. "At least we're not totally sitting ducks! Sometimes I take information instead of money for the eggs from my farm. As you know, the war is southward now, and the enemy is not so well organized as you think. Anyhow, Mortera was a plunderer more than a soldier. Then I think his drinking got the best of him, and he wandered off."

222

"But my brother might bring back others . . . "

"Yes. I expected him by now. We have sealed off this house except the back entrance which is quite heavily overgrown now. Soon, the time will be right to escape."   ·

For the next few days, Ben did little more than sleep in the kitchen near the house's only functioning heater.

"This won't do!" he complained to Maria.

"*Paciencia!* You are healing faster than you think."

With a makeshift crutch Ben made his way to the utter shambles of his father's office. Cherished books were torn and ruined, family pictures ripped to shreds. Someone had used an axe on the computer.

Finally, with dread, he forced himself to look at the vault. The door had been shot open.

Empty.

For hours after searching the office, Ben lay on the mat, staring at the ceiling.

Not only had the sacred book vanished, but any records of contemporary affairs, private letters, legal documents, military and civil correspondence —— all were gone. Ben had studied relics of civilizations which had been swept from the earth, leaving little, if any, written word. Was this to be the fate of Cumorah, then? To have her history obliterated by brutes? Was he to fail in this most vital mission, to forfeit the trust his father had bestowed upon him?

Shadows of nightfall increased his despondency. Jagged blades of darkness stabbed into the room, widening their wedge, squeezing out the light. Securing his weapons, Ben at last fell asleep.

5

The thud of heavy boots in the atrium awakened him.

"Señor Ben!" Maria whispered. "Come with me!"

Ben made out her shadowy figure in the dawn. He grabbed his weapons and, hating his clumsiness, followed her as quickly as he could. They hurried out the kitchen door and clambered into the back compartment in Enri's big market truck.

They were not alone. Dozens of chickens clucked and fluttered sleepily in response to the intruders. The presence of one very large sow completed the menagerie, with the smell fitting the decor.

"What's going on?" Ben whispered just loud enough to be heard over the truck's idling engine.

"That neighbor, Gomez, and his wife Juana, have been snooping around, and we must get out."

Ben peered out from the air holes in the truck's wall. Clutching by the feet one chicken in each hand, Enri conversed vigorously with a burly Latin. Juana, the wife, stood by, her mouth frozen in a vacant smile, revealing a silver upper right tooth.

"*Sí, hombre,* I take this livestock to the troops, and you are making me late!"

"I shall turn you in to the authorities for using this property. You have no right to do this," the other man whined. "This property belongs to the people!"

"Here, you covetous scum. Have a free lunch. A gift . . . from the people . . . of the order . . . of Voltaire!" Enri spoke rhythmically as he flailed his opponent with the two chickens. He bashed the man's head with one bird and with the other raked the beak across the face and eyes till the man screamed in pain and fury.

As Enri floored the accelerator, the truck lumbered off, leaving the would-be "squealer" bellowing. The woman remained motionless as the chickens squawked and flapped away.

"If we're lucky, we'll be over the border within three hours," Maria explained. "Fortunately the phone lines are down so that *estupido* back there can't do much about us. Enri will avoid the larger towns, but he doesn't expect to arouse much suspicion with a chicken wagon. The back roads aren't as fast, but we'll see fewer people. However, if he makes any stops, we must hide under this old army canvas. Enri has bags of chicken feed here, and we will have to look like a couple of old bags!"

Ben chuckled and dragged his large frame into position, ready to lie prone at an instant's notice.

After an hour the truck jolted to a stop. Ben flattened himself under the canvas and discovered he had failed to clear the area of all chicken droppings.

Maria heard a familiar voice and hesitated. The top of the truck's back door was yanked open, leaving only mesh wiring to restrain the livestock.

With pistol poised, there stood her son Francisco.

"*Mamá!*" he exclaimed in sudden recognition.

"Francisco?"

"Why are you riding in the back? Such luxurious accommodations, *Mamá!* Really, now!"

"I. . ."

The two officials wrinkled their noses. "Such a stink!"

"Does your mother always choose such irregular modes of transportation?" the comrade said with a smirk.

"*Hijo,* please!" Maria pleaded. Then, regaining her nerve, "It's the smell of money. Food for the soldiers. We're going to market."

'Cisco guffawed. "Is he going to sell you, too? *Y, Mamá,* what have you under that canvas . . . eh?"

At that moment the sow, Toda, made her move, grunting in irritation, and distanced herself from the harsh voices at the back of the truck. She waddled over beside Maria and flopped her immense body fully upon Ben's still form. Maria prayed the men didn't hear Ben's slight moan under the immense weight.

Both men laughed uproariously. "If you had hopes of smuggling out any equipment, your pig squished them good." 'Cisco wiped his eyes. He paused to regain his composure. "Well, what are you waiting for? Get going! Oh, *mamacita* . . . stop back after the delivery and share some money with me. Our troops could use a few beers." He slammed the door and waved them on.

"Ben!" Maria shouted over the racket. "Can you breathe?"

Hearing the muffled "yes", she coaxed and prodded, but the huge beast would not be moved. Finally, after what seemed like an eternity, the truck began to climb a steep incline. Gravity did Ben a favor when Toda rolled back slightly.

"You all right, Señor Ben?"

"Surviving." Each clung to the sides of the truck, anticipating a forward lurch when the descent began.

Down the steep hillside with chickens flapping wildly in the air, the truck gathered speed.

"He must be doing one hundred!" Ben hollered over the squawking fowl. "Did he lose control?"

"I don't know! Hang on, in case we stop," she shouted back.

Toda calmly braced her massive bulk against the front.

Finally Enri leveled out and came to a gradual stop. He threw open the door and peered in.

"We made it to El Triunfo. Sorry about the last stretch," he said after confirming all his cargo was still alive. "We came to the last check station at the border, and I just told them my brakes were out. We were doing 120 kilometers when we roared past them. I didn't want to deal with any more nosy border guards like Francisco. What happened back there, anyway?"

Ben stretched and brushed off the dust of battle. "My life was saved by a capitalist pig!"

6

The refugees had a meal and refreshed themselves.

"I need to meet someone in Bahia Verde," Ben said, "clear over on the gulf coast. Must be a bus to take me there. Do they accept Cumorah money?"

"Nonsense, my boy. We can take you. I know where to make currency exchanges. The roads are decent. We should arrive by late afternoon. You are long overdue to be reunited with your father. Maria and I will stay the night in Bahia Verde, then on to San Estéban tomorrow. I have connections there."

Bahia Verde was a remote town which barely occupied a spot on the map until the influx of Cumorah refugees swelled its population. Word was out that Solano's *Guardia Nacionál* had fled there, and opposition to the terrorist guerrillas was gathering. The village boasted a small airport, as well as many hotels and cottages which were rapidly filling with soldiers and future freedom-fighters instead of tourists.

Enri's "connections" included people in Bahia Verde. He knew where to eat dinner to catch up on all the gossip.

As Ben dug into a generous serving of *arroz con frijoles*, a tall slender man in a broad-rimmed sombrero approached him, speaking with a Zarahemla accent.

"*Buenas tardes, joven*. Benjamin . . . son of Zephan Benamoz?" The man extended a friendly hand. "My name is Mike Clayton."

"*Mucho gusto, Señor*. You have news from my father?"

Mike's face registered heavy gloom. "Son, it is my lot to bring you bad news. Your mother did make it safely to Zarahemla after the Solano assassination. All information from Solano is in my possession, and I shall publish it in its entirety. At least I can do that much. But . . . "

"My father?"

Mike paused and laid a gentle hand on Ben's shoulder. "Your father's plane was forced down by the weather. The pilot landed in Frontera, just over the border, by the Rio Sidon. What actually happened is unclear . . . "

Ben regarded Mike expectantly.

"The report said Zephan went to check on an urgent message from an unidentified source. After the call, he went outside the hangar in a downpour, slipped on the river bank, and drowned."

The Second Book Of
Benjamin

Fiery Serpent

THE SECOND BOOK OF BENJAMIN

1

Zarahemla
November 2079

Beth MacRay studied the story from the international press wire service. "Zarahemla extends diplomatic recognition to New Ammonihah. 'Our administration's aim in Cumorah was to get Solano out before Zarahemla elections,' says assistant State Consul Horace Verman, 'and we did it!'"

New Ammonihah continued to fill all the front pages, while Solano's murder, now old news, had occupied a tiny square on the inside last page of *Zarahemla Post.* The murderer remained at large, the article had stated, but readers could be assured the assassination was the work of a lone, crazed fanatic, and no conspiracy was involved.

Beth reflected on the past year's events. Territorial control of Antionum had been given away to a dangerously unstable government, against the express wishes of Zarahemlans. Among the Mediterranean nations, the Ashley administration had driven staunch Zarahemla allies from power, creating a vacuum for terrorist-trained agents to fill. The Ashley administration's final act had been, in

231

collaboration with the international media, to engineer the betrayal of the free Cumorah republic.

Beth sighed and hoped Chief-Judge-elect Elidor would do better.

She wearily straightened her desk. Only one week of substituting for Dan's regular secretary, yet it had seemed like an eternity. Not at all like the usual exciting journalistic realm in which the popular Dan MacRay worked so ably. But of course this week he was away from home, seeking truth on the Cumorah issue. Oh boy, it would be great to see him again. Still, he remained depressed over Solano's death. Must be prepared to cheer him up.

Methodically, Beth locked her desk, the cabinets, and her briefcase. She glanced around the office, seeking anything else which might need closing, clasping, or fastening down for the weekend. Must be a subconscious desire to lock up the gloom and leave it behind.

On her desk the buzzer sounded. What else . . .

"Beth, a gentleman from Cumorah is here with an urgent message for Dan MacRay. He has letters, but says the documents are only for you."

Beth unlocked a drawer which held a small revolver. One couldn't be too careful. "All right. Call security and stand by. Send him in."

The visitor's tall athletic frame filled the doorway. He wore a stylish Western suit. Ducking slightly, he entered the room. Though not smiling, his mouth was set firmly, revealing a charming dimple. He looked boyish, harmless, but looks could be deceiving. *Who is this man?*

"Please stay where you are and open the letter," Beth stated coolly, keeping her hand on the revolver in the drawer.

The man showed her two individual pages.

"Now, come here, keeping one hand on each page. Hold them up so I can see the message."

His face unreadable, the stranger's cold gray eyes never left her. Slowly he followed her orders.

Beth's eyes widened as she read the letter and studied the enclosed photographs. "You are the grandson of this man?"

He nodded.

She relaxed a little. "I apologize for my hostility. Sometimes we get explosive messages."

The stranger flashed a handsome smile, responding in an easy voice. "I understand, ma'am. You are wise."

Beth dismissed the guard and dialed the unlisted number at her cabin.

"Dan?. . . Good to hear your voice. Don't go away. You won't believe the surprise I have for you!"

"Come on, *amigo*," she said. "Let's go see my husband." At last. A bright spot in an otherwise rotten week.

2

With his considerable weight, Dan MacRay flung open the door to face his wife, who stood on the step with a tall, very good-looking stranger. "Would you look at that?" he declared. "I go away for a week and my beautiful wife winds up with another man!" He chuckled. "Have you no shame, woman?"

"You're the one who should be ashamed!" she scolded. "I bring you the friend of a lifetime and you stand there insulting us!" Fustily she pushed aside her husband's substantial self and moved into the living room, tugging the mystery man by the hand. "Dan, meet Benjamin Benamoz."

Dan stared blankly into Beth's laughing eyes. Now it was her turn for fun, and he was totally at her mercy.

"Oh, Dan, how can you be so dense?" she exclaimed in mock exasperation. "Here, Ben, grandson of Amoz ben Gideon, give him the documented evidence," she ordered the grinning visitor.

The mystified journalist was handed a single sheet. On it was a photocopied picture of Amoz ben Gideon with his wife, son, and grandsons, dated 2067. Under it was duplicated a page 529 of the book of Joseph with verses 4 and 5 shaded.

Next to the familiar passage, Dan read in his own handwriting the message he had penned over a decade ago.

To my cherished friend, Amoz———
I know as surely as I live that this testament
is true. May this book be a blessing in your life.

"Little Benjamin . . . not so little anymore. I remember that day," Dan said in a hoarse whisper. "You were there." Overcome, he held the young man close for several long moments. "How on earth did you end up in Cumorah?" he asked finally.

"It is a long story, sir, and I shall enlighten you, presently, if you have the time."

"I have plenty of time. You must spend the weekend with us," Dan replied cordially.

"But first, regrettably I have an urgent message." The younger man's face was filled with pain. "It's a copy of Anastasio Solano's letter of resignation, which he sent to Chief Judge Ashley, who is at this moment wining and dining arms smugglers from the Tartarean Coast." Ben's hazel eyes were a smoldering gray. "I believe you are aware of the Central Committee's role in the fall of my country."

MacRay read with heavy heart Solano's last message to the world before his death:

On the advice of numerous emissaries from the Committee, and with the desire of peace for my country, I hereby resign the presiding office for which I was popularly elected. My resignation is irrevocable.

I have fought against encroaching tyranny of global proportions, and I believe that when the truth is known, history will say I was right.

"My father, Zephan, who was a personal advisor to Solano," Ben continued, "is missing."

"Again, may God forgive us." Dan's voice was choked with emotion. "I know this is too little too late, son, but let me do something for you. Anything."

Ben started to shake his head, then paused. "I am going back to Cumorah to find my father, sir. When I return, we will investigate Solano's murder."

3

Keeping on the outskirts of Frontera village's tiny airport, Ben combed the river banks, searching for some clue to his father's disappearance.

"Zephan is alive," Ben's mother had said.

If Papa is alive, I will find him. And Papa would remember where to find the lost testament.

Quicksand sometimes appeared innocent, and the path along the river was very faint. Here and there, rough-hewn poles rested loosely in forked branches pushed into the ground at uneven intervals. This makeshift handrail was unstable at best, and not to be trusted.

Ben paused in a small semi-clearing where the trail stopped at a patch of heavy overgrowth. He fingered the hilt of Abiram's sword, which had become like a family emblem. In the surrounding jungles, the weapon might come in handy. He studied the area and felt to be near where his father had been. Zephan might not even have fallen into the river. In fact, his enemies could have dragged him off to prison in the very "ambulance" supposedly sent to rescue him.

A curious relic caught his eye. Ben edged near the water and gazed further up river. Barely visible through gathering mist and dense vegetation, a large sculpture of a serpent head encircled in flame stood in the wilderness. How best to get a closer look?

For the hundredth time, what could possibly have lured his father out here . . .

Something rustled behind him. Ben whirled, whipping out his pistol at the same instant.

"Why, Benjamin! You look like a gringo cowboy! You wouldn't kill your brother, would you? See? I'm unarmed. Put that thing away!"

Ben lowered his weapon.

"That's better!" Haman seemed quite confident. "Mama said you had gone to Zarahemla! Tsk, tsk! She told us not to lie!"

"What are you doing here?" Ben asked, wary.

"I have business here. I was going to ask you the same question! Although I knew you were coming here. It is our business to know everything."

"So your business is to know everyone else's business. Since you know so much, where is Papa?"

"Even if I knew, I wouldn't tell you. It would be classified."

"Why?"

"He was considered hostile to the new order in our society."

"Was?"

Haman shrugged. "Well, he isn't around any more."

"Don't you care? How can you speak so casually when our own father is missing?"

"He did nothing for me. He means nothing to me."

"Haman, do you know what happened to Brother Bianco?"

"How should I know? I have more important things to do than worry about your silly prophets."

"Not my prophets, Haman. God's prophets. Papa is an Apostle of the Lord. You know very well the prophet and apostles are all sustained as prophets, seers, and revelators."

"Ha! Our father, a prophet. That's a good one. I've never been able to stomach these childish fables about the prophets. But our father, a prophet of God. That's too much."

"You had trouble accepting Brother Bianco, too, didn't you? At least I finally understand why people in the Bible were always reviling against the prophets. Those people had the same problem you do."

"Really." Haman's voice was thick with sarcasm. "So, Mr. Know-it-all, what is my problem?"

Ben smiled disarmingly. "You and I have always had some pretty rousing discussions, haven't we? For old times' sake, let's see if I understand you. You think Papa has no business being a prophet because he's not perfect, right?"

"Right."

"If prophets were perfect, none would need to bear witness of the Redeemer, would they?"

"You are rationalizing Papa's faults."

"The Lord chooses his apostles; they don't choose Him," Ben replied. "He works with those who don't rebel against Him, Haman."

"Papa was always moralizing. What a bore."

"Is it because he is your father, and you know him so well?"

Haman nodded reluctant acknowledgment.

"Well, Paul said we have fathers of our flesh who corrected us, and we are supposed to obey them; shouldn't we even more so obey our Father in heaven?"

"There you are, quoting the Bible again. I don't understand it."

"Take Moses, for example. The people rejected him over and over again. But he was a just man to whom God had entrusted His authority. What I meant was, if people can't obey God's word through a prophet who lives among us, how can they know and reverence our Father, who is in heaven?"

Haman folded his arms and tilted back his head. "Look, Ben, I don't have to listen to your preaching. You're beginning to sound as bad as Papa did. You know how I always hated it. We just couldn't get along."

"This is why the people rejected Moses, Haman." Ben became more earnest. "You know what happened to them. Is it worth it to revile the prophets, rebel against God, and risk the consequences?"

For an instant fear flickered across Haman's face, but as quickly it vanished. "You are afraid of God, just like a child," he said in a loud voice. "But God is no longer relevant. Face the truth, Ben, and grow up."

"But why do you hate Papa so?" Ben persisted.

Haman sighed heavily to show his impatience. "I don't hate Papa. He can believe what he wants to." He glanced at his costly watch. "I simply have much more important things to do. But if Papa gets in my way —"

"You were the last one to see him, Haman." Ben cut in, his voice hard. He moved closer to his brother.

Haman stood his ground. "Now, let's not be making loose accusations."

"Did I make any accusations? Tell me what happened that day, Haman."

"He came out here for one last look at the land before leaving it forever."

"In the driving rain? It doesn't make sense."

"As a matter of fact, the rain had ceased, and I brought him out here to show him something. An old Mulekite relic. You know how Papa always liked such things. See, over there?"

Ben stared at the strange figure he had been studying earlier.

"Come over here; you can see it better," Haman said. "Hang onto this rail."

The view was better just on Haman's other side. Ben reached for the rail and stumbled over something. He felt himself slipping like a rock into the quicksand.

"Hang on!" Haman shouted.

Ben clung to the rail, but it left its flimsy supports and hit the swamp beside him with a loud slapping sound.

"I'll try to help you!" Haman called. He grabbed the rail, now slimy with muck, and it slipped from Ben's hands. Haman held out the rail, suspending it in midair.

Ben felt the overpowering suction draw him into oblivion. Haman still held the rail out over the water, but the more Ben kicked to grasp at the elusive pole, the greater the drag upon him.

Heavy and slick, almost like sea kelp, mangrove-like branches enabled Ben to pull himself away from the sand trap near the bank. The dense plant growth, however, together with the strong current, demanded all his energy. Cumbersome foliage obstructed his vision, and the tangle of branches gripped him like human arms, ever pulling him downward.

The sword slipped away . . .

Ben took a deep breath and went down. He felt the sheath, with the strap caught on a branch, resting precariously on a steel cable which ran along the river bottom. The weapon once again secure in his possession, Ben pulled himself along. The cable ran under the weeds, but beneath him the river current had turned into whirling pools of suction. Only by holding onto the cable with all his strength, he avoided being sucked into the swirling vortex. Pulling himself along the cable as it started to ascend, Ben thought his lungs would burst.

Finally free from the undertow, Ben surfaced, kicking with all his might to push up a heavy blanket of weeds and make an air hole for himself. A tiny air pocket was like the breath of God, keeping him alive. His head came up under a huge leaf, and he thrashed his arms to push the slippery mass out of his way and get his bearings.

Haman would be far up river by now, if he had lingered, and would be obscured in the gathering mist.

Of more immediate concern were the thick vines which seemed to grab him the tighter with every kick, but Ben extricated with difficulty the sword to slash himself free from the tenacious fetters.

The relic, standing alone in the wilderness, seemed closer as he looked up the river. He had been a fool. If he hadn't been so curious about that thing, he wouldn't be in this fix. Again he dove for the cable and pulled himself along until he saw a shaft of light pierce the dark water ahead. Surfacing in fewer weeds and more water, he pulled himself along the cable with his head above water.

The cable led from the water toward the relic, ending at a hook concealed in bushes at the base of a tree. Ben waded out and perceived he could reach for and touch that artifact. No, the object was much farther than it seemed.

At last he pulled his tired, waterlogged body out onto the Jershon bank of the river. His pack was rainproof but not airtight. His sandwiches were sopping, as was his change of clothing. It was a marvel the underwater jungle hadn't simply swallowed his entire, bulky, awkward frame.

As Ben studied the area all around him, he had a distinct impression of being watched. Again his eyes scoured the wilderness. The Mulekite relic now appeared to be on a foot hill, against a backdrop of the wilderness called *Hermounts*. Ben decided since he had come this far, he might as well shed the extra water and go see the relic.

He took one boot off, dumped out the water, wiggled his toes, and shook his head to alleviate the ringing in his ears. No. What was that sound? With the slight dizziness from his recent exertions, he did not immediately identify the source of the vibrating sound.

5

Beneath the dense umbrage on the river bank, a branch began to move. Ben watched in horror as a bushmaster appeared from the green jungle overcast, extending in its full length to over eight feet.

His pistol was drenched and jammed. To kill the creature with the sword he would have to get within striking range. To retreat to the water meant he could be a hostage for hours. Ben could only try to put distance between himself and the snake before it coiled for a strike. He made a run for freedom, keeping his eyes forward, heading for the strange figure on the hill.

He did not look back to see the serpent close the gap and coil around his leg.

At the same time it struck his heel, Ben drew his sword, hacking at the monster, severing it into pieces with the sharp blade. When the snake released its grip, Ben grabbed a large rock and crushed its head.

He drained the wound as best he could, then continued toward the Mulekite relic, looking on the way for any possible shelter.

When he reached the huge image of the fiery serpent, he could see why his father's curiosity had been piqued. Throughout this land, many ancient ruins bore the mark of a serpent. This widespread manifestation continued to mystify worldly scholars, but the answer could be found in the book of Joseph. Descendants of Abraham through Joseph had come to this land, bringing with them a dual symbolism of the serpent. Moses had fashioned a brazen serpent in the wilderness to heal through faith those who had been bitten by poisonous, or fiery serpents. As the brazen serpent was lifted up to heal the afflicted, so the Holy One was lifted up in atonement for his people. In Hebrew typology, the brazen serpent became a type of the Messiah. Thus had a thread of the Redeemer's vast influence been retained among new world peoples. The sign of the serpent was held sacred, representing the law of Moses and signifying the power and authority of God as held by Moses and all of God's prophets.

For a moment Ben almost regretted having destroyed the snake which had threatened his own life. Then the opposite half of the dualism took shape in his mind. The serpent had also appeared in many forms, declaring himself to be the glorious Son of the Highest, and demanding worship, but he was only a mirror image, the antichrist used by Satan in the garden of Eden. Though Pharaoh, political superior to the prophet Joseph, did not possess the authority of God, he sought to obtain it through every possible imitation. Thus the crown of Pharaoh bore the image of a serpent, but it only served as a blatant expression of false doctrine which lacked the divine signature.

Ben stared at the immense grinning serpent, or *coatl*, looming before him. Long ago the Messiah had come to earth. Humbling Himself, He lived among the people as a serpent dwelt in the dust. After He returned to the heavens whence He came, the people forgot His teachings, and abandoned His divine spirit. The people only remembered somehow the power of God had been among them briefly, then ascended into heaven like the graceful quetzal bird.

Despite the warnings of prophets, people turned away from God and followed idolatry, worshiping the work of their own hands. Again Ben regarded the graven image before him. It was merely a corrupt outward form, only one of man's many futile attempts to create his own distorted version of the Creator.

When the Messiah returned, would men know Him, or would they gaze vacantly past Him to their own gods of technology, war, vanity, or nature? As Isaiah had wondered, would the work say of him that made it, he made me not?

Ben felt a fresh wave of grief because he never had a chance to teach Solano about the ancient Christians in this land. And Anahí never had the chance to tell Solano she finally sighted the exquisite quetzal.

Ani! Where are you? Why did you tempt death to return to Granada?

Nagged by the feeling someone was watching him, Ben kept his eyes moving, fearful of ambush while in his weakened state. He felt more than heard the water's rhythm, washing over a gentle silence. He wanted desperately to sleep. A wild bird's cry came to him on a breeze from the *Hermounts*, like the haunting, breathy call of a pan pipe, a familiar voice from a remote corner of antiquity. Good. If the bird ventured to call for its mate, it must be safe . . . or was it a warning?

A rush of wings confirmed his suspicions. Something, or someone, flushed that wild parrot out of its concealment. No, it was not a parrot. Its heart-shaped chest was red like crimson. On wings like the mountain snows, it soared on an updraft, sweeping the air with a curtain of plumage, shimmering green like the emerald waters of Bahia Verde, like the Hill Cumorah in spring. The quetzal rose so high it became a speck, a white star on sapphire, high above the earth.

Fiery venom seared his heel, and a wave of weakness engulfed him. Ben urgently needed to press on. Where? He could not move, not even lift his head.

He collapsed on the ground and pleaded with God: *O, Eternal Father, who can heal the nations, and all manner of diseases, and the unclean, an even those afflicted with the spirit of evil, I beseech thee, heal me of this poisonous venom.*

Then he blacked out.

6

The high sun of noon awakened Ben, and he sensed he was not alone. He sat up with a start, instinctively reaching for his pistol. His eyes met those of a native Mulekite who returned his glance with a riveted stare.

To his surprise and relief, Ben discovered on his wound an herbal dressing which had kept the swelling minimal. "Thank you." Ben looked at the man with cautious gratitude.

"I know you," the Mulekite replied.

"You know me? Ben." The young man pointed to his chest. "Squanto."

"Squanto?"

"Your father calls me that."

"You know my father? I don't understand!"

"Your sword." Squanto pointed to the magnificent weapon lying beside the young man. "He made some."

"Squanto! My father . . . does he live?"

"*Sí, sí.* I fished him from yonder swamp where you were. Almost died. Your father kept his name secret for long time, to hide from the enemy. The enemy pushes many into the swamp. Your father was lucky. Others were not so lucky. He said, put a rod in the river."

"The cable? It saved my life!"

Squanto hastily made a fire, roasted chunks of meat, boiled water for tea, and as quickly extinguished the small blaze.

Ben was famished. The meat tasted like chicken, but rather tough.

Squanto nodded at the meat. "*Serpiente.*" He grinned, hefting the sword admiringly. "When you cut him, you make good steaks!"

"Squanto, do you know anything about that fiery serpent?"

"Mulekite tradition tells us the Holy One visited this land anciently."

"Interesting."

"Your father said he has ancient records of my people."

"This is true, Squanto. Where is my father, then?"

"*Paciencia.* I will take you to him. First, we take Ponistas on . . . uh, merry chase?"

Ben chuckled. "But we are across the border!"

"No matter. Enemy will search the river banks and find Ben's sock."

"My sock?" Ben's eyes widened. He stared at his bare foot, which gave off a scent of juniper and basil from Squanto's treatment.

"Sleeping in modern city made me foolish. I did not see the missing sock." Though obviously chagrined, Squanto shrugged. "No matter. We are smarter than the Ponista dogs."

"Let's go back and get my sock."

"No. We will not find the sock, but enemy will find us in the morning. They will come with jeeps, maybe tanks. We will go ahead before them, tonight. The night, she will cover us. Where we go, they cannot come. Where we go, is your father. But the path is in Cumorah, *un poco.* Come. We must hurry."

Ben wrinkled his nose. "What a souvenir to leave in my beloved Cumorah . . . one stinking sock!"

7

Haman Benamoz shared a hearty meal with his comrades. Gluttony among several soldiers repulsed Benamoz, who was a light eater. One exception was Major Andrei Kovac, the supervising officer from the Tartarean Empire, who seemed to have iron self-control. The man kept himself aloof, saying little. Haman felt threatened by Kovac's mysterious demeanor.

Haman found himself drinking more wine than usual. *Who cares? Ben's death is for the cause. This nervousness shows weakness. Toughen up.*

Lieutenant Odón Pelegri was staring at him. "What is it, Odón?" Haman forced himself to sound casual.

"We finally found out who murdered Captain Mortera, Haman. Leb sent word that your brother, Benjamin, was responsible."

Ah, so Ben's death was merely an execution. "Don't worry. I've handled it. Ben was here today. He accidentally took a little swim. No point in wasting time dragging his body from the muck."

Lieutenant Pelegri seemed satisfied, but Haman's respite was brief.

A soldier burst into the room, holding an article of clothing. "Sir! We found this by the river, and tracks leading east, on the north side of the river!"

Haman paled under Pelegri's glare.

"But . . . Nobody can survive in that swamp! Zephan Benamoz is gone. And so is his youngest son. The last of the Canosa threat is eliminated. Odón, I had my orders, and I'm thorough."

"How do you explain this? Does this look like your mother's stocking? And do dead people walk away and leave tracks, eh?"

"But . . . "

"*Basura!*" Odón Pelegri was livid. "How do I know you didn't help him to escape? I've a mind to kill you! It would be easy. Just leave your body somewhere and tell the world press the peasant death squads did it!"

"I made you, and I can break you, ungrateful *chancho*! I could do the same to you, and no explanation would be necessary!" Ignoring his telltale perspiration, Haman glanced at Andrei Kovac. The major's face was unreadable. Haman forced a conciliatory tone into his voice. Pragmatism was a handy defense. "*Basta.* Enough, comrade. The enemy advances while we squabble amongst ourselves. Let us not waste any more time!"

Pelegri left with the others to organize a search, while Haman Benamoz did some serious thinking.

8

After wrapping remaining meat chunks in large pieces of snake skin, Squanto stuffed it into his back pack, then made Ben some strong tea from the *uña de gato* herb. "One more chance to clean poison out of you before we go," he said.

Ben noted his friend's muscular build. Squanto was not soft. The young man knew his own weary plodding was no match for the native's noiseless stealth. Squanto left Ben's remaining sock far from the trail, then periodically rubbed bushes, trees, and the trail with the meat, to dilute the human scent, and sidetrack the dogs.

Later in the afternoon the two men reached an impasse on the north side, where the *Hermounts* wilderness began to create a natural boundary. As they entered the river, Squanto began throwing meat periodically into backwashes where the water was mossy and murky, and onto the Cumorah side, which was up wind from the dogs' position. The Mulekite winked at Ben. "This confuse them *un poco*," he said.

As the elevation increased, the banks rose sharply on either side of the river, which abruptly became shallow and turbulent. Ahead they heard the falls roar as the river cut a deep canyon through mountains in search of the distant sea. The fugitives emerged on the Cumorah side and continued at a rapid pace, with Squanto still throwing his morsels into the wind.

Cliffs rose sharply, and Ben's anxiety peaked. He and Squanto were on the wrong side of the river, standing on a mere shelf! Eastward, the land jutted up steeply yet another several hundred yards. The Land of Jershon, and safety, lay on the other side of angry waters, three thousand feet below.

Squanto threw more meat into the river. "The meat will wash up down river, if crocodiles do not eat it, first." He smirked impishly.

Ben paled in horror. "You mean where we crossed the river crocodiles were. . . .?"

Squanto's toothy grin broadened. "No matter. They do not eat *us*!"

244

All the while the Mulekite was taking out gear. First, a sturdy, stainless steel rod which he lengthened into what looked like a javelin, with a piton on the end. Swiftly he tied a very long nylon line to it, with a large clip on the loose end. "See that lone tree on the other side?" Squanto shouted over thundering falls. He threw the javelin and it made an arc across the canyon, over the gaping chasm to land near the tree, thirty yards from where they were standing. The Mulekite then jerked on the rope with all his weight to test it.

Squanto took the last piece of meat and leaned over the edge, tossing the chunk gently so it caught on a small branch partially down the cliff wall.

The Mulekite clasped a safety harness on Ben, and another on himself. "Do as I do," he said simply. Then he clipped on the line and jumped, swinging down to hang suspended, halfway down the opposite cliff. The steel rod, jutting outward, lessened his impact against the rocky wall. Swinging to the rugged precipice, Squanto scaled its face on the remains of an old rope foot bridge hanging over the edge.

Ben grimaced. *That's easy for him to say!*

Squanto hurled the weighted clip back across the canyon. When Ben caught the clip, the sound of yelping dogs reached his ears. Still, he hesitated.

Oh, well. Better to be dashed to pieces on the rocks below than face the wrath of his enemies. Besides, God had spared his life thus far.

He jumped. The rod bent like a fishing pole, allowing him to bounce and cushion the shock of his falling weight.

Squanto had belayed the line on the tree, and hauled on the line as soon as Ben swung to the cliff.

The last few feet, Ben moved himself along, hanging by his hands on the rod, his feet suspended, tingling, over the raging river a thousand yards below, until he reached the bridge fragment.

The cliff was concave at a sharp angle so the bridge swung in open air like a fragile ladder. Ben knew the nylon cable would hold him. But would this ancient bridge give out under his weight? If so, he would be forced to scale the overhang by holding on with his fingers. This would slow him down. The lowering sun was shining full on his back. If he did not reach the top in time, his pursuers could easily pick him off with a high-powered rifle.

Could the dogs see him? The crashing water now muffled any clamor of dogs and men. No time to think about that now. He concentrated on his objective. One cross-tie on the ladder did break on the left side, but he had gripped the frayed bridge on both sides. The sturdier rope joint in his right hand held fast. All the while, Squanto, bless him, was pulling steadily upward on the nylon safety line.

At last Ben reached the top and scrambled up over the edge. They scurried into a ravine behind the tree.

"*Hombre*!" Ben exclaimed. "How did you and Papa do this?"

"We walked through the mountains, which takes many days. This way is a short cut. Your father told me how to do it with a rod. He calls it *barra de hierro*, an iron rod."

"How like my father."

Ben studied the land northward. A tiny meadow stretched away from the river, vanishing into the mountains. He gazed up at the wild olive tree which had saved him from tumbling to his death in the gulf below. Known for long life, the tree was perhaps even a thousand years old, maybe two.

The dogs' howling had now reached a high pitch. Ben allowed himself to peer from the ravine to the canyon's other side.

The dogs could see the meat hanging on a branch several yards down but were unable to reach it and whined hysterically.

"*Basura*!" Pelegri yelled to Kovac over the roaring water. "Those blamed dogs are after that meat, not our man!"

"Major!" A scout reported, scratching his head. "The trail seems to have vanished, sir. We must have lost it somewhere back there."

But Major Kovac, not so easily foiled, took in the situation with binoculars. "Ah," he said. "See that old foot bridge hanging down on the other side?"

"It has been broken for years," replied the scout. "Too many lost their lives in trying to repair it."

"Perhaps, but it is swinging slightly, as if recently used," the wily major observed.

"That's impossible, sir," the scout insisted. "They could never get across without the bridge. This place is deadly. Our ancestors called it Gulf of Misery. Either those men are far down river or they have plunged to their death."

"Very well," Kovac replied with grudging admiration. "Let's see if we can go back and pick up the trail, but night closes in, and I fear we only waste time chasing after a wild goose. "

9

Ben and Squanto toiled all night through the rugged mountain terrain, and at dawn they arrived at a small village.

"Here we are in the land of the Mulekites," Squanto said.

"It is a wild and remote land."

Squanto nodded. "Best reached by sea. My ancestors came out from Jerusalem at the time Zedekiah, king of Judah, was carried away captive into Babylon. My people carried no records with them, so their language became corrupted, and they denied the existence of their Creator. Anciently, my people met others from the house of Israel in this area."

"Squanto, how do you know this?"

"Your father taught us, from what he called the stick of Joseph."

A tiny cabin nestled against mountains on the north, looking down on the immense Bahia Verde, and beyond, the Caribbean Sea.

Squanto knocked briefly. "¡Hola! Zephan! I bring a surprise!"

The man who stepped out on the little porch, his left shoulder sagging slightly, was as stately and calm as Ben had always remembered him.

"¡Hijo mio!" Zephan embraced his son fervently. "I was afraid I would never see you again!"

"Nor I, you, Papa."

After assuring his father of the family's well-being, Ben reported his unsuccessful attempt to obtain the book of Joseph.

Zephan received the news with bitterness. "So the swine have taken our most cherished possession." He groaned. "I am grieved. I have betrayed a trust, Ben."

"Do take comfort, Papa. Dan MacRay still possesses a copy of the book."

"Thanks be to God. And I am so grateful you are safe!"

"Now that we are reunited, Papa, what will you do?"

"I have not wanted to endanger your mother by trying to contact her, at least until things settle down. But now I must get back to Zarahemla."

"Solano was a dear friend, Papa. Can we bring his murderers to justice?"

"It is an evil pattern. We have seen this before, and we will see it again. More than a playwright, Shakespeare was a historian. The words of Cassius, when he assassinated Caesar, were almost prophetic. *How many ages hence shall this our lofty scene be acted over in states unborn and accents yet unknown!*"

Ben declined his father's favorite snack of peanut butter and purple onion rolled in a tortilla.

"This exile has its drawbacks, but I am comfortable, and I love the people. I would like to come back here and bring Sarita, but there will be no retirement for me, I'm afraid. Do you know what happened to Brother Joseba?"

Ben groaned. "No. Nothing since Ponte seized him."

"According to Haman, he was only to be questioned and released. First we must try to help Brother Joseba."

"I know, Papa."

"We have another urgent matter to attend to. I will send Abiram and Alison to settle here. Much work is here to do, teaching the gospel. The people are ready to receive it."

"But can Abiram be spared, when we have so much tribulation?"

Zephan smiled. "You know the work goes on, no matter how hot things get. Besides, Abiram has a very special mission."

"Here?"

"The time is coming when the Egalitarians will destroy the free press in all urban areas. Government censorship in Cumorah is already widespread. Abiram will establish a press here in the wilderness, so we can continue to publish the glad tidings."

"True to your calling, you sound prophetic, Papa."

Zephan shook his head. "It is not me, Ben. I am but an instrument. The Lord makes known his will for the sake of his kingdom."

The two men conversed for a while about the fall of Cumorah and Solano's tragic death, then lapsed into a melancholy silence.

Ben paused, listening. Surely he heard piano music. Someone was playing Tchaikovsky's "None But the Lonely Heart" with passion and poignancy. Anahí . . . ?

"Papa, what is that? You have a piano around here?"

"Huh? Oh, that. Well, we built a little chapel over there for our Sabbath meetings. Actually, it is possible to ship some things here by sea. So I bought a small upright piano for . . . " Zephan grinned. "Come on. I'll show you!"

10

Quietly father and son let themselves into the small chapel's foyer. Involved in her music, the pianist did not notice their entrance.

"She plays much sad music, lately," Zephan whispered. "A release for her. . . Oh, well . . . I'll leave you two alone, and let her tell you!" Zephan slipped out, smiling broadly.

Ben stole across the room, staying at her back, and let her finish the piece. Then, softly, "Ani!"

After one speechless moment, she flew into his arms.

Finally, she pulled away gently.

"Leb. . . " Ben could not conceal his anxiety. "Did he. . . ?"

"No! No, Ben. I was protected."

"Who in the name of thunder nearly pulverized my skull?" Ben asked.

"Pedro Aguerros. He's sorry, though. He didn't mean it."

Ben gave a low whistle. "What's he like when in earnest?"

"He is only twelve years old, Ben. Those Ponista terrorist training camps take in children and make demons out of them! But Pedro is a fine young man, and he is an excellent scout.

She led Ben to the window. "Pedro is coming now."

"Anahí?" Pedro ventured shyly into the chapel. "Señor Zephan said I should come here, that I had some explaining to do!"

"Indeed you do!"

"Ah, Señor, I know it will be *difícil* for you to forgive me, but try to believe I am a genuine defector!"

"Why did you defect?"

The boy's eyes filled with tears.

"When terrorists killed his parents a couple of years ago," Anahí interceded gently, "he had nowhere to go, and ended up in a Ponista camp."

"Anahí was very kind to me." Seeing her nod encouragement, Pedro went on, trembling. "When I saw Leb nearly kill you, his own brother, I learned terrorists had murdered Anahí's family, and I knew something was very wrong. I had made a terrible mistake."

"It takes a big person to admit he was wrong, Pedro," Ben said. He turned to Anahí. "And how did you escape Leb?"

"He got more than he bargained for." With a mischievous smile, she reported her skirmish with Leb.

Ben's immense relief tumbled out in hearty laughter. "Ani, *mi corazón*, I will not risk losing you again. Will you marry me?"

"Yes." She clapped her hands together, and he caught them in his, drawing her to him. "But when?"

"Now. Tonight. We can be married for time and eternity in the temple in Sheffa before we go to Zarahemla. And who better to marry us than my father?"

The Book Of

Dan

"Liahona, which is , being interpreted, a compass;
and the Lord prepared it. And it did work for them
according to their faith in God."

THE BOOK OF DAN

Zarahemla
2082

1

Almost three years, and the investigation of Solano's death seems to be going nowhere," Mitchell Hunt said. "Sounds like a coverup to me."

"One advantage we have is that the terrorists are counting on our ignorance of a hidden history."

"History?"

"About the remnant of Jacob," Zephan said.

"How do you figure?"

Zephan frowned. "There is but one place the assassins could unearth the name, *Amalickiah*. It is found only in records held sacred by the house of Yeshurun."

"Why would the terrorists use that particular name?"

"Whoever this so-called modern Amalickiah really is," Zephan said, "I suspect the Zarahemla press will idolize this person or terrorist group."

"You are way ahead of me," Mitchell Hunt said. "The press? Lionize a terrorist?"

"Then Egalitarians will pin the blame for Solano's assassination to someone they don't like. This is precisely the strategy Amalickiah used to cover up an assassination."

"You think they will use this ancient trick?"

Zephan nodded. "It is a pattern. Thus saith the Lord: Satan goes about deceiving the nations. How better to deceive entire nations than to suppress the truth and publish lies?"

Hunt selected a licorice stick from a jar on his desk and leaned back in his chair. "Is this deception deliberate?"

"By a few, perhaps. Most people in the news industry simply obey those who pay their bills. This is a kept press, Mitch, just like in the old world where I came from."

"Now you mention it, Zephan, I see what you mean. But who —"

"Combinations of global corporations, interlocking directorates too complex to describe. But one thing all seem to have in common —— an affinity for the Egalitarian philosophy."

"The Egalitarians do seem to love terrorists. Supposing, heaven forbid, they succeed in covering up the true identity of Amalickiah. Do you have any idea whom they would blame instead?"

"Someone very close to me." Zephan became extremely agitated. "Mitch, I believe the Egalitarians will make an example of Joseba Bianco."

"Are you sure?" Hunt said, astonished. "Why would they target someone as harmless as Mr. Bianco? They even released him after the confrontation with Ponte, didn't they?"

Zephan shrugged. "Yes, even they could not find a reason to detain him. But he still spends more time in prison than he does out."

"Why?"

"He calls people to repentance, and Ponte claims this agitates the people."

"Mr. Bianco, causing a disturbance?"

"Repentance is hard work, Mitch. We are always looking for a way to get around it, an easy way. We hate to repent, but we love to listen to flattery."

Hunt looked puzzled.

"Supposing someone claims he can save us from bondage without having to give up the iniquity which enslaves us. Doesn't that sound good?"

"Oh. Are you are talking about some religious preachers?"

"No. I am talking about self-adoring politicians."

"What do you mean, Zephan?"

"Many politicians and demagogues don't like to keep God's commandments, so they set themselves up as a light unto the world. They make their own rules, even their own religion. It is a religion of men, not God, but they set up their own prophets, and even create a false image of Christ. In the eyes of men, it looks like a great church, but in the sight of God, it is abominable."

"Do they have a name?"

"Usually it is a pleasant-sounding name, but the scriptures call it Babylon."

"Hmm. A political church. But our country is very adamant about separation of church and state."

"I also believe in separation of church and state. But it can be abused in unexpected ways. Under this very pretense, Babylon exercises extreme intolerance, even persecution, against all churches except herself."

"What if people choose their own prophet? I heard Ponte formed his own religion. In fact, didn't the people in Ammonihah elect him to be their prophet?"

"No true disciple of Christ would aspire to be God's prophet. Nor is it God's way to force anyone's beliefs. It is an ancient practice to enforce one's ideas with money and political power."

"Oh, I see . . . Hunt tied his licorice stick into a knot and nibbled on the middle of it. "I never did trust Ponte, anyway. But why would the Egalitarian press want to smear a prophet of Yeshurun, like Mr. Bianco? He speaks the truth, but he certainly has no money or political power to enforce *anything*."

"The Egalitarians are afraid of that truth, Mitch. Truth would expose them."

"I always wondered why tyrants tend to oppress people of faith. Now everything is clear. Mr. Bianco could be in grave danger, Zephan."

"And Ponte's thugs could easily intimidate someone into betraying him. I must get Brother Joseba out from Cumorah, Mitch, before it is too late."

"If only I knew how," Hunt said, gnawing on the candy as a dog worries a bone. "Dalton Mortfield, our defector from the Egalitarian camp, has been acting strange since the assassination, and I'm having him watched. He worked for Kingerman in Cumorah, so considering the source, his intelligence may all be bogus. He may be a plant to derail the investigation. He says Kingerman is fighting

255

terrorism in his own way, but they had a disagreement over policy. Whatever he knows, he's not talking until he's ready."

Zephan nodded.

Hunt scratched his head absently. "Sometimes the ideological lines are pretty blurry, Zephan. I mean, for Ponte no act of terrorism is too vile. Kingerman, on the other hand, keeps his hands clean, preaches world peace, and loudly proclaims his aversion to terrorism. Those two men seem to be on opposite ends of the political spectrum."

"Ponte and Kingerman may have different styles, Mitch, but you'd be amazed at how close together they really are. Both want to be kings: one wants to be king of Cumorah, the other wants to be king of the world."

Hunt shook his head. "The world is a bowl of mixed nuts, all right. For now, we have Miles Potter to worry about. He has fled to Cumorah and needs to be extradited. You know, he's the one who incites racial violence and finances his crusades with drugs."

"I'll take that case. Maybe he can lead me to Jaime Canosa."

Hunt groaned. "One of my best men, missing."

Zephan stood. "Mitch, I must go to Cumorah. Canosa and Joseba are my best people, too. I cannot rest till I find them."

Carrying snapshots of numerous suspects, Zephan met with Farley Bunker, a ZRI agent vacationing in the Caribbean isles.

"What is this all about, Benamoz?" Bunker, young, unmarried, and more daring than the devil himself, had recently been moved from a line in Antionum which he had been working.

"Relax. This is cleared by the department."

Bunker studied the photos. "I can brief you on many of these. You think the order of Voltaire had something to do with Solano's assassination?" he smiled. "I'd give you an *A* for originality, but I thought of it first."

Zephan was not smiling. "I said nothing about the Chief. I want names, not opinions. In the most recent transactions, who are the buyers still at large?"

"In Zarahemla, Orton Beck is a big buyer, but he isn't a kingpin. He works for many others. I've found the dominating cartel to be massive. Not just south, but worldwide, including the land of Tartarus, the Philistines, and members from the Community of Nations." Bunker raised his eyebrows. "And the agents are not your mere jungle junkies, but some who appear to be respectable bankers and merchants, citizens above suspicion."

Zephan's face remained without expression.

Bunker looked around. The beach was empty except for a woman and her child playing in the waves a hundred yards away. "My source told me there was a big conglomerate. Beck has a huge network, with headquarters right here on the island. His dealers are even all indexed. I almost had the conglomerate's name. Then my operative got killed, and I was moved. Glen Turley in Zarahemla has taken on the file."

Back in Zarahemla, Zephan found Turley to be less cooperative. "You've done this without a go-ahead from Hunt," he said. "I ought to have you fired."

"I do have Hunt's authorization, but I am also wrapping up an investigation specially requested by Cumorah's Chief Judge before his untimely death."

Turley grimaced.

Zephan knew he had scored. "Some of our agents are already in great danger," he went on. "You can help, or further imperil them."

A week later Director Hunt summoned Zephan into his office. "I have a letter from Chief Judge Elidor's Security Advisor, Archibald Kingerman."

Zephan gave a low whistle. "That man is everywhere!"

"Says here, 'the Attorney General's Office requests your agents to discontinue the Solano investigation until further notice. Any further action by your department at this time would not be in the public interest, as it will be seen as casting doubt on the World Court's decision to seal the archives for fifty years.' "

Zephan was speechless.

"Well," Hunt said, "not much we can do against . . . Uh, best leave it alone."

"I am still worried about Brother Joseba, and Canosa is my kin. I must return to Cumorah. Time is growing short."

"You know that place better than any of us, and you are certainly the best man to go," Hunt said with a trace of a smile. This man's determination alone would probably accomplish the work of three men. "But," he added, lifting his hand in warning, "You are not to go alone, Zephan. Cumorah has become the headquarters for a massive drug cartel. This cartel is the leverage point for every other secret combination in the world, and it is the deadliest of all."

Within days, Glen Turley died after being thrown from a sixth story window. Orton Beck was gunned down while leaving the Golden Triangle Casino. Farley Bunker mysteriously vanished.

2

"Elidor will cover for me," Verman bragged as Kingerman's coterie filed into the cushy Dermucker Foundation headquarters. "In fact, my appointment as State Consul is in the bag. Now I'm working for the International Banking Complex, and I can't be touched."

"Many inmates said the same thing," Mortfield said.

"What's to worry about?" Verman asked. "Look at Senator Penlock, the most powerful man in Congress. He couldn't stay sober long enough to scare us. With Kingerman as Security Advisor, and Rupert Banberg running interference for the Pyramid, we're all clean."

Mortfield gazed out the smoke-colored window at a huge planetary dome, the Dermucker-financed Pax Universalis building. "Don't be so sure." He turned to Kingerman. "Do you have that POW situation locked up?"

"Sealed and delivered." Kingerman snickered.

"You had a stroke of genius, Arch," Verman rattled on, "when you decided to send little Oliver Beck off to the Cumeni war. When Oliver didn't come back from the Cumeni war, his mommy got suspicious and hired private investigators. Orton had gotten too sloppy. You can't take too many chances with the mafia. Things were getting sweaty, and Beck became a liability. Now with Beck eliminated, the old lady dead from cancer, and the boy conveniently languishing at the Taj of Little Tartarus, there in Cumeni, we can rest easy about one more troublesome family."

"Wrong," said the ever-watchful Mortfield. "Young Beck came back in '81 with the Project Homecoming spearheaded by that Benamoz family."

Verman gasped. "Blast! Do you know what story Beck could tell?"

"Nonsense!" Kingerman's every move, even his smile, was one of consummate laziness. "The Empire terrorists helped us out. Oliver D. Beck is so messed up with cocaine he'll do anything to get the stuff. He's known in Zarahemla as O.D., overdosed." Everyone laughed. "Fear not. O.D. is our man."

"Solano's testimony has been published in book form," Devon said with forced casualness.

"That book must be destroyed!" Verman exclaimed.

"Skip the knee-jerk reaction," Kingerman said with mild annoyance. "You act as though we are guilty of some crime."

"Well, aren't we?" Mortfield's voice was tight. "According to his book, supporting insurrection and mass murder of dissidents is a major crime."

"Well, that's politics for you," Verman said.

"Listen to Mortfield, the assassin!" Kingerman scoffed. "Sporting a conscience, now, are we? Do you have some problem with our handling of the assassination probe?"

"He liked Solano." Devon chimed in. "He fought beside him in the Empire wars."

Kingerman clucked. "Not a luxury we can afford, my good man. Our goals are lofty, but sometimes we have to be ruthless to achieve them, you know."

Mortfield shrugged. His plan had been to remove Solano from office, not kill him. They didn't know he had gone to great pains to avoid pulling the trigger, only to be foiled by car bombs of which he had not been informed. He had to say something to deflect the scrutiny from himself. "Solano's publisher is a member of Yeshurun."

"Them again," Verman grumbled.

"Some maverick press in Jershon run by a man named Abiram Benamoz, " Devon added.

"Benamoz!" Kingerman was suddenly alert.

"You know him?"

Kingerman nodded. "And if he's anything like his father was . . . "

"Worst thing is," Devon went on, "the book is all true. Real history can seriously disrupt our disinformation program, even after all these years of censorship in the schools."

Kingerman laughed. "I'm surprised at you, Devon. Since when was truth an issue? The book is only the truth as Solano saw it. Don't you see how easy it will be to discredit Solano's testimony?

Yeshurun is so peculiar and eccentric no one will take them seriously. Trust me."

"But Dan MacRay is promoting the book, and he is my most popular columnist. I found out he is a good friend of . . . " Devon muttered something.

"Guess who else is back," Mortfield cut in. "Zephan Benamoz."

Kingerman swore.

"Haman's father?" Verman asked.

"Yes," Devon said. "You know, he opposes Haman in everything. Haman thought someone had, uh, dispatched Zephan, but Haman's brother found him and brought him back, and he's asking questions about Amalickiah."

Mortfield bit his lip. Had he said too much? How much *did* they know? Of one thing he was certain: he would not rest until Solano's murder was avenged.

"We control the investigation," Kingerman said.

"Yes," Devon continued, "but Haman said Zephan was very close to Solano, and he has the tenacity of a badger. No one has said anything, but I can put two and two together."

"It doesn't pay to underestimate the adversary," Mortfield said quickly. "Need I spell it out for you? There are still Solanistas around, and a very smart one is working for ZRI."

Kingerman's eyes narrowed. "You're right, Mortfield. Zephan Benamoz must be stopped."

3

SHOCKING NEW EVIDENCE REOPENS SOLANO CASE

Solano's assassins bear a code name of "Amalickiah", according to Global Police. This unusual name is found only in an ancient record possessed by Yeshurun. According to expert investigators hired by General Kemen Ponte's administration, this new evidence links the Solano murder to members of Yeshurun who were disaffected with the former Cumorah leader. An anonymous source confirmed that prior to his untimely death, Solano had broken off with his Yeshurun supporters. Yeshurun, a branch of the house of Israel, is considered by many to be an extreme religious sect.

The rift appears to stem from Yeshurun radicals who objected to Solano's efforts for world peace. Increasing evidence points to a "climatological conspiracy" as the cause of the leader's death. Specifically, a climate of hate and fear created by Yeshurun is directly responsible for the assassination.

"Concerning this crazed fanatic who murdered Solano and six other innocent men, we can only assume he has ties to a hate-filled fringe of Yeshurun," says Kemen Ponte. Ponte, freedom fighter and new Chief Judge of Cumorah, has had his hands full reviving that nation's troubled economy. "We cannot deny this development poses tremendous danger, not only to the people of Cumorah, but to the entire world, until this terrorist is apprehended. But we can be assured the world police will soon have this criminal in custody."

Pillars of Zarahemla society, quick to condemn the violence, have rushed to support our ally, Mr. Ponte.

"Yeshurun is a dangerous force who breathes fire and speaks a rhetoric of fear, suspicion, and hatred. Yeshurun is obsessed with defeating the order of Voltaire," says Harvey Dermucker, a founder of Pax Universalis.

"Yeshurun represents all that citizens of the world fear most," says Horace Verman, official in the Elidor Redmund Administration.

"This religious movement is an ignorant and backward element in our society," says Rupert Banberg, CEO of the International Banking Complex.

"Yeshurun's religious opposition to the order of Voltaire condemns them," says Archibald Kingerman, Security Adviser and executive in Pax, "but they refuse to bear their collective responsibility for the bombing of Solano. As an expert on Yeshurun history, I can assure you the name 'Amalickiah' is unique to that history, and is found nowhere else. All members of Yeshurun are implicated in the murder, by simple logic of association," Kingerman told the *Post*. "It doesn't take a genius to figure this out," the world leader concluded.

Benjamin read this article aloud to his wife while she cleaned up after the evening meal. "Since I'm no longer in the military, I promised my father that I would pursue my career as a writer. Dan MacRay has kindly secured a job for me at the *Zarahemla Post*." He rattled the newspaper with dismay. "But this is what we find on the front page!"

"Do people really believe those lies?" Anahí wanted to know.

"It appears this press takes us for a nation of fools." Anahí smiled. "Do I detect the creature emerging?"

With a mischievous grin, Ben crossed the room and covered her eyes with one hand, arranging at the same time to hold her in his other arm. "Here, you be the blind and impartial judge, oh, thou soft-spoken one. I have a riddle for you, or a paradox.

"For generations, Zarahemla schools have taught this people to be skeptical of God's word. By their own experience the people learned to distrust politicians and journalists who lie frequently. Yet for information and interpretation of reality, these same skeptical people continue to rely upon whom? The same kept press, intellectuals, and politicians who have deceived them all these years. Is this skeptical . . . or gullible? How do you answer?"

Anahí opened her mouth to speak, but the telephone squawked.

"Dan MacRay, here, with an invitation to another gala party on Irreantum Avenue, core of the capital's high-rent district."

"You are very kind, Dan, but I'm not in the mood to mingle with that type of people, and they're not especially fond of me, either."

"Now, now. You don't see Dan MacRay getting intimidated by political correctness, media drivel, capital city psycho-babble, globalist high-handedness, militant immorality, or any other assault by proponents of current philosophies of men (or women), do you?"

Ben chuckled.

"See there? When Dan MacRay laughs, the nation laughs with him."

"That's what I mean. You can get by with it. I am just like my grandfather, who was very outspoken, and my father is no diplomat, either. No one will elicit apologies, whimpers, and pleas for mercy from me. I might offend somebody."

"Aw, the only time they get offended is when you tell the truth."

"Then it can't be helped."

"That's more like it. Otherwise, it can be pretty boring, unless you find drinking cocktails with a bunch of jackals entertaining. We'll pick you up at eight."

4

Benjamin paused at a buffet table to sample caviar, the only identifiable item nestled on platters of food. He observed the mansion's opulence and noted sequined apparel on glamorous guests. Tuxedo-clad ambassadors, diplomats, local and foreign officials and dignitaries, the high-ranking and the common, and anyone in between, all crowded the great and spacious ballroom. Journalists, merchants, and movie stars trod the luxurious carpet, arm-in-arm with lesser-known but presumed socially and politically ambitious persons. Women sailed by in a rustle of glittering gowns and expensive perfume. Heavily jeweled fingers lifted dainty champagne glasses. Sensual lips pecked clean-shaven faces bulging with appetizers.

Martini in hand, a slick-haired young man sauntered past Ben, Dan, and Beth. Leaning on the fellow's unsteady arm was an exquisite Latin woman, wearing a low-cut dress and heavily adorned with costly jewels.

"That man is Oliver D. Beck from the State Department staff. Don't know what he does, except draw a salary from the taxpayers," MacRay said. "As I recall, he's in drug enforcement, but looks like he's on something himself. Ironically, his nickname is O.D. The wench on his arm is Delia Matagorda, ambassador from Cumorah, and darling of the Ponista terrorists."

"Dan!" Beth grinned impishly. "Why so cynical?"

"You're not exactly idyllic, yourself!" he said. "Oh, and look over there. Enter Ted Lipscomb, essence of Romanticism. Truly a Noble Savage. Rousseau himself would be proud! And Lipscomb is an Egalitarian, Ben. He even has that bright-eyed, I'm-going-to-save-you-from-yourself look."

"My brother Haman follows the same philosophy, and believe me, they are not as harmless as they look. Now Haman is a leader in Cumorah."

"Well, if it isn't the MacRays! Are you still writing your newsletter, Dan?"

"Trying to," Dan replied politely. "Ted Lipscomb, meet my good friend Benjamin Benamoz, who has just put away his military fatigues to join us in the arena of ideas."

Lipscomb slapped the boy on the back. "Good! Good! After all, it's our ideas which are behind the battles with bullets, anyway."

"Your ideas, is right," Dan said.

"Just be careful, Ben, not to become a stodgy old historian like Dan, here!"

"Same old Lips!" Dan retorted. "A single page in history is worth volumes of your theories, and Benjamin has memorized several books of history, haven't you, Ben?"

Lipscomb's eyebrows shot up. "Whole books?"

"Ancient religious history."

Lipscomb smirked. "Come now, you don't believe those Bible myths, do you?"

Ben shrugged. "Who can argue with history? Either it happened or it didn't. God's prophets tell us it happened; politicians tell us it didn't."

Dan laughed.

Ted Lipscomb lifted his nose. "So what do these books of yours have to say?"

"In some ways it's like reading today's news, only the prophets showed life through God's eyes. It's called reality." Ben winked at Dan.

"But it is so outdated," Lipscomb said. "Everyone knows science has proved that all those myths about creation are false. The Bible is no longer relevant for us today."

"On the contrary," Ben replied. "The word of God through his prophets is more relevant today than ever. For example, Isaiah prophesied about Elidor and her friends."

"Really? What did he say?"

"As for my people, children are their oppressors, and women rule over them. O my people, they who lead thee cause thee to err." Ben's face was serious, but his eyes were laughing.

"Your Isaiah had an objection to women who rule?"

"Only to those who choose to rule by the precepts of men, rather than God."

"Religious people always criticize their government," Lipscomb complained, "like that horrible house of Yeshurun. Can you believe the awful things they've done? I hear their members deal in drugs, too. I just hate Yeshurun, don't you? It's their hatred which causes all this violence. Terrible group. Such hatred, and a climate of fear."

Ben glanced at Dan. "Remember what this man said. I will prove a point with my wife."

"Smart man, this friend of yours," Ted said to Dan. "I tell you, Yeshurun is one big conspiracy."

"History is full of conspiracies," Ben said. "And without a doubt, many conspiracies exist today. But your analysis is flawed, Ted."

"Really, now."

"You see, men's plottings are fragments of a much larger pattern."

Lipscomb blinked.

Dan smiled. "You're getting too deep, Ben. So. Beyond our petty politics, what is the essence of our earthly conflicts?"

"It began before Cain and Abel. In fact, before Eden. The conflict concerned the right to reign over Adam's descendants. There were two plans presented."

"Which were——?

"Self-government under God or rule by man's dictates."

"Oh." Lipscomb took a deep draft on his drink. "Now, about our new Chief Judge, Elidor. She is a woman experienced in leadership, nation-building, and effecting major change in society."

"Right," Dan said. "Elidor is the absolute paragon of Egalitarianism."

"You mean that?"

"Sure. With modern liberation, Elidor has proven beyond doubt that women can abuse power just as much as men." He laughed.

"How dare you!" Lipscomb said.

"Dan!" Beth jabbed with her elbow at her husband's ample side.

Ted turned to Ben. "He's hopeless. Doesn't the Bible talk about helping the poor? We in our government have eliminated the poor in our society."

"Yes, Elidor's solicitude for the poor and unfortunate is definitely fervid —— "

Lipscomb shot a gloating look at Dan. "See?"

"—— but is her sympathy false?" Ben asked. "In the name of helping the poor, Elidor's administration has funneled millions in grants to banking chums in her hometown."

Lipscomb was indignant. "Are you implying that Madame Chief is guilty of wrongdoing?"

Ben smiled. "Just the facts, sir."

"Humph."

"Elidor claims that without her programs, people will perish from poverty, crime, war, or whatever," Ben said. "On the surface it sounds necessary and urgent, but one must be careful, lest he be deceived."

"What do you mean?"

"Your programs have offered your so-called bread of life to all. But the poor are exploited by your programs. Rather than trusting in God and building personal character, they are dependent upon you for their bread, like slaves. Isaiah spoke of grinding the faces of the poor."

"You make no sense. For centuries, religious leaders told us money was the root of all evil. And what did we get? Poverty, crime, and war, that's what. Without Elidor's programs, where would people be? They would die, that's what."

"And who does Elidor think she is? A light unto the world? She thinks we can't live without her, eh?" Ben laughed. "Well, I'll tell you. I wouldn't trust her with *my* life!"

Lipscomb stared, aghast, and fumbled with his silk tie. "You . . .you would dare speak against the Chief Judge?"

"Nothing personal," Ben said. "I know Zarahemla's laws. I studied them when I left Cumorah's tyranny and became a legal citizen here. Don't worry. I believe in obeying the laws of the land. But I don't have to agree with them or the people who decree them. We have free speech. I am free to express my opinions."

"You are opinionated, for sure."

"As is the biased, so-called free press here. If the *Post* can lie about Yeshurun, then I can tell the truth about the order of Voltaire."

"We all have our own version of the truth. And all this old biblical history you claim to know so much about. What does it have to do with anything modern?"

"God doesn't change. And we are still accountable to Him."

Lipscomb slapped his forehead with the palm of his hand. "You better be careful, young man. You speak like a fanatic. I wouldn't talk about God in public discourse if I were you. It just isn't done. Let me tell you a secret." Lipscomb glanced around furtively. "My boss, Karl Devon, told me a recent poll revealed almost half of the population say God speaks to them personally. Now, isn't that a scary thought?"

Ben smiled. "What are you scared of, Ted?"

"Don't tell me you hear the voice of God, too!"

"Absolutely," Ben said quietly. "God doesn't yell, so if we don't listen, we'll miss it. The prophet Elijah described it as a still, small voice."

266

"Good grief. What does an old prophet like Elijah have to do with modern society?"

"Everything. We owe our heritage to God's law and the prophets. Especially the prophet Mosiah."

"Who on earth was Mosiah?" Lips demanded.

"Mosiah is the father of this country!"

Lipscomb laughed. "In all my social studies, I never heard that one. You claim to know so much about history. Are you sure you don't have your countries mixed up? You must be referring to Cumorah, I'm sure. No. I mean, General Ponte created Cumorah, and Zarahemla was established by Pax Universalis."

"Originally the prophet-king Mosiah established the reign of judges in Zarahemla." Biting back an insult, Ben pressed on with forced patience. "Mosiah was the ancient prophet who taught the people of Zarahemla how to govern themselves," he explained.

"Just one minute!" Lips argued. "You are basing history on prophets. The existence of prophets assumes there is a Bible, and the Bible is a fairy tale. Nowadays, educated people don't buy such poppycock. Only a few radical people still believe in the Bible."

"Are you a member of the Egalitarians, Ted?" Dan cut in.

"I am. Wouldn't be anything else."

"Your insignia is a wolf in sheep's clothing, which comes straight from the Bible!"

"No!" Lipscomb colored. "This can't be true. I won't believe anything so ridiculous."

Dan grinned. "It is pretty bizarre, isn't it?"

"Well, it must be a lie. Probably perpetrated by Yeshurun."

Ben laughed heartily.

Lipscomb frowned. "I don't get what there is to laugh about. Yeshurun has always opposed us, and there is no lie too big for them to use against us."

Ben glanced at Dan and broke into fresh laughter.

Lipscomb glared at Ben. "Obviously this young man does not grasp the seriousness of this matter. After all, people's lives are involved here," he continued haughtily. "You don't care about people. Elidor is a very warm, caring person. There is nothing she wouldn't do for us —"

"Sure. Give up all for carnal security." Dan interrupted, declining an hors d'oeuvres tray. "Keep it up and we'll have neither freedom nor security."

Lipscomb pounded a small table with his fist, rattling the hors d'oeuvres tray. "When there is too much freedom, and personal freedom is being abused, it is time to limit it."

"And who would you have limit our freedom?"

"Those who know what is best for everyone."

"That sounds rather arrogant, doesn't it, Ted?" Dan countered.

"What do you mean?" Lips looked puzzled. "Most people simply don't know what's best for them. They have to be forced to do what's right, but it's for their own good. It's the only compassionate thing to do. It's their only salvation!"

"Is it?" Dan said, softly.

Momentarily disconcerted, Lips paused to empty his glass, and sputtered. "You say such mean-spirited things about our leaders, but our leaders are much more kindhearted than you are. They always use their power to help people."

"'He that thinks absolute power purifies men's blood and corrects the baseness of human nature, need only read history to be convinced to the contrary.' Those, my gullible and well-meaning friend, are the words of John Locke."

Lipscomb's face lacked comprehension. "With all the useless history you drum into this boy's head, he certainly needs to be taught what political agenda is correct. But you have no agenda!" he said.

"I agree with you," Dan replied affably. "I have no agenda. I only speak the truth! The people have the right to know. Isn't this your slogan?"

"Truth is all relative!" Lips said.

"That," Dan said, "is the motto of those who lie for a living."

Lips opened his mouth, but said nothing.

Laughter floated over to them.

"It's my father!" Ben said. "See you around, Ted."

5

"Zephan!" Beth extended her hand. "A pleasure to see you again."

"The honor is mine." Zephan bowed. "To begin with, allow me to present my wife, Sarita. Uh-oh. Here comes Delilah."

"You mean Lady Macbeth," Sarita said.

Delia Matagorda ignored Sarita and sidled up to Zephan, eyeing him openly. The Jershon sun had bronzed his face, making a warm brown contrast to his tumult of white hair. His steel-gray eyes consumed everything. Exile in the wilderness had given him strength unusual for middle age. The lustful Delia, weary of Ponte's velvet tyranny and Haman's flabby petulance, found the power of Zephan's bearing to be irresistible.

"Ms. Ambassador! What an unexpected pleasure! Delia, you know my wife, Sarita. Meet Dan MacRay, journalist, historian, and educator. Dan, meet Delilah Matagorda, the flower of the Ponista desert!" Zephan announced grandly, with a sly grin.

She sighed with mock annoyance. "It's *Delia*, silly, not Delilah!" Tearing her gaze from the handsome Zephan, Delia studied the big journalist's nonconforming apparel, right down to his cowboy boots. "Educator?" she said. "I have been in the education business, myself, for years. Last year, for the Revolutionary Education Award, I was the winning candidate! What do you think of that, Zephan?"

"Hmm? Candidate?" Zephan responded absently. "Candidate for what? Retroactive child sacrifice?" Zephan was amused by his own joke.

"Wherever you were educated," Delia said, "they failed to teach you any manners!"

"Sorry, madame ambassador," Zephan replied. "I was taught truth and justice, however, which momentarily overrode my training in diplomacy. We also learned much from Shakespeare. Right, Sarita?"

"Indeed. 'More needs she the divine than the physician,'" Sarita remarked, quoting Shakespeare.

"'Now does he feel his title
  Hang loose about him, like a giant's robe
  Upon a dwarfish thief.'" Zephan quoted back.

"What are you talking about? Who is Shakespeare?" Delia asked, mystified.

"Shakespeare was a great playwright, and we are talking about Macbeth, who was a powerful king. Isn't Kemen Ponte powerful in Cumorah, like a king?"

"True."

"And you are like Lady Macbeth, the queen."

"I see." Delia looked flattered.

"'What need she fear who knows it," Sarita went on, "when none can call her power to account?'"

"How very interesting." Delia stifled an exaggerated yawn. She caught sight of Mitchell Hunt's solid figure nearing the group and whisked Zephan off to the dance floor.

"Looks like Delia is quite intent on monopolizing Zephan for the rest of the evening," Sarita said.

"I know a designing woman when I see one," MacRay drawled. "Delia could be a trap."

"Zephan calls her 'Delilah' for a reason," Sarita said.

"I think she suspects he is working for us," Hunt said. "Speaking of spies, who is that gent, yonder?" Dan glanced at a man by a far table, talking to an ambassador from the Black Sea Democracies. "Looks like an agent."

"Colonel Kovac from the Black Sea Democracies. Agent of FSB . . . *apparatchik*, you know." Hunt explained. "He's been around for a long time. Zephan's father knew him." He shook his head. "The Benamoz family came here to get away from people like him. He keeps me on my toes. Doesn't say much. Just watches."

"He gives me the creeps," Beth said.

"There is still no satisfaction on the Solano case," Dan said. "I'm flying to Cumorah to ferret out the facts."

"That should be a real fiesta," Hunt said, unsmiling. "Elidor's administration won't let our agents touch it."

"This is why your intrepid reporter is going. Reporters have immunity."

"Don't count on it. Besides, the *Post* will probably fire you."

"No problem. I have an independent publication, now. I don't need them. Besides, Ben can fill my job skillfully. Maybe I'll even give it to him as a belated wedding gift. And he won't have to tear himself away from his lovely bride to do this dirty work."

Hunt grimaced. "I don't know which is more frustrating — the Solano case or the ongoing drug investigation. A couple of my men will want to go with you. We can sure use more answers."

After a time, Zephan gave Hunt a signal to follow as he, Delia, and Oliver Beck left the party.

6

At O.D.'s penthouse door, Zephan looked down into Delia's eyes. She did not stint on her wiles, and her perfume made him dizzy. He felt the evil from this woman who sold herself to enslave others.

He recalled from the book of Joseph an ancient chief judge who sent his servant in disguise to learn secrets from a band of assassins. It was their intention to destroy their brethren, or subject them to bondage. The people's only desire was to defend their lands, their liberty, and their church. But at times one had to be clever, and defend them by stratagem . . .

"What are you thinking, *mi amor*?" Delia's voice was low and provocative.

The danger of her nearness was more than a notion. He could see a stiletto concealed in the bodice of her dress. "What do you think?" Zephan countered mysteriously. With her breath on his neck, he jammed his hands into his pockets to grasp a small apparatus. *Pray for me, my beloved Sarita.* Sarita's gentle face came to mind. *Delia knows the identity of Amalickiah, Solano's assassin. I'm doing this for justice, Sarita . . . for us. Sarita, dear one, pray for me . . .*

"Why don't you come in for a while, Zephan?" Delia murmured.

That's suicide. What does she want from me? "The city lights are truly breathtaking tonight, are they not?" *Better get this over with.* Stroking her hair, Zephan gently engaged a tiny bugging device in the tangles of her thick tresses. Delia's face was upturned, her eyes closed, lips poised for a passionate kiss. He studied her face for a second, praying for the right thing to say . . .

"I think I'm going to be sick," he exclaimed suddenly.

Her eyes flew open. "What is it, darling?"

"I don't know. Maybe it was the punch. But I didn't drink any. Maybe it's the flu. I don't want to expose you! I'll get a cab. Give me a couple of days, and we'll try again. Good night, Delia!"

Zephan turned abruptly, fled down the street and around the corner, where Mitchell Hunt was waiting. He jumped into the car and flipped on his radio. Zephan and Hunt could hear Delia climbing the stairs to Oliver's room, swearing vehemently in Spanish.

7

The romantic element in her assignment foiled, Delia entered the room for a business meeting.

Zephan and Hunt could hear the voices of three or more men, and identified with certainty Oliver D. Beck's nasal tone. Others in the group were recognized as the discussion continued.

Hunt jotted down the names of persons they could discern. He and Zephan stared at each other, aghast at the expansive drug network Delia and her friends were unwittingly exposing.

"Let's get down to business. Hunt and the ZRI know enough to be dangerous. Bad enough if the agents from the Black Sea Democracies get exposed, but if we have one more fiasco, Verman will kill me with his bare hands. Cumeni was a perfect halfway station, until Cabrios was forced to eliminate some of his men to take the blame away from himself."

"I must admit, darling," said Delia, "Señor Verman's State Department did a beautiful job of creating the right image in the press. Why, I even heard some in Zarahemla express admiration for Cabrios, for having the courage to shoot his own men for drug trafficking! 'Fomentio may be a terrorist,' they said, 'but he's got high morals when it comes to drugs!'"

Laughter.

"Better yet, while Cabrios was performing for the world press, Rameses was able to score a telling blow against his old enemy, Yeshurun."

"How?"

"Old Joe Bianco finally died in prison yesterday morning. It's on the records as a severe head injury. Of course, it's not clear whether this injury occurred before he fell or as a result of his falling."

Laughter.

Zephan said nothing, but bowed his head. Hunt sensed his friend's overwhelming grief.

"The drug enforcement agency is clamping down in Sheffa," O.D. was saying, "so we better steer clear of those ports. Someone will assure safe passage for the cargo. Ponte's crowd still has a powerful lobby in the capital."

"For my part, I can't wait to get my hands on Zephan," Delia said.

"And I can't wait to get my hands on you, you little dish!"

"Must be Penlock!" Hunt said.

Penlock's voice was very close to the device.
"Ouch! Cut it out, Ellsworth. Pig! I'm not in the mood!"
Delia grumbled.
"But Delia, darling . . . ", came muffled words on the device.

"Uh-oh!" Hunt whispered. "We've got to split!"

"Come on, Delia! Let down your hair! Hey! . . ." Penlock
gasped. "Delia, you're bugged."
She screamed.

Gradually accelerating to a good clip, Hunt sped down the
empty streets until they reached a safe place to talk. He knew Zephan
had something heavy on his mind.
Zephan's eyes were dark with misery. "I thought the press
would savage Joseba, but I never thought the Egalitarians would go
so far as to have him killed . . . " Mitchell," he said, "I must resign
immediately. I did not ask for this, but I must now turn from my
secular labors and dedicate my life in calling people to repentance."
"But you can't leave me now, Zephan!" Hunt's voice was
almost pleading in its tone. "We need men from Yeshurun, for their
integrity. They are valiant warriors for liberty. I have no one to
replace you."
"The Lord will provide . . . but not Benjamin. He is much
more valuable where he is. The press will try to cover up the truth
about Brother Joseba's death, but Ben will publish it. Presently I
must return to Cumorah. Canosa may be trapped there, and I must
recover valuable family records."
Hunt was aghast. "You can't do this! It is a hot bed of
apostates from your faith. They have even joined with underground
bands of the Tartarus empire! Nowhere will you find more bitter
enemies of Yeshurun. Look what they did to your prophet, God rest
his soul."
"They will know I have renounced my worldly duties. My
mission is solely for the welfare of my family, and for Yeshurun.
There are reasons . . . I only do what I must."

8

Zarahemla
Palace of Chief Judge

Karl Devon, maestro of the mediarchy's daily charades and image-creator of the present Chief Judge, strolled into the opulent office and took a seat by the window. He smirked at Arch, who stood unprofessionally close to his protege, Elidor Redmund.

Archibald Kingerman had made the shallow, vacant little Elidor from a female of no consequence into the most powerful woman in the world. With her dyed blond hair swept into an elegant coiffure, perfect at all times, Elidor deftly drew attention away from her forgettable face. What she lacked in countenance, however, she more than made up for with her adorable figure, ever clad in the latest fashion.

Through his carefully managed public relations, Devon was sure everyone thought Elidor was the most intelligent woman in the country. What the public didn't know wouldn't hurt them.

"Arch," Devon whispered, "you are the envy of every man in the capital. But Elidor is an unusual name . . . is she any relation to —"

Kingerman uttered an obscenity. "Of course not! I may be many things, but I'm not incestuous!"

Arch waved off Devon and peered over Elidor's shoulder as she made last-minute notes before meeting with her advisors.

"Quite a night, wasn't it?" he whispered, blowing in her ear. "Ah, the symbolic consummation of union between Eastern and Western empires!"

Elidor idly traced her penciled check marks and toyed with her bone necklace. Centered on the necklace was a tiny skull, with thin bones hanging on either side resembling the phalanges of some animal. "Different," he murmured. "Where did you get it?"

"Like it?" She giggled. "Got it at a boutique in the Diversity Fair."

"Why, Elidor," Arch teased, "are you sporting parts of endangered species?"

"Of course not! I have a conscience!"

Kingerman's face lit up when Haman slipped unannounced into the room. "Greetings, old friend!" The two men embraced.

Rupert Banberg, financial genius, brushed his usual imaginary dust from his chair and seated himself with care.

Karl Devon stared at State Consul Horace Verman on his left. How much longer could the lid be kept on Verman's extensive drug connections?

Devon chuckled to himself. Well, while the public was mesmerized by some grisly murder trial on television, Verman had been confirmed in the Senate without a hitch, despite blatant evidence of his great risk to national security. In order to maintain most preferred trading status with the Empire, Verman had suppressed intelligence that the Tartarean Empire had nuclear weapons aimed at Zarahemla. Verman had an ability to cut deals with terrorist despots worldwide, but senators were much more tolerant these days. Not so isolationist. Zarahemla citizens didn't care, as long as they were distracted by the continual slaughter and sleaze served up on the evening news by Brackenlaw's networks. You could always count on MBS to say "watch the birdie". It had worked well so far. Globalist policy makers had been given a free hand for decades now, even in upholding quite bloody regimes if necessary, to push forward the cause of Pax Universalis. Karl himself was surprised at the progress made by the Egalitarian ideology.

Nevertheless, Verman's ways were outdated. Too messy.

Karl Devon basked in self-satisfaction. The future belonged to such as himself, a master of deception when occasion required, a guru of human philosophies, a molder of opinions . . .

"Fellow Citizens, the world is shrinking, " Devon quipped. Everyone laughed.

"Reports, please," Elidor began promptly. "Horace?"

"Since subjugation of Cumorah, the remaining nations in the Western Hemisphere are falling in line nicely," Verman said. "Therefore the Zarahemla Republic is now effectively bound to all the proper allies. With the Western Economic League in place, we are moving swiftly toward a single currency, and our convergence plan is right on schedule."

"So the West is now totally compliant with the enumerated liberties set forth by the order of Voltaire," Elidor continued, her face smug with glory in her efficiency.

"Not quite. It seems there are a few stubborn individuals who resist," Devon said.

Haman cleared his throat politely. "I'm afraid I share Karl's concern, Madame."

275

"You must be mistaken, gentlemen." Elidor moved to a nearby computer, rapidly retrieving data to prove her desired results. "Everyone in my jurisdiction has the right to housing, health care, education at all ages, and subscribes to the correct political agenda in every detail. In the name of preserving the environment, my agencies own more land than any other government in the world. All military forces fight under the Pax Universalis flag." She paused, studying the screen, then shook her head. Elidor was very sensitive about her competence. "Just as I promised you during my campaign, all rebels to the international agenda have been subdued. The World Tribunal does not report a single maverick nation."

"The problem is not a nation, but certain people's minds," Devon said in a flat voice.

Elidor turned to Archibald Kingerman, smiling. "This shouldn't be a problem for you, Arch. You are so good at getting people to change their minds."

Kingerman sighed. "Unfortunately, my dear, some people do not respond to, uh, treatment."

"Some!" Haman said. "Might be millions, all over the world. We have been unable to number them."

"Who are they?" Elidor asked, looking alarmed.

"The house of Yeshurun."

"I've been warning you," Rupert Banberg whined. "This planet has too many people. Only those who respect Mother Earth should be privileged to live here. The rebellious ones must be exterminated. Moslems, Buddhists, and especially Yeshurun, have got to go!"

"Banberg, you are a hopeless racist!" Devon said, making no effort to conceal his impatience. "But Yeshurun is not just one race, or even one nation. Centuries ago its people were scattered throughout all nations. Bah! They have no identity to worry about."

"That is the danger!" Banberg wagged a warning finger. "The centerpiece of their religion is to gather their people, you know. And they're gathering, all right, causing nationalistic turmoil.

"Oh, just another church," Elidor said.

"Not just another church, Elidor."

"How are they different?"

"They believe in prophets, and that God talks to them."

"The Bible was discredited years ago. Every child's education has been carefully cleansed of the religious dogma and incorrect political attitudes espoused by their parents. With euthanasia legal at 65 now, this problem will be blotted out soon."

"Not just biblical prophets, Elidor." In his excitement, Haman forgot his formality. "Not just old dead men from a dusty old book. Living, breathing prophets, who say God speaks to them. That's how Yeshurun is different. Do you see why it's so dangerous? These are lunatic ideas."

"You're right, Haman," Banberg chimed in. "At this very moment Yeshurun has those prophets and priests planted in every nation, building up armies and raising the ugly head of fundamentalism. Fundamentalism is a dirty word for planetary survival."

"A military threat, then?" Elidor asked.

"Yes, yes," Banberg said. "I've studied these people, and the more I learn, the more frightened I become. Listen to this. They believe their Christ will come down and lead their armies to overcome the world, which they call Babylon. And this is why we must eradicate them, because they are totally untrainable —— impossible to subdue. But this is the worst part . . . " Banberg lowered his voice for dramatic effect. "They are taught as children to hate Voltaire! It is part of their religion; it is ingrained in their very culture. Don't look at me like that. I know what I'm talking about. I'm talking about the fastest growing religious group —"

"Not just a religion!" Haman's voice had become shrill. "It's a way of life."

"Not easy to blot out this whole culture," Devon said. "Besides, these people believe the land westward is their inheritance!"

Elidor remained unconvinced. "Let's calm down, here. We're getting entirely too excited." Her tone was one of a mother soothing her frightened children. "Everything is under control," she continued. "Private property is illegal. The traditional family is all but gone, and all the prejudices with it."

"Not this family!" Haman said. "Yeshurun still believes in the God of Abraham, and like the old myth, their seed compares to the sands of the sea."

"Why so many?" Elidor asked.

Arch fingered the centerpiece on Elidor's necklace. "Their 'nonpersons' grew to maturity!"

"What do you mean?" Elidor paled. "You mean, all these years this group has opposed the Pax doctrine on the family?"

For a moment no one spoke.

"You can't mean these people were allowed to live in open defiance of . . ." Elidor stopped, her lovely lips parted in amazement and indignation.

"You know what it means, Elidor," Kingerman said quietly. "And trust me, you know the political implications of that meaning."

Bristling, Madame Chief snatched a pencil. "I want names!"

"Zephan Benamoz!" Horace and Arch chorused immediately.

"What Zephan knows could hang us all!" Verman added, his voice cracking.

"The ZRI is virtually infiltrated. Benamoz' demise is only a matter of time." Elidor regained her composure, and her voice became cold, imperiously calm. "Every man has his price. He will sign the Pax Code of Human Rights, and his influence will be nullified."

"We have to catch him, first," Kingerman said. "He's burning all our bridges. He is hot on Miles Potter's trail, he has stopped up all our handy leaks in immigration, and he's going to find Solano's real murderer or die trying."

Haman gave a rare smile.

"Karl," Elidor continued in her best executive's voice, "use your expertise to get inside the minds of this people. Find out what drives them. I want to know what will pierce their armor and crush them once and for all."

Haman leaned over and whispered something to Kingerman.

"Tell them, Haman."

"There is something which Yeshurun has. Something behind their fanaticism . . . it unites them . . . "

"Yes, go on. What is it?"

"A book, a history of their people. They regard it as scripture. It's a rare possession. If that can be destroyed, I think we would see their rapid demise."

"Excellent!" Kingerman said.

"The only way we are going to do it, Elidor," Devon said, "is through an insider in Yeshurun."

All eyes turned to Haman.

"Don't look at me. I'm not one of them. Oh, they tried to throw me out of their membership. My father accused me of dealing in drugs."

"They know?" Verman was on his feet.

"Relax, Horace." Haman was enjoying his importance. "That was a long time ago. I convinced my father I had quit the drug trade so they left me alone. But when I joined the government in

Cumorah, they accused me of supporting groups opposed to the doctrines of Christ, and I was excommunicated. How do you like that for political motivation? I hate Yeshurun, and I'm glad to be out."

"If I can't use your services any more, Haman, I must have someone else on the inside," Devon said. "Who do you suggest?"

Haman considered for a moment. "My brother believes in the order of Voltaire, but I don't think he has been excommunicated from Yeshurun." His face brightened. "Yes! My brother, Leb."

9

Dan MacRay rented an airplane for the trip to Bahia Verde on the Sheffa border, where they would enter Cumorah on their fact-finding mission. Zephan acquired the necessary supplies. Dan contacted Mike Clayton to ensure safe passage on this strictly civilian mission.

An hour before departure time, Dan received a call from the ZRI, requesting permission to send along an operative whom the agency refused to name. Dan was only told the agent would meet them at the airport near the capital.

When the passenger was thirty minutes late, Dan's anxiety grew. Further delay could jeopardize Clayton's carefully laid plans.

Zephan peered out the window. "It's O.D. Beck."

"Of all the . . . " Dan made a gesture of exasperation. But something told him to forbear.

The sun began to slide behind the horizon. Dan brought the aircraft near the water in Bahia Verde, but circled without landing.

"This part of the bay is mined," Beck said. "You'll have to beach her."

"A good thing we brought the amphib," Dan said. "Even so, the beach looks like a postage stamp! Somebody down there in a jeep is signaling us to come in. Must be Mike."

Setting the plane down on the beach, Dan glanced at his watch with chagrin. Forty-five minutes late.

The men battened down the plane and gathered up their gear, but their welcoming committee had disappeared. Where did Mike go?

They sauntered up to the empty jeep. What was going on? Finally, Mike emerged from the dense jungle on the edge of the beach. With a relieved smile, Dan walked up and extended his hand.

To Dan's amazement, Mike's face blanched. Abruptly he turned and retreated into the forest.

"Now what the devil does that mean?" Dan demanded.

Zephan frowned. "Something is wrong. Mike knows me. Beck, do you —" Instantly Zephan was face down on the ground, his hands quickly tied behind him.

Dan, also bound, prayed they wouldn't get their legs broken. Where was Beck? Was he responsible for this?

Before them stood a bearded young man of medium stature and angry countenance.

"Leb!" Zephan said under his breath.

Leb glowered at his captives, but did not acknowledge his father.

Several terrorists frisked the prisoners. On Dan they found a small tape recording device and some cash; on Zephan, nothing.

On O.D. were discovered several grams of cocaine.

"We'll decide in the morning whether you have betrayed us," Leb said.

Like other rural settlements scattered in the foothills of the Hermounts, Frontera had once been a center of bustling trade and exchange of ideas. But after modern highways passed it by, this village was like the nineteenth century revisited. With his hands tied, Dan struggled to keep his balance as the jeep lurched around sharp turns, swerving to miss pedestrians. There were no curbs, so the buildings on either side crowded into the streets, leaving only a narrow passage, and few alternatives for a pedestrian in the path of a speeding vehicle. Homes and businesses were so close together they appeared to be one long building, with the stucco walls painted in various hues. Rays from the sinking sun made the colors more garish than ever.

The jeep came to a halt in an old plaza before a large antiquated municipal building. The three men were taken into a dank and decaying jailhouse and shoved into a small cell with one cot and a slit window. In keeping with the primitive surroundings, chains were clasped about their wrists and ankles. It was a strange sight: men in business suits with chains on. By the light from a single bulb dangling from the ceiling outside the cell, the prisoners managed to push the mattress onto the floor and lie down with their heads on the dirty mat. The close air and oppressive heat made sleep difficult.

At dawn, without explanation, Dan was unshackled, but Zephan remained in chains. Soon a crowd, mostly young people, began to gather in front of the cell. They were backed up into the jailer's office, and they spilled into the plaza.

"Where did they all come from?" Dan asked. "This town doesn't hold this many people." He heard the snort of a bus as it pulled away. "College students."

Zephan nodded. He identified many from Ammonihah. Some had come from Granada.

National administrations came and went, but through it all, students attended their classes in cheerful oblivion. Their world, like a cocoon of trendy doctrines carefully spun for them by their teachers, would swing to and fro in the prevailing winds of the daily political climate. Students were easy prey for *agents provocateurs* from the Anti-Hate Committee, who offered the same solution for everything: blame someone else.

"Do you know why we're here?" one of them asked.

"A hate crime unit for social studies," another replied.

"Actually," a girl said in a shrill voice over the din, " I heard this man is a spy. I've never seen a real spy before. Isn't it exciting?"

The visitors came in a steady stream, spouting whatever "educational concept" they had been spoon-fed the day before. Zephan watched the vacant young faces which filed past him. He had the sensation of seeing into their minds and hearts, and their lives. Some understood well the words they were parroting. Most did not. Some had been taught eternal values by their parents and had willfully chosen rebellion. Some of their parents trusted public opinion-makers more than themselves. Other parents, timid of their peers, and to avoid the dreaded label of "opinionated", failed to pass on family values to their offspring. Most of these youngsters, having been taught nothing at home, entered worldly institutions unprepared, their empty heads a vacuum for idolatry. Sad to see young minds corrupted by default.

"Isn't there someone here to tell us what we should think about this? Cisco! You're the one with all the brains."

A male voice rose above the others. Zephan could not see the speaker at first, but the voice was familiar. "No, Cromwell says we're supposed to take notes and draw our own conclusions."

281

"How?" The girl with the shrill voice had stayed behind to ask questions. "Who is the subject?"

"That's obvious —— the one in chains."

"Oh, my."

"The newspaper said he is some kind of high priest for Yeshurun," said another. "Of course, Yeshurun is outlawed throughout occupied Cumorah now, you know."

"This is why Cromwell says Zephan Benamoz is trying to use a disguise. He is really a spy."

"A spy for Yeshurun," said one with a hollow voice.

"No, my friends, he is a spy for God!" said the one called Cisco. Laughter.

"Remember that other fellow, Joe Bianco?" This was followed by a chorus of loud groans.

"Bianco claimed to speak for God. Some people called him a prophet. Remember?"

"Yeah. Old Bianco tried to run our lives, and said it was God speaking. The newspaper said he died, but it said not to mourn, because he was an enemy, anyway. I for one won't miss him."

"Me, neither. All he ever talked about was good and evil. He was so extreme."

"Yeah, then he proceeded to spell out everything he thought was evil. Bianco told us what not to drink, how not to spend our money, what movies not to see. He even said we should all get married, and then he told us who not to marry!"

"To him, everything was too clear. The old geezer had a pat answer for everything. But it's not so simple."

"He even told us we shouldn't listen to certain kinds of music! So rigid, and narrow-minded."

"Bianco was very blunt, and plain. Not sensitive at all to our feelings. I like someone who can understand us."

"Bianco was intolerant of our lifestyle."

"How rude!"

"I know. I was quite offended."

"Me, too."

"We all were."

"Now, if a real prophet came around, I know I would listen."

"Like Moses?"

"No, of course not. Moses was just a myth. He didn't do all those things some people say he did."

"How about Isaiah?"

"No scholar would accept him. He was no prophet. How could anyone see so far into the future? That's impossible. He was phony."

"A prophet in our day?" said the hollow voice. "I can't imagine it. But have you heard about that new universal religion who elected Ponte as their prophet? "

"They are converting some church pulpits over to the new religion. Ponte uses old Yeshurun chapels for meetings with women Pax volunteers. I think he uses the scriptures for more practical purposes than those old churches."

"Now, Ponte seems more like a prophet whom I would like. I like the way he talks, and he relates to us. Ponte doesn't think he's too good for us. He feels the way we do. Yeah . . . maybe Ponte is a prophet."

"Ponte is so handsome!" said a girl with a breathy voice.

"Some people have already said Ponte is a prophet. He is sure better than Bianco. I couldn't endure listening to that old creature. Why, Bianco was nothing but an old farmer. What did he know? A real prophet of God wouldn't talk like that. So harsh and inflexible. Hateful."

"Nobody liked him."

"Yes, he was very unpopular."

"The whole house of Yeshurun is like that. They are opposed to everything. They see no good in the world. To them, everything is evil."

"Cromwell says it's because they are taught to hate change. Their God does not change, they say, so why should they? So they are unenlightened. Strange people. They love modern conveniences, but they hate modern ideas. Cromwell says Ponte came along just in time."

"Yeah, he saved our economy."

"Better yet, he finally made the Voltaire world view enforceable by law."

"I'm surely glad you can give us all these answers, Cisco," said the shrill voice.

"Of course. This is my field of expertise. We must use every possible means to raise awareness in the modern world. We must stamp out all obstacles to world harmony."

The girl with the breathy voice sighed heavily. "Fortunately Ponte's administration finally banned the Yeshurun culture. They always made me feel so uncomfortable."

"Yeshurun. I *hate* it."

"Me, too." And several students spit in Zephan's face. He wiped the spittle off with his sleeve, but said nothing.

The talkative one finally emerged from the pack. So. It *was* Francisco Mundo — the neighbor boy. He had put on weight. Whatever he was doing these days agreed with him. He looked sleek and well fed. His mother, Maria, never gave up believing Francisco loved her, in his own way. But the boy never listened to her, and reality had not improved his hearing at all.

"Don't you know you are not welcome here?" Francisco was the first to address Zephan directly. He puckered up to spit.

Zephan smiled sadly. "Your mother never treated her neighbors like this. A wonderful woman, Maria is. How is your mother, Francisco?"

The boy blanched. He refrained from spitting, and said no more.

But several others spat upon Dan, too. "If I wanted to stoop to your level, you little punks," he said hotly, "I'd spit right back."

Zephan signaled him to be still.

Like children at a zoo, the visitors noisily tramped outside to lunch on festive foods before going on to the next attraction. But Dan and Zephan were given no food.

Dan was relieved that the few visitors who returned following afternoon siesta did not stay long. He peered at Beck, slumped in a drunken heap in the corner. His siesta seemed to last all day. That Beck fellow had been no help at all. What could Mitchell Hunt have been thinking? And where in the name of thunder was Mike Clayton?

"I do not understand their behavior," Dan said aloud. "Why are they so vehemently against Yeshurun here?"

"This is the part of the tame olive tree which withered away because of pride, Dan," Zephan explained. "Their roots go back to the book of Joseph. They were a branch of Joseph, delivered from Jerusalem by the hand of the Lord. They were a people highly favored of the Lord, even above every other nation, kindred, tongue, and people. All things were made known unto them. They were visited by the Spirit of God, conversed with angels, and were spoken unto by the voice of the Lord. The people had the spirit of prophecy, revelation, and many spiritual gifts. They were saved from famine, sickness, and all manner of diseases; they waxed strong in battle, and

284

were not destroyed. The people were brought out of bondage time after time, and in due time were even taught by the Holy One. The people finally went against the light and knowledge they had received. A couple of centuries ago, when the knowledge was restored, many were leaders in Yeshurun. But once again Ammonihah became exceedingly rich and prideful; they left the church and fought against it, and they passed their hatred on to their children. This has continued into the third and fourth generation, and they are foremost among those today who persecute us. Even more than our worldly enemies, these are the most stiff-necked."

"Why did you come here, Zephan?"

"To find a kinsman. And to preach repentance." Zephan smiled. "A prophet does not always do what is easy. Still, I know in my heart there are a few who can be persuaded to repent. Even one soul is precious in the sight of God."

Dan looked upon Zephan with compassion. This, at the hands of his own son, who was particularly intense in his torment.

At dinner Dan and Zephan were again denied food. It was not so bad for Dan, but Zephan had no excess fat. Yet Zephan did not complain.

10

The second day brought more sophisticated visitors — members of the Anti-Hate Committee, judges, lawyers, and teachers who were the profession of Voltaire. Chief among them was a man in his early thirties. He wore a well-tailored, pin-striped suit, crisp white shirt, and a silk tie. His hair, though thicker than Zephan's, was already gray, and his face had the color and texture of overcooked pasta. "This place is just like all these mountain villages," the man said. "It stinks! It reeks! It's putrid! Vile! This place should be condemned. Destroyed. Burned."

"Hello, Strobe Fenley," Zephan said. "We meet again."

Fenley smiled. "You just can't stay away, can you, Benamoz?"

"We agree on that, at least. I thought you would leave the country and never come back."

"The difference is," Fenley continued, "I am a legal administrator, with authority to prosecute you to the full extent of the law. And your presence here is against the law."

"Not in Cumorah, where the law of Mosiah may hang by a thread, but has not yet been demolished."

"You are under Pax Universalis now," Fenley said. "Cumorah ratified the treaty, remember?"

"I have no official capacity," Zephan replied. "I am here as a servant of God, strictly to minister to the people of Yeshurun who were ravaged by the war."

"Under the Pax treaty, Yeshurun is a nonentity. Banned. Defunct. Eliminated. Nonexistent." Fenley snapped his fingers, apparently enjoying his command of words, and his control over other people. "Do you understand me, Benamoz? You are a *persona non grata*. An outlaw. A criminal."

Zephan said nothing.

Fenley removed a sheaf of papers from his briefcase and began to read aloud. "'The Pax edict orders the security police to arrest and prosecute all persons disseminating printed matter, film, photographic, audio and video material designed to propagate and incite social, racial, ethnic, or religious hatred.'"

"*Religious hatred?*" Dan repeated in amazement.

Zephan laughed.

"Somebody as guilty as you are has no room to laugh," Fenley snapped. "But I can make it easier for us all." His tone became stiff and polite. "We know you are guilty on several counts, but all that can be forgotten. All you have to do is sign this Code of Human Rights. Then we can let you go home, and I can get back to work."

Dazed but wary, Zephan took the document and read it.

By the authority vested in it, PAX UNIVERSALIS hereby establishes a League of Religions. Under it, all citizens will enjoy the following rights:

-FREEDOM OF FAMILY ASSEMBLY: *as defined by the family of nations*

-FREEDOM OF PERSONAL PROPERTY: *No one has the right to use her or his possessions without concern for the needs of society and Earth*

-FREEDOM OF EDUCATION: *Education will be compulsory and available free to all. Each graduating child will possess a fully developed personality, respect for the principles enshrined in the charter of Pax Universalis.*

-FREEDOM OF RELIGION: *Everyone shall have the right to freedom of thought, conscience and religion. This right shall include freedom to have a religion or whatever belief of his choice, and freedom, either individually or in community with others and in public or private, to manifest his religion or belief in worship, observance, practice and teaching.*

Zephan shook his head and handed the paper and pen back to Fenley. His hand was trembling. He sat on the cot.

"Get them some water!" Beck shouted suddenly from the corner. "Can't you see they're starving to death?"

Without a word, Fenley walked away deliberately and returned with two glasses of water.

"Thank you." Zephan took the glass and drank.

"How about it?" Fenley tried to press the pen and document into Zephan's hands.

"No," he said simply. "That is all."

Fenley returned several times during the day with his group, always with the same demand. A teacher expounded on the benefits of the Code of Human Rights. A psychiatrist analyzed Zephan; he soothed, cajoled, theorized, hypothesized. A world expert on creeds was called in, and systematically debunked every religion known to man, except the new universal ethic.

A judge threatened him: "You know what happened to Bianco. Knowing this, would you dare to preach again in this land?"

But Zephan answered them nothing.

At sundown Fenley returned one last time, alone. "What do you have against the Code of Human Rights? You who would fight for religious liberty. Are you so stubborn you don't even want freedom? Why do you not answer all those fine people? Now they are all angry. Do you know why they are angry? Because in the past you have plainly spoken against them, and against our administration. From the very start you have found fault with our laws. There is no such thing as an evil law, Benamoz. All our laws are enacted for the good of mankind. The only evil is your criticism of society, which you expound in terms all too plain. You call our cultural practices evil. People don't like to be called immoral. They don't like somebody like you telling them what is sin and what isn't. Your idea of sin is irrelevant to our society. A sin is a personal matter, and it is evil to speak about those things so plainly. It is embarrassing and offensive. It is unkind, and as of July of '79, it is illegal. Don't you know I have power to deliver you up to the world court? Ponte wants every last remnant of Yeshurun driven out, and he has the world power to back him in it."

"This is because we teach truth, and we are effective," Dan said.

Fenley ignored him. "Ponte alleges you are subverting our government. He says you are moles. Spies! But I will give you one last chance. You can still retract all your words. I demand you speak immediately. This instant! Now! Without further delay!"

Zephan said nothing.

"You have spent my patience, you stubborn old fool. As far as I'm concerned, you can stay in this jail indefinitely. I hope you rot! Decay! Dissipate! Disappear!" Fenley yanked up his briefcase and stalked out.

Dan watched him go, then turned to Zephan, but he was embarrassed to put his thoughts into words.

"What's on your mind?" Zephan asked.

"Well, uh." Dan gulped. "To tell you the truth, Zephan, I, uh, . . . didn't see anything wrong with that freedom of religion clause in the document."

"It is the height of arrogance."

"But why?"

"Who do these Pax Universalis king-men think they are, anyway? A light unto the world? They presume to dictate what religious freedom shall include. Freedom of worship is an inalienable right endowed upon us by our Creator. To presume to grant or deny this right is to mock God."

Dan gave a low whistle. "Now I understand. But why didn't you say this to Fenley?"

Zephan sighed. "You know Fenley. His mind is made up. What would I accomplish by contending with him? The entire document is wrought by designing men who seek the overthrow of all nations. It is unworthy of debate. We stand unalterably opposed to its purpose. There can be no compromise with such doctrines."

That evening, Dan and Zephan each were given water, but they were to receive no food until Zephan signed the document. Everyone had gone but Leb, and Beck was finishing his evening meal outside the cell. Beck must have struck a deal, because he received food, but he looked sickly.

"Benamoz doesn't look like a prophet," Beck said to Leb.

"Aw, underneath those street clothes, he's dressed like a prophet," Leb said. "In the Bible, the Jews used circumcision for some kind of covenant. Well, Yeshurun no longer stresses that, but they still have covenants. Can you imagine, in this day and age, promising to do everything God tells them to do? God even tells them how to dress. They are not allowed to wear expensive clothes, because somebody might end up looking better than somebody else."

"Really?" Beck was curious.

"Yeah. They act as if they wear the armor of God or something." Leb laughed. "Get this, Beck. All you have to do is keep clean and evil will stay away from you!"

Beck laughed.

"As if their faith could protect them from harm. How's that for a fairy tale?" Leb laughed again, more loudly. "Hey! Want to see something? Stand by, Beck. You are about to see the dismantling of a prophet."

Dan gasped.

"I warn you, your heart is as black as that beard of yours," Zephan said quietly. "If you lay a hand on us, and defile that which is sacred, you will incur the wrath of God. You know better, Leb."

"Okay, okay." Leb backed away suddenly. "I was just joking."

"It is not a joking matter. "

"Touchy! My father is really very modest," he said to Beck. "But I think they do it to keep their women modest. Yeshurun men are very selfish about their women. I could bet you ten *onties* of silver you would never find a Yeshurun woman who is scantily dressed."

"The bet is on," Beck said. "I could use the money."

"Nah," Leb said idly. "Hey, speaking of money . . . " He whispered something to Beck, who nodded.

At night came extra guards, who soon fell to drinking, laughing, and talking among themselves. They bragged about their exploits as soldiers. The soldiers had been in many areas in the world, crushing rebellions, herding refugees, fighting, killing, plundering, rampaging, taking prisoners. If the Pax forces had brought peace anywhere, or done anything praiseworthy, they did not speak of it that night. The men seemed bent upon surpassing one another's tales of murder, rapine, torture, and mutilation. The guards began to compare the physical characteristics in different races of women and children upon whom they had visited their vile acts of terror and perversion.

Dan lay on his back staring at the ugly light bulb hanging from the ceiling. He was disgusted, shocked, and horrified. He wanted to rip into those guards, but restrained himself. Next to him, he knew Zephan was awake, probably thinking about another prophet, in an earlier era, who had been in a similar situation.

Suddenly Zephan rose to his feet and thundered, "Silence! You fiends of the eternal pit! I rebuke you in the name of Jesus Christ. Be still! I will not endure such language. Cease such talk, or you or I die this instant!"

He ceased to speak and stood tall, in terrible magnificence, chained, without a weapon, calm, unruffled.

The guards begged for pardon and quailed before him as if they were seeing the avenging angel. Their weapons clattered to the floor, and they shrank back, crouching and trembling in silence until the change of guards.

"Criminy, Father, you don't have to get so emotional." Leb hurried from the room.

Oliver David Beck said nothing, but his mouth hung open and he remained stunned and blinking for a long time.

Dan felt transported back to an oft read account of an earlier servant of God, who had also censured such vile behavior. Dan shuddered. It was like a *déjà vu* ——— as if he were reliving history.

Now and then, nobility and courage would stand out like an anomaly in the patterns of evil which repeated consistently with every generation. Powers and principalities, empires, and princes of darkness, could determine the fate of kingdoms with the flourish of a pen or the push of a button. But he, Dan MacRay, had been permitted to see a prophet's dignity and majesty: in chains, at midnight, in a dungeon, in this obscure village.

11

Early in the third day, Dan looked out the narrow window over the main street. Centered in the plaza was a ceiba tree typical to this region. In the jungle it reached heights nearing two hundred feet. In these parts the natives accorded a sacred nature to the tree, for it was reminiscent of a "tree of life" symbol found widely in native folklore. The tree was laden with large white flowers representing the premortal stage of the soul in its journey toward heaven. Dan marveled at this land of contrasts: ethereal beauty and ugly realities.

A few hundred people had gathered near the tree, as if anticipating some special event, and they seemed in a festive mood.

Zephan's chains were removed, and the prisoners were led from the quarters into the plaza. Off to the side, Strobe Fenley sat at a table selling tickets. A microphone and speakers had been set up on the old courthouse steps, apparently to announce a prize. Fenley had collected large sums —— not just paper money, but *amnors* and *ezroms* of pure silver, the old Cumorah money. It looked like a raffle, or a lottery. Zephan laughed out loud. Fenley averted his eyes.

Finally, upon Fenley's urging, Beck moved forward carrying a small bag and jingling the coins within it. He took the microphone and addressed the crowd. "Ladies and gentlemen, standing before you is Zephan Benamoz, who some have called a prophet of God. He claims God talks to him, and he believes in visions and angels. Yet he thinks God doesn't want him to sign the Code of Human Rights. Can you imagine? God being against a universal ethic?"

People began whistling and catcalling.

"Benamoz is an impostor!" someone said. "I knew it. They told me he would be a fake."

"God doesn't speak. Otherwise, why don't we hear him?"

Suddenly the microphone hummed at a high pitch, and everyone stopped. Beck seized the moment to regain control of the fickle crowd. He rattled the coins so all could hear, and the sound of money seemed to calm them. "Zephan Benamoz," he said, "here we have six *onties* of silver, and everything in Fenley's coffers over there. It amounts to one tenth of the silver treasury in the entire province. We will drop the charges, grant you freedom, and all this is yours, Mr. Benamoz, if you will do one small thing."

With those words, everyone was quiet.

"I repeat, all this is yours, if you will sign the Code of Human Rights and give the universal ethic your blessing."

"Oliver David Beck, I know what is in your heart, and you are lying! You are pandering to this wicked and perverse generation. You are conniving with these lawyers and hypocrites; laying traps and snares to catch the holy ones of God. At this moment your only desire is to make me go against all I believe and deny the true and living God. After you have destroyed me, you will give the money to one of them." Zephan gestured toward the crowd.

291

The people began to shout again.

"I don't believe him!"

"He is a fraud, not a prophet! He will defraud us!"

"Show us an angel!"

"The man is insane!"

"Stone him!"

A stone hit Zephan solidly beneath the left eye.

Dan spotted the perpetrator.

"Maybe that will improve your visions!" The speaker was a small but cocky young man in a business suit. There was laughter, but all at once Dan MacRay held the young man by the collar. "Fenley!" he said in his booming voice. "Arrest this man! He's guilty of a hate crime."

Fenley froze in confusion. This was not turning out as planned. He nodded at two guards, who closed in on Dan, but were no match for the big man, who, having grasped the young man's tie, flung him down on the top step. Grabbing one guard by the hair, and the other by the ear, he dragged them up the steps. "Now sit down and listen!" He commanded them, and they obeyed, sitting on the steps in a row like naughty school boys on detention. Dan ripped the pocket off the young man's white shirt and used it to blot Zephan's bleeding face. "We would be pleased to hear from you now, Brother Zephan."

Zephan turned to the wonder struck Beck.

"Why don't you just give them back their money? It's money they want, isn't it, Beck? These people are here for a lottery. This was Leb's idea, wasn't it?"

"Where's Leb?" Fenley bellowed, and weaved his way nervously past the confused onlookers, but Beck would not relinquish the microphone.

Zephan continued speaking directly to Beck. "Not only have you lied to me, Beck, but you have lied to God. He knows your thoughts, and by the power of his Spirit, I can perceive your thoughts. You have a subtle plan to deceive these people and set them against a prophet of God. Do you think these people care whether I believe in God? All they want is money."

"You are right," Beck said softly. "I have wronged you greatly. I hope someday you can forgive me." Then he raised his nasal voice and spoke into the microphone with uncharacteristic firmness. "These two gentlemen are the only honest men here. They are held under false —"

"Ladies and gentlemen, may I have your attention?" At last Fenley wrested the microphone from Beck and set the guards upon the prisoners.

"As administrator, it has become necessary for me to cancel this discussion." Fenley tried to keep his voice calm. "An, uh . . . educational debate was scheduled, but the subject you have raised has not been approved for a public forum. It is far too controversial. This is an issue of Yeshurun, a culture which is no longer legal in Cumorah. These men are outlaws, and have somehow found their way over our boundaries. They are guilty of hate, and the Anti-Hate Committee has been looking all over for them. Please make way. You can see these men are dangerously unstable."

"Hey! That one looks like Dan MacRay!" somebody yelled.

"Oh, you must be mistaken," Fenley said quickly. "What would he be doing here? Ladies and gentlemen, please relax," Fenley said. "Everything is under control. Now, if I can just have your attention, we will proceed with the drawing for the lottery. . . "

Dan and Zephan were returned to the jail and handcuffed. Beck did not return until long after dark, and he had been severely beaten. He managed a wan smile in spite of his profuse perspiration and convulsive shaking.

His addiction. "Guard!" Dan yelled. "We have a very sick man here! Get a doctor!"

The guard turned abruptly and walked out, and an uneasy peace settled over the three weary men.

And Zephan filled the silent dungeon with song.

"Faith of our fathers, living still,
In spite of dungeon, fire and sword.

"Faith of our fathers, we will strive
To win all nations unto thee,
And thru the truth that comes from God,
Mankind shall then be truly free.

"Faith of our fathers, we will love
Both friend and foe in all our strife,
And preach thee, too, as love knows how,
By kindly words and virtuous life.

"Faith of our fathers, holy faith,
We will be true to thee till death!"

Dan added his rich base to Zephan's resonant baritone.

"Redeemer of Israel,
Our only delight,
On whom for a blessing we call,
Our shadow by day and our pillar by night,
Our King, our Deliv'rer, our all!

"How long we have wandered as strangers in sin,
And cried in the desert for thee!
Our foes have rejoiced when our sorrows they've seen,
But Israel will shortly be free."

A door screeched somewhere, and footsteps announced the guard had returned. But he brought no doctor, and he hung back in the darkness.

"I know he's hovering behind the wall, listening," Zephan whispered. "Let's not disappoint him." They sang with greater power than before.

"The Spirit of God like a fire is burning!
The visions and blessings of old are returning,
And angels are coming to visit the earth.

"How blessed the day when the lamb and the lion
Shall lie down together without any ire,
And Ephraim be crowned with his blessing in Zion,
As Jesus descends with his chariot of fire!

"We'll sing and we'll shout with the armies of heaven,
Hosanna, hosanna to God and the Lamb!
Let glory to them in the highest be given,
Henceforth and forever,
Amen and amen!"

The prisoners were not disturbed for the rest of the night.

12

It was still dark when Beck awakened Dan and Zephan. "They're moving us," he whispered. "This may be our chance." Hastily he dug from his pockets pieces of bread he had saved from his last meal, and gave them to his companions.

Blindfolded, they were shoved into a jeep. Two men in the front seat were speaking rapidly in Spanish.

"What are they saying?" Dan whispered.

"I'm not sure," Zephan replied. "The Cumenite accent is so fast it's hard to make it out. Heard something about an island called Calaveras."

The jeep stopped, blindfolds were removed, and Dan saw that Beck was also a prisoner. Through the darkness they could scarcely see to board a small motor launch which headed for an island across the bay.

Large clouds veiled the moon, dimming its light. The prisoners picked their way through human bones which looked to be deliberately arranged on the beach.

Dan and Zephan exchanged a look of disgust.

"*Los nativos* eat some hostages!" The driver, a lean Mulekite, jerked his thumb toward the skeletons.

Dan marveled as he and his companions stumbled at gun point through the dark woods. What had gone wrong? Had Mike Clayton turned? Hard to believe. Must be some explanation. But would he, Dan MacRay, nationally-known journalist, be dead before he found out the truth? How could Mitchell Hunt have made such a ghastly mistake? Was Beck such a traitor that his presence had doomed them all? He glanced at Beck, who said nothing.

Dan shuddered. Was it to end like this?

They climbed up a steep hill and arrived at a clearing in some deserted barracks. A monstrous light glared down upon them.

The night seemed unending. It was still dark when Dan was again blindfolded, taken outside, and shoved into a waiting helicopter. Beck tumbled in beside him. Zephan was left behind on the island.

Snatches of dialogue between Leb and the pilot were in reference to the sick man.

"Whoever you are," Dan yelled in English over the engine, "I am a member of the press, and my friend Zephan is a harmless pastor. What have you done with him?"

"We get big money for the especially nosy ones, like you, MacRay," the pilot said in heavily accented English. "As for your friend, he costs us more money every minute he's alive!"

The pilot laughed.

When the pilot's companion opened a door of the craft, a thunderous rumble of water could be heard below.

"Want to swim?" asked the pilot.

Dan shivered as he felt a rush of cold air. He was closest to the door. He was worth more alive, but what would they do with Zephan?

Blindfolded, his hands locked behind his back, Dan hadn't a prayer of survival. No way to reach out and grab onto something. He would fall through the air like a sack of cement. Frantically he tried to work his hands loose. This was all so unbelievable. Despite horrible experiences in the past, never had he experienced such terror as at this moment. All he could do was pray the end for all of them would be swift.

Something did come to pass swiftly. Dan felt himself shoved hard, but he hit the ground immediately, landing on his side.

"Roll!" yelled the pilot.

Dan rolled away from the water sounds and heard Beck land nearby. Then the sound of the chopper diminished until it was gone.

Again Dan moved away from the river and cried out when he started rolling down a steep decline, but seemed to hit the bottom of a ravine. He rubbed his head on the ground and managed to slip off the blindfold.

Minutes later, or was it hours? Above the roaring river another sound surfaced. Was the same helicopter returning? No. A reluctant dawn revealed a chopper bearing the PAX insignia, hovering low, spraying bullets. Lingering semi-darkness offered only partial protection.

O.D. was hit. The order of Voltaire, shooting at one of their own?

After one round, the chopper headed for a clump of trees, where it opened fire on a flock of sheep before disappearing.

Dan shook his head vigorously as if to awaken from a nightmare. *Pure insanity! Am I dead or alive?*

13

Bahia Verde
Resistance Headquarters

On the scratched and worn desk before him, Ben studied his
inventory of weapons and supplies. Those would improve after the
raid. He pulled out a nautical chart and spread it before his associates.

"See, in Bahia Verde, just over the hill from here, there is a
narrow strip of land jutting out." He pointed with a stubby pencil.
"Just offshore a few miles is this tiny island called *Las Calaveras*. The
island is in Sheffa waters, but the Ponistas have set up a Cumeni-style
terrorist training camp there. We have word on prisoners of war
being detained there. If the hostages are still alive, we will find them
there."

Ben sized up his troops. Squanto, the native of Mulek who had
rescued Ben from the river, had arrived quickly upon hearing about
Zephan's capture. A magnificent warrior, Squanto could do anything.
Pensado, immense in stature, commanded everyone's respect.
Whatever inadequacies Pensado had, he compensated with heart,
courage, and sheer strength. The remaining men trusted those two
implicitly.

Then there were the hostages. Dan MacRay could draw a huge
ransom, but Zephan they wanted out of the way. Poor Papa. His life
was usually in mortal peril. He was a good man. Why did other men
hate him so?

With fierce determination Ben focused on the task at hand. "So
here is our plan. The skeleton tower we have constructed will pass
for a lighthouse at night. Our intelligence informs us that tonight the
Ponistas are expecting a small vessel from Antionum, loaded with
arms and ammunition sent by the Central Committee."

Murmurs of disbelief arose from the troops.

"I know, men. Those terrorists have too much help," Ben said.
"Their vessel will be steering for the island, whose light is timed for
one flash every ninety seconds. First, we place our little makeshift
lighthouse up on our sandbar after dark. Their ship is due at 4:40 in
the morning. We must strike swiftly before they make a decision on
the hostages. As soon as the ship is sighted, I will take a small band of
men on the island and overtake the lighthouse guards. They'll douse
the lights and we'll fire up ours. The ship will be guided to our light,

and before that little ship knows what happens, she'll sail right into our hands! Then, we move in and take the island."

"Do you intend to use *that* as part of your weaponry?" Squanto asked.

Hanging on the cabin wall was an enormous sword.

"The sword of Laban." Ben unsheathed the weapon and held it, studying the inscription with reverential awe. "My brother made several of these replicas, just like the ones my father told you about. Might come in handy."

14

Overcast but calm, the night was perfect. Inspecting the troops, Ben found them prepared to overtake the Antionite vessel and proceed to the island of Calaveras. All was ready. Time for a last minute conference with his men.

"They will outnumber us four to one. Be mindful these men are hardened, highly trained, ruthless killers. You are fully authorized to defend yourselves and do what is necessary for victory."

The men nodded.

"We must take out the guards in total silence. Squanto, take the ship quickly and land at the island. Our weapon supply is meager, and we need the enemy's equipment. Only a small detachment of their men will be assigned to unload the weapons. We will fan out into the trees and bring any and all prisoners to the clearing, or training area, here." He made a mark on the map. "Once we have Miles Potter in custody, we will compel him to talk. Now, if there is no further discussion, we will report to the High Command."

Everyone knelt while Ben offered a humble prayer.

15

Squanto and his men brought in the ship expertly to find the lighthouse alarm dismantled, with the guards bound and gagged. As expected, the cargo detail consisted of only a few men who were quickly overpowered. Squanto's band immediately advanced on the island. Pensado, the giant lieutenant, was sent with a team to capture

Potter while Ben took two men to search for the hostages. Squanto secured the island and gathered his little band at a dimly lit training area near the main headquarters. But Pensado came empty-handed. Miles Potter was not in his quarters.

Squanto inspected the soldiers with satisfaction. The great supply of sophisticated weapons they had captured made him feel secure. All the terrorists had been surprised in their sleep, disarmed, and bound. All, that is, except Potter. Now, as soon as Ben arrived . . .

"Drop those weapons, or I shoot these prisoners!" As weapons dropped to the turf, a terrorist sneered in Squanto's face.

Must be Miles Potter. Squanto silently cursed their failure to apprehend this murderous leader.

"Missing a few men?" Potter snapped. "Now your men, not mine, are bound and gagged down on the ship." Potter laughed raucously. "Such a pity. The Resistance should have sent a man instead of a fool to do this job!"

Potter held a white-haired man in front of him, pointing an automatic at the prisoner's temple. Zephan! Squanto saw a warning in his friend's eyes and averted his gaze.

The other prisoner was aged, stooped and emaciated. Squanto hoped to God Dan was also alive somewhere. Potter's comrade stood ready to fire on Squanto's band.

The Mulekite broke into a sweat and tried desperately to stall. Where was Ben?

"What have you to do with these poor prisoners, sir?" Squanto's eyes searched the darkness behind his foe. "We have only come to retrieve our people."

"People are our business!" the terrorist said. "Do you think I would give up political prisoners? You — "

Behind him, his companion grunted. The terrorist turned his head, but felt an excruciating pain in his gun arm; the weapon dropped from his grip like a hot rock. His feet were knocked from beneath him. Suddenly he lay flat on his back, pinned beneath a heavy boot. He gazed up at a sword point held to his throat. Ben!

Ben stiffened. He had severely injured, not Potter, but Leb. "My own brother! Give yourself up, Leb. As much as I despise you, I wouldn't kill you, as you would your own father. Unlike you, I do not delight in bloodshed."

Leb gaped, speechless. His arm. No feeling. Was it there? He felt strangely unwhole. A warm wetness soaked his right side.

"Do you know who this poor old man is? Our own Grandfather Canosa!" Ben said.

"Grandpa Canosa?" Leb whimpered. "I didn't know . . . I did not recognize him."

"Small wonder!" Ben hissed the words through clenched teeth. "The way you and your ilk have treated him. And Papa! How could you do this to our own father? Innocent men, Leb! What have you become? Are you past feeling?"

Like an electric pulse the rebuke ripped open a shell of bravado and withered Leb's arrogance to the core.

"Where is Dan?" Ben pressed the blade persuasively.

Ben. That sword. It pricked poisoned recesses in Leb's memory, releasing unspeakable fear, a horror of torment beyond boundaries of death. "Anything!" he shrieked. "I'll tell you where he is."

16

Dan MacRay awoke with a bad headache. Above him, long fingers of sunlight reached through an olive tree to poke gleaming rays into his eyes. Except for the river's incessant grumble below, only the hum of a locust throbbed with the increasing heat.

Plik. Plok. He began pounding his light steel chains against a sharp rock. "Can you move?" he said to Beck. "We must get out of here. They will be back."

"You're right!"

Dan started violently. The voice had come from the ravine. "Mike!"

Mike Clayton raised his head cautiously above a boulder. "Come!" he said, quickly removing their handcuffs. "We'll get him to the hospital across the border. I have horses."

"What in tarnation happened back there?" Dan helped Mike get the wounded man onto a horse.

Clayton frowned. "Hunt blundered. By the time you arrived, Ponte's men were here. I didn't dare let on I know you. Almost cost our lives. No bureaucracy deserves the name of intelligence," he said with a wry look.

"They knew we were coming?"

Mike nodded. "Beck had a rendezvous."

Dan gasped. "Beck is — "

"Not what you think," Mike went on. "He got addicted during the war, but is working for us. He's all we've got. At least what's left of him." Clayton shook his head. "Beck's been through a lot. Hope he lasts till we bust this cartel. Now the other side suspects me, but they still think he's one of them. One narco-terrorist camp is on Skulls Island."

"Speaking of skulls . . . "

Clayton scowled. "Cursed terrorists have no respect for the living nor the dead. Those are remains of a nineteenth century shipwreck on rocks lying seaward of the island. They dug up the bones to use for some occult rites."

Dan reined in to guide the horse carrying the semiconscious Beck. "The global empire would gun down their own man?"

"One drug addict means nothing to them. The empire was actually gunning for its enemies, among whom you are now the most famous, Dan."

"I'm surprised Leb isn't back already."

"With a dangerous cliff on one side and impossible mountains on the other, he probably figured you wouldn't get far," Mike said. "Besides, last night Ben raided that camp. With luck Leb may be behind bars soon."

By the time they neared Zephan's old cabin in the Jershon wilderness, Beck's condition had become precarious. High fever had pushed him to the edge of delirium.

There in the tiny clearing they found Ben, Canosa and Zephan.

"Zephan!" Beck cried out in a hoarse voice. "Are you a ghost?"

Zephan laughed. "No, Beck. Ben rescued me."

"I think I know what hell is like," Beck said. "You were innocent, and I was wrong. You could have been killed, and it would have been my fault." Tears coursed down his face. "I hate myself for what I did to you back there in Frontera. But you are alive. I've never been so happy in my life." He broke down and sobbed. "What is the matter with me? A grown man, and I am blubbering like a baby."

"It is the Spirit, pricking your heart," Dan said gently.

"This man needs a blessing." Zephan reached under his shirt, pulled out a tiny flask of golden liquid, and grinned triumphantly. "They didn't find my consecrated olive oil."

Taking the sick man by the hand, Zephan said, "Oliver David Beck, do you believe in the power of Christ?"

"I did when I was younger, Zephan. When I came home after my POW days in Cumeni, I was a wreck. But I married the love of my life, and had a precious little boy. When they were killed by a drunk driver, I never got over it, and I blamed God. Yesterday, in reviling you, I was lashing out against God. But when you spoke, I knew your words were true, and I had always believed it."

"If you believe in the redemption of Christ, you can be healed."

Beck nodded hesitantly. "Yes, I'm certain I have a little . . . faith."

"It is enough."

Zephan and Dan laid their hands upon Oliver's head, blessed and prayed for him, and he fell asleep on the cot.

The others sat on the porch to make plans. "The time finally came when my two sons faced each other," Zephan said. "I'm grateful you prevailed, Ben."

"Leb wouldn't agree with you," Ben said wryly.

"Nor will the cartel," Clayton added.

Again Zephan embraced his beloved kinsman. "Such a blessing to have you back, Jaime." He looked at Clayton with sudden pain in his eyes. "Does he know?"

Clayton nodded slowly.

"My Aurelia is gone," Canosa said dully. "Cancer. And it hasn't been very long, has it?"

"How can we help you, *hermano*?" Zephan's voice was filled with compassion.

"It can't be helped. I will return to ZRI. What else can I do? And what have I got to lose?"

"We have already won a great battle, thanks to you," Clayton said.

Canosa laughed without mirth. "Watch me. I'm not through yet. In fact, I've only begun to fight."

Clayton pursed his lips. "Mr. MacRay's capture has caused a huge uproar in the world press. The land will be crawling with jumpy revolutionaries and confused Pax troops. Right now we need to reach Mitch and let him know you three are alive."

They all turned as Beck opened the cabin door and walked out, smiling. "I'm a new man, in more ways than one."

"I shouldn't be surprised," Dan said. "But every time things like this happen, I am amazed. Your cuts and bruises from the beating are gone. No more black eye, no more welts."

Clayton stared. "I thought you were a goner, Beck. How is the bullet wound?"

"Much better. But I'll have a scar as a souvenir." Beck grinned. "I actually hope they will give me a sling or a cast at the hospital. I can use the evidence against those buzzards for shooting at defenseless people."

"The fever's gone?"

"Every whit. When I woke up, I practically leaped out of bed. I've never felt better, especially my soul." He turned a serious face to Zephan, and knelt at his feet. "You really are a prophet of God, Zephan. Back there when I was so hateful, you read my mind. Then you healed me. You healed me! How can I ever thank you?"

"David, *mi hermano*. It was not I. My son Ben holds the same power to act in God's name as I do, and Dan and Canosa, as well. Some day you can do as we have done, if you repent, obey, and keep yourself worthy." Zephan smiled with obvious embarrassment. He stood, drawing the young man to his feet. "Don't thank me, but your Father in Heaven. It is He who delivered you. I am but his humble servant."

Beck experienced an unfamiliar feeling. The prophet had called him "brother". He was no longer "O.D.", the piece of human wreckage. He was a child of God, a soul of great worth to his Father in Heaven.

17

True to Hunt's prediction, the *Zarahemla Post* fired Dan immediately upon his return. Ben helped him clean out his desk.

"I am truly sorry this happened, Dan."

Dan smiled. "Not a problem. If a man is measured by the enemies he makes, I shall wear this as a badge of honor." He tossed several rough drafts into the waste basket, then, brushing the dust from his hands, he turned a serious face to his young friend. "The real pity is that my investigation failed. My mission has been thwarted."

"Your profile is too high. Let me go."

"Ha! And get you fired, too."

Ben shrugged. "With all due gratitude, Dan, I can't seem to accustom myself to a desk job. At least not as long as the Solano murder goes unsolved. I never figured on being an investigative reporter, but no one else is doing it, and I simply cannot leave the truth buried. Will you help me fund the effort?"

"Why, sure, son! Well, I'll be . . . Your family doesn't lack for guts, does it? " Dan stroked his chin. "Hey! Wait a minute! This is just too dangerous!"

"Look. This is not an impulse. I have it all thought out, but I must act quickly while the world is still focused on the hostage episode. I have numerous covert contacts on the Jershon and Sheffa side of Bahia Verde, but I am almost unknown in the public eye. I grew up in Cumorah, and know the land. I can be in and out of there within twenty-four hours."

Dan still looked skeptical.

"Leb is out of the way."

"Yes, Ben, but Haman is a devil."

"I know him well, and I won't take any chances, believe me. My father and I know how to deal with him. I will meet my father, and we will come back together, to ensure our safety."

"Your father is going back again, so soon? That's suicide."

"Oh, not to Cumorah, sir. My father is brave, but not stupid. He is going to Sheffa and other border areas for a regional conference and to instruct missionaries like my brother. Then on to Antionum for another mission conference. The Antionites are a stiff-necked people as well, but they're not due to fall under the Pax yoke for a few more years. Papa wants to strengthen our people in that area."

"Does he have any protection?"

"The very best. Mitchell Hunt won't let anything happen to him. Besides, he has diplomatic immunity, because he is a religious representative, not a political official."

Dan frowned. "I hope you're right. And how does your wife feel about you going to hell again?"

Ben laughed. "You mean, to hell *and back*, sir. She's not happy, of course. But she feels more strongly than I do about Solano. He was like a father to her. Somehow, we owe it to his memory to do what we can. Besides, when she prays, she calls down the angels to protect me. You can't beat faith like that."

"I see I can't stop you." Dan engulfed the young man in a huge bear hug. "You just see to it you don't become a memory, too. And by all means, come back to that angel wife of yours."

"Thanks, big guy. I'll be back before you know it. You have my word on it."

18

Dalton Mortfield replaced the telephone receiver with trembling hands. Kingerman wanted to see him, immediately, and it sounded ominous.

But Mortfield hadn't told anyone, except Mitchell Hunt and Zephan Benamoz. Benamoz was no longer with the agency, but he was bound by law not to disclose classified information. Hunt said Zephan was a prudent man.

Mortfield had swept his house for bugs, in case he talked in his sleep, which he was certain was not his habit. As far as his liaison with Kingerman and company was concerned, nothing had changed. He had been scrupulously precise about that. Once he had seen nothing could be done for Solano, he had kept silent, for his own safety. How could they possibly know? The answer was obvious. There were moles in ZRI, just like he had made himself a mole in the Kingerman ranks.

Mortfield sat still for a long time, collecting his thoughts, then finally resigned himself. He had known from the start the magnitude of danger in this game he was playing. And he had lost. It was very simple. So he would face it like a man, and die like a soldier. It would have been smarter to have stayed a soldier, rather than listening to that little voice in his mind. Still, one had to be true to himself. Good grief. This was starting to sound like Shakespeare. And why not? If he was going to die, he might as well do it in style.

Now calm and deliberate, he took out a piece of paper, wrote a short note to Mitchell Hunt, and affixed his usual precise signature.

Mitch,

I have been summoned to Kingerman's office. I suspect he knows everything. If this is the case, God only knows, and perhaps you know, who betrayed my trust. If I am found dead, regardless of the coroner's report, this is to inform you it was not by my own hand.

He dated it and sealed it into the special pouch, along with other files he had been holding until he could safely deliver the whole package

305

with all the answers. On the way to Arch's office he left his package in the prearranged drop box, and noted with mild irony that his appointment with death corresponded to the proper drop time.

He had left Mitch nothing for weeks. Well, they would be surprised this time. That the packet was too little too late left him feeling desolate. His life's work devoted to politics, and what would it yield? Emptiness. If he died before the day was over, who would remember him? Or even care? For the first time in his life, it occurred to him that perhaps there was something beyond politics, after all. He almost longed for that intangible idea, or so-called "faith", which many people clung to when faced with death.

As he took the elevator to Arch's office, he gave himself a mental slap. He was not defeated yet. By thunder, he was not going in there unarmed, and he would die fighting if necessary.

"Come in, come in, Dalton." Arch waved him to a chair. "Oh, help yourself to a drink. Make yourself comfortable for a minute while I finish this infernal paper work."

Mortfield skipped the drink and sat stiffly on the couch, browsing through *Universal Affairs,* the power elite's propaganda organ. Funny. He had just been thinking about "faith", and here in the magazine, somebody named Cromwell talked about establishing a League of Religions of some sort. This was extraordinary, for this publication had been purely political for decades. But whatever was set forth in this magazine inevitably became policy. So. It appeared that the elite were taking a different approach. Surely there was little to gain by dealing with a bunch of religious milksops. But Solano himself had been religious. At least this angle might temper the violence. Maybe it wasn't such a bad idea.

Certainly Arch seemed affable enough. Even pleasant. Mortfield looked around. No one had checked his weapon. Maybe he was just getting paranoid.

In stocking feet, Arch padded in from the kitchenette, drink in hand. "Don't get up." He settled in an easy chair with his back to the window.

The sunlight from the window behind Arch made his face look dark. Mortfield could not make out his host's expression, but he thought Arch was smiling.

"We know, Mortfield."

Mortfield went cold. He thought his life might flash before his eyes, but there was only emptiness. His tongue was dry, his lips could not form words.   "You —"

"We know *everything.*"

"What is there to know?" Mortfield said thickly. "I have done nothing . . . " Beads of sweat sprang from his pores. He restrained himself from going for his weapon. Arch had not moved. He did not appear to be armed.

"No need to lie, Mortfield. We know about your liaison with ZRI." Arch said nothing for a moment. He just sat there, smiling.

Heart pounding, Mortfield watched him, and waited.

"Relax, Mortfield. You've done us a favor."

Mortfield blinked.

"You want to nail Solano's killer," Arch went on conversationally. "I don't blame you. We all want to resolve this case. Trust me. The longer this killer is at large, the greater the threat to world peace. You can help us, but no more mistakes, Mortfield."

"Mistakes?"

"Something obvious going on at ZRI which you seem to have overlooked. Something we told you before, but you weren't listening very closely, were you?" Arch's voice was cold as steel. "Think, man! Who at ZRI knew Solano best?"

Mortfield remembered his debriefing with Mitchell Hunt. Zephan Benamoz was there. Zephan Benamoz had been close to Solano. Very close. He had seemed determined to avenge Solano.

"Aha, my boy. I can see you are thinking now. Who, Mortfield?"

"Zephan . . . Benamoz."

"Devon told the world about Yeshurun's disaffection from Solano just prior to the murder. Remember, Mortfield? This is information you should not have forgotten. Who stood to benefit from the assassination, especially after the rift?"

Mortfield remained rigid, pale and mute. So Zephan had betrayed him. Was Zephan Benamoz a murderer? Maybe. The man's enraged attack on his own son in the Frontera jail was a matter of record. If Benamoz had not been restrained with chains, Leb would be dead by now. Zephan was brutal to his own sons. This, at least, according to Haman. But could he trust Haman? And why would Zephan Benamoz do anything to help allies of Ponte, his rival? Ponte claimed he wasn't responsible for the bombing. But he didn't trust Ponte, either. Mortfield felt smothered with dark confusion.

"Mortfield, how well do you know Zephan Benamoz?" Arch asked softly.

"Not well, sir. I do know his son, Haman." *But I detest the man.* If Zephan was anything like his son . . .

"Zephan is a high priest of Yeshurun. Does this tell you anything? It is common knowledge that members of Yeshurun are religious fanatics. They pretend piety, but in reality they crave power as much or more than any of us. It's obvious. Else why would they be connected with the bombing?"

"I know little about religion, sir. I never believed in mixing politics and religion."

"I couldn't agree with you more. Separation of church and state. But these days, churches are meddling in the affairs of state. They are making everything political, and they are forcing our hand. The only way we can control those oddballs is to unite everybody into one religion. To build our power base, we get all nations to sit down together and give up those core beliefs which cause all the problems. Then, by sheer numbers, we squeeze out the few remaining who oppose the peace process. But first we have to punish the troublemakers. That's where you come in." He stood abruptly. "This meeting has been most fruitful. I trust you will take full advantage of your position, Mortfield, and see Zephan Benamoz apprehended. Then we will interrogate him properly and put this matter to rest permanently."

Mortfield left Kingerman's penthouse with a mixture of relief and confusion. He was so preoccupied he did not see Haman pass him on the street.

"I know you're here, Haman. You didn't have to slam the door. And you're late."

"I know, Arch. Sorry. It's those blasted airlines. Or actually the passengers. I had all my papers in order, and they waved me on through, but there are so many suspicious people in Cumorah these days, you know. Some people really held up the line, and I was getting so impatient ——"

"Yes, yes. I didn't ask you here to listen to all your excuses."

"Why am I here?"

"Your father still didn't sign. Your brother failed. Made an absolute idiot of himself."

"It's not my fault —"

"Shut up!"

Haman flinched. He didn't like it when Arch was angry.

"I want your solutions, not your complaints," Arch went on more calmly. "Let's face it. Your father stands in the way. He couldn't stop the Pax treaty from taking effect in Cumorah, but it's different here in Zarahemla. People aren't as easily swayed here."

"Look, Arch. He was a high-level government official in Cumorah, and he still couldn't stop it. Now he's totally involved in his old religion. He no longer does politics."

"But your religion, Haman —"

"Not my religion!"

"Excuse me. You know your father's religion teaches direct opposition to Voltaire, and he is even against the Egalitarian agenda. Yeshurun has never deviated from its position. I know their history. Their teachings are ideologically incorrect. Your father has no right to teach such ideas."

"I wouldn't worry. He's so caught up in all those rituals and traditions he doesn't even think about anything else. He's just a crazy old man, with his religion for old people."

"How old is he, Haman?"

"How should I know? In his sixties, maybe."

"Hmm. Well, while you have been busy in Cumorah, Haman, your old man has been inciting racial and religious hatred in Zarahemla. He is anything but harmless. He has picked up where Canosa left off."

"Well, Canosa is gone, and I see all the reports. I don't think my father is as knowledgeable as Canosa was. My father never even mentions Egalitarians or the order of Voltaire in public."

"Your father is much craftier than Canosa was. Zephan never spells it out, but his words are much too plain, and his meaning is clear. When he speaks of Gadiantons or the order of Nehor, his followers listen, and they know exactly what he is talking about. Yeshurun is growing at an alarming rate in Zarahemla, and their vote must be reckoned with. His words are too plain. Somehow, he must be silenced."

"He's getting old. He can't last forever."

"It's amazing how much influence one man can have in a lifetime. But they do get senile, don't they? He is getting crazy, isn't he?"

"I've told you this all along."

"Crazy enough to murder Solano?"

"Good grief, Arch. You're going to have to do better than that. They were like brothers."

"Don't brothers ever fight?"

"Yes, but —"

"Zephan is a very powerful man. He likes to be in control. You told me yourself how he used to control you."

"True . . . "

"Look at all the power and respect Zephan enjoys since Solano's death. What if you were he, Haman? Would you want to share the power with someone like Solano?"

"No, but —"

"Zephan is no different from you or me, Haman. All men are the same. They have to have power, or they can't really be men."

"But this is insane —"

"Exactly! Your father is an old man, Haman. Insanity is common among old people. Maybe he wishes he hadn't killed Solano. No wonder he acts crazy. People do strange things when they are insane."

"I don't know . . . "

"Of course it's no reflection on you, Haman," Kingerman said gently. "It's not your fault. But you must face reality. Your father has probably cracked. He may have reached the point where he doesn't know what he's doing. We've all seen the bizarre things people do when they take their religion too seriously. But this isn't just old age, is it? Think back, Haman. Remember when I first met you, when we were teenagers? Your father was a control freak way back then. He was in league with old Joe Bianco, and if they'd had their way, we would have all been in jail. Remember?"

Haman remembered that day long ago. How ashamed he had been of his parents. Maybe his father really was insane. Now people were calling Zephan a prophet of God. This, even though he had killed Solano . . . "But he couldn't have killed Solano!" he found himself saying. "My father may be mean, but he is not stupid. If he were involved in the assassination, he would have stayed away. He would have established an alibi, and he would not have endangered his own life by being in the vicinity of the crime."

"Haman! What's this I hear? Are you defending an enemy of the order?" Kingerman paused, scrutinizing the young man. "Do you still support our objectives?"

"No! I mean, yes!" Silently, Haman cursed his father. Why did Zephan have to survive the swamp? If he were gone, this wouldn't be happening. Because of Zephan, Haman's commitment to the order was being doubted. "What I mean is, my father . . ."

"Yes?" Arch drummed his chubby, bejeweled fingers on the end table beside him.

Haman shifted from one foot to the other. "I mean, it's not my fault . . . "

"Haman, you're standing," Kingerman said. "Sit down. Relax. I can see your dilemma, and of course it's not your fault."

"I. . .didn't think my father would do such a thing."

"Oh, he didn't kill Solano."

Haman sighed.

"But we wouldn't want it known who Amalickiah really is, would we? You made an oath when you joined with us, Haman. Do you remember what that oath is?"

"We swear to protect our fellow Voltairists from harm or legal liability under all circumstances. All plans of the order are sworn to total secrecy for our own protection. Violation of the oath is subject to the laws of the order, and the penalty is death," Haman quoted.

"Very good. Then you understand your obligation to protect Amalickiah at all costs. But it is not only our law. We do it for our friends. If the true Amalickiah were revealed to the world, it might turn out to be a close friend of yours, one who has helped you to the position of power you enjoy today. We wouldn't want to jeopardize your position, would we?"

"Not at all."

Kingerman smiled lazily. "I know this is a great test of your allegiance, Haman. We all must go through it. But you are special. You are the only one in your family who has been willing to go against Yeshurun traditions. That takes courage, and I respect you for it."

Haman gripped the arms of his chair. The most powerful man in the world was praising *him*.

"I realize this is difficult for you. It is for all of us. Sometimes we are called upon to subordinate our personal concerns for the good of the world. This time it is necessary for you to sever family ties for the cause of peace. It is a much greater sacrifice than is required from many of us. But you will be rewarded for your sacrifice. You will be a hero in the eyes of the world, and you will never want for anything."

Haman felt growing pride in the privilege of belonging to this great brotherhood.

"Here, my friend, let me make it easier for you. Think of all your fellow Voltairists have done for you."

"I am overwhelmed by their kindness, sir."

"Now, what has your father ever really done for you?"

"I can't think of anything worth mentioning."

"He is old, and he is no longer useful to society. He is a prophet in an illegal and dangerous religious group which violently opposes all the important global purposes we stand for. On the other hand, Amalickiah is a bright young man with great potential, and he will make great contributions to the world. Actually, he did us a favor by removing Solano. Now, Haman, if you were in my place, and you had the burden of bringing about world peace, and you had the excruciating responsibility of deciding who should live and who should die, would there be any doubt in your mind?"

"No, sir."

"Do you see why we must sometimes do difficult things for the good of the world?"

"Yes, sir."

"Do you think you can do what is required of you, Haman?"

"Yes, I know I can do it."

"Good. I knew we could count on you. I thought for a moment there I might lose you."

"Oh, never, sir."

Kingerman stood up. "Now, don't worry. I'm not asking you to do anything rash. But keep an eye on your father, Haman. That's all I ask. Be alert. I know this may get difficult, but remember, I am here for you. You can talk to me. Trust me."

Haman left Kingerman's place feeling noble. They were demanding a great deal from him, but it was worth it. They were asking great things of him because he was special. He had courage to defy Yeshurun. The order was so wonderful. After all they were truly egalitarian. He felt confident, powerful. He could fight the entire house of Israel if they asked him to. And Arch. There was no better friend in the world. No matter what happened, Arch always seemed to know what to do; he could handle anything; he was always in control.

19

Zarahemla Republic Intelligence Headquarters

Jaime Canosa emerged from the debriefing in a deep, reflective mood. A battle against the cartel had been won, but not without great cost. The beast had claimed two of his grandnephews. Haman was slippery as the devil, and Leb's only remorse was in getting caught. Zephan had done much good, but in so doing had earned a growing list of enemies. At least he was retired now, so he was out of danger.

Mitchell Hunt bid Canosa farewell and saw the old gentleman to the door. Zephan had said the Lord would provide his replacement. But he never dreamed it would be Canosa again. The man's experience alone was worth a dozen lesser recruits. He was a man truly bowed down by the trials of life, but not broken. His fighting spirit was an inspiration. When the time came for him to die, Canosa would take scores of enemies with him. He must be kept in reserve, however. A low profile was essential. If his enemies found out he was not only alive, but back with the agency . . .

Did Canosa know the truth about his wife's death? Heartbreaking, those Clayton reports. That Aurelia Canosa's death was really caused by poisoning could no longer be denied. The cancer had been induced years earlier, during their first visit in Antionum. It was a favorite trick among agents from Tartarus, and they were getting bolder. They had infiltrated the entire continent, Zarahemla and the lands northward, Antionum in particular; they were getting by with murder, and smiling all the while.

Should he tell Canosa the truth, or should he be mercifully silent? What would be Canosa's wish? Hunt sighed. Sometimes he hated his job. This was a vital service to his country, but all this knowledge could be a curse.

One could not afford to make too many mistakes in this position. His tactical error, a miscalculation in timing, had endangered some of his best operatives. He wanted to retire, but he had too much going right now, and he must stay as long as the agency was still independent of Elidor's lackeys. He didn't have much time, for her forces were steadily infiltrating the agency. It had become increasingly difficult to know who to trust and who to watch.

At last he was seeing fruits of months and years of hard and hazardous work. Numerous consensual searches at corner grocery stores in the heart of the capital had caused dozens of drug lords to be arrested. Hordes of drug-toting illegal aliens from Cumeni, Antionum, and nations overseas had been successfully checked. The notorious drug-runner and instigator of mob violence, Miles Potter, was finally behind bars.

But the work was far from finished. The main cartel still was not busted. Investigations had revealed foreign drug lords were recruiting and training children as young as twelve years old to enter Zarahemla and act as drug dealers, couriers, smugglers, and crack-house managers. Lords of the lesser cartels were financed by, and reporting to, kingpins in the Pyramid cartel. Debriefing of Jaime Canosa had yielded volumes of damaging information on Haman Benamoz, who was used shamelessly by Cabrios, and probably everyone else. Paths of a probe done in cooperation with the drug enforcement agency all led to a handful of powerful political officials deeply entrenched in the government of Zarahemla Republic. Hunt's operatives had identified two code names in the Pyramid hierarchy. "Plague" was head of the drug underworld. "Rameses", however, was another matter altogether. He was the secret head of the order and orchestrated both the criminal underworld and the legitimate political elite. From his position he had not only flooded Zarahemla with drugs, but he had also served as a liaison with Ding Po of Tartarean Empire, who established an arms ring with Zarahemla street gangs. ZRI was within moments of nabbing Rameses, but a leak to the *Post* by Elidor's administration ruined the sting.

Whatever his real name, Rameses was a citizen above suspicion, a pillar of polite society.

By liberating Canosa and bringing Miles Potter and his band to justice, Ben had almost singlehandedly cleaned out a nest of hard-core conspirators, severely crippling the Pyramid Cartel. In more ways than one. Hunt smiled. The medics had been unable to save Leb's arm. Leb Benamoz had been literally and unilaterally "disarmed".

Then Benjamin Benamoz had done something unexpected. He had deployed his religious associates to teach Christianity to the thugs in prison. Those Yeshurun people may be peculiar, but they were persistent, and little by little the outlaws were beginning to listen. Ben's brother Leb was not among those who were responding positively, but to everyone's astonishment, Miles Potter was.

The temporary lull was no reason for apathy, however. Incidents of violence, though fewer at present, were more deadly than ever. Now Haman's circle of power had been penetrated, and he would be extremely volatile, capable of any atrocity . . .

"You must be on to something, Hunt," was Clarence Rook's terse comment over the phone. "As of today, the city mayor has ordered Project Nix Narc terminated."

Hunt said nothing.

"And by the way," Rook said to the palpable silence on the other end, "the media isn't helping, either. You better take a look at channel thirteen."

20

Hunt switched on Warner Brackenlaw's News of the Hour and found Ted Lipscomb interviewing Kemen Ponte, head of the notorious Ponista regime in Cumorah.

"Ladies and gentlemen," Ted said with a broad, cheerful smile. "Tonight, News of the Hour brings you to the city of Frontera, Cumorah, for a live, exclusive interview with the esteemed General Ponte. With him is his Minister of Interior, Haman Benamoz."

Hunt felt helpless rage sweep over him. The incompetent fool had just violated a cardinal rule of national security by revealing his location in such a highly sensitive area.

"General." Ted used his most ingratiating tone. "We are deeply grateful to you for granting this interview. Let's get right to the point. Some people say you should be granted the Dermucker Peace Prize for stepping down so graciously and ceding your power to Pax Universalis. How do you feel about this honor?"

The General hesitated. "Well, not all the power ——"

"It was the only honorable thing to do," Haman interrupted with a slickness which would rival Ponte's. "It is in the best interests of democracy to grant power to the people."

"Truly noble words, sir," Ted gushed. "I'm sure no one would doubt you are working for peace! Tell me, Mr. Benamoz," he continued. "You have worked side by side with clergymen, haven't you? Now that you are in politics, do you believe in separation of church and state?"

315

"We believe all ideologies are entitled to equal forum. All, of course, except those which promote religious hatred. The Anti-Hate Committee's responsibility is to regulate religious activity and make sure the country is free of hate." Haman leaned back with a benign smile.

"What does the minister of Interior do? Preserve natural resources?"

Haman smiled indulgently. "The name is internal security, not interior. We are funded primarily by the Ponte Foundation, and we are committed to enforcing the Anti-Hate Committee's laws."

"Like a war on the causes of war?" prompted Lips, pleased that he had added a clever phrase which was not in the script.

"Yes, you might say."

Hunt stared in disbelief at the television. *The Ponte Foundation is a front organization for the Empire's secret police.*

"Sounds wonderful!" Lipscomb was beaming.

"General, whom do you blame for the recent hostage situation in the Caribbean area?"

"Radical Solanistas, of course. There is no doubt about it."

"Mr. Benamoz, I understand you are the son of Zephan Benamoz, called a priest or apostle by the house of Yeshurun. Do you think your father should mix religion and politics?"

"Absolutely not!"

"But in your country, you work with the churches, do you not? Would you care to explain?"

"That's different!" Haman said. "As long as the churches stay in harmony with the Anti-Hate Committee, they have complete freedom. No one criticizes anything. We have freedom to do anything except criticize."

"Your policy is sensible. But some people's ideology is not exactly in vogue these days," Lipscomb simpered.

"Exactly. Yeshurun is a prime example. Their people still believe in prophets, and they believe the original biblical religion has been restored, exactly the same as the primitive church. With it came all those old prejudices, which explains why those of Yeshurun continually criticize everything from schools and society's experts on raising children, to government and moral preferences, to the order of Voltaire itself. Criticism is so negative, you know. You can see why my father's outdated religion has no place in a hate-free society like ours."

Hunt watched Haman. The snake was going to spit venom.

316

But Haman's face was a picture of kindness. "Don't you see, Ted?" he spoke personably. "All this bloodshed could have been avoided but for my father's misguided thinking! We are extremely pleased we could arrange the hostages' release!"

"Ted, you know Haman is lying!" Hunt shouted at the television.

"That is very kind of you, sir," Ted was saying.

There was Haman's smile again.

"Gentlemen, our time is spent. One more question. Mr. Benamoz, as you know, agreement to disarm has not been unanimous among the *Resistencia* of Cumorah, and as your new ally, we share the frustration you must feel. We simply cannot understand why they so childishly refuse to accept defeat." Ted rolled his eyes, with that oh-we-are-so-embarrassed-by-these-stubborn-nationalists look. "Furthermore, we all know Yeshurun is violently opposed to the order of Voltaire. Is it logical to assume, then, that your father, as a member of Yeshurun, would sympathize with this radical faction?"

"Of course."

"In fact, your father was purportedly a very close friend of Solano, am I correct?"

"Yes."

"Everyone knows the *Resistencia* leaders all hide out in the neutral states of Sheffa and Jershon, on the other side of Bahia Verde. Let's speculate for a moment. Suppose Zephan Benamoz were, at this moment, lending aid and comfort to the resistance, across the bay from here. Would it bother you if your own father were in such close proximity to the seat of your government, working in direct opposition to you?"

Hunt gasped. How did Ted know the location of Zephan? Sure. He was ostensibly making a mere supposition. Lips didn't know what he was saying. All he did was read the copy. It was an obvious tipoff, right over the air waves. Zephan was solidly on indisputably neutral ground, but this did not concern his enemies.

If Haman was surprised, he did not show it. He kept his face without expression, and said nothing.

Ponte warmed immediately to the *periodista estupido*. "No bother at all, señor. We have already won! Pax Universalis works with us, so the order of Voltaire can carry on with new life!"

"Thank you for your time, gentlemen. We'll be right ba—"

317

Hunt smashed off the television and grabbed the phone. You couldn't be too careful. You could trust these terrorists to do exactly what they want, and they were never known to respect neutrality. To be on the safe side, Hunt decided to contact Clayton and revise the time and meeting place with Zephan.

21

Manuel Fernandez lovingly guided his shining boat through the gentle current of Bahia Verde. How blessed he was. He and his family had managed to escape Cumorah, but they arrived penniless. Then this opportunity presented itself. He and several of his former associates from the plantation in Cumorah worked, scraped, and saved to buy this rickety old, bi-level touring cruiser. She was headed for the graveyard, but her pitiful condition made the price attractive. Still, it wouldn't have been possible without the largesse of Dan MacRay, who financed a complete overhaul and brand new engine. After the barnacles were removed, and the ship's hull sealed tight, good as new, Manuel and his friends sanded, scraped, and painted, refinishing the topsides and the interior. At last the little boat was finished, and it was a joyful day when she was christened the *Liahona*, meaning "compass". It was a fitting name for the mission which gradually became Manuel's own. The Fernandez Tours came to include the transport of refugees, especially people of Yeshurun, from Cumorah's yoke of iron. Hundreds of refugees had been carried to freedom through Manuel's efforts.

But the ultimate reward came tonight, when he had the honor of carrying a prophet of the Lord along on his journey. In preparation for the arrival of their prophet, the people in Sheffa had given themselves to much prayer and fasting. The Lord had rewarded their faithfulness by pouring out His Spirit upon the gathering; they had the spirit of prophecy, and of revelation, and when the speakers taught, they taught with power and authority of God. The days of conference had been joyful and uplifting.

There were forty passengers tonight. It was a trifle overloaded, but Manuel hadn't the heart to turn away gentle brothers and sisters in the faith, who all wanted to join in the *despedida*, or farewell, for their beloved prophet. They had come straight from meetings, and were still dressed in their Sabbath best. It was only a short trip.

318

though. Everything would be all right. Manuel wished he felt the same confidence about his dear friend.

"I still wish you had body guards, Zephan," he said.

Zephan chuckled. "Body guards are for political figures. A decrepit old shepherd and his gentle flock are not a threat. You know missionaries and pastors of Yeshurun do not enter lands where they are forbidden by law. I have strictly limited my ministry to neutral lands, and we have scrupulously observed the laws and ordinances of local authorities. They have all been most gracious. I am confident of our safety." Beneath the awning light he took a small radio from his pocket and turned it over in his hands, checking all the functions. "Besides," he said, loosening his tie, "when I get to the Jershon shore, I'm to radio Clayton, who is waiting to fly me to Antionum. If I need anything, I have only to call him."

Suddenly he looked up at Manuel. "On the other hand, Manuel, if my work is finished, and it is my time to die, all the body guards in the world cannot protect me."

Manuel flinched. "Please don't say that —"

"We thank thee, O God, for a prophet,
To guide us in these last days."

The passengers had burst into song, and their harmonious voices rose over the drumming engine, bearing an *Himno de Sión* through the quiet night.

"We thank thee for sending the gospel
To lighten our minds with its rays.
We thank thee for every blessing
Bestowed by thy bounteous hand.
We feel it a pleasure to serve thee,
And love to obey thy command."

Gradually another engine's roar drowned out their voices. A boat raced toward them at an alarming speed. Manuel spun the helm and turned sharply to the starboard. What was this reckless fool trying to do? Ram his boat?

But the immense craft pulled along side, towering over Manuel's little boat. On its side was the insignia of the People's Democracy of Ammonihah. "Ahoy, the *Liahona*. Cut your engines immediately or you will be fired upon!"

For a moment, all was silent, and Zephan listened. No crickets, no frogs, no other boats, only the water lapping softly against the side of Manuel's boat. Too quiet. A shiver scurried up his spine. Something was wrong.

A blinding light exposed him. "Stand by to be boarded." The voice was familiar.

"Come in, Mud Ball!" Zephan radioed Clayton desperately. "Mud Ball, do you read me?"

Nothing. Only bellowed commands and the thud of rubber soles upon the deck. "Passengers go to the upper level so we can search the cabin. Move it!" A thickset man with heavy jowls was giving orders. This gestapo wore casual slacks and expensive windbreakers, but displayed prominently on every jacket was the ubiquitous Pax insignia.

"I found him, General."

"Well, well, so you have, lieutenant. We want you, Zephan Benamoz."

Ponte. *I'm a dead man.* Aloud he said, "What are you doing? This is a neutral zone, you are trespassing, and your search is unwarranted."

"You are to report for questioning. You are charged with conspiracy in the murder of Solano."

Manuel gasped. A woman aboard stifled a cry.

"Don't worry," Zephan said to his people. "The power of God is greater than the soldiers of Babylon."

"Silence!" barked the lieutenant with the jowls. "Keep quiet and no one will get hurt."

"Take me, then, and leave these people alone." Zephan's voice was calm.

"You've always been an intelligent man, Benamoz. You avoid resistance, and your people will remain unharmed."

Once again, the clank of chains. Zephan turned and looked up at his people. "When I leave, carry on. Keep singing!"

"Brother Zephan," Manuel whispered. "We will wait for an hour and pray for you."

Zephan watched from the Cumorah cutter's broad transom as it pulled away from Manuel's humble little ship. He could hear some women weeping, but the people resumed their singing, loud as they could, as they disappeared into the night.

"When dark clouds of trouble hang o'er us
And threaten our peace to destroy,
There is hope smiling brightly before us,
And we know that deliv'rance is nigh.
We doubt not the Lord nor his goodness.
We've proved Him in days that are past.
The wicked who fight against Zion
Will surely be smitten at last.

"We'll sing of His goodness and mercy.
We'll praise Him by day and by night,
Rejoice in His glorious gospel,
And bask in its lifegiving light.
Thus on to eternal perfection
The honest and faithful will go,
While they who reject this glad message
Shall never such happiness know. . ."

Zephan was aware of someone beside him, studying him. Mortfield! What could be the meaning of all this? But Mortfield's face was not friendly. Zephan perceived a tremendous conflict boiling inside this man.

"Ponte wants to see you below deck, Benamoz," Mortfield mumbled.

Zephan stumbled awkwardly down the companionway to the cabin, where Ponte sat at a polished, gimballed table, sipping an iced drink. His free hand rested on the neck of a Tequila bottle, but he was not drunk. He was very much in control.

"At ease, Mortfield." He raised the bottle toward Mortfield, who declined. Then he glared at Zephan. "You can't have any of this. It's against your religion." He laughed. "Be seated, gentlemen."

Zephan eased himself onto a bench that doubled as a bunk, and stretched out his legs. The chains cut into his flesh, especially the one on the right, which was connected to a heavy weight.

"So, Mr. Benamoz, what do you have to say for yourself?"

"Before you deceived this nation, the people had religious freedom. They were peace loving and industrious. Now the people are lazy, immoral, and bloodthirsty."

"Go on. I find this highly amusing."

321

"Why do you set your heart on riches, so you have legalized plunder? Why do you teach the people to steal from their neighbors? Why do you punish the faithful, and reward idolatry?"

"Idolatry!" Ponte laughed. "Isn't he quaint?"

"Where is your wife, Ponte?"

"She is at home in the state mansion, enjoying all the luxury the state can provide. What does this have to do with ——"

"Why do you commit whoredoms and spend your strength with harlots? Why do you cause this people to commit sin, so the Lord has cause to send me to prophesy against this people?"

Mortfield was shocked. How did Zephan know? Ines Ponte was pretty, in a shallow, vacant sort of way. Obviously she hadn't a grain of sense in her head, for she worshiped Kemen Ponte. It was a convenient marriage for Ponte, who needed a wife to enhance his appearance as a respectable world leader. His first act upon moving into the mansion was to bind the Palace Guard to secrecy regarding his extramarital affairs. Ines was a stupid and silly woman, but she did not deserve this. A certain protectiveness had kept the guards silent about Ponte's secret, until one of them fled for his life due to an infraction of Cumorah's new free speech laws. When he arrived in Zarahemla, he found Mortfield, and confided the guards' private joke about Ponte as the "Casanova-in-Chief."

Ponte pounded the table with his fist. "Enough! I don't have to listen to this character assassination."

Zephan laughed. "Since when was character an issue with you, Ponte? You have no character to assassinate."

Ponte, livid, opened his mouth to reply, but was interrupted.

"We have docked, sir."

"Already? " He checked his watch. "Twelve minutes flat. Excellent. Eight minutes to go. Very well. Come on, Benamoz. You can answer for a more serious assassination."

Back on the deck, Zephan attempted to disembark, but stumbled and fell, nearly slipping off the dock into the water below. The weighted chains would have sunk him speedily to the bottom, twenty feet down. Mortfield grabbed his arm and pulled him to safety, then steadied him, helping him toward the beach.

Slowly Zephan put one bleeding foot in front of the other. He did not look at his unexpected rescuer. Did he detect a hint of compassion there?

Ponte arrived to walk beside them the short distance across the well-lit beach to the waiting limousine. Lieutenant Jowls trailed close behind.

Suddenly Zephan spun around and stared toward the place on the bay where they had left the *Liahona*. "No! No!" he cried out. His voice was filled with terror. He fell to his knees on the beach, and bowed himself until his head almost touched the sand. "Lord God Almighty, how can we witness this awful scene?" His voice rose in anguish.

Those with him stood in stunned silence and stared.

"Stretch forth thine hand, oh God, and exercise thy matchless power, and save them from the flames." Zephan remained crumpled on the ground, his hands clasped over the back of his head as if anticipating a devastating blow. He groaned repeatedly, and must have been murmuring a prayer.

Ponte looked at his watch.

At that moment an explosion convulsed the evening air, reverberating across the water, and orange flames leaped into the sky.

"It's a good way to get rid of a few weirdos," Jowls said. "There are too many people in the world anyway."

"My, my. Those terrorists are at it again," Ponte said. "Sheffa should have voted for Pax protection." He clucked. "Such a pity."

Mortfield swore.

Zephan was on his feet and reaching for Ponte's throat. "You lied," he said, but Mortfield restrained him.

"That's it, Mortfield. Call off your dog," Ponte said mildly. To Zephan he said, "I would not do that if I were you, Benamoz. You have seen your people cast into a lake of fire and brimstone. Would you dare preach again in this land after what you have seen?"

"There is a pattern here, Ponte," Zephan said. "These are not the only murders laid to your charge."

"Why did your God not save them?" Mortfield asked, but his voice held more curiosity than rancor.

"The Lord revealed to me that he received those forty souls up unto himself, in glory," Zephan said to Ponte. "God allows men their agency, for good or evil, and he has suffered you and your accomplices to do this evil thing, because of the hardness of your

323

hearts. And the judgments which he shall exercise upon you in his wrath will be just."

"Are you threatening me?" Ponte said.

"I don't need to," Zephan said simply. "The blood of the innocent shall stand as a witness against you, and cry mightily against you at the last day."

Ponte shoved Zephan into the back of the air-conditioned limousine and pulled a partition to separate them. "Whew!" he said conversationally. "At least we don't have to listen to that raving madman for a few minutes. I couldn't bear another word."

"This was unnecessary, Ponte," Mortfield said through his teeth.

"What?"

"In the name of everything decent, man, don't play dumb with me. You know what."

"So what of it?"

"Good grief, have you no conscience at all? You were responsible for that bombing, and you know it. Doesn't it bother you?"

"Bother me? Why should it? I'm proud of it."

"The murder of forty people is something to be proud of?"

"Stop blubbering like a woman, Mortfield. This is war, stupid. People get killed in wars. Besides, it was only a bunch of those Yeshurun people. They are a blight on the planet."

"Blowing up a boatload of innocent, defenseless people, after promising them safety is terrorism," Mortfield said. "It's mass murder."

"I will inform Rameses about your attitude." Ponte jotted some notes in a small book. "He will not be pleased."

"I guess it really doesn't matter, does it?"

"What do you mean?"

"Benamoz is onto you, Ponte. He knows who Amalickiah is."

Ponte lit a cigarette and took a long drag, savoring the sensation before exhaling. "We can't let him get away with that, can we?"

"He knew that boat would blow up before it even happened, Ponte."

"I noticed. Those people are spooky, I tell you."

Mortfield brooded as the chauffeur pulled up to the Ministry of Internal Security. He couldn't shake the memory of those people.

Their hymns had wrenched something in his mind; they had reached for the highest within him. *And how does Zephan Benamoz know these things? He is an extraordinary man. Or is he?* Yet Solano had known this man well. Presumably they were very close friends. As a friend of the Yeshurun people, Solano had spoken often about them, and Mortfield had listened carefully, probing for weakness which could bring down the enemy. Solano was told that God still speaks to man, and called it revelation. In fact, this religion was tightly bound to this thing called revelation from God. Even their own prophets claimed Yeshurun could not survive a day without it. If this so-called revelation was their ultimate weapon, though, how did one fight against an intangible?

Zephan had mentioned something being revealed to him by God. Nah. It was too hard to believe. It might have been one of Zephan's purported visions. Then again, maybe it was a revelation. No. It was probably a psychic phenomenon. Whatever it was, of one thing Mortfield was convinced: Zephan Benamoz was not Solano's murderer.

"Zephan Benamoz knows entirely too much," Ponte said. "He is a dangerous man."

22

Ben slipped out of the forest and walked across Parliamentary Square in Cumorah, using the darkness as cover. Smoke was billowing from somewhere, further blurring identities of people moving about the square.

Here Zephan's countrymen had made their last vote as free men, before the arms embargo, before the revolutionaries took over. The buildings had fallen into disrepair, except for one newly remodeled edifice, the Ministry of Internal Security.

The structure was a giant thing, towering over every other building in the neighborhood. Modern in every way, it sported over its palatial doors an enormous logo of Voltaire: a global map, cradled in traditional olive branches of peace, over which was superimposed a money sign. And something else — subtle, almost subliminal, but unmistakable to the discerning eye — a serpent embracing a sword. A type and shadow throughout Hebrew religious history was the brazen serpent, a reminder to the house of Israel to look to Christ for protection against a wilderness of disbelief and fiery serpents of deception. The order of Voltaire had borrowed this revered cultural symbol and prostituted it to worldly purposes.

A *dèjá vu* of his narrow escape from the poisonous serpent in the Hermounts wilderness left Ben a sense of foreboding.

On the building's exquisite facade, windows stared like obsidian eyes down on the glow in the square.

Ben's one-day penetration was over, with no measurable success. But with his former homeland now enemy territory, he would be relieved to get out. He was running a little late for his Jershon rendezvous with his father, but the smoke, together with a commotion, aroused his curiosity.

Ben rounded the building and elbowed his way through the milling spectators to a bonfire. Soldiers, all clad in gloomy Pax Universalis gray, fed the flame with boxes of printed material. Books. And ...? Bibles. Despite the heat Ben felt chilled by old memories.

He approached a bored-looking young official. "Pardon me, I'm just passing through. This seems like a strange place to incinerate litter."

"Not litter, really," the young man said. "Just old books. Nobody uses books in school. Just television. We only have high tech, you know. This is the reason for this holiday, you know. Everything new. Get rid of the old."

Ben could not help himself. "But this is an outrage!" he blurted out. "Like the Dark Ages!"

"Huh? The what? You mean, before computers?"

"Yes, when people still had to read and write, as in history."

"You don't have to know history. We're starting over with the new order. Everything is totally egalitarian now. Books are classified B.A.R. now, so they totally aren't important."

"B.A.R.?"

The youth looked incredulous. "Man, where have you been? You know, before the Age of Relativism!"

"Oh."

"All these books are too hard to read. You know, their language is so old. Like hundreds of years old! So they've all been standardized, and written for television, so we can understand them. Everything we need to know is on television. It's easier and less boring. You know what I mean?"

"And who programs your television?"

"Oh, it's all government-approved, you know. Man, I wouldn't trust anybody else. Our teachers can depend on only one source."

"Have you ever had to answer a question such as, *why?*"

"What do you mean?"

"It's what people do when they think."

The youth shrugged and chomped with increased vigor on a wad of gum. "Look, man. I don't know what you're talking about. And what do I care? I'm just doing my job. And I don't like working when everybody else has the day off to party."

"They pay you. To burn books? To destroy your national heritage?"

"I think it's wonderful that our youth are serving society this way." A thin young woman stepped up to Ben. Straight dull hair, fine as flax, hung in limp threads to her shoulders. In bland skirt and faded blouse, she looked like a faceless figure in a child's stick-drawing. Black-rimmed glasses formed the only contrast on her person. She held a small boy by the hand.

"I want my Emmett to do this when he grows up. Not be like his father. Basil was . . . you know, one of those Yeshurun weirdos. They believe the father is patriarch in the home, and they frown on women working outside the home, unless absolutely necessary. It was a necessity for *me*, but I couldn't convince him. He insisted he made enough money to provide for the family, and he refused to let me get a job, unless I made money at home. But I wanted to get away from home! The children were driving me nuts. All we had on his job was an old house that needed work, a junker for me to drive, rags for me to wear, and a tiny TV. All our neighbors had big screen TV and saunas. Everybody else lived in great big, spacious homes. But not us. Basil wouldn't hear of it. All he could ever say was our house was paid for and we were out of debt. Big deal. I was so humiliated.

"And to make things worse, I had to stay home and wash diapers, wipe snotty noses, cook meals, and wash dishes. Basil kept saying it was noble to be a mother. He just said that so I would stay home and be a slave. I deserve better. I tell you, his religion is a curse. I'm glad they finally outlawed it in this country." The woman rolled her eyes. "Ugh! Can you imagine such antiquated thinking, in our day and age?"

Ben did not answer. He tried to edge away, but she was clutching his sleeve. How did he manage so often to get trapped by these women who insisted on telling him their life story?

"Basil wanted me to stay home and teach my own children," the woman rattled on. "Can you believe it? What could I teach those children in a tacky little house with no high tech-facilities? Poor

327

Emmett would have been stuck at home with his brother and sister. He would have received no socialization with his peers.

"But when I confronted Basil over this, he ranted and raved about how the community schools were teaching our children immorality! I don't know where he gets these ideas. Good grief. It's illegal to teach anything about morality at all. Teachers are totally neutral. How could the children be taught immorality?

"Basil was just saying such things because he didn't want to pay taxes. Really. How childish! Just because the experts wouldn't allow him to express his own silly ideas."

"Might there be some truth in what he said?" Ben asked.

She ignored him. "Oh, Basil was a tyrant, I tell you. Everybody knows that the family is the smallest democracy at the heart of society. Parents and children should be equal before the state."

"What if your child decides he has the right to join a street gang, or some kind of cult?" Ben asked.

The woman hesitated, obviously surprised. "Then I would gently try to persuade him to choose a better course," she replied.

"Then you would be using the biblical world view in which children are required to honor and obey their parents to the extent that the parents honor and obey God."

The woman shook her head vigorously. "I would never impose the Bible on my children."

"Have you read the Bible?"

"Of course."

"Then you do not understand."

"Basil threatened to keep the children home and teach them himself," she droned on. "By then I had enough. I reported him to the authorities. When they threw him in jail, that's when we split up, you see. It cost him a fortune, but he finally got out of jail. He said he couldn't afford to send me much money. I told him to keep his dirty money. I didn't need it. I now have my dream job. I teach at a brand new Pax school, and in two years I will be principal. I got my reward for alerting the authorities. Well, Basil left the country, of course, and he took Emmett's brother and sister with him. Can you imagine the audacity of the man? Emmett chose to stay with me, of course." The woman replaced her irritated look with a vapid smile. She rambled on in a childish voice, with eyes too bright, and the plastic cheerfulness of a well-programmed secular humanist.

"Emmett isn't going to be like other men, are you, dear? Emmett's going to be a world citizen-servant, aren't you, dear? Tonight we are celebrating. In two years we will have a pool and new car, after all," she continued. "This is the last time we will have to burn books, you know. Today is historic, because from now on we will write our own history. It is like a whole new evolution of humanity."

"Do you mean the great day in history Professor Cromwell always raves about?" Ben asked. "Supposedly the day when a water puppy crawled up on the land, decided to be a land animal, and became man's progenitor."

"Yes! That's it!" she exclaimed.

"Is that what we are celebrating here?"

"Yes, you might say so. Isn't it exciting?"

"So! This is how the world celebrates Water Puppy Day!" Ben laughed.

"You offend me with your sarcasm!" She raised her voice. "How can you be so rude?"

"Human nature, including your animosity, madam, has not changed."

The woman swept the child up into her arms. "I wanted my son to be part of this momentous day." She kissed him. "Don't listen to that man. Isn't it wonderful, darling?"

The child did not respond, but only fixed a bewildered stare upon the fire.

Ben turned to go. There was nothing he could do here. Better get out before he was recognized. This woman and her babblings had only made him later than ever.

Ben heard a violent cough behind him and felt a hot breath on his neck. Beneath his jacket, he gripped a revolver and pushed ahead, not looking back.

"Don't turn!" came a hoarse whisper. "Just move out from the crowd."

Ben hurried for the forest. Maybe he could lose this fellow. But the man grabbed his arm, and he turned.

It was Beck.

O.D. grinned. "Sorry to startle you, *amigo*. Look. To state the obvious, it's dangerous for you here."

"I'm on my way back to Jershon to meet my father."

Beck rubbed his eyes. "Great. Just what I need, and me fresh from rehabilitation. Clayton assigned me to sniff around the Ministry of Internal Security here, and it's killing me."

Beck gazed past the acrid smoke to the Ministry building. "This looks like a fancy version of the interrogation center in my POW days," he said bitterly. "I hear Ponte has reduced the practice of torture to a science. From the outside, you'd never know the horrors which go on inside that place. It's heavily guarded right now. Whoever is in there must be important."

23

To Zephan, the immense lobby in the Internal Security building resembled a shopping mall. Several large fountains sprouted water from pieces of junk metal fused together, twisted beyond any recognizable shape, painted in garish colors, and sometimes called "modern art". Coins were scattered on fountain floors. Heavy railings around the fountains all had conspicuous signs in red and white letters warning: KEEP OFF. The smaller print read: "Your coins support the Anti-Hate Committee. Give generously." Stale air assaulted the visitors. Odors of antiseptic exuded from the fountains. Imitation trees in dim artificial light gave a plastic jungle effect, except for the vast white marble floors. The walls were filled with so-called art work —— thick paint gobbed onto costly canvases. Zephan wished he had not noticed the few pieces with discernible subjects, for their obscenity was an affront to him.

With startling swiftness, two large police dogs bounded up to Zephan and overwhelmed him with their affection.

"Fabian! Fabiana, come!" Haman appeared, laughing, at a doorway a few paces ahead.

"Welcome to New Ammonihah!" the young man said cheerfully.

"Nice dogs, Haman." Zephan stroked the well-groomed animals.

"They're wolves, Papa. Committee mascots, actually," Haman said with an urbane smile. "These are hallowed halls in which you walk. This is a chief administration building in the New Ammonihah Republic."

Their feet slapped on the marble floor. "Actually, this is the Anti-Hate Committee building, and they let me share it," Haman added with obvious pride. "Isn't it beautiful? I have always loved this place. It makes you feel so warm and comfortable." Haman chattered on with the enthusiasm of a child playing "let's pretend". If he was disturbed by his father's chains clanging on the marble floor, he gave no sign.

When they reached the entrance to a large conference room, Haman touched his father on the arm and said, "Now, Papa, don't worry. They just want to ask you some questions. All you have to do is say the correct words, and you will be out of here in no time."

In a palatial room guards shoved Zephan to his knees on more marble floor. Centered on the floor was an inlaid design of the Voltaire logo. A few red carpeted steps led to a stage-like platform, also of marble. Cushioned benches were to the right, as if for a king's counselors. Designated for those in high official capacity were chairs and couches covered in brocade, with jeweled arm rests. The furnishings were so overdone they could satiate the most gluttonous tastes.

Zephan beheld a dozen men and women, clad in business suits, faces intent, each sitting in a plush chair. To them, this was all in a day's work.

Ponte was there. He and Jowls clasped leashes on the two wolves.

Gold velvet curtains hung at every window except at one on the opposite wall, which was a strange stained-glass window. Under the title, "Toward a Perfect World", a mural depicted two persons striking the earth's global sphere with hammers. Beneath this scene, many people in medieval garb knelt to worship stacks of books advocating doctrines of men. But the most astonishing part on the piece was a crest, mounted above the globe, of a wolf wearing the skin of a lamb.

Absurd. Amazing. Zephan could not help himself. He laughed. "Welcome to New Ammonihah!"

The voice's owner was also familiar. "You!" Zephan exclaimed. His heart plunged. Here, seated in something resembling a royal throne, was the mastermind, the archenemy, the kingpin, code-named Rameses, but Zephan knew he would never reach Mitchell Hunt with the evidence.

Zephan's captors seated him in a straight-backed chair and offered him a drink, which he declined.

Rameses rattled some papers and cleared his throat from deep within the folds of his massive neck. "Zephan Benamoz, we have reports you have been stirring up hate among the people, and you have accused Ponte of cheating on his wife."

The onlookers laughed.

"Now, Zephan, I want you to explain in detail what you were illegally teaching in our land. Jury, take this down carefully."

"I was captured in neutral territory, and it is you who are acting illegally. Nevertheless I will tell you what I was teaching. With pleasure I will testify of the word of God at every opportunity." Zephan said. "There is one true God, and you shall have no other before Him. Not even money."

"Man has created God in his own image," Rameses said. "As we evolve into more intelligent beings, our gods become more kind and merciful, less selfish in dispensing justice and equity. Your God of Moses is much too harsh and vengeful. Our people do not have to worship any god at all, if they do not want to."

"But they do want to. They worship money, power, movie stars, athletes, their possessions, animals, the earth. They even worship trees."

Ponte laughed. "He is daft, Rameses."

"You shall worship no graven images," Zephan continued, "especially not the corrupt images on television, which the people worship by the hour.

"Do not profane the name of God or speak obscenities.

"Keep the Sabbath day holy; do not force others to work on the Sabbath by selling and buying worldly goods and entertainment on the Sabbath day."

Zephan looked at Haman. "Honor your father and mother."

Haman rolled his eyes.

Zephan turned to Ponte. "You shall not kill, or anything like unto it. This includes population control, mercy killing, gender selection, expediency, abnormalities, undesirable characteristics, ethnic cleansing, international police actions, rebellion against the dictates of society's leaders, complicity of family, or any and all political reasons or pagan rites not covered in the above —"

"Hey!" Ponte said. "That is straight from the manifesto. Where did you get it?"

"I'm sure you would like to know."

Ponte was agitated. "There was only one man who knew —"

332

"Impossible," Rameses interrupted. "This only confirms he is a spy. Continue."

Zephan's gaze remained on Ponte. "Adultery is still a sin."

"Sin!" One onlooker hissed.

Someone giggled.

"You shall not steal, even if it is legal for our rulers to take from one class and give to another.

"You shall not lie, and bear false witness against your neighbor, as you are about to do to me."

"Father, you are always so suspicious!" Haman said.

"And you shall not covet —— not as an individual, not as a group —— and you shall not use your voting privileges as a means to plunder and satisfy your private coveting," Zephan continued.

"See how rude he is?" Ponte said to Rameses. "Clearly these words violate the anti-hate code in this nation. And he keeps saying I am causing people to sin. Of course, this is impossible. We are no more capable of sin than our pet wolves over there."

"It doesn't matter," Rameses said. "Those old Hebrew commandments are made to be broken."

Every time Rameses spoke, the jury would laugh, as if on cue for a comedy show.

"I also teach the Creation, the Fall, and the Atonement," Zephan said. "These cannot be broken."

"Not here, you don't teach such dogmas," Rameses said. "Our society does not permit it."

"This man teaches that men are all fallen creatures," Ponte said. "It is pure religious hatred, ignorance, and bigotry, and it is against the law. Everyone knows, and science has proven, that humans are, not fallen, but the highest form of animal." He stroked the wolf nearest him. "We are as noble as a wolf, like Fabian, here."

"You think you can get rid of God and avoid moral responsibility through this so-called equality to animals," Zephan replied quietly. "But God will not go away. Even you, who hate Him, are created in His image."

"This is too much," Ponte scoffed. "We can't believe in something we can't see. And can you imagine some living body rising from a corpse buried in the dirt, and calling it resurrection? These are impossible miracles spawned from a child's imagination. This ignorance must be stopped."

"So our fate is worse than that of a fossil. You condemn us all to extinction," Zephan said.

333

"Then there is no hope," Mortfield said, momentarily forgetting himself.

Zephan's countenance lit up. "On the contrary, my good brother. God does not create anything to be destroyed."

"This must be so," Mortfield said thoughtfully. "If not, there would be no point in our existence. What justice would we have? There must be some reason we are here on earth in the first place. Why are we here, anyway?"

"To be tested," Zephan said.

"For what purpose?"

"God's work is to bring to pass immortality and eternal life for His children."

"This sure sounds better than being buried forever in some hole in the ground," Mortfield said. "But eternal life requires perfection, doesn't it? Nobody can be perfect."

"Here is the good news, Mortfield!" Zephan exclaimed. "Were it not for the atonement, we would all perish. For this cause God sent the Christ, to make an atonement, so we could overcome our imperfections. The Atonement brings us both mercy and justice."

Mortfield marveled at the kind look he saw in the prisoner's eyes. How could Zephan face his tormentors without malice? Where in this man could be found the hatred and violence of which he stood accused?

"Here in Ammonihah we have one universal ethic," Ponte said. "Your silly traditions about a Creation and a Fall cannot be proven, so it is against our law to believe them. Therefore your laughable notion of a Savior and Atonement is totally irrelevant. We stick to those facts which have been scientifically proven by our own Pax educational, scientific, and cultural council. We had no disagreement until you came along. You are an enemy of world peace, tolerance, international harmony, and everything else good and decent."

"I understand that you want world peace," Zephan said patiently. "But those who use their philosophies to turn others away from God will never bring peace, but are in sore need of repentance."

"Repentance! This is religious hatred!" Ponte insisted angrily.

"Because I have told you the truth you are angry with me," Zephan said.

Haman leaned over and spoke softly to his father. "I will help you. I have considerable influence with these people. Just say what I tell you to say, and you will get a light sentence."

334

For a moment Haman was again standing by the swamp, holding the lifesaving pole out to his father, hovering it in the air, but never quite within reach. "I don't need your help, Haman," Zephan said.

Haman turned to the onlookers. "Ladies and gentlemen of the jury. I warned you my father was a visionary man. You can see for yourself he has a vivid imagination!" He got the laughter he was looking for.

"No wonder!" Rameses said. "The Bible is in sixteenth century language. And old people do tend to conjure up the most unusual notions. Senility, you know. Hmm, we have laws to deal with that problem. But you say your father is not yet sixty-five years old, Haman?"

"No, but some people lose their minds much earlier!"

Zephan stood erect, his chains rattling. "Because I have spoken the word of God, you have judged me to be mad. Why persecute me for telling the truth? Remember Saint Paul, who was ridiculed and reviled. But all this did not destroy the reality of his vision. He had seen a vision, he knew he had, and all the persecution under heaven could not make it otherwise, and though they should persecute him unto death, yet he knew, and would know to his latest breath, that he had both seen a light and heard a voice speaking unto him, and all the world could not make him think or believe otherwise. So it is with me. No matter the frequency and density of your words to the contrary, I know what I know, and the truth is the truth. Who am I that I can withstand God, and why does the world think to make me deny what I have actually seen? I know what I know, and God knows it, and I cannot deny it. I don't dare, for by so doing I would offend God."

Mortfield permitted himself a covert study of the prisoner. What he saw shocked him. Zephan had aged, but his physical strength was not diminished. There was something else about him. Other faces in the room were half in shadow, despite artificial light. But Zephan seemed to stand in a light all his own.

Mortfield watched Zephan move past two thugs to stare out the window into the night. The older man was observing the burning of books in the bonfire below. The expression on his face was not anger and defiance as Mortfield expected, but deep sorrow.

Haunted by the prisoner's eyes, Mortfield tried to turn away, but his gaze was drawn irresistibly to the lone figure on trial.

335

Zephan's white hair was in disarray. His fall on the dock had reduced his shirt to a tattered white remnant, revealing shoulders of a man accustomed to strenuous physical labor; this in marked contrast to Rameses' flabbiness and soft hands.

Rameses' pencil-thin mustache was the only slim feature on his body. He looked like a lazy, overfed aristocrat. He should have a beard, too, to cover up those expanding chins.

Though in chains, Zephan stood straight with a bold assurance which Mortfield found unnerving. The prisoner emanated a strength and energy Mortfield did not understand. Could be that faith Solano had mentioned on a few occasions, which Mortfield had dismissed as trivial.

Somewhere, he had seen this before. A twinge of familiarity tugged at Mortfield, until he remembered one afternoon spent in Solano's art gallery. To his mind leaped an image from a single painting: an ancient, white haired prophet standing in chains before his enemies —— a fat, surly, degenerate king of some sort, flanked in a court by savages, all drunk. The king even had wild beasts on chains, lurking about before him.

The painting had depicted a scene from another era, long ago, but here was he, Dalton Mortfield, viewing with his own eyes, history repeating itself. This was uncanny. A dread revelation sank through him like a leaden ball to the pit of his stomach. Zephan Benamoz was an innocent man.

"My, my." Rameses was saying to his audience. "Haman, I'm afraid I must agree with you. Your father does appear unstable. A fanatic like this man is a public menace. He is obviously insane."

Assenting murmurs trickled from the onlookers.

"Papa!" Haman whispered. "Now is the time to plead insanity."

"Haman," Zephan said slowly, "Remember the Bible? What does it teach us about bearing false witness, or in other words, lying, as all these people are doing?"

"Papa, the Bible has nothing to do with this! This is a life and death matter," Haman said urgently. "Just for the moment, forget all that. Just deny the Bible for now, and then you can get yourself out of this little, uh, predicament."

"The Bible is the Word of God, Haman, and you know it!" Zephan's words cut through the air. "And God knows you know it!"

Haman's voice rose in exasperation. "You are making things difficult."

Zephan did not move.

"Then at least recall your words!" Haman said.

"Truth transcends all the foolish moments, my son. All these things are types and shadows of days to come. But God will avenge the blood of the saints, for he will no longer suffer their cries from the dust."

"Papa!"

"I will not recall the words which I have spoken." Zephan remained firm.

"What does it matter?" Rameses said. "Your Bible and all its foolish myths will soon be forgotten."

"And if it is not forgotten? What if the people turn to God, not you?" Zephan's notorious laugh attested to his defiance. "You threaten to destroy the Bible, Rameses, but there is another testament, which proves the Bible is true, and exposes the enemies of Christ, like you! The Lord spoke to the prophet Abinadi, saying: I will preserve the record of Joseph for other nations which shall possess the land. Even this will I do so I may discover the abominations of this people to other nations."

"Rameses!" Ponte shouted. "Do you hear this unmasked hostility against us? He is quoting the book of Joseph. This book is full of treason, Rameses! I have heard these prophets from Yeshurun preaching before. They call down God to destroy the nations! That book should be burned."

"As usual, Ponte, you have perverted the truth," Zephan said calmly. "You have even twisted the everlasting decree of God, which is: this is a land which is choice above all other lands; wherefore he who doth possess it shall serve God or shall be swept off."

"See what I mean?" Ponte shrieked.

"Your fear is totally unfounded," Zephan continued. "God gave us this land, but we have a responsibility. Behold, whatsoever nation possesses this choice land shall be free from bondage, and from captivity, and from all other nations under heaven, if they will but serve the God of the land, who is Jesus Christ."

"It may sound innocent, but it is pure religious hatred!" Ponte insisted. "Rameses, that book is hate literature. I have seen passages from it which would shock you. It is bursting with violence and criminal acts, including assassinations."

"Yes, of course. The book of Joseph. Hardly a bestseller." The spectators laughed.

"It is history, and it is the truth," Zephan said. "This nation's mainstream is searching for the truth, and you make it difficult for people to find it. "

"You forget, Zephan, the masses only read on a fourth grade level."

Whose fault is that? "The prophets have spoken plainly. Look to God and live, they tell us. Nothing in those words could lead people to err."

"You are an educated man, so you don't understand," Rameses said softly. "Their very ignorance makes the masses unruly, and they must be protected from the few who are prone to violence. We must carefully screen out anything which might incite them. Why, even if the wrong things are said over the radio, people go crazy."

"You mean things said over the radio which you don't agree with, like the truth."

"So. Is your book of Joseph true?"

"As the Lord God liveth, it is true."

"Now, Zephan, you know that truth is relative. This is why it is illegal for you to declare your book as the absolute truth."

"Do not fight against truth," Zephan said. "The book of Joseph contains the word of God. If you harden your heart in unbelief and reject this book, it shall turn to your own condemnation — for the Lord God has spoken it."

Rameses made a gesture of disgust. "I cannot tolerate this fear-mongering of yours. But, no matter. We now have a new church which can arbitrate all these things for us. Discussions like the one we are having will no longer be necessary. Isn't this right, my colleagues?"

"Right!" barked the jury in unison.

"Ha! But my dear Zephan, how you do weary me with these trivialities. And this when you have a very grave problem, indeed." Here Rameses leaned back on his cushions and regarded Zephan through narrow, half-shut little eyes. A lazy smile stole across his fleshy face.

The jury leaned forward.

"My dear man," Rameses continued. "You may have broken the very laws against which you so loudly preach."

Zephan said nothing.

The spectators' mouths opened slightly.

338

Zephan half-expected them to salivate.

"Zephan Benamoz, I know you are in a very delicate position. You are accused of conspiracy in the death of Chief Judge Anastasio Solano. I know if you are found guilty, you will be shamed before your people, and you will lose your religious power. Now, we don't want that to happen, do we? But unlike your ancient God, I am much more merciful. I offer you a plea bargain. You give us a copy of that book of Joseph. In exchange, if you do happen to have any dirty little secrets, we will never mention them! We will never breathe a word that you are clinically insane! Right, my colleagues? This little episode would not leave this room, would it?"

"Never!" was the choral response.

"See? The Committee will edit all the hate-words out of your book and publish it. The people would have their book, we would drop all charges, and you would walk out of here a free man! I am a fair man. Trust me! You can't lose. This is an offer you surely won't refuse." Rameses' tone was conciliatory. "How about it, Zephan, my friend?"

"So if I refuse your offer, what will you do?" Zephan asked. "Burn me at the stake?"

"See?" Haman mumbled. "He is definitely insane."

Rameses uttered an obscenity. "What do you take us for? Barbarians? We are much too civilized to do such a thing. Besides, you have no room to speak of barbarism. Zephan, who was Amalickiah?"

"He was an assassin."

"Zephan, where did Solano's assassin get his code name?"

"From the book of Joseph."

The spectators gave a collective gasp.

"I told you the book should be burned," Ponte said to the group. "You can see it is pure hatred."

"Burn the book!" the spectators chorused.

"You can see, ladies and gentlemen," Rameses said to the group, "this man has no shame over what his people have done."

"Rameses, why do you hate my people, the house of Yeshurun?"

Rameses smirked. "Ladies and gentlemen, Zephan asks me why I hate the house of Yeshurun. The answer is appallingly obvious to the most ignorant simpleton, but I will tell him. It is because Yeshurun is responsible for the death of Solano, of course."

"Of course," said the spectators.

"Our history is known to outsiders," Zephan said. "It would be easy for someone who dislikes Yeshurun to use such a name to cover up the identity of the real criminal."

"Have you no moral conscience?" Rameses said in a shocked whisper. "How dare you utter such hatred? Only a member of Yeshurun would imply such a thing."

The jury began to whisper among themselves in shocked tones.

"Rameses, you are afraid of Yeshurun. You are afraid of the justice of God."

"Correction, Zephan. I am afraid of what a madman like you might do if you are turned loose."

"We dare not turn him loose," said one of the spectators.

"Rameses," Zephan continued, "you don't want this nation to be free under God, do you? Rather, you want the sole right to rule over this people. Self-government under God is a threat to you. Someone might find out the truth and bring down your unlimited power. You fear the word of God and his prophets as the Third Reich feared the archives of Judah in Warsaw!"

The man called "Rameses" smashed Zephan across the face, tearing the skin mercilessly with his bejeweled hand.

The jury clapped and whistled.

"No decree can change eternal truth!" Zephan retorted, unflinching.

"My dear man, you attach entirely too much importance to yourself," Ponte said. "Your followers will soon forget you, and this little house of cards which you call the house of Yeshurun will collapse when you are gone."

"What power shall stay the heavens? As well might man stretch forth his puny arm to stop the Sidon river in its decreed course, as to hinder the work of Almighty God from going forth."

"We have power to change the course of your mind, don't we, ladies and gentlemen?" Rameses said. This was met with ribald laughter, and Jowls brought out a vast assortment of needles and vials.

Rameses addressed his lackeys. "You have heard this old man's ravings. But we will take no action without jury consent. Would you agree this man has, uh, shall we say, lost touch with reality?"

"Yes!" they chorused.

"Insane?"

"Yes!"

"Insane enough to be guilty of murder?"

"Guilty!"

"Guilty of conspiracy to murder Solano?"

"Yes! Guilty!"

"Guilty it is."

"He pleads insanity," Haman said in a small voice.

"All right, Haman, you win," Rameses said. "Secretary, add 'insanity' to the verdict. So what's the sentence, Haman?"

"Why, uh, treatment for insanity, of course!" Haman turned to his father. "See, Papa? I got you a lighter sentence!"

Mortfield raised his head slowly and looked at Zephan. He knew this man would never escape. Their eyes locked.

Zephan felt compassion for this ambiguous man who tried so hard to discern what was right.

But Haman's excitement over his apparent success quickly transformed into a perception of self-importance, even power and dominion. "Mortfield!" he commanded. "Strap him down for treatment!"

Something broke inside Mortfield. He wanted to scream. *Haman, you fool! This is your father, who is twice the man you will ever be.* But he said, "I'm going to be sick. I need some air." And he fled.

Ben and Oliver Beck moved away from the bonfire and reached the woods. "Four of five other witnesses to the Solano murder are gone," Ben said. "Three dead and one escaped to Jershon. Without revealing my identity, I asked the one survivor, an old bartender at that hotel where my parents waited for the plane. He said he did his own investigation. According to his words, he had a stack of affidavits from other hotel occupants present that day, who testified they had heard a violent argument between Solano and Zephan Benamoz. Of course the bartender said these documents were at his home in a safe. Two of these so-called witnesses said the morning of the murder they saw my father loitering suspiciously around the vehicles in question. He said there was only one conclusion to draw: Zephan is Amalickiah."

"He was a plant, Ben. Someone pays him to spread disinformation."

Ben groaned. "I know."

"By now he will have reported to his controllers, and they will have identified you. Your life is in danger. Take my advice, Ben, and just be the best of journalists. You are needed there, and this is lousy business for married men. You had better scram, or you will be making a widow out of your lovely wife."

"You're right. This trip was a waste, and I feel very uneasy about my father. If they're spreading such rumors about him —"

Gunfire drowned out his words. It came from the Security building. Both men turned to see a figure running across the square. Beck fumbled for his field glasses and managed to spot the person just as he clambered into an unmarked car and rolled away with his lights off. Across the square, two men cranked up the siren in a police car and tore out diagonally across the plaza, scattering people in their path.

Beck lowered his field glasses, stunned, and fiddled with his radio. "It's Mortfield! And he looks like he's seen the devil himself."

Rameses rummaged through his desk. "Haman! What can we use for a gavel? This must be official, you know. Here's a revolver, but let it not be said that we are violent."

"Let's just drink to the verdict!"

"Charming idea. Drinks all around, Haman. Except to dear old Zephan, of course. He doesn't touch the stuff. A little difficult to drink when you're strapped to an operating table, anyway."

This evoked riotous laughter.

"Lift up your glasses, all. At last, Solano's murderer is brought to justice, and we can feel safe in our beds, once again!"

"I have always wanted to know what this one would do," Rameses said idly, taking up a hypodermic.

"Ladies and gentlemen, of all descendants from the primordial amoeba, this Zephan Benamoz is definitely a malignant mutant variety. Would you agree?"

Laughter.

"Ah, Zephan, this will all be very scientific," he continued. "Millions will benefit from this experiment. What have you to say, old man, before we make a New Man out of you?"

Zephan turned in agony to his son. "I beseech you, do not do this, Haman. Depart from this company now, before it is too late. Look to God and live. I pray with all the energy of my heart that this may not be an everlasting farewell, my son."

"What are you talking about?" the young man shouted. "You are insane! Totally lost from reality!" But suddenly Haman was afraid.

Zephan faced Rameses. "You can kill the body, but you will never have my soul. May God have mercy on you, but as for me, I forgive you."

Rameses said nothing. He motioned the thugs. "Take him away."

Zephan stared at the onlookers, who were talking among themselves, and taking notes, as if they were attending a business seminar.

A huge brutish man moved forward and grasped a metal railing on the bed where Zephan lay. "Ouch! That's hot! This thing feels like it's on fire! Look at his face. It's glowing white all around him. Hey, what's going on, here?"

"Oh, Divine Redeemer!" Zephan exclaimed. "I know that my Redeemer lives."

A hulking figure in military uniform barged out from the crowd. It was a woman, almost as big as the man. "I can handle this," she said. "Are you afraid of a raving lunatic? Get out of my way."

"Haman, Haman, why won't you face the truth?" Zephan called as they wheeled him out. "You will shed innocent blood!"

Haman looked from Rameses to Ponte. They had been his friends for some years, now. "Listen to him!" Haman said. "He's screaming blood and murder! He won't be . . . killed . . . will he?"

Rameses smiled reassuringly. "Of course not. Only subjected to routine treatment for insanity. He's suffering from severe paranoia."

"That's what I thought." Haman sighed. "But my father is suspicious of everyone. 'Never trust in man!' he always says. I guess that is typical paranoia, isn't it?"

"Well done, my boy." Rameses clapped Haman on the back. "You have done a brave thing."

"Thank you, sir." Haman avoided looking toward the door through which his father was taken. "It was difficult, but your confidence in me helped me through it."

"Good, good." Rameses smiled again. "Uh, Haman. I know you're tired, but there is one more thing."

"Anything, sir."

"Do you know where Zephan kept his copy of that book of Joseph?"

"Yes, but my men already cleaned out his house. I'm sure it has been burned with all the other hate literature."

"Excellent. Take a few days off, Haman," Rameses said. "When you come back, I will be sure you get a promotion and are paid twice your present salary. Trust me!"

"Thank you, Rameses! You are so kind!"

24

ZRI Headquarters

Mortfield's car plunged off a cliff. Murder. Mortfield's warning note had been received some time ago — just long enough to let him think he was safe. The poor man was brutally used. Now he was gone, and with him the best chances for solving the Solano case.

Torn with anxiety, Mitchell Hunt paced the floor, fighting a sense of encroaching doom. He glared at the phone, which so far had only brought bad news. His frantic calls had not gone through yet, and he didn't trust the lines anymore. This cursed cartel was pervasive, but at least it was flesh and blood. The cartel was only the lower jaw of the beast.

Before he retired, Zephan had taught Mitchell about the larger scheme, a great struggle for world dominion. He called it pressure from above and below. Below were the seething pits of the narco-mafia, where the body count was obvious. But above were the powers which slowly corrupted the minds of men. These casualties were more subtle, because the deceived appeared abundantly successful. Nevertheless, this spiritual deadness could be found in corporations, the press, the government, even the ZRI itself. And good grief, here at ZRI they were supposed to know who were the good ones and the bad ones. Good men were caught in this deadly vice-grip.

Zephan was on an errand for the Lord, but how safe was he? Historically, priests, despite their peaceful ways, had been known to arouse more ire than political agents. Since the events in Ammonihah, the people of Cumorah, particularly those of the Anti-Hate Committee, were filled with hatred.

Still no word from Clayton. Zephan was well within Sheffa, and neutral territory. Why hadn't Clayton picked him up and reported in by now?

Hunt slammed his fist on his desk in frustration. His men had almost cracked the Pyramid; they were hot on the trail of Rameses. Then that silly mayor pulled his head into his shell. The enemy had the advantage of impenetrable secrecy. In the meantime Egalitarian forces were like a beast, consuming the life out of everything. And Rameses was behind it all. Who the devil was he? Swallowing up good men . . . Mortfield, and now . . . Dear God, not Zephan. Please!

With sweaty hands Hunt picked up the phone. Clayton. "Mudball, where are you?" he shouted into the silent phone. It rang in his hands.

"They got him, sir." Clayton's voice was barely audible. "They killed Zephan. And it was by the hand of Rameses."

"We interrupt this program to bring you a special report," the radio blared. "The assassin of Solano has been apprehended. Zephan Benamoz, former aid to Solano, was captured this evening while attempting to penetrate the Cumorah border. After thorough cross-examination before a judge and jury, Benamoz was found guilty of murder . . . no, make that conspiracy to murder. Zephan Benamoz answered perfectly the description of the dreaded terrorist and assassin known as Amalickiah. But he pleaded insanity, anyway.

"Due to his mental condition, he was sentenced to psychiatric treatment. However, the patient's condition was quickly assessed as utterly hopeless. In Zephan Benamoz' raving lunacy, the implicit plea for mercy was unmistakable. Pure compassion forced doctors to do the unavoidable. Benamoz was euthanized.

"Zephan Benamoz was involved in a larger conspiracy. Accomplices in the conspiracy were said to be in a drug cartel called 'Pyramid'. This could possibly implicate the house of Yeshurun further, or maybe the Arabs, we are not sure which . . ."

"An urgent message for you, sir."
Hunt awoke with a start. "What time is it?"
"Just after four . . . a.m."
Hunt followed the silent emissary to the safe room. "Beck! At least *you* are alive!"

Beck put a finger to his lips. "Mortfield is, too. How he escaped that wreck, heaven only knows. The enemy thinks he's dead, which will protect him. He took a long leave of absence, and we're not to try to find him. The work is really getting to him, Hunt. And this thing with poor Zephan about did him in."

Hunt nodded, understanding.

"But to his everlasting credit, he left us this." Beck held up a box of tiny tape recordings, regarding it like a chest of rare and precious gems. "Last night Ponte blew up a boatload of forty innocent people. Yeshurun folks."

Hunt gasped.

"Of course, such information is not considered newsworthy by the kept press. Nor is Zephan's capture in neutral territory, the sham trial at which Rameses presided, or the disclosure of Amalickiah's true identity." He patted the tapes. "Mortfield was there through it all, and everything is on these tapes."

Hunt gave a low whistle. "And the identity of Rameses?"

"Mortfield said Canosa will lead you to Rameses."

Parte Ultima

Zarahemla

2089, A.D.

The Second Book Of

Zephan

THE SECOND BOOK OF ZEPHAN

1

Home again. Zephan stared around him —— it was familiar, infinitely familiar. On the horizon lay a shimmering sea . . . Lake Tantagua? The Caribbean? No, too smooth, like glass.

Beyond a long series of steps, he beheld a structure of ancient design, reminiscent of Solomon's temple. He ascended three flights and paused at a three-tiered fountain. The largest level, a vast deep pool, reflected the sky, a celestial hue, graduating to the second and third levels. Each was smaller and ever deeper blue.

Where am I? It looks like the House of the Lord.

Bougainvillea, flaunting brilliant magenta. *Is it Canosa's villa?*

He smelled gardenia and orange blossoms. Must be heaven.

His eyes were drawn to the beautiful House. Just two more flights of stairs. Zephan leaped two steps at a time. Somehow at the top was another flight, and then another, and another. But the seventh flight was indeed the last. All at once Zephan's forehead struck something solid, but he could not see anything. He realized the House was beyond a great glass wall, extending endless miles left and right, the most enormous window he had ever seen.

He hesitated.

"Zephan ben Amoz."

Zephan whirled. From his right came a calm, kind voice. Zephan measured the voice's owner, a man of indeterminate age and slight in size, with farseeing eyes. Thick silver hair edged the back of his head, with thinning hair on his crown. Though the man's features were not striking, his blue eyes were without guile. His aura bespoke undeniable benevolence. The face seemed so familiar. He was dressed in a fine suit, all in white, including his shirt, tie, and shoes, and he sat at a small table. Behind the table a fig tree, barely putting forth leaves, gave little shade. The speaker paused over a thick document behind stacked books and papers. As he stood and moved forward, donning a pair of thick, outdated glasses, his face crinkled up into a warm smile. "The power of God is greater than all the soldiers in Babylon."

"Brother Joseba!" Zephan laughed. "I did not recognize you at first without those silly glasses of yours!"

"Well now, I must admit you were much happier to see me than most people who have passed by these portals lately. Oh, it has been a joyful reunion with our brothers and sisters, and many who were confused on earth felt relief to find out the truth. But those who fought against Zion were surprised and disgusted to discover they had to report to our own Brother Joseph."

Zephan pictured those who had sent him across the veil, and could only laugh.

"So where am I? This looks like earth."

"You're close. Welcome to the world of spirits, Paradise Region."

"Am I close enough to go back and visit my new grandson? I never got to see him."

The prophet nodded. "Later. But only with special permission."

"I thought I died!"

"Indeed you did! Mortally speaking, at least. A martyr's death, no less! Aside from that, though, you're really very much alive. It's amazing how much can change in just the twinkling of an eye."

Zephan looked longingly toward the beautiful House, but it had vanished, obscured by a heavy mist. "Then may I proceed to the House of the Lord?"

"Not now."

"But I must!" Zephan Benamoz, big, dignified, fearless, sat down on the step, his face wet with tears.

"I understand your desire to see Father," Joseba said. "And you have earned it, my friend. But for now, a colossal task lies ahead . . . "

Zephan drummed his fingers against the glass and was surprised to hear no sound. "Let me guess." He grinned. "I'm the new window washer!"

Joseba chuckled. "Fortunately for you, we shall not have time for that. Cleaning is not necessary, anyway."

"True. Not a speck on it! How do they do it?"

"Glass is sand in its purest form. Everything here has passed through the Refiner's fire. You know. No unclean thing—"

"Can enter the kingdom of God. Of course."

"Do not forget this, Zephan. It will be a key for you later on."

Zephan nodded toward the vast window. "So what is this great barrier?"

"It is figurative," Joseba said. "A veil between the eternal past and the eternal future. The circumstances under which you come are grievous, but I am infinitely pleased to see you again, *hermanito.*"

"*Hermanito?* Little brother! So Spanish is spoken here?"

"Among other languages. Spanish is the most widely spoken language in Yeshurun," Joseba replied, "but don't let it fool you. The gospel is being preached to every nation, kindred, tongue, and people. We are a worldwide religious body."

Zephan tilted his head. "Do you not find this . . . intimidating?"

Joseba nodded slightly. "I understand your concern, but remember, Babylon has been organized on a world scale for centuries."

"That's what I mean. We in the church of the Lamb are not losing sight of the individual, are we?"

Joseba shook his head. "The adversary's approach is collective, but salvation will always be an individual matter. Our Father in Heaven knows each of us by name. Even the hairs on every person's head are numbered," Joseba said, stroking the top of his head. "I made it easy on Him. But see? They're starting to grow back."

2

"No time to waste!" Joseba declared. "More than seven years have passed since you left. Seems like minutes, doesn't it?"

"Okay, so what is this task?"

"Look in the glass, Zephan."

From the glass, now dark and cloudy, Zephan's reflection stared back at him. "I only see myself."

"Neither can people see beyond themselves." Joseba leaned over a map of the western hemisphere.

Zephan searched the older man's face. "Where do we begin?"

"All you need to know will be revealed to you presently."

"Sounds like an intelligence-gathering mission."

"Indeed it is. You learn fast. You know more than you realize. But I am getting ahead of myself, for the people are losing sight of God's dealings with them, and without a history there will be no gathering."

"Without history, no one can know the future."

"We must move fast. We are still regarded as a single-nation church. By wiping out Cumorah history, the enemy seeks to stop the gathering," Joseba said. "Of course, Satan does not know the mind of the Lord."

"Ponte and company certainly wasted no time in rewriting all school books," Zephan said. "People seem to believe everything they read and hear. And now in Zarahemla the Bible is illegal, too."

"Yes, the Bible, which we value so much — and a great history. Yet people trample it under their feet! Do they remember the pains of the Jews? Do they thank the Jews for the Bible?" The prophet suddenly slashed through the whole map with heavy, rhythmic strokes, dark, parallel lines crisscrossing one another. "Wo unto them that fight against mine ancient covenant people, saith the Lord."

Zephan looked at the map, scored and scarred by Joseba's pen.

"But many on the isles of the sea are not ashamed to wait for Him. And the time has come that He manifests Himself unto all nations. After He made Himself known unto the Jews and also unto the Gentiles, now He manifests Himself unto the Gentiles and also unto the Jews. Thus the last shall be first, and the first shall be last.

And out of the mouths of two or more witnesses, the truth is established."

3

Zephan paced the landing and stopped suddenly. "This other testimony . . . it must be the book of Joseph. It will convince people the Bible is true."

Joseba smiled. "You are beginning to catch the vision of your calling."

Zephan stared at Joseba's crisscrossed lines, which seemed to merge into the sea beyond, like an infinite fisherman's net. "Benjamin loved that book so much he memorized the whole thing, " he said slowly, the pain of his loss returning. "But now . . . "

The prophet pressed his fingers together into a symmetrical spire. "Go on."

"I felt unshakable foreboding that the book might be lost . . . that someone might . . . " Zephan froze. His words fell into a dry well of darkness, echoing back a thousand times from legions of empty souls. "*Hermano*, I must go back to them."

"Yes, my brother. But if you return as an angel, it is very serious business."

"This is urgent, *hermano*! The stick of Joseph is now hidden in enemy land." Zephan pressed his lips into a firm line. "Joseba, my descendants may dwindle in unbelief!"

"Let us not be hasty. Remember the Word is never wasted. God has chosen you, and refined you in the furnace of affliction to carry on this work. But we must be certain we are effective instruments of God's will. We must have a plan."

4

"*Hermano*, we have seen the adversary." Zephan sat down, trembling. He turned to a blank page with only a line down the center. "Now what about our side? What is our team's name?"

The older man gestured toward the distant sea. "We are as numerous as the sands of the sea. You from the tribe of Joseph, I of Judah, but all of us the seed of Abraham. And of course, everyone has the same Father of our spirits." He winked. "Which is why we are brothers."

"Quite a family tree!"

The prophet drew a horizontal line on a chart before him. "Even two branches of the prophet Abraham's descendants can be complicated. Imagine a time line seven thousand years long!"

Zephan gawked at the great window, now white, as two black dots centered in the white expanse sped away from each other toward vanishing points in either direction, leaving a horizontal black line as far as the eye could see.

"Hey! How did you do that?"

Joseba laughed. "We use computer technology, too, without the hardware. Every Sabbath, numberless concourses of people arrive here to be taught the gospel of the Holy One. Computer animation comes in handy! Now, the house of Israel, and Ishmael's descendants, and Keturah's. It all began in the Third Seal, or third thousand years," he continued, walking to his right. "'Tomorrow, and tomorrow, and tomorrow, creeps at this petty pace from day to day, to the last syllable of recorded time . . . '" he muttered. "Yes, here we are, near the end, almost finishing the sixth seal." He circled a tiny segment on the line.

"Our side, the hosts of God!" Zephan whistled softly. "Excellent! Let's get organized right away. I know just the man to lead . . . "

"Negative," Joseba replied, but with eyes smiling. "Trouble is, the moment someone starts organizing, then people place their faith in the organizer, rather than the Lord. People begin to substitute politics for virtue. Never forget that Israel's Commander-in-Chief is none other than the Messiah himself."   Zephan's   eyes widened. The mist before the House of the Lord had gathered into a luminous white figure, resembling a lamb.

5

"But the work is not yet done," Joseba said.

"So what do I do now?"

"In your present state, very little."

Zephan was on his feet. "What do you mean?"

"Remember, you are beyond the veil. Your own options are limited. The resolution is now up to your descendants, through their faith."

Zephan nodded. "I see. But what if they don't . . . "

". . .and your faith!" Joseba cut in with a chuckle.

356

The Book Of
Ammon

THE BOOK OF AMMON

1

It was the occasion of graduation at Zarahemla campus, Yeshurun University. The event was moved to the stadium to accommodate a record multitude.

Ben's wife took his arm and with him crossed a crowded parking lot. Ben watched her at his side, taking long strides to keep up with him. Anahí frequently wore white for a practical reason, to keep cool in Zarahemla's torrid heat while she labored in horticulture. Under Brother Joseba's tutelage at Solano's mansion, Anahí had developed great interest in this hobby. Invariably she emerged from her expanding gardens as pure and fresh as the roses which thrived at her touch. Even with a flame-hued rose in her hair Ani seemed, as usual, oblivious to the entrancing effect she caused. It was her very nature, however, more than outward appearance, which commanded Ben's respect. Ani was intelligent, but without guile; her mind was a sure compass to discern truth from error. Once again, Ben thanked his God for this choice daughter of Zion.

Ben was attending this graduation as an honored alumnus, and for Anahí, a graduate from a secular school, this was a special event. "Excited?"

"More jealous, I think," she said. "Your sojourn at the Yeshurun academy was a joyful one. My college days were a constant battle. By the way, who is the keynote speaker?"

He shrugged. "Some mystery guest, for the bicentennial . . . "

"Papa, look! It says H-O-M-E." Young Ammon was tugging at his father's suit jacket.

Sure enough. The car pulling into a slot beside them looked unusual. The tail lights spanned the vehicle's entire back end, but with individual squares. Someone had blacked out certain squares, so the lights looked like digital letters, spelling the word "home".

"Good evening, Bishop," someone said to Ben.

It was Enrique Cordero, who had married Maria Mundo, the Benamoz' former neighbor in Cumorah. Poor Maria's son and daughter-in-law were killed on Manuel Fernandez' boat, so she and Enri were raising her little grandson, Aaron. "Hermano Cordero!" Ben greeted him. "Your car is unique."

"This is our grandson's handiwork. We came home and found open paint cans and uncleaned brushes which he had 'borrowed' from our neighbor without permission. Hardhearted old man that I am, all I saw was the permanent black paint on the tail lights of my new car. And of course, I saw red." Enri grinned. "The poor little fellow pulled many weeds and cleaned many chicken coops before I finally understood. When he said he was trying to send a message to his parents in heaven, we didn't have the heart to finish out his punishment. He now understands that vandalism is vandalism, no matter what the motive, and his repentance seems sincere. We decided justice had been served, and mercy was in order. It was a good lesson for us all, and I now proudly own a one-of-a-kind automobile!"

Anahí dabbed at her eyes, glad for once she had forgotten her usual light touch of eye makeup.

2

Even the stadium was overflowing, but the Benamoz family had seats reserved near the front. The seat for the featured guest was still empty, but finally the master of ceremonies began his introduction.

"Ladies and gentlemen, you can see by our numbers that we of Yeshurun are no longer provincial, as we once were. There were times when we feared to surrender even the slightest portion of our theology. The presence of our guest tonight proclaims to the world our break with the past, and our new enlightened eye toward the future. We are now a world class culture, and here to give us our new world view is an expert from the Ponte Foundation. Through long, tireless effort, and dedicated teaching, this individual has worked himself up through the rank and file of our growing church. We are proud to claim him as our own. Please welcome Dr. Nils Cromwell."

Anahí gasped in stunned disbelief as the audience broke into thunderous applause. She turned to Ben, but he ruefully shook his head. "Sorry, *corazón*, I would like to leave, too, but I must report on what he has to say."

Cromwell was exuberant. "Ladies and gentlemen, I bring you greetings from Messrs. Dermucker, Banberg, Kingerman, Ponte, and Cabrios, all from the Ponte Foundation. On their behalf, I bring you a grand vision for all. And who better to usher it in than the creme de la creme, even the noble and great ones of Yeshurun?

"Your rapt attention now, my fellow believers, while I unfold our marvelous plan for the Millennial Era. One night, the 150th anniversary of Pax Universalis, I had a vision. I'm sure it came from God."

"The Lord's anointed don't speak publicly of their sacred experiences," Anahí said to Ben.

"Imagine an interfaith organization designed to achieve in religion what Pax Universalis has done for the nations of the world politically!" Cromwell said. "Think of it! For decades, nations of the world have had the moral courage to meet around the table and discuss their differences. But the world's religions haven't even spoken to each other!"

Cromwell leaned forward confidentially. "My fellow believers, after that long, sleepless night, I was reborn as the prophet of a new day. This is the vision we have all been looking for, but I need you to help me implement it. Who better than Yeshurun to spearhead a drive to thrash out specifics for a new universal ethic?"

A few in the pensive crowd nodded slowly.

"A special friend has ordained me to this important mission. In his modesty, he prefers to remain anonymous," Cromwell continued, "but I assure you he has authority. Already I have been gathering supporters, raising funds, and creating the structure, which is to be modeled on Pax Universalis. Our goal is to open world headquarters in Zarahemla city within a year!

"We have all been anxiously waiting for the return of Christ. And when our image of Christ returns, his first visit will be to Pax Universalis to see if his dream of world unity and brotherhood has come true. He is waiting for us to do our part. When he comes, will we still be torn apart into fragmented churches, or will we have the new League of Religions ready for him?

"My fellow believers, are we worthy to call ourselves brothers and sisters when we are divided by absolutes? How can we be a global family if we continue to bicker among ourselves?"

"He has a point, there," someone said to Ben.

"Let us do away with our strife, my fellow believers," Cromwell said. "Not everyone's idea of truth is the same. For example, if you believe exclusively in the God of Israel, you may have to alter your views a little to accommodate the world. It is time to address specific duties regarding our global responsibility. It is Yeshurun's turn to be silent about man's duties to an absolute God. It is Yeshurun's turn to surrender some core beliefs, if necessary. Intelligent people can be tolerant of other beliefs, such as Kemen Ponte's Tower of Understanding, or nihilism from the land of Tartarus, or Rousseau's Idyllic Imagination. It is time for Yeshurun to yield to the pantheistic collective."

Many in the audience wore a look of awe, perhaps for the speaker's erudite language.

"And what is truth?" Cromwell said. "Is anything which offends people ever right? What do you think is right and wrong? Does it agree with what everyone else thinks? And does it really matter what you think? In a perfect world, do we have a right to impose our absolute perceptions on others? This is the Age of Self-Authority. Does the notion of sin offend you? Then pluck it out. Some people are forever speaking of sin, and what harmony do we get? The answer is obvious."

Thousands of heads nodded in acknowledgment. Of course, it was obvious.

"Here is an important example," Cromwell continued. "The old, traditional family has been nothing but a breeding ground for torment and abuse. The new global family will sweep aside the divisive dogmas of sin, punishment, atonement, and other obstacles to world peace. Fundamentalism, which has caused so much strife throughout the world, will mellow under the governance of a League of Religions. Encourage your congressman to vote in favor of the Pax

Charter for the League of Religions. Insist that your representative support the Pax Code of Human Rights."

The audience remained attentive.

"It is time for reform," Cromwell said. "The Universal Ethic will give us a new Ten Commandments: Thou shalt not offend others with rigid moral absolutism."

Laughter.

"The new Sermon on the Mount will enshrine Tolerance as the highest virtue ——— the only virtue.

"You are glorious, beautiful, and brilliant people. You are the chosen ones. This is your mission as much as it is mine. It is up to you."

"Listen to his flattery!" Anahí snapped. "This man reminds me . . . of . . . "

"Korihor," Ben finished.

"You mean, that antichrist in the book of Joseph?" Ammon said, a little too loudly.

"Shhh!" someone hissed behind them.

Ben turned. It was the blank-faced, flaxen-haired humanist he had met in Cumorah years ago.

"How can you say such a thing?" the woman whispered fiercely. "Dr. Cromwell is more Christlike than you will ever be!"

"Shhh, yourself!" Anahí retorted rudely.

Suppressing his amusement, Ben pulled his wife close to him, and together they stared at this gullible woman with the glazed eyes and plastic smile.

The woman finally averted her face and turned adoring eyes to the speaker.

"Children, I am deeply moved by your support." Cromwell wiped his eyes with a large white handkerchief, easily seen by the multitudinous spectators. "I urge you, vote for the League of Religions, and together we can solve all the world's problems, be they religious, economic, or political in nature. I invite you personally. Come, follow me. Together we shall succeed, and nothing nor no one shall stand in our way. No corner of the globe will remain unaffected. Our earth will fit the Universal Ethic like a hand in a glove. In a perfect world, our attitudes will be changed permanently, *and then there will be no turning back.* Thank you." He blew his nose and sat down. He received a standing ovation which lasted for more than an hour.

To Ben's surprise, the *Zarahemla Post* published his article opposing the Nils Cromwell speech.

"Dr. Nils Cromwell is widely revered due to his exalted status in the academic field, but he claims to be a prophet of a new day," Ben wrote. "So let us be discerning, for many counterfeits can be found in the world today. Can anyone accept doctrine as authority, when it springs from some secret and unknown source? The father of lies is the founder of works of darkness. He leads the unwary by the neck with a flaxen cord, until he binds them with his strong cords forever. But the Lord God worketh not in darkness.

"A wolf among us today is a skillful imitator of sheep," Ben wrote, "but what is behind his words? Is he intemperate, irreverent, or immoral? And what are his fruits? Are his doctrines like venom from a poisonous serpent, perverting the ways of the Lord?

"Our learned Dr. Cromwell has informed us that our planet will fit his 'universal ethic' like a hand in a glove. One critic has warned: Watch out for gloved hands that control planets."

Nils Cromwell multiplied his appearances, both to Yeshurun and to other communities.

As a journalist, Ben covered Cromwell's speeches for the *Post*.

"I'm here because I want to redefine the meaning of citizenship," Cromwell said.

"The original laws of this country granted us a radical amount of freedom, assuming that we would use our freedom responsibly . But now people are too irresponsible, and everyone is saying there is too much freedom," he continued. "When personal freedom is being abused, we must move to limit it."

Cromwell appealed to the elitism and micro-management tendencies among Zarahemla's university faculties. "I prefer the philosophies of Voltaire, myself," he told them.

"Illuminators of group thought have synthesized this new religion," he told faculty members. "The new history will play a role of an undogmatic Bible to the world. It will hold the world together mentally. Our Universal Ethic will exert a very real influence upon everyone who controls administrations, makes wars, directs mass behavior, and feeds, moves, starves and kills populations."

This comment was met with laughter.

"You see how the implementation of this new Ethic could spread like a nervous network, a mental control system encircling the globe," he said. "We can replace competition with voluntary service. To harness our youth for the Cromwell Youth Program, we must capitalize on their idealism, and what the churches taught them about sacrifice. After all, who can disagree with the ancient proverb from a historic king? When you are in the service of your fellow men, you are in the service of your God. Who is God, ladies and gentlemen, if not society?"

University professors were taking copious notes.

"Now, we all know how most teenagers are."

Laughter.

"Teenagers are totally incapable of compassion unless they are forced to it," Cromwell said. "Let's be realistic. We must intervene to solve the nation's social ills. You must teach the youth that their duty to society transcends any other loyalty. I hate to say it, but you must expect volunteerism to be compulsory, because it has to be done. If we want it to be realized, we have no other choice. The Cromwell Youth Program should be the shock group. Each youth should be made to see that he may have to work with people whose doctrines he may not understand, whose doctrines he may not immediately adopt. But he must be made to see that we are the people who are showing him the right way," Cromwell said.

"And to parents who will not vote for the Cromwell Youth Program, I would calmly say: Your child belongs to us already. What are you? You will pass on. Your descendants, however, now stand in the new camp. In a short time your descendants will know nothing else but this new community.

"Let's talk about mass psychology," Cromwell told his spellbound listeners. "Education is a powerful ally of human oneness. The new Ethic will be one of self-actualization. But the populace must not be allowed to know how its convictions are generated. Verses set to music and repeatedly intoned are very effective."

Again, laughter.

"Influence from the home is obstructive to our new Ethic," he warned. "In fact, two powerful forces stand in the way of global harmony: one is inflexible religion; the other is nationalism. The only way we can overcome this disunity is to ratify the Pax Code of Human Rights."

"There is no law against a man's belief," Ben wrote. "Therefore, Dr. Cromwell's activities are not illegal, yet. But once he imposes his belief system by law, it will be the beginning of enforced priestcraft, and the end of religious freedom, and we will be bound to obey it. Let us not forget the numerous examples in history in which the Jews started out being affable, and compromised with foreign rulers. That which began as mild restrictions led to unspeakable atrocities, because our Jewish brethren would not give up their religion. We in Zarahemla have more political freedom than any other nation, and we have the privilege of voting. Our God, who favors no person, race, class, or circumstance over another, has spoken: it is not right that any man should be in bondage one to another. Let us, therefore, oppose this untoward Pax legislation, and stand fast in our God-given liberties, before it is too late."

Cromwell spoke from pulpits across the land, but especially to Yeshurun. "Your book of Joseph is too Christ-centered," he told people of Yeshurun. "This book is offensive to the rest of the world," he continued. "It speaks far too much about the Biblical Christ. The day of Biblical literalism is past. Christ is whoever we want him to be. He does not have to conform to the religion of the house of Israel.

"We live in the post-modern age," Cromwell said. "In biblical days, an ethnic God performed little miracles for his people because they were so backward. But today we have miracles of our own making. Look at our advances in technology! Let us take pride in the products of our own genius. It is the tendency of certain elements in our society to accuse and judge other nations for their diverse moral codes. We should not accuse other nations of sin, my fellow believers, simply because in other lands, each one lives and dies according to his own measure of morality. We should be ashamed of ourselves for focusing on sin all the time, and making other peoples, and ourselves, feel guilty. See how stressed and frenzied we always are!

"I offer an easier way for us all," Cromwell said to the people in crowded chapels and cottage meetings. "Why label as sin those things we all are going to do anyway, and which we know we enjoy? Go ahead. Enjoy yourselves. Free yourselves from this burden of sin. Think of it! A perfect world is free from sin. Such freedom! No tyranny from consequences, guilt, repentance, atonement, and all those tiresome old dogmas we've been fighting over for centuries.

With the wars gone, we will truly be one global family." Thus he went about gaining signatures and endorsements, and although he never directly asked for money, he began receiving immense donations.

"With but one great League of Religions," Cromwell continued, "we will all be in harmony, and truly we will be brothers and sisters. With one great harmony, who can be offended? So some people don't believe in a biblical God, or a particular savior, or the atonement, or all that . . . what of it? It's time all those uncomfortable doctrines were put to rest, and absorbed into the greater whole. The important thing is human oneness and true brotherhood."

4

The hour was late, and Ben knew Dan MacRay was still waiting outside the bishop's office to see him. He rubbed his eyes, certain he would feel less fatigued if he had hauled cement blocks all day. At least in such work, he could leave behind the day's encumbrance and go home. Not so with the sin-laden people who had streamed into his office all afternoon. As bishop he could only counsel, and each person must bear his own accountability, but much as he tried to be detached, Ben deeply loved his people, and could not totally unburden himself of his concern for these unhappy individuals. Surely the most miserable would be Nola Stormer. If only she could be rescued in time from the dreadful step she was about to take. Ben knew it was about this urgent matter that Dan, her home teacher, had come to consult him. He had never seen Dan so agitated.

"I have phoned several times a day, but no one answers," Dan said. "I left messages repeatedly, but no one returns my call. Finally I visited her apartment, but her roommates are hiding her. I explained in a most civil and kind manner that I was her minister, and was there to help her. Her roommates seemed united as a stone wall in opposition. As often as I dared, I continued visiting until finally those girls told me not to approach their apartment anymore, or they would call the police on me for harassing them."

"I see."

"But we have one more slim chance," Dan continued. "Every day at different times, I drove slowly past their place, in hopes I might glimpse Nola. I didn't, but finally, today, one roommate, Cristina, did speak with me. She flagged me down around the corner

367

from her house to avoid being seen. She said she did not agree with her roommates, and she was afraid for Nola. When I asked who the father of Nola's baby was, so I might speak with him, Cristina looked terrified. She refused to answer my question, but she did tell me the name of the clinic where Nola is going to sacrifice the child."

"When?"

"Tomorrow morning at seven o'clock."

Ben grabbed his briefcase. "Let's go."

Arising early to make the two-hour drive, Ben and Dan arrived at the clinic with a gray sunrise. In the gloomy dawn they made out figures of a man and woman at the clinic's back door. "That's Nola!" Dan said. "You take the front—"

But Ben had already leaped from the car and was sprinting halfway to the couple. He hailed them, but they vanished into the building while a guard hastened to lock and bolt the door. Ben rapped on the glass door. "Please open up! I must see that lady!"

"Who are you?" the guard said through the glass.

"Bishop Benamoz. I came to minister to her."

The guard's face registered no expression. "Well, wait here." He walked away from the door without unlocking it.

Dan joined his friend. "That front door is locked up like a tomb. I can see people in there, but no one answers."

The guard still did not return, but a police car roared up, siren wailing, and two officers came on the run, weapons ready. "You are under arrest."

"This must be some mistake," Ben said, but he and Dan allowed themselves to be hand-cuffed without resistance.

"Benjamin Benamoz? Dan MacRay?"

"Yes."

"Then it is no mistake. You are charged with harassing and assaulting patients and workers at this facility. You will be held at the Public Safety Building."

Dan and Ben were released the following morning; the charges were dropped, but no explanations were given, and no apologies.

Weeks passed, but no word from Nola. Ben and Dan could only pray she would come to them and let them try to salvage something from the wreckage of her life.

Late one evening after work, Ben went to his office to use the time alone for some urgent correspondence. He was soon deep in thought and study.

"Men are free to choose liberty and eternal life, through the great Mediator of all, or to choose captivity and death, according to the captivity and power of the devil," the ancient prophet Nephi had said.

Again, and with growing concern, Ben studied the text from all Nils Cromwell's speeches. With his teachings, the man was herding people en masse down a broad road to destruction. Now it appeared Cromwell's philosophies were making inroads into Yeshurun as well.

A knock at the door. And he thought he would have some time to himself?

One look at the visitor and he knew it was going to be another long, draining interview. She could not be past her twenties, but she was gaunt, like a person three times her age, wasted by some devastating illness. Her fine blonde hair was almost colorless, giving her a ghostly appearance.

In the past months Ben had seen scores of people weighed down with sorrows from grave sins, but none bore the tragic countenance of this girl. The look in her eyes would haunt him for years to come. "Nola Stormer?"

She drew back. "How did you know?"

Ben smiled. "You are the only sister in my congregation whom I have not met before. A pleasure to meet you at last." He shook her hand warmly and ushered her to a seat.

After a prayer, he let her pour out her heart, and it was worse than even he had anticipated.

"Who was the father?" he asked.

"Nils Cromwell."

Ben winced. This brought Cromwell's tally of Yeshurun women to six in the past year. What did those women see in him? "But this man is much older than you are, Nola."

"Forty-two. And married."

"However did he seduce you?"

"It was an intellectual exercise."

Ben stifled his disgust and kept his voice neutral. "Please tell me about it."

"He was a guest professor, giving a course in Roman Society. I needed the course to graduate. It would not be offered again for two years, and Cromwell would complete it in only eight weeks. Dr. Cromwell was my uncle's friend. I figured that should be to my advantage. It sounded ideal, so I took it. The first day he told us we had only one major assignment. It would be difficult, he said, but it must be done to pass the class. The assignment was to personally violate one moral code, either in our family or church, and then write a thirty-page paper on our experience. We could not interview someone else who had done it. Only personal experience would be accepted. Many of my friends had told me in great detail how they had been deflowered. I had never even so much as been tempted by anyone, because I know I am homely." She sighed and continued in a monotone. "I decided to make up a composite of their experiences and pass it off as my own. It would be a lie, but I figured by so doing I would be violating my moral code and comply with the assignment."

Ben waited.

"The weeks passed, and I was pleased with my cleverness. I was sure I would get by with it. Cromwell seemed to like me. He was always watching me. I thought it was because I was the only member from Yeshurun in the class. Even though I had not told him about myself, somehow people seem to figure it out when you are from Yeshurun." She hesitated. "On the other hand, perhaps he found out from my uncle — he knows everything about everybody.

"Every day Cromwell complimented me on what I wore," she continued, "but most especially he always told me what a beautiful figure I had. I started to believe him. No one had ever even given me a second glance. Oh, I had been told often that I am intelligent, but no one had ever made me feel so pretty before. He was flattering me, of course."

"In one sense he was telling you the truth, Nola," Ben said. "Even in the world's eyes, none is more beautiful than a daughter of Zion who is pure and undefiled. Unfortunately, Cromwell looks upon purity and chastity with a predatory eye."

She moaned and closed her eyes for a moment. "He was so brilliant and famous, and I was proud to be the object of his attention," she went on. "I made up my mind to enjoy it while it lasted. Every day he taught a philosophy from one man or other."

"Yes, it is the trend in universities."

"'Reality is but a model created by our class, gender, and racial persuasions,' he told us. 'We must revise literature, law, history, and religion to conform to a new reality. Our law must be based on scientifically proven facts, not on the words of some old prophets and their imaginations. The founders of our law, and especially the prophets, were placed on pedestals in our childhood, and the time has come to knock those false heroes off their pedestals.'"

She shifted in her chair. "By this time I was hanging on his every word. I was only too happy to adopt him for my new hero.

"But he said, 'Man is but another species of animal. How are we different from any other animal, since our purpose in life is but to eat, drink, and reproduce? Heroes are another false reality. The true reality is that which brought us into being. Better to worship the sacred earth, which gave us life. If there had been no water, there would be no fins; if no air, there would have been no wings, if no land, there would be no legs.

"'You can't deny it. At an early stage the fetus of a child cannot be distinguished from the fetus of an ape, or a pig, or a horse. If Adam *arose* from a monkey, then a baboon, then a gorilla, how can anyone say Adam *fell*? You can see man didn't need God to create him. Then, when we remove the biblical icon called the Fall, why would we need a savior or an atonement? So any intelligent person can see it only takes a moment to topple the pillars of the Bible. The Bible can no longer stand in an environment of scientific facts.'"

Nola covered her eyes and dug her fingers into her scalp. "This was the reasoning he pushed upon us day after day, Bishop. After awhile, I could no longer discern what was right. I no longer could dispute his logic."

"'It is easier to accept the scientific evidence than to believe, with blind faith, that some mystical God created Adam through an incredible miracle,'" Cromwell said. "'Since man has figured out for himself how he developed, we should only be accountable to ourselves, shouldn't we? Why should we be subject to the arbitrary whims of so-called good and evil dictated by some unseen God? It is time to accept a new reality. One which is useful. Your parents' values and version of history may have been practical in the past, but it is useless for the future,' he said.

"I began to feel ashamed of my ignorance," Nola said.

"At last we turned in our papers and a Roman-style banquet was held for the final week," she continued. "We all dressed in togas and had a great time, except my classmates kept teasing me, calling me the Vestal Virgin. Champagne was plentiful, and I decided to have some, too . . . I know, Bishop. It's against our health code. It was not the first time I tasted liquor, because my mother hasn't kept her covenants for years, and my father is a Gentile. They like to drink for social occasions. Besides, if Cromwell found out, I could tell him that although I was still a virgin, I had violated two moral values to make up for it.

"When dinner was over, he asked me to stay after everyone left. We talked about many things, and had a few more glasses of champagne. Then he tore up my paper and told me he knew I had tried to deceive him. He said he would have to fail me, because I had missed the key learning experience in the course. I was uncertain what to do. He took my hand and drew me to him, and looked into my eyes.

"'You look entrancing in that toga,' he said. "But I imagine without your toga, you must look a lot like the Greek goddess, Venus. Only the statue I saw of Venus had no head. But Venus was all heart and hormones. No brain. But oh, what a divine figure! Looking at you, I know now what Venus' face must have looked like. Best of all, you have a fine mind, with the figure of Venus in the bargain. Come here, my little Venus.'

"By then I was slipping fast. He began to look like a Greek God, himself, with his wavy hair and bedroom eyes.

"'You are so beautiful,' he kept saying. 'No one will ever love you as much as I do. I adore you.'

"'You mean, you want to marry me?' I asked stupidly.

"He laughed. 'Have you learned nothing from my class? I said nothing about marriage. Marriage is an unnecessary tradition. You are free to experience all without the bonds of those old traditions, remember? Tell you what. I'll give you a second chance. You wouldn't want a failure on your lofty academic records, would you? What would I tell your uncle? Come on. Just for a moment, for the sake of experience, for an experiment. Experiment! This is what experience is all about, isn't it? Just for a moment, pretend you have the body of Venus, but you keep the mind of the Vestal Virgin. We will perform the experiment on your body, but in your mind you'll stay a virgin. It's easy, see? Mind over matter!'"

"When I still hesitated, he said, 'what if you never marry, my darling? You may never have another chance to have this experience. No one will ever love you again as I do at this moment. Don't you love me, too?'

"'Okay,' I said at last. 'But what if later I am with child?'"

"He laughed again, and caressed me. 'You are so quaint,' he said. 'This is what is so adorable about you.' He put on a mock frown. 'You are also stubborn. I have been teaching you for weeks now, everything starts out as a lump of protoplasm. How will that matter a few years from now? The only reality is *now*. You will not be *with child*, as you call it. Human beings are but a higher form of animal. It is perfectly natural for animals to do it, isn't it? Why should we deprive ourselves from doing it? All flesh is just a mass of cells. We can do what we want with our flesh. Are we not here to subject our flesh to the will of our minds? Any excess tissue which may develop is a perfectly natural occurrence. The, uh, little experiment we are about to perform is perfectly natural, too, isn't it? As long as our minds are in control, we can overcome any perceived consequences to the flesh. Do you understand me?'

"He assured me there was a pill I could take the next day which would take care of everything. I could pretend nothing had ever happened, he said . . . Well, now I've done it. But I couldn't get the pill. The doctor told me it was a potent drug, and I had to get my parents' consent. My parents may be social drinkers, but they are decent people and I knew they would be furious. My parents live far away in Sheffa, so I just hoped nothing would happen, and did nothing. But I was pregnant. I called Nils, and he said he would arrange for a simple surgical procedure I could get at a certain place without parental consent. Soon I felt the little one kick, though, and I panicked. I called Nils again and said I couldn't do it. He said to be firm. 'Mind over matter', he said. 'That's all it is, Nola. Just a little piece of matter. All the other girls did it,' he said, 'and they have never regretted it.'

"'But they are Gentiles', I said.

"'You and your eternal beliefs,' he grumbled. 'You miss the whole point,' he insisted. 'My theory works just as well for Israel as it does for Gentiles. It's time you gave up these silly superstitions, Nola. If you didn't want to learn from me, you shouldn't have taken the course. Stop acting like a stupid freshman.

"'How would all the other girls in my classes ever pass the course if they always worried about minor consequences?' he demanded. 'Students might refuse to complete my assignments. They would fail to learn the important concepts I am teaching; it would destroy my scientific credibility; it would undermine my authority.

"'Your uncle is funding my work, Nola,' he said. 'If he finds out I made an exception for a Yeshurun girl, or anyone else, it will ruin credibility in my scientific experiments, and he will cut off my funding. This I can't afford.'

"I told him what he could do with his experiments, and his money, and I hung up. After that, he called me incessantly. 'You're making entirely too much of this, dearest,' he would say. 'It's really nothing. Millions have done it.'

"One day he got ugly. 'Your uncle knows about this, Nola.'

"Then I was scared. 'But I am his niece!' I protested.

"'It makes no difference!' Cromwell snapped. 'Indeed, it's worse. You know how your uncle feels about Yeshurun. You know he will do anything to destroy it. In fact, he put me up to this, just to bring you down. I'm sorry, Nola. I. . .I didn't know I would fall in love with you. But if you really loved me, you wouldn't do this to me.'

"Finally I agreed to go through with it. By this time, the baby was almost full term. Nils went with me and held my hand the whole time. He kept saying he knew it was a painful decision for me, but he said over and over how brave I was. He kept saying it didn't matter how late I did it; the important thing was that I had the 'courage' to do it. They gave me a drug so I wouldn't know what was happening. I felt no pain. I was not brave. I was a coward. But when it was all over, . . . oh Bishop, it was so awful. I thought I didn't want to die, but when I saw . . . I just wished I had gone ahead and died."

Ben frowned. "Was your pregnancy healthy?"

"Absolutely."

"But Nola, I have investigated the medical journals extensively myself. World medical experts have testified that normal full term pregnancies do not in any way endanger the mother's life."

"Oh, I know."

"Then what were you afraid of, Nola?"

"My uncle."

"Who on earth is your uncle?"

"Arch Kingerman. Do you know him?"

"Yes, I do," Ben said.

"But you don't know what it is to cross him. You don't know how many people have been killed for doing far less than I did."

Ben clenched his teeth. *Yes, I do.*

"I was conscious enough to hear the most pitiful little cry. I know I heard it. They can't tell me he wasn't born alive! Then my baby died. And then after it was all over," she said, "and I saw that baby thrown on the floor with its brains sucked out, I screamed. But not Cromwell. He laughed! Here I had done all this to spare his life as well as mine, and how does he thank me? He wanted to take me out on the town, and celebrate victory for his theory! I wanted to kill him myself. Now I am battling cancer. God is punishing me."

"If only I had reached you in time."

"You tried to ——"

Ben nodded. "I got to the clinic door just as they closed and locked it in my face. This was after your home teacher had tried for weeks to see you."

"I never knew."

"Sister Stormer, why did you not come to me sooner?"

"I was afraid of my uncle. And I thought . . . I thought you would condemn me."

Ben groaned. "Nola, Nola. I am here to help you, not condemn you. It is not in my power to either save you or condemn you. It is in the Lord's hands."

She turned to him a face of unspeakable anguish. "Bishop, the baby . . . it was . . . a little boy. And he looked just like me!" She sank to her knees and pounded the floor with her fists. "Oh! What have I done?" she wailed. "What have I done?" She remained prostrate, sobbing uncontrollably.

"Look at me, Nola." Ben raised her to her knees. "Your little son is alive in Christ. He was sinless, and is safe in the highest realm, to live with his Father in Heaven forever."

She dried her tears. "Thank you. Oh, what comfort that sweet knowledge brings. Of course my little one does not deserve the hell I have brought upon myself."

"We would all be in hell without the atonement, Nola. Listen to the words of your Redeemer. 'Behold, I came into the world not to call the righteous but sinners unto repentance; the whole need no physician, but they that are sick.'"

"Have I any hope at all . . . ?"

"You were deceived by Nils Cromwell's subtle craftiness," Ben said. "But you must face the truth. Your sin is deeply grievous to the Lord. However, the Final Judgment is not yet in."

"Is there still time?"

"That depends on you. Do not procrastinate the day of your repentance."

"I'm dying anyway. Perhaps it will atone . . . "

"Only One could do that," Ben said gently. "Jesus died for you. He is the Christ, your Redeemer, the Atoning One. Cast your burden upon the Lord, Nola."

"I can't, Bishop. He is the Son of God. He is perfect. He would not understand."

"Yes, He is the Son of God," Ben said softly. "For that very reason, just as lies have brought destruction to your door, so liars assaulted Him. You see, most people did not believe He was the Son of God. Many claimed He was merely the son of Mary, whom they called a fornicator, and they persecuted and reviled Him all His life for it. He descended below all things for people like you who repent, Nola. The road of repentance is not easy, but it is worth it. Total repentance is required from us, but even after all we can do, there is still no other way nor means whereby we can be saved, only through the atoning blood of Jesus Christ. Do not reject His gift and let His suffering be in vain. Will you not now return unto Him, and repent of your sins, and be converted, that He may heal you?"

After Nola left, it was too late to start anything, so Ben began to clear his desk, getting ready to head for home. Another knock at the door was loud and firm. Who else could be coming at this hour? "Come in."

It was Haman.

Ben breathed out slowly. "What do you want?"

"A fine way to greet your brother. I was on my way back from a meeting with Arch, and I saw that girl leave your office sobbing her heart out. What did you do to her, Ben?"

"I gave her hope and comfort."

"I'll bet you did." Haman smirked. "I can hear it now. You told her what Papa drummed into our heads for years. You told her about the horrors of human sacrifice in history, didn't you? How the Canaanites fed their baby boys to the fire to appease the war God Molech; how the Lamanites sacrificed Nephite women and children, then cannibalized the remains; and how the Nephites did the same thing in anger, hatred, and vengeance. Some comfort."

"Do you know this girl? How do you know what her problem is?"

"Arch told me about her. He said Yeshurun was making a big deal about it, as usual."

"Well, how different is it from the Canaanite abominations?" Ben began to pace.

"Plenty. You know I abhor those instances from history as much as you do, Ben. Papa was always ranting about furnaces and altars in public places. But those people were primitive. Barbarians. I personally find it revolting, like what some people do in their back alleys, even today. But what's wrong with a small clinical procedure, in a sterile environment, by a licensed health care provider? And certainly no one does it in the name of religion."

"The gods of hedonism disdain true religion, but crave your worship. The ancients justified violence and depravity with hatred, vengeance, or victory in war. But now it is done as a lark. And cannibalism has become the subject of movies, jokes, or situation ethics." Ben's voice was heavy with weariness.

Haman shook his head with an indulgent smile. "You are a fanatic."

Ben sunk into his chair and closed his eyes. "I have just seen the utter desolation of a young mother who beheld her baby, dead on the delivery room floor, at the hands of a medical professional. How can you tell me I shouldn't care? Are you beyond feeling, Haman? Or is it pride?"

Haman opened his mouth but said nothing.

"It must be pride," Ben continued. "If you acknowledge that what Nola did was wrong, then everything you and your friends have been rationalizing all these years is wrong, too. You could never admit that, could you?"

"You're talking insanity. I don't have to listen to your preaching. I'm not in your religion any more, remember? And don't you dare tell me to repent!"

"So, Haman. And where are the remains of your little daughter, hmm? Being consumed as medication, or perhaps in someone's beauty cream?"

"Huh? What are you talking about?"

"The fruit of your own loins, Haman. We Benamoz men produce many male children, and we love them more than ourselves. But you, Haman, have begotten a girl — the first girl in this generation. And you destroyed her when she was only ten inches long."

Haman shrugged. "Good grief, Ben. It's just family planning. What Delia did is perfectly legal. She believes in population control just like a religion. She thinks it is more harmonious with nature to keep the population down. After all, families have to be planned just like the economy has to be planned. What's wrong with that? Delia is doing her duty to the world. It is her preference, and she is not rude about it like you are. On the contrary, she has been most pleasant. Delia is, shall we say, pleasantly pro-planning. Yes, that's it."

"You treat this abomination as if it were a preference in wines, or resort areas."

"Since you're determined to talk about sins, what about cigarettes? I think it is a disgusting habit," Haman said.

"As is your cigar habit," Ben shot back.

"And racism! It's the mother of evils."

Ben continued straightening his desk. "Spare me the hypocrisy, Haman. You think anyone who does not agree with your politics is a racist."

"Let's talk about how splendidly the economy is thriving," Haman said. "That's much more important."

"Yes, let's," Ben said in an agreeable tone. "After all, human sacrifice is not a single issue. It has far-reaching consequences, even on your precious economy. Zarahemla population is aging, Haman. Where will Elidor get taxes for her welfare programs, hmm? Certainly not from the old and dying. But there will be no young wage-earners, Haman. Do you know why? Zarahemla has killed one third of each new generation, that's why. We are flooded with immigrants from Ponte's Cumorah, Haman. Perhaps foreign people will do the nation's farm work you and your friends disdain to do. Perhaps others will fill the gaping chasm in our population caused by your family planning massacre. But someday people of integrity who have worked hard all their lives and provided for their children will want to enjoy the fruits of their labors. Do you really think, Haman when that time comes, we will care for the likes of you and you crowd —— a bunch of selfish old Egalitarians who sacrificed thei own progeny, hmm?"

"You are merely biased," Haman argued.

"I suppose I am." Ben sighed. "Biased in favor of the huma race."

"But those are just biased demographics," Haman said. "Those statistics were thrown out when the family planning laws were passed."

But Ben would not be distracted. "Why didn't you give your baby up for adoption, Haman?"

"What? And have it grow up and —"

"Not *it*, Haman. *She.* Mercy! I would have adopted her myself."

"Now you're making a big deal about it again. It's only a piece of tissue, anyway. Why all the fuss over a lump of protoplasm — "

"With a face and a beating heart, and a spirit."

"Well, it's what Delia wanted. I can't deny her a choice to do what she wants, can I?"

Ben shook his head. "Why don't you honor our God, the giver of all life, as much as you do the gods of Babylon, Haman?"

Haman tried to avert his eyes, but could not escape Ben's compelling gaze. He started toward the door.

"You can talk like a Gentile if you want, Haman, but you cannot change who you are. You are the remnant of Jacob, *hermano,* a child of covenant Israel. Our families are forever."

"Ha!" Haman turned with a sly look, as if some secret knowledge had suddenly restored his threatened pride. "And how do you expect to prove this identity of the remnant, except in the written scriptures, which are banned? You place far too much value on your miserable race, Benito. These days everyone has his own view."

"So what's wrong with mine?"

"Your view offends everyone. In a perfect world, we can't have so many churches. How can we have peace with everyone fighting over those old traditions?"

"I understand. So you think the world has no room, except for one universal ethic?"

"Exactly. We have never had room for all those wars the Bible has caused. But at least the Bible is gone, now. And as for the book of Joseph . . ."

Ben froze. Did the Egalitarians know where to find the last copy of the other testament?

"After Solano's assassination I went back to our house to look for the book of Joseph," Haman said. "But I was too late. The Pax peace forces had already torched and gutted every Yeshurun home. There was nothing I could do."

379

So the Benamoz home was destroyed. Ben was sick at heart.

"It's just as well," Haman said. "The book of Joseph is illegal under Pax law. That book was nothing but trouble, anyway."

"I —"

Haman waved off Ben's response. "I know, I know. It is said you memorized the whole book. You even quote it in your newspaper articles. You always were too smart for your own good. But now there is nothing you can do . . . " Haman shook his head. "Hey! You know what? If you try to publish the book of Joseph anew from your memory, it will be totally discredited. Now, how about that? Looks like your law and the prophets are ashes. Ha! Here you are worrying about the human race, and Yeshurun could become extinct. Extinction!" Haman laughed. "Do you get it? In the human race, the strong will survive, Ben. But Yeshurun! Now there is an endangered species for you. Such a pity!" He sniffed and made a show of wiping his eyes. "And you will have no history to verify that you ever existed. One more generation and you will not only be extinct, but you will be forgotten! Yes, indeed. Such a pity." He slammed the office door with all the irreverence he could muster, and his laughter could be heard echoing through the chapel halls as he left.

6

Ben decided to join other bishops in writing a private epistle to their brethren and sisters of Yeshurun.

> We exhort you in the words of Saint Peter: "Beware of false teachers among you, who deny the Lord that bought them, and bring upon themselves swift destruction. These teachers speak evil of the truth, and many follow their pernicious ways."
>
> Many women and men of our faith have been led to commit whoredoms. Daily we see more broken families in our offices, and even more people who are leaving the faith, following after these idolatrous philosophies.
>
> We ask Zarahemlans to pray that our leaders will lift the ban on the printing of sacred literature. Until then, we enclose passages concerning Korihor and Sherem, antichrists in ancient

history. We urge you to study these words diligently, that you might be aware of these doctrines in our day.

We affirm the words of a modern prophet: "Virtue cannot be purchased with money, but may be enjoyed by all people, even those of humble birth and humble circumstances, as well as the rich, as much by the high school student as by those who are professors in universities. Everyone may enjoy these great blessings by living for them.

"The lack of chastity, fidelity, and virtue causes rivers of tears to flow, breaks numerous homes, deprives and frustrates armies of innocent children. Loss of virtue has toppled many nations and civilizations."

Thus hath the Lord declared to Jacob: "For I, the Lord God, delight in the chastity of women. And whoredoms are an abomination before me."

We cannot tell you all the things whereby you can fall, for there are divers ways and means, even so many that we cannot number them. And you should not be commanded in all things.

But this much we can tell you, in the words of the prophet-king in Mosiah's times: "If you do not watch yourselves, and observe the commandments of God, and continue in the faith, even endure to the end of your lives, you must perish. And now, O people, remember, and perish not."

Despite the private circulation of the epistle, it reached the hands of Ted Lipscomb. Smug with his big scoop, Ted then discussed it with Nils Cromwell on MBS' News of the Hour show.

The *Zarahemla Post* was swamped with letters to the editor, demanding Ben's resignation. Haman, who led this campaign, accused his brother of religious extremism and writing hate literature. Arch Kingerman heaped praise upon Cromwell and accused Ben of "Sein Canosaism". Banberg and Ponte added their enraged letters. "Do we wish there were no such person on the planet? Yes," Banberg wrote. "We have a law against using such words," Ponte wrote. "How dare he even think such a thing? To teach hate to a congregation is carrying freedom too far. Benamoz should be imprisoned until he learns some manners."

A sleek limousine rolled up to the *Post* building. Harvey Dermucker and his body guards got out, waded through swarming reporters, and used every elevator in the building for his entourage to ascend to the top floor. There he went into the chief editor's office alone, shutting the door in disappointed faces. After awhile he came out smiling, nodding and waving, but saying nothing. Back in the street, the limousine doors were closed, again in reporters' faces, and they were again disappointed. Five minutes later, Devon fired Ben. The reporters were not given that story, either.

7

Bahia Verde
Land of Sheffa

The MacRay cabin in Sheffa was equipped as a retreat from Zarahemla's hectic pace. Activities to relieve a journalist's tension ranged from fishing, swimming, sailing, and gardening to weight-lifting, target practice, and boxing.

Benjamin Benamoz, continually battered by a hostile press, availed himself of the more rigorous activities. He had become a crack shot and his hands were heavily calloused from boxing. He could run, hike, and pummel the bag for hours and not feel fatigued. But, all this —— for what? He was numb to pain, physically, but he felt no relief. His enemy was not flesh and blood, but an idea, a human philosophy that spit in the face of justice. Pride and envy stalked the halls in academia, poisoning the minds of students who became journalists, lawyers, judges, teachers, and politicians. Truth and justice were the casualties. Like the Nephites of old, the people had divided into classes: the elite class, the idle class, and the working class. And Yeshurun was not immune to it. Class warfare was rampant in the political arena and was creeping into the churches.

Cumorah had succumbed to lies, and Zarahemla was ripening in pride and envy. Lies had overthrown Solano and destroyed the free Cumorah republic. Lies had killed Zephan Benamoz. Lies had massacred millions through the centuries, and continued to enthrone tyranny worldwide. Zarahemla was now ruled by liars who, failing to learn lessons from history, embraced the very lies which would lead to their own destruction. Elites lied to the rabble, gushing a fervid but phony solicitude for the poor and unfortunate, buying votes in the name of false charity. Rabble lied about their indolence, selling their liberty for a crust of "free" bread promised by politicians, and hours of circuses provided by the media. Self-adoring   elites

382

squelched liberty because it interfered with their agenda for power. The rabble despised liberty because it demanded too much from them — to work hard, and to think.

Many people mistakenly thought the Egalitarian philosophy was a battle between rich and poor, but in reality it was pressure from above and pressure from below to crush the people in the middle. Although they hated each other, the elite and the rabble were united in one thing — hatred of middle Zarahemla who worked hard for an honest day's pay and tended to obey the commandments of God. Middle Zarahemla centered society. It was the back bone, the strong mid-section which kept the nation going with gut fortitude.

A solid middle represented a threat to corporate monopolies, international meddlings, and enforced experimental philosophies, thus arousing ire in the elite. The indolent envied small businessmen, professionals, and skilled workers for their excellence, independence, and modest holdings. Anyone with more than the "have-nots" was to be despised, exploited, and brought down. Law-abiding middle citizens brazenly enjoyed the fruits of their labors, opposed subsidies, and insisted everyone work, and each pay his own way. These showed no sympathy for the idle, who found such an attitude unforgivable. At least the elites were sympathetic, showed guilt about their wealth, and tearfully promised to use tax money for an easy life, total security, and pursuit of pleasure for the underprivileged. The idle class believed crooning words from the elite.

Solano had been unsympathetic to the idle class and had refused to cooperate with the elite. He had championed the obdurate middle citizens. Zephan Benamoz had not shared his wealth, except with the churches, who were deemed by the rabble to be discriminating and inefficient in the redistribution of wealth. Zephan was a member of the prosperous Yeshurun, which was portrayed as a rich and fanatical people. He was propertied middle class, and not to be trusted. So when elites said Zephan had betrayed and murdered Solano, the rabble, always greedy to consume upon their lusts any sensations, however false or evil, believed it.

Justice was lost. Solano's murder would never be avenged. And now, Papa.

Ben stopped and leaned against the deck railing. *Papa! What can I do?*

The bigger the lies, the more people believed them. Of those who wanted to believe those lies, the numbers were increasing. And Haman was chief among them.

Ben's heart was grieved, for he saw the people were wicked and perverse; their hearts were set upon gold, and silver, and upon all manner of material goods. He also saw their hearts were turned to great boasting in their pride.

Silently, Ben bowed his head and began to pray for Zarahemla and her leaders . . .

Dan MacRay turned up the television volume to drown out Ben's staccato assault on the punching bag outdoors.

Now, here was a young man in excellent shape, manifesting a quiet, hardened fitness. Zephan's looks lived on in the boyish face of his son. Ben's eyes were like blue flame, smoldering with turmoil. A look from Ben could leave a person feeling unsettled, as if his thoughts and heart had been discerned. Physically, Benjamin Benamoz had the aspect of a dangerous man.

Unlike Dan, who liked to clown on the electronic media, Ben was a writer, who used his pen like the proverbial sword. His work was well-researched and not vindictive, but his plain words could cut asunder the proud, the envious, and the deceitful in society. The Holy Spirit was Ben's editor, and the Spirit's power carried his words into his readers' hearts.

Dan's words were mere sounds, bitten off and swallowed by the air waves. But Ben's writings were as a marble witness against him, a stumbling block which the powerful would strive ruthlessly to remove. The young man's courageous stand against Cromwell and his elitist associates had wrought a cleansing effect upon Yeshurun. Many new souls entered the fold, and the weak had garnered strength from Ben's leadership. Alone on the great and spacious fields in the world, withstanding the winds from Babylon, Yeshurun was comparatively small.

Small, perhaps, but not inconsequential, because Yeshurun was united. During the centuries of the Great Apostasy, other sects of Christianity, as well as Judaism and Islam, had suffered tremendous schisms. These continued in modern times with no healing in sight, because no one could rise above the precepts of men. Yeshurun was a restoration of the primitive church as Jesus himself organized it in the Meridian of Time. This restoration included a living prophet, a righteous man whom the Lord himself chose to lead the church in his absence from the earthly realm. The prophet of God, then, was the key to Yeshurun's solidarity. Other religious bodies, determined not to accept a modern prophet, either clung to dead prophets from previous dispensations or settled for confusing doctrines that spring from sincere but unauthorized individuals. The inevitable result from these misguided tours through life was unending turmoil, while Yeshurun enjoyed comparative tranquility. Yeshurun had her detractors, to be sure, but the issue was greatly simplified. Apostates either repented or fell away. On the other hand, those who accepted the living prophet could benefit from daily contact with the mind and will of God as revealed through his appointed servant. The faithful, therefore, remained anchored to the rock of Christ, which is revelation, while all others, deprived of that anchor, were tossed to and fro and carried about with every turbulent wind or subtle breeze of human doctrine.

Refugees from Cumorah had swelled the ranks of Yeshurun in Zarahemla, bringing with them a temperance which forged new strength among their backsliding neighbors. Merchants were compelled by the renewed emphasis on Sabbath observance to decide upon a course to follow. Finding business at an all-time low on Sundays, merchants either closed in observance of the Sabbath or moved from the Yeshurun community.

In his corner of the vineyard, Ben urged unwavering support of the Lord's prophet. Thus under Ben's leadership, a new prosperity developed in Zarahemla city; many families progressed both spiritually and temporally, and the membership expanded to a formidable block of influence. Politicians frequently courted favor, clothing their envy in the language of the faithful. But to his people Benjamin Benamoz had taught well the law and the prophets, and Yeshurun did not buy the demagoguery of hypocrites.

Forces bent on destroying the patriarchal order of families were advancing on society. Nevertheless, Calandria and Ramira, who had known Anahí at the university, came to visit her, seeking help for themselves. Anahí taught them the divine law, and the two women were cleansed from their moral corruption by the power of God. Calandria soon married a choice son of Zion, but the two women taught the truth unceasingly, and brought hundreds of men and women from decadence to the strait and pleasing way of the Lord.

385

These acts of healing and mercy only incensed those who saw their recruits being taken from them. Radicals became more domineering in pushing their doctrines in the education system. Holding to Leviticus 18, Yeshurun parents refused to send their children to schools where students were taught and encouraged to violate the eternal verities of God. This enraged those who were receiving tax money to teach abominations to Zarahemla children.

Ben's wife was a coordinator of cultural activities for private schools and home-educated children for the entire region, and Yeshurun families enjoyed comparative serenity. Under her leadership, dependence on government schools dropped to a meager twelve per cent.

Yeshurun leaders in Zarahemla were opposed to the formation of church units in any other language but English, the official language of Zarahemla. Anahí was called upon to teach English as a second language to immigrants, who consequently integrated smoothly into society.

Dan saw further manifestation of good fruits from his own spiritual labors as he co-taught holy scriptures with Anahí every morning at six a.m. —— a series of classes for the youth, known as seminary. Their theme this year was taken from the words of the prophet Helaman in the book of Joseph:

And now, my sons, remember, remember it is upon the rock of our Redeemer, who is Christ, the Son of God, that ye must build your foundation; that when the devil shall send forth his mighty winds, yea, his shafts in the whirlwind, yea, when all his hail and his mighty storm shall beat upon you, it shall have no power over you to drag you down to the gulf of misery and endless woe, because of the rock upon which you are built, which is a sure foundation whereon if men build they cannot fall.

Unfortunately, however, Ben still had enemies . . .

On the television screen, the day's headline was made by a man in priestly apparel, including a hood which partially obscured his face.

"God has commanded me to avenge the death of Zephan Benamoz. I will not stop until I have poured out Haman's blood upon the ground. In this I have the blessing of his brother, Benjamin Benamoz."

"The Ministry of Justice is tightening security to prevent Marcados and other religious activists from carrying out this assassination attempt," the newsman concluded.

Dan shook his head vigorously, as if to throw off seeds of doubt the media had planted. Media reports had been pure myth right from the start, he reminded himself angrily. He, of all people, should know.

Still, of the entire family, Ben manifested the most difficulty in accepting the painful loss of his father. He had been subjected to unprecedented venom from his enemies. Had he cracked under the pressure?

Berating himself for even asking such a question, Dan resolutely marched outside and stared at his young friend's muscular shoulders. *I must know for certain . . .*

"Now that you are the strongest man in the land," Dan said mildly, "what will you do? Kill Haman with your bare hands?"

"I admit the idea of strangling him has crossed my mind. But Haman was not directly responsible for Papa's death. Yet he knows the truth and prefers to believe the lies; therefore he is more accountable. He is so stubborn in doing what he knows is wrong, my patience with him is spent. If I were in his presence, and armed, I fear what I might do, Dan."

"Shoot your own brother?"

"Nah, not really. If Haman were gone, others would come in his place. Legions, who all believe sincerely in lies. What can I do, line them all up and shoot them?" Ben said with a sardonic smile.

"Your humor is getting to be as absurd as mine. Well, at least Haman has left the church."

"But he cannot leave it alone."

"True. And Cromwell has managed to polarize us all. You called him a modern Korihor, Ben." Dan sucked in his breath.

"I never publicly labeled him in any way. The media somehow learned of a comment I made privately to my wife. Is a man no longer free to speak his mind to his own family?"

"Now that I'm running for Chief Judge, I don't dare say anything."

Ben gave Dan one of his unforgettable looks and said with his usual bluntness, "In the name of all that's decent, Dan, now is no time to compromise your principles. That is what character is all about. You have character, and it is an issue. Stand firm, and give the people a choice."

Dan hung his head. "I stand corrected," he said softly. "Your father's courageous spirit is alive and well in you, my son."

"What has happened to our justice system, Dan?"

Dan shook his head.

"Many good people, even among the faithful, have come down to believe in the works of the Egalitarians. Any decent man deplores stealing. But let the same man walk into the voting booth, and without hesitation he will vote for legalized plunder. Thus he can dig a pit for his neighbor and partake of the spoils through the priestcraft of his leaders."

"It's human nature, Ben. Ask anyone on Central Avenue, and he will virtuously denounce such baseness. But in the name of democracy, he will believe anything is acceptable. In society's name, he will coddle criminals and even sanction murder of the innocent."

"So many good people are being deceived. God did not send us here to be victims of deceit."

"As journalists, we have an obligation to truth." Dan laughed without mirth. "But obviously our kept press doesn't share our devotion to duty. While our editors cut and cower, whole nations are being deceived."

"It's like the parable of the wheat and the tares. This is what torments me so, Dan. It only took a few tares to destroy all Cumorah. Now I see it happening in Zarahemla, and I can't stop it."

"I learned something when I was about your age, Ben. Maybe it will help you. When I began my career as a journalist, I began to uncover much evil in the world. I saw, as you say, tares, everywhere, among the wheat. I wanted to expose all evil and yank out every last tare by the roots. Then a wise teacher made me study deeply Jacob's allegory of the olive tree, in the book of Joseph. The Lord of the vineyard instructed his servant to clear away all the bitter fruit. But he warned not to clear away all the bad fruit at once. Thus the good would have a chance to grow, increase in strength, and overcome the evil. In other words, the Lord says not to pluck up the tares while the blade is yet tender, lest you destroy the wheat also."

"I understand."

"So the Lord wants the wheat and the tares to grow together, until the gathering of the wheat, when it is time for the field to be burned."

Ben hurled a rock into the field beyond. "Thanks. I was beginning to think I would never be able to reconcile myself."

Dan gave him a sharp glance. "The name Reno, or rather Raul, Marcados mean anything to you?"

"Never heard of him."

"Some priest, supposedly —— getting all manner of media coverage. Claims he's commanded by God to kill Haman and that he has your blessing."

"I have been extremely cautious not to accuse my brother in public. I have tried to avoid attention, but this ugly publicity follows me relentlessly."

"It's not you, Ben," Dan said quietly. "It's what you stand for."

"Did ZRI find anything on Marcados?"

"Just a Raul Marcados who was a peasant kid in Cumorah decades ago. Period. The probe ends there. No more information on him at all." Dan frowned. "According to Hunt, no record of any affiliations with Cabrios or Ponte. But this fellow, priest or not, has money. Much money. His face looks familiar, but I can't place it."

"Marcados is not a priest, Dan," Ben said. "Where does he get so much money? And no true man of God would even advocate murder, let alone carry it out himself."

Dan let out a deep breath. "The Ministry of Justice isn't interested in investigating. Their agents are focusing all their manpower on you and me. The Order would like nothing better than an excuse to see us in jail or executed."

"It's destroying our family, Dan. Why?"

Dan had no answer.

"My own bitterness is eating me. I know it. I worry that this frame of mind will cause me to be insensitive. What if, at some crucial moment, I fail to hear the still small voice of the Spirit?"

"It's still your father, isn't it?" Dan said gently.

Ben's face filled with pain.

Dan put a hand on the young man's shoulder. "Leave it alone, son. Nothing you do will bring him back."

8

Benjamin cherished his weekly visits at the MacRay's vacation home in Sheffa, where dinner could be enjoyed with a view of the bay at sundown. The dining table was at one end of the family room, from which a television was conspicuously absent. Overstuffed bookshelves filled every available wall space. Since MacRay had read nearly every one of the tomes, dinner conversation invariably resulted in a rich educational experience.

But this night everyone else was out for the evening. Ben sat alone at the table, studying Lehi's vision and the olive tree allegory in Dan's solitary book of Joseph.

Ben focused on the sacred texts before him. Somewhere in the word of God he would find the answer he desired. Next to the book of Joseph was an equally rare copy of the Bible. Ben smiled at Dan's account of smuggling the Bible out from Zarahemla. Ignorant young border guards, mystified by the sixteenth century King's English in which the old volume was written, had not recognized this black market antiquity so sought-after by the present regime. He opened the old Bible and turned its pages with reverential awe.

"Dan is right," he muttered to himself. "I must find peace with God."

Suffering and persecution we have endured, and we hope to be able to endure all things.

And yet the remnant of Jacob had survived through the centuries.

Now our enemies threaten our homes, our families, our freedom to worship, and our very lives. After all we have endured, is the remnant finally to become extinct?

Ben turned to Dan's single remaining copy of the book of Joseph.

Inasmuch as ye are not guilty of the first offense, neither the second, ye shall not suffer yourselves to be slain by the hands of your enemies.

More than seven years since my father was killed, and the killer remains free. By the law of Mosiah, capital punishment is required for murder. If we spare the murderer, my father's innocent blood will come upon us. We will not be guiltless for failing to bring about justice. Justice is now apart from the written law and subject to the whims of men, judges in particular.

Our people are forced to pay for lies to be taught their children and are thrown in jail for opposing these abominations, while murderers go unpunished because of their money. Where is justice?

Now, a just law was given by Mosiah. A punishment was affixed, which brought remorse of conscience unto man. Now, if there was no law given —— that if a man murdered he should die —— would a man be afraid to commit murder?

And also if there was no law given against sin men would not be afraid to sin. And if there was no law given, what could justice do when men sinned, or mercy either? For they would have no claim upon the creature.

But there is a law given, and a punishment affixed, and a repentance granted; which repentance, mercy claims. Otherwise, justice claims the creature and executes the law, and the law inflicts the punishment. If not so, the works of justice would be destroyed.

For do you suppose that mercy can rob justice? I say unto you, Nay; not one whit. If so, God would cease to be God.

But God ceases not to be God, and mercy claims the penitent, and mercy comes because of the atonement.

Therefore, whosoever will, may come and partake of the waters of life freely; and whosoever will not come the same is not compelled to come.

And thus God bringeth to pass His great and eternal purposes. For behold, justice exercises all his demands, and also mercy claims all which is her own. And thus, none but the truly penitent are saved.

As Ben studied the Word, and pondered, the Spirit softened his heart. And with all the energy of his soul he begged the Father to remove anger from him. He mourned for his brother. *If only Haman would repent.*

And it came to pass that Benjamin humbled himself exceedingly. Again he pondered the psalm of Nephi:

Why should my heart weep and my soul linger in the valley of sorrow, and my flesh waste away, and my strength slacken, because of mine afflictions?

And why should I yield to sin, because of my flesh? Yea, why should I give way to temptations, or let the evil one have place in my heart to destroy my peace and afflict my soul? Why am I angry because of mine enemy?

391

Awake, my soul! No longer droop in sin. Rejoice, O my heart, and give place no more for the enemy of my soul. Do not anger again because of mine enemies.

O Lord, I have trusted in thee, and I will trust in thee forever. I will not trust in the arm of the flesh; for I know that cursed is he that putteth his trust in man, or maketh flesh his arm, or shall hearken unto the precepts of men, save their precepts shall be given by the power of the Holy Spirit.

Proverbs 20:22. *Say not thou, I will recompense evil; but wait on the Lord, and he shall save thee.*

The gentle warmth of the Comforter enveloped Ben, and he fell asleep, peaceful at last.

. . .He beheld the cliff where he had escaped from the Ponista dogs. The foaming river tumbled recklessly over cragged rocks in its canyon bed.

He saw, not the olive tree, but an exceedingly tall tree, with pure white fruit. Someone stood beneath the tree, eating its fruit. Papa!

Zephan beckoned to his son to come eat of the fruit. Abiram walked forward in his no-nonsense way, and he ate the fruit. Haman and Leb trod the same path. They struggled and finally arrived at the tree. Zephan beseeched his eldest sons to partake of the fruit, but both men turned from their father and refused the fruit.

Ben was running . . . running on a narrow, treacherous path. . .running toward the tree and his father. The going was slippery, only negotiable by gripping an iron rod to his right.

There, on the other side of the path he saw another rail. Next to the plain, simple, and straight rod of iron, the rail at his left hand was gorgeous, in a flashy way. It was ornately engraved with exquisite little images, all in gold and silver. So easy to reach. Yet it was slick to the touch, for it was encased in long and giant neon lights, which flashed exceedingly bright rainbow colors. Quite gaudy, really.

A host of men and women in business suits clutched the nearby rail. It was crowded, and Ben could only find room to touch the rail with his finger. At first it felt pleasant, and he wanted to grasp it with both hands. The others had long since

392

given up trying to extract their hands. Since they could not, they loitered, chattering among themselves.

But Ben's left hand was stuck fast in a gummy, adhesive substance on the rail. The pleasant sensation was gone. He had no feeling at all. His nerve endings were dying, and numbness was creeping up his arm. In a panic, Ben exerted all his strength to withdraw his hand from that rail. In so doing, the rail broke. He saw it was hollow, and the gold was only a thin layer of paint over slag — the dross and refuse which Ben had seen in great heaps at Grandpa's steel mill.

Suddenly the rail vanished, and so did those people. Only their laughter remained, echoing as from a great empty building.

Boiling up from the turbulent river was a hideous dragon, the king of this world, the archenemy. The dragon's face was that of a man vaguely familiar, its head bearing a crown like an ancient pharaoh. But the creature had the arms of a woman. Many arms. Soft, inviting, irresistible.

Abiram appeared, carrying a long sword. He slew the beast, which then subsided into the swirling vortex of the river.

At last Ben reached the tree. He ate the fruit, which was large like a melon, pure white, and very white.

"I did not know any fruit could taste so good, Papa."

"You have labored long and diligently in pruning, cultivating, and nourishing this tree, my son, so it is sweet to your taste. It is sweet above all that is sweet, white above all that is white, and pure above all that is pure."

Ben's mother was there, for Zephan would not eat alone.

"It is delicious beyond description," Sarita said. "The more we eat, the more we desire." And she, Zephan, and their two sons got down upon their knees and scooped it up, eating it by double handfuls.

As Ben reached for another piece of fruit, the tree transformed into a soft figure. The creature was white, but it had an aura which was even whiter, beyond description, and large as a cloud, but it was pure light. Radiance flowed into all space; it filled the entire earth. A glow encircled Ben, and warmed him, and it filled him. He thought he would never again be hungry, thirsty or cold. He was feasting on the love of God. And the creature was a lamb. . .

Ben awoke slowly, unsure whether the moisture on his face was sweat or tears. For a long time he pondered the dream, but understanding eluded him, until the counsel of an ancient prophet came to mind.

> And now, as the preaching of the word had a great tendency to lead the people to do that which was just —— yea, it had more powerful effect upon the minds of the people than the sword, or anything else which had happened to them —— therefore Alma thought it was expedient that they should try the virtue of the word of God.

Depression, morbid melancholy, consuming hatred. All were gone, leaving in their place one clear objective. Ben would fulfill his promise to his father. He would return again to Cumorah and find the family's sacred testament.

9

Zarahemla
Palace of Chief Judge

Karl Devon lingered after the monthly business meeting. When he and Elidor were alone, he switched on a taped conversation.

> "For example, Isaiah prophesied about Elidor and her friends."
> "Really? What did he say?"
> "As for my people, children are their oppressors, and women rule over them. O my people, they who lead thee cause thee to err."
> "Your Isaiah has an objection to women who rule?"
> "Only to those who choose to rule by the precepts of men, rather than God."

Elidor frowned. "Religious hatred! Who is speaking?"
"Dan MacRay, of course. And that young fellow named Benjamin Benamoz —— Haman's kid brother. This is how Haman knows first hand about the Yeshurun crowd. These fundamentalists

are not going to give up their core beliefs easily," Devon complained. "They do not like the new universal ethic."

"I know about Benjamin Benamoz," she said. "He's been mounting that hate campaign against poor Nils Cromwell. He's bringing back Canosaism."

"We stopped it. I fired him. But there is something else."

"What, Karl?" Elidor batted her new eyelashes.

"It's their culture . . . the Yeshurun attitude. They are fiercely opposed to the order of Voltaire specifically and everything we stand for in general. Their people are taught this from infancy, and they won't allow their children under control of state child care. You can't change the thinking of these people, Elidor. We must find an ultimate solution . . . something which exterminates their culture once and for all."

"Karl! You're starting to sound like Rupert Banberg! That man is genocidal. You know we could never get by with such a thing."

Devon pouted. "But their way of thinking must be erased. To them, everything is good or evil, Elidor. Yeshurun people are much more inflexible than Banberg could ever be. You know, they always quote some old prophet on 'rulers of darkness in this world, spiritual wickedness in high places', and other such hate literature. And listen to this!"

"Our new Chief Judge, Elidor, is a woman experienced in leadership, nation-building, and effecting major change in society," another voice, very familiar, intoned.

"Right," a third voice said. "Elidor is the absolute paragon of egalitarianism."

"You mean that?" The second voice sounded astonished.

"Sure. With modern liberation, Elidor has proven beyond doubt that women can abuse power just as much as men."

Laughter.

"How dare they say such things about me?" Elidor clenched her fists, then quickly relaxed them.

"There's more. Wait till you hear this."

395

"And who does Elidor think she is? A light unto the world? She thinks we can't live without her, eh?" Laughter. "Well, I'll tell you. I wouldn't trust her with *my* life!"

"You are opinionated, that is for sure."

"As is the biased, so-called free press here. If the *Post* can lie about the house of Yeshurun, then I can tell the truth about the order of Voltaire."

"Where did you get this?" Elidor's face was white, but as always, her rage was in control.

"Ted Lipscomb."

"That idiot!"

"It's authentic. For such a fool, he's more an asset than a liability. After all, his stupidity got us Zephan. And he did defend you, Elidor."

Elidor nodded. "I didn't know the little pimple had it in him."

"I was surprised myself that the mindless stooge pulled this off at a cocktail party more than seven years ago."

"Hmm. That was before . . . "

"Now, Elidor. There is no 'before'. The world started with the new order of Voltaire in 2084. The break with the past is total. All history is irrelevant, except to empower Voltairism. Remember?"

"Where do they get their teachings against Voltaire?" she asked.

Devon slapped his forehead. "Darling, you are a genius! How could I forget? Cromwell has been after me to squelch their publications, which are totally incorrect, ideologically."

"What are you talking about?"

"Their history. Their records. All we have to do is get rid of those."

"Then what are we waiting for? But you told me these people just quote old writings from 600 B.C. Nobody pays attention to that old stuff any more. What does it have to do with us?" Elidor said, her self-assurance returning. "Bible influence is not a threat. Hasn't been for years. Take it easy, Devon. Give the government a little credit for efficiency."

Karl's eyebrows shot up. "You don't get it, do you?" he said. "Look at this, Elidor!" Holding the written transcript with a trembling hand, Devon hammered it with his index finger. "He's using the words of their prophets against the Order."

396

Her lip curled. "But if we don't believe in those prophets, we don't need to worry."

"Exactly! Millions of people do believe this!"

"Zephan is dead."

Devon gave her a dour look. "Do not underestimate a martyr's power."

"You worry too much. He's gone, and this whole bother has gone with him."

"Look here. The writings of their dead heroes are used as hate literature, and I hear rumors about making this journalist the next Chief Judge!"

Elidor's face paled. "Who?"

"Dan MacRay," Karl replied softly. "Can you believe it? A man of Yeshurun with the gall to run for Chief Judge."

"And using religious hatred in his campaign. I've always hated him, but he must be very shrewd. If we destroyed all the Bibles, where could he be getting this hate literature?"

"His references were found among old manuscripts he tossed in the trash when he left the *Post*. It's like a disease, Elidor! Perhaps the Bible is gone, but MacRay is quoting the book of Joseph!"

"The book of what?"

"Joseph, alluded to in the Bible." He swore. "No sooner we stamp out their blasted Bible then they dig up more old scrolls and metal plates which support the Bible!"

"Are you sure it's a problem?"

Karl came up on the balls of his feet. "A problem! These testaments are the keystone of their religion. You wanted the ticket to their inner sanctum, Elidor. Well, this is it. People don't read the Bible much anymore, because it's too hard to understand, but that book of Joseph preaches all the same stuff as the Bible, only it's plainer. I've seen passages from it. It is easily understood, and it has all those dogmas in it Nils Cromwell has been trying so hard to eradicate. As long as any copies of this testament are in circulation, it's going to interfere with the Universal Ethic, because that Joseph testament is reviving people's belief in the Bible!"

"That would make us a backward society all over again," Elidor observed.

"Nils says that book of Joseph contains some very damaging information about his ideas. That book could destroy him. If the public finds out the truth ——— " Devon caught himself.

"You're right," Elidor cut in. "We can't let that book get into print."

"Nils can't fight this thing alone," Devon added quickly. "We must help him."

"That does it! You have done your homework well, Karl," she congratulated him. "But we can't just burn books like Haman did. It's barbaric."

"Accidents happen at publishing houses, you know. It will just give us reason for tighter control over the press."

She smiled. "And we also have paper shredders!"

Devon nodded.

Elidor sat at her computer. "How many books do you figure are in circulation?"

"Not many, presently, but it only takes one to reproduce many."

"So." Her tone was brisk. "We dispatch the PAX Peace Force to police the libraries and bookstores. The commander can easily stage a vandalism incident while they're at it, to justify our taking control. In the mean time, we must quickly ferret out any individuals found possessing it."

"Easy. We start with Dan MacRay."

Eyes narrowed, Elidor projected her cold fury onto paper, heavily underscoring the name. "Definitely Dan MacRay."

10

It was Ammon's eighth birthday. In Yeshurun tradition he had reached the age of accountability, and on this birthday afternoon he was to be baptized. Dan MacRay was called upon to give a brief discourse, after which Ben would baptize his son. Dan arrived early at Sarita's cottage in Sheffa, to accompany the family to the chapel.

Ammon greeted him at the door, and Dan scooped the little boy up into his arms. "How's my favorite little brother today?"

"Grandma has a surprise for you!" Ammon said.

"Too bad Beth is busy tonight." Ben appeared at the door, fiddling with his tie, then came down the steps to join them on the patio.

"A pity indeed," Dan said. "She has sprung more than her share of surprises. Would do her good."

"¡*Hola!* You can come out now!" Ammon squealed with excitement, wiggled out of Dan's grasp, and charged past his father.

Oliver Beck emerged from behind Ben, the child leading him by the hand. "He's going to be —"

"Just one minute, Ammon," Sarita broke in gently. "First things first." She regarded Beck with warmth and affection, her eyes glistening. "Oliver has been examined thoroughly, and ever since the blessing Zephan gave him, he is pronounced clean, every whit. No traces of drugs. No infirmities. The doctors cannot believe it."

Ammon was hopping up and down on one foot, then the other. "Now, Grandma?"

Sarita nodded laughingly. "Yes, *nieto.*"

All at once very serious and grown-up, Ammon leaned slightly on the porch railing and pretended to adjust the microphone at the podium, as he had seen his father do at meetings. He stood very straight and tried to make his voice deep like his father's. "We are pleased to announce . . . " He turned and put his arm around Beck's waist. "Come stand beside me, my good brother," he said huskily. "We are pleased to announce —— " Ammon lost his poise and again hopped up and down, grinning jubilantly. "Papa's going to baptize Brother Beck, too!"

After an early supper, Ben settled at the table on the patio. Anahí sat on a swinging chair under an enormous oak tree which dropped leaves and twigs on the concrete.

"Anahí, this is the most delicious birthday cake I've had in a long time." Dan MacRay swiped a dab of the rich icing from his serving and licked his finger with relish.

"It's made from *pan de San Juan,*" she said.

"Mm, better than chocolate." Dan tested his weight on one piece of patio furniture he had helped Benjamin repair.

Ben surveyed with satisfaction the pleasant cottage he had built for his mother. Resulting from Zephan's "trial and conviction" in the media, the Zarahemla government had classified him as a liability. Pension was withheld from Sarita, despite hearty attempts by Clarence Rook and Mitchell Hunt to overturn the "verdict".

"Skip the government pension. I will care for myself," Sarita had insisted.

The press had declared Zephan Benamoz a public enemy, and consequent persecution had driven Sarita to Sheffa, where she took up residence a few miles from Dan and Beth MacRay's vacation home. Ben, too, had recently purchased a second home in Sheffa, where it was safer for Anahí and their son, Ammon. Since he no longer worked for the *Post*, Ben was gradually breaking his ties with Zarahemla.

Sarita worked at the hospital. She also loved working with Anahí and her grandson, selling produce from a vegetable garden and small grove adjacent to the cottage.

Sarita heard the familiar gurgle and hiss of sprinklers in the grove and smiled as Ammon appeared from among the trees. "Ben, remember when you worked as Ammon is doing?"

Ben nodded, biting his lip. Ammon reminded him powerfully of Zephan. Same thick hair with auburn highlights, wide-set gray eyes.

Dan turned to Beck. "Are you sure you're out for good, Beck? You must hold the world record for hospital stays."

Beck shook his head in wonder. "After the ordeal in Frontera," he said in a low voice, "Zephan brought me to Zarahemla, and took me into his own home. He knew I had lost my family . . . everything. He forgave me freely and never mentioned my betrayal again. He administered to me in my tribulations and strengthened me in the Lord." His voice caught. "You people are wonderful, Dan." "We are human, just like everybody else," Dan said. "But perhaps we repent more often."

"We changed his diet to conform more closely with the Word of Wisdom," Sarita said briskly. "You should have seen all the junk this *muchacho* was eating!" She winked at the young man. "But here in Sheffa we have found many plants and roots of excellent quality, which God has prepared to remove the cause of diseases."

Beck wrinkled his nose but smiled. "This angel woman refused to let me expire. Haven't eaten and drunk so many green vegetables in my entire life, but I must admit I haven't felt this good since I was a child."

"Then how about a jai alai game?" Ammon fastened a bold, hazel-eyed gaze on Beck and waited, ball in hand.

Beck's face softened. "Sure, *jovencito*," he agreed, ruffling the boy's hair. "Where do we play?"

The boy led Beck to a nearby field.

Beck warmed up, serving gently. As the boy connected, the ball sailed out of his reach. Beck raced with all his might to recover the ball, barely returning it. Ammon jumped high to reach the ball, but missed. He tumbled to the ground, laughing.

"You are a good player, señor." The boy gave a happy sigh.

"Just call me David, like your grandpa did. I only let people I really like call me David. Haven't played this in a long time. Feels good. Say, you're pretty big for eight years old, aren't you?"

"Uh-huh. Like Papa was."

"I used to play jai alai with my son. He would be about your age by now, Ammon."

Ammon kept an easy volley going with Beck. "He would be?"

"He and his mother were killed by a drunk driver several years ago."

Ammon was quiet.

"Sorry, *joven*," Beck said hastily. "War is cruel, and leaves loved ones behind. Should have killed a piece of wreckage like me and left your grandfather." They played in silence for a while.

"Mama knows I miss Grandpa to play jai alai with. She's glad you can."

"Do you hate the people who killed your grandfather?"

"I did at first, but then the other day Grandpa told me he forgave uncle Haman."

Beck stared at the boy. "Wait a minute! Your grandpa told you that? But I thought he was dead!"

"Well, yes, but he is an angel, now," Ammon replied matter-of-factly. "Grandma was there, and she saw him, too. He said he couldn't reach my father, because my father has kept himself very busy so he wouldn't have time to be sad about Grandpa. Grandpa told me not to worry and made me promise to pray very much, and keep the commandments. Then he said something I do not understand. Could you help me?"

"I-I'll try." Beck looked away. The child's eyes were breaking his heart.

"He said 'Do not trust in the arm of flesh.' What could it mean, *Hermano* David?"

Beck buried his face in his hands. Finally he looked up and peered bleakly at this innocent lad who had unknowingly held a mirror up to the pain-ravaged soul of Oliver David Beck. In that mirror David saw himself as a child Ammon's age, sitting at his mother's knee. An ancient Proverb came back to him: *Trust in the Lord with all thine heart, and lean not to thine own understanding.*

"Those who trust in the flesh," David began slowly, his voice shaking, "do not love God as your parents taught you to do."

"What do you mean, David?"

Beck did not answer immediately. The boy led the way to a small cove where a sizable work boat was tied up.

David felt the smooth varnished boat railing, admiring the craft's excellent condition.

"Squanto's boat," Ammon said, as he climbed into the cockpit. "She came in at Calaveras. Squanto uses it for fishing and sells his catch. Come aboard."

"Squanto helped Papa capture this boat," the child explained as they descended below deck. "Papa told me he and the others cleaned out many bags of white powder, sewn into mattresses and stuffed in the bilge."

"What was that stuff, Ammon?"

Ammon shrugged. "Some kind of drugs."

"Think carefully, Ammon. Who was the top man in charge of that drug shipment?"

"No one told me his name," Ammon replied slowly, shaking his head.

David grinned. "Their commanding officer was not God, then?"

Ammon's response was a tolerant smile. "Of course not, David! Such people don't love and follow God, they . . . Oh, I see."

"Now, I have a question for you," said David, taking a seat in the cockpit.

"How could I help you?"

"Well, I noticed the chapel where we were baptized, as well as all our meeting houses everywhere, are many, but small. Is it because they refuse to pass a collection plate?"

"No, David." Ammon laughed. "Papa says exchanging money in church offends the Lord. Besides, tithing and offerings are something personal between each family and their bishop."

"Does your father get any of the money?"

"Gracious, no!" Ammon exclaimed. "That would be priestcraft, and my father would be cursed if he ever took any money for performing his priesthood duties. Everyone must earn his own money, like King Benjamin in the book of Joseph. Every chapel and temple is paid for by tithing and offerings. We have smaller buildings where we have fewer people."

"So how big is your father's congregation?"

"About average. Four hundred on the rolls, two hundred active. If it gets any bigger, we divide the ward," Ammon informed him. "Papa says the Lord likes the congregations small so the bishops and other elders don't lose track of anybody."

"I see." David was impressed. "You may not know the answer to the next question."

"I'll try."

"The chapels are not only rather small, but also simple, with no elaborate adornment. But the most unusual thing is . . . what I mean is, we are the only Christian church without a cross. Why do I never see a cross?"

Ammon frowned. "I know the answer, but if I explain it like Papa did, it might make you . . . uh, sad. But Papa's words are always very plain, and I don't know how else to say it."

"Your father has always been very blunt. Go ahead. I'm used to it."

"Well, uh. How did your wife and son die? I mean, were they hit by a car, or a truck?"

David winced.

Ammon placed his small hand on his friend's arm. "I'm sorry."

"It's all right. I asked for it." David was moved by the boy's sensitivity. "It was a head-on collision with a speeding pickup truck."

"You would not make that truck into a monument in memory of the accident, would you?"

"Absolutely not."

"Likewise, the cross is an instrument of torture. Why would we want to place a big old cross in all our buildings? Jesus died on the cross. But He lives! And because He lives, we can all live forever." Ammon looked into David's eyes. "I know my Redeemer lives. And he wants us to remember him as the living Christ, not the dead."

David shook out and recoiled a line on the deck, wondering if the boy noticed the hot tears that landed on the lines. The child could not have known David had been forced by his father's business associates to fight in an unnecessary war in Cumeni. David saw scores of his friends die for nothing; he saw what terrorists did to Zephan's friend Canosa. David himself was held a prisoner of war by Cabrios' terrorists for years. It ruined his life. He hated his father for it, but he did not care about himself. Then, the woman of his heart, and his son . . . taken from him. Why Deborah, and little Davy? It was all so brutal, so unfair. And so senseless. David had spent his life seeking revenge, but it was hopeless. He had only become more miserable.

Ammon cocked his head. "Are you all right, David?"

David studied Ammon for a long time, wishing desperately to see his own little boy again. *He lives! And because He lives, we can all live forever.* The agony of the cross was no more. Not for the living Christ. Never again for Oliver David Beck. The boy's powerful testimony lifted him from the depths of his sorrow. He would see his family again. Right now, his loved ones were probably in the arms of the risen, living Lord.

"Papa says all things, even our chapels, testify of the Redeemer and his atonement."

David held the boy close to him. "Your words . . . God's word . . . has healed me. More than you'll ever know."

At length, Beck's trained eye could not resist scanning every inch of the craft. Ben had been thorough, all right. No sign of ship's logs, either. Beneath a metal plate concealed under the hatch to the engine compartment, however, was a hiding place known only to traffickers. With his knife David quickly unscrewed the plate and found a tiny log book. "From the desert with love, X-816," were the words in the final entry. David recognized the secret number of "The Plague", code name for Horace Verman.

"We're lucky the supplies survived those bandits on the border." Dan grinned with satisfaction as he helped Sarita with the dishes.

"The hospital is grateful for your help," she said.

"By the way, I hear factions in Cumorah are seeking to rebuild ties with Zarahemla," Dan said as he joined Ammon's parents on the patio.

"Too late," Ben said with bitterness.

A deep sigh escaped Anahí.

Wind chimes sang incongruously into the long, awkward silence, and Dan remembered. "I have a surprise for you, too!"

"Sounds good," Anahí said with attempted cheerfulness.

"Hmm. You don't say." Ben kept his tone bland.

"Is that all you have to say about the biggest publication in history? Ben, I'm going to have the book of Joseph published in its complete and original form!"

Ben jumped to his feet. "That's it! We've got to hurry, Dan. I suspect we'll have stiff opposition."

"I'll do everything in my power," Dan said. "I'll get started Monday, as soon as I get back to work."

11

Zarahemla suburbs

Beth fumed over the unexpected traffic. Now she would be late with dinner, and Dan's favorite ice cream was probably turning to soup. Closer to home the traffic became more dense and more puzzling. Despite plans for Dan's campaign for Chief Judge, he would never hold a press conference at his private home. About this he was very adamant about. What could be going on?

She slowed to a stop. The drive was clogged with vehicles bearing the PAX insignia. Officials from the international police force were crawling all over the place like a horde of killer ants. The entire block was staked out. Special forces stood battle-ready at their stations, their machine guns leveled on the doors and windows of the house.

"Anyone remaining in the house has ten minutes to appear with hands up and surrender all weapons," a brassy female voice blared over the loudspeaker, "and then we will send in tear gas."

Beth spotted him, towering over a mob of reporters. "Dan!" She jumped out of the car and scrambled over the crowded lawn.

"Make way!" the officers were saying.

Dan? Handcuffed?

Beth elbowed through a jungle of camouflage battle fatigues, pushed aside government-employed assault weapons, and threw her arms around her husband. "How can this be happening, in our own land?"

Dan leaned down and kissed her tear-stained cheek. "Don't worry about me," he whispered. "Beth, you must run for your life, my love. And take with you a message. Tell our flock the remnant of Joseph is in shreds."

12

Sheffa

At Sarita's house, Ben and Ammon brought in the last baskets laden with tomatoes, red and yellow onions, lettuce, avocados, potatoes and corn, while Grandma made signs with the pricing. Anahí washed the produce and placed it in boxes to take to the local market.

Ammon grinned. "This place is bountiful, like the lands in the book of Joseph."

"Makes all the hard work worthwhile, doesn't it?" Ben said. "With last season's orange crop, this will have been a prosperous —"

"Ben! Ben!" someone called him.

"Sounds like Beth MacRay. Back here, Beth!"

Beth flung herself in the swing, her eyes two points of fright in a usually calm and dignified countenance.

"What is it, Beth?"

Beth gripped an arm of her chair. "The Central Committee arrested Dan."

"In the name of all that's decent, why?"

"These persons shun all that's decent and civilized. He is charged with ideological incorrectness. In other words, speaking, writing and publishing material critical of the Order."

Sarita dropped her marker and stared. Anahí was at Beth's side, an arm about her friend's shoulder.

"Our home is utterly demolished. It may go up in flames before I return, but that I can handle." Her voice broke. "But what will they do to my husband?"

"Don't worry, Beth," Ben said. "Dan has a huge following. The Committee will never get away with this."

"That's not all," she went on, miserable. Fists clenched at her forehead, Beth bowed forward with closed eyes. "Officials confiscated his books and files, and shredded them all on the spot."

Ben felt his stomach turn over. Her pitiful sigh answered his unspoken question.

"Ben, the book of Joseph is —"

"I know."

Anahí and Ben exchanged a glance. No words. Numb with dread, Anahí gave a slight nod.

Ben knew what he must do.

"No, Ben!" Sarita rushed to her son and clung to him, stifling her sobs. She said no more, but he knew what was in her grieved mind and broken heart. *You can't go to that evil place, Ben. I won't let you! They'll kill you. I can't bear to lose you, too!*

Gently Ben held her for a long time, stroking her, calming her. "I will come back to you, Mama. The Lord always prepares a way for us to keep his commandments."

The Third Book Of

Benjamin

THE THIRD BOOK OF BENJAMIN

1

Tantagua border, Land of Cumorah

At the women's insistence, Oliver Beck was to accompany Ben. They acquired tourist visas with false identities, made extensive preparations for living in the wilderness, decided to go into Cumorah from the land northward, and tried to foresee every possible difficulty. About one thing Ben was adamant.

"If one of us gets detained for any reason, the other must go on," he said.

Beck shook his head vigorously. "If something happens to you, *hermano*, I will not leave you. I am sworn to protect you."

"Then you might as well stay home!" Ben replied. "I am not a child, Beck. I am on an errand for the Lord, and He will provide a way for me to accomplish it."

Beck whistled softly. "Very well. You know your way around Granada better than I. The worst part will be getting past the border."

In the twilight the border official, a hard-faced woman with hair pulled up tight beneath her cap, peered at the visas and scrutinized the tourists' faces. Despite the government's rather extensive advertising campaign, few tourists had appeared in the seven weeks since borders were opened. "How did you know the resort was reopened?" she asked sharply.

While Beck kept his hat yanked down over his eyes and feigned sleep, Ben whipped out a shiny brochure. "We want to get an early start in the morning. Nothing like fishing in Lake Tantagua!" he chatted. "Wish I'd never left, but I went east for school, you know, and couldn't get back in. Fishing permits in Sheffa are so expensive!"

"Any firearms?" The official rummaged through their gear, pocketing various items.

"No, the only thing we plan to shoot is our cameras!" Ben laughed nervously.

"Money?"

"Sufficient for our needs."

"You may exchange your currency inside, and please bring your cameras for inspection." The official spoke with extreme politeness, then mumbled something in a walkie-talkie. "If you'll step inside and sign a few forms, you'll be on your way."

"The way so many broads are running things these days, it's like a female gestapo!" Beck laughed without humor. Grumbling, he ambled toward the office. Through the small window he glimpsed at least a dozen armed troops.

Immediately Beck made up his mind to be a decoy. But how to warn Ben? He could see the young man climbing from the jeep and walking slowly beside the woman, speaking with her. Few women, even the most hardened, could resist Ben's charm. At least this would help lower her guard.

Once he gets here it will be too late. Don't look in the window. You didn't see anything. These troops must think we're very stupid. Let's hope so.

"Ben! Go back to the car and get more film," Beck yelled in English. "I see a Trojan horse, here. We can't miss it!"

"*Un momento!*" One more disarming smile for the woman, and Ben turned, sauntering toward the jeep.

Nonplused, the woman hesitated.

Good job, Ben! Beck paused as if waiting for his companion to obtain the desired film, then forced himself to continue blissfully

412

toward the office. Nothing for it. Might as well give them their meat.

Once inside the vehicle, Ben ducked down as if retrieving something on the floor, ignited the engine, and floored the accelerator.

Beck did not look toward the retreating jeep. God go with you, my friend. "Now, gentlemen," he said in a loud voice, "what did you want me to sign?"

2

Think. Ben evaluated his situation as he sped down the road. Tantagua would be alerted and crawling with national police. He had to get rid of the jeep with its telltale license plate. Fortunately darkness was on his side, and he knew the city well. He pulled up on the city side of the lake and doused the lights. Then he removed the license plate, hauled out a small bag of essentials, and flagged a taxi.

"Where to, *Señor?*"

"Nowhere, for you. Just let me rent your car." Ben flashed a wad of Zarahemla currency.

Wide-eyed, the driver took the money.

"If you keep your mouth shut, you'll get your car back. It's a matter of life and death. Thanks, *amigo.*" Ben handed the startled cabby another generous tip and rolled away, blending into a fleet of taxis, all bright green Volkswagen beetles, on Cicero Boulevard.

Where to go? Haman had said the family home was torched and gutted. Even if by some miracle the book of Joseph still existed somewhere, how would he ever find it?

He zipped by the hospital. Same one where Papa got hurt. The west wing still was not restored, but the rubble was gone, and the building's remains had become a more permanent structure.

That doctor who offered to help. What was his name? . . . Escudo.

Ben hurried down the hall. "Dr. Escudo still working here?"

"Yes, he works emergency, and he's with a patient. May I help you?" The nurse studied the young man's face.

Ben sighed. "No. Will he be long?" He noted the broad-shouldered woman with a box-like figure.

"We will call him as soon as he is available." She smiled. "Just wait here."

413

Back at the desk, the nurse appraised the harried stranger. The man did not appear to be injured, but looked vaguely familiar. She searched papers in the drawer and whispered to another nurse, a thin brunette. "I think I've seen that man. Trouble is, I can't remember if he is on the wanted list or not. Do you know him?"

The brunette stared at Ben. "Nope. Wish I did. "

Ben waited, and waited. Thirteen minutes. That broad-shouldered woman . . . where did she go? She didn't look friendly. If the officials found him here, what could he do? He scanned the building, searching for a possible escape.

Twenty minutes. He could wait no longer. The shriek of sirens was incessant. By now his pursuers had probably found the abandoned jeep and cabless driver. And the green cab parked down the road would soon look suspicious.

Could Escudo still be trusted? He had no choice but to find out . . .

Finally he stood and forced himself to walk toward emergency. Slowly. *Don't hurry.*

The sound of footsteps at the entrance drew his unwilling glance.

It was the gestapo woman from the border.

The words "armed and dangerous" reached his ears. *Run!* was the message his adrenalin pumped to his brain.

Don't run. Ben turned his back squarely to his pursuers and walked with steady steps toward the familiar laundry room.

He could feel their eyes on his back, their weapons trained upon him. The hall seemed endless. Were his footsteps too loud, or was it his heart pounding? He shut the laundry room door, cringing when it squeaked. Donning a smock and mask, he hurried after a nurse toward emergency, where he found Escudo washing up.

"Good job, Beatriz," Escudo told his assistant. "Makes me think of Sarita Benamoz. That woman was an angel in a nurse's uniform."

"She taught me all I know," Beatriz replied softly.

"Wonder if she made it across the border all right."

"Sarita Benamoz is safe," Ben said.

Escudo whirled, puzzled.

Ben slipped off the mask.

"Zephan's boy?"

Ben nodded, replacing the mask. "In trouble again, sir. I've got to get away from here."

With the sound of heavy footsteps in the hall, "Shoulders" burst into the room, closely followed by the gestapo woman. "Doctor, they're looking for a spy."

With a meaningful glance, Escudo placed his arm on Ben's shoulder and abruptly the two men turned their backs on the officials. "This patient may die!" Escudo exclaimed he and Ben rushed out the ambulance entrance. "Get him in here immediately!"

"So your jeep is at the lake," Escudo said quietly as he drove the ambulance around the corner to where his car was parked. "How did you get here?"

Ben indicated the beetle parked half a block away, looking especially green under the street lamp.

Escudo grinned. "You're in luck. You'll be one in a million." He tossed Ben the keys to his own white beetle. "I'm sorry about your father, Ben. He was a good man," he said. "See that you get what you came for and get out. You know what these people are capable of. *Vaya con Dios, hijo.*"

"Thank you, sir. I won't forget you."

As Escudo walked slowly back from moving the ambulance, the border patrol, with a fierce looking woman in the lead, and weapons ready, pushed past the frightened nurses. "Where is the patient?" she demanded.

"Put those things away. If you shoot the doc, who will fix the people you injure? That's better." Escudo donned a look of studied sympathy. "Poor man didn't make it. They took him to the morgue."

"Who was the patient?" the militant woman asked, her mouth twisted with suspicion.

Escudo frowned. "We don't make a practice of interrogating dying human beings," he retorted dryly. "We are sworn to heal the sick and wounded, and we have no time to discriminate due to name or political rank."

"Of course, Doctor." The officer's smile was unpleasant. "Actually we have been informed the Minister of Internal Security, Haman Benamoz, has a brother who is visiting. The Minister wishes to extend his hospitality. This man was last seen driving a green taxi."

415

Escudo laughed. "Come now, officer. First you burst into my facility demanding confidential medical information. Then you expect me to identify our visitors' vehicles. What kind of outfit is this, anyway?"

"It is the law, you insolent man," the officer replied with icy contempt. "It is Pax Universalis."

"Sergeant!" her companion shouted, pointing out the door. "A green taxi is parked over there."

"Get the number, " she commanded. Like the edge of a whip, her voice cracked orders into her portable radio as she left the room and ran toward her car. "Search the hospital, the morgue, and the neighborhood. Roadblocks at every exit. Put the entire area under surveillance. We'll try to flush him out."

"What are you gawking at? Let's get back to work!" Escudo snapped to his nurses.

3

The sun was well up in the sky by the time Ben arrived in Granada. He drove up the winding road to his old home address, passed the huge bamboo tree which guarded the driveway, and braced himself to expect the worst. Then he saw the house. The outer structure was still intact, showing no signs of fire.

Ben concealed the car and approached the house. Too many beer cans and cigarette butts to remove. It would take a back hoe to plow them under. At least this indicated someone had lived here. No one would inhabit a building that was ashes inside.

In the garden, the tall bougainvillea bush had been torn out by the roots; birds of paradise had broken under mounds of rubbish; but here and there among the weeds a rose bloomed, defying neglect, gloom, and defeat. Perhaps something remained inside . . .

He entered the house, weapon in hand. Assured he was alone, he stood still in the silence and viewed his surroundings. Someone was camped here, but it had not been destroyed. So Haman had lied. For once Ben was grateful for his brother's deception.

He checked the phone. Dead.

A grease-encrusted sink brimmed with his mother's prized dishes. Half-emptied food cans sat neglected upon the table, while cockroaches scurried across the floor and soiled tablecloth. Empty

Rubbish was cast upon the floor with utter disregard for decency. In the refrigerator, gray mold had taken on mossy dimensions, while spore-encased items on the shelves resembled bizarre creatures from a science fiction movie. Ben shut the door quickly and groaned.

The bathroom reeked, and the once-shining white floor was gray with dust, hair, and grime. The commode was caked with crud, lime, and cigarette ashes. The showerhead was broken, the tub clogged and half full of slimy water; the ceiling and walls were black with mold.

Fighting his gag reflex, Ben began in the kitchen. He washed the dishes, cleaned the sink, forced himself to scrub the refrigerator, and hauled out trash. Next he found unused cleansers under the bathroom sink and worked in there until a human being could use the facility without fear of disease.

Mama's feather duster was still in its place by the pantry. He removed a thick layer of dust and swept, scrubbed, and mopped the floor, trying to decide what to do next. He discovered the stereo still worked and turned on Zephan's favorite concerto, scratched but usable. The familiar strains wrenched at his heart. Papa. *Papa, what would you do?*

At last the place began to look civilized. Sunshine burst through the windows, flowing through multiple crystals of Mama's chandelier to create colored patterns upon the wall.

Were Papa's book shelves still intact?

The shelves were untouched, but the family Bible, the largest book of all, was missing.

He heard a door close softly, and cautious footsteps in the hall. Ben whirled, pistol in hand.

When a woman and little girl appeared, Ben lowered his gun. A smirk on the woman's face did not hide her fear. One upper right tooth was silver. So it was Juana Gomez, wife of the greedy neighbor who had driven out Maria and Enrique.

"Who . . . are you?" she stammered. "Don't shoot. I can explain."

"I own this house," he replied. "If you don't interfere, you will not be harmed. Where is your husband?"

"Dead. He drank too much, and talked. He was eliminated. I was just released because of the *niña*." She nodded at the child. "The new government promised to pay me support."

As an informer? "Very well, Juana."

"You know my name?" she asked, startled.

"I know all about you. You have already talked too much."

His words had the desired effect. Genuine fear crawled over her face. Poor ignorant woman. She only knew enough to be dangerous to both sides. No doubt she could be bought, though, and his cash would look better than Ponista promises. He handed her a wad of money. "Look, I won't let on that you slipped up if you will help me with this one thing."

"What is it?" Her tone became friendly.

"Where is my family Bible?"

"Oh, is that all? It's in the pantry on a stool. It was just the right size to help me reach high shelves."

Ben cut her down with a look of disgust, retrieved the scriptures and headed for the library. "Now, don't bother me. There is more money where that came from, but if you breathe a word to your Ponista friends, I'll see you regret it," he said.

In the library he sat at a table so he could watch the woman. How much time did he have before the Ponistas discovered him? He must hurry. But this time he would not leave without the book of Joseph. Where could it be?

He perused the Bible, stopping to ponder various passages. *Out of the mouth of two or three witnesses shall every word be established.* Could a nation's history survive on oral testimony of a lone man who, at best, knew only fragments of the true story?

Zephan had said the ancient testament was buried in the ground. Those records were not lost or forgotten, nor did they survive by accident. After purposefully concealing their writings, ancient prophets and their people were destroyed in a violent religious war.

Cumorah was suffering a religious war of sorts.

Zephan Benamoz was a careful man, one accustomed to jeopardy of life and liberty. He would never leave documents so vital and sacred where chance could assist the tyrant. At once Ben knew his father had hidden the records somewhere, beyond the grasp of a spiritually hardened and benighted foe. But where?

He read on, but it was getting late. Soon it would be dark. He glanced in the family room. Juana was asleep on a couch with her little girl. Probably exhausted from her daily ordeals. Now was the time to find the book and get out of here. But how?

His glance fell on a passage in the New Testament: "Ask, and ye shall receive."

Searching for other passages on prayer, he came to Matthew 6:6.

"But thou, when thou prayest, enter into thy closet, and when thou hast shut thy door, pray to thy Father which is in secret. "

Okay, I'll try it. Which closet shall I use?
He made his way to the master bedroom, where the walk-in closet was recessed so as not to diminish spaciousness in the main room. The closet, lined with cedar wood, was comparable in size to a small room, yet was not immediately apparent to the casual observer.

With the fragrance from cedar, a mixture of memories invaded Ben's mind. As a youth, terrorized by two bullying brothers, Ben had often hidden from his pursuers in that closet. Reflection on the safety in those moments from the past brought him comfort.

Few clothes were left hanging. Looters had seen to it. Zephan and Sarita were not given to excessive and costly apparel, anyway. Determined to pray, Ben lowered himself to his knees, but started to lose his balance. To his surprise, he felt dizzy.

He thrust his hand out to steady himself, and the wall before him gave slightly beneath his weight.

Ben discovered a well-concealed track supporting the panel before him. Lacking lubrication, the panel required considerable exertion to be moved. Ben slid it aside, and almost fell down the stairs before him. A flip of the switch illuminated the staircase. He shut the panel behind him and carefully descended the stairs, pawing at the cobweb shrouds.

Ben discovered shelves lined with food supplies and equipment. Several barrels, sealed airtight, labeled and dated, contained enough corn, grain, rice, and varieties of beans to feed a large family for more than a year.

The large room was carefully sealed against humidity and unusually dry, with everything beneath a thick layer of dust. On a table in the most remote corner lay stacked letters and documents, and a well-worn copy of Shakespeare's *Macbeth*. One of Zephan's more prized possessions, no doubt. Also, a sword identical to the one Abiram had made. This sword had long been unsheathed, except in a blanket of dust.

Brother Bianco had told him about an earlier prophet who discovered wagon-loads of ancient records inside a cave. The original sword of Laban had also been found. It was unsheathed, and on it were written the words: *This sword will never be sheathed again until the kingdoms of this world become the kingdom of our God and his Christ.*

Ben brushed away the thick dust and sneezed. First, he uncovered a personal journal of his father's. Inside was a picture of his grandfather, Amoz ben Gideon, and his grandmother, Marta.

Born of Amoz and Marta ben Gideon, Zephan ben Amoz had the blood of Judah in his veins. His mother, Marta of Lithuania, descended from Ephraim.

A reticent man, Zephan Benamoz had been silent about his past. At that moment, Ben felt great love and compassion for his father. Zephan Benamoz had taken secrets from his past and locked them up in this closet.

4

Ben took a small towel from a supply of linens and blankets and reverently removed dust from the writings he had found. Where was the book of Joseph?

Pages in ancestral journals, bursting with carnage and destruction, exuded the chill of death and filled Ben with desolation. The twentieth century had suffered the reign of evil, with blood and horror on the earth. Still, Ben read on with eerie fascination, oblivious to passage of time.

At length he looked up, disquieted by a sensation of another presence in the room. He glanced behind him and saw nothing. Still, he felt something . . . somebody? He shuddered.

Must be fatigue.

He stood unmoving, his eyes inspecting every inch of the room. Not a sound. All was still. Or was it?

Did something pass by him? No, nothing. It was *someone.* Or so it seemed.

A small cloud arose from the sword, as if someone blew off the dust. Ben drew back, his heart pounding, and he dared not blink, until a drop of sweat rolled into his eye. *Who was there?* Of a certainty, not a living soul knew about this place . . .

Finally he moved. He picked up the sword, startled at the drops of dried blood upon the blade. He studied the floor. More drops of blood. How did he miss this before? Someone besides Zephan knew about this place and must have used it for refuge in the recent conflict.

Ben edged toward the stairs with journals in hand, and his eyes again swept the room, searching for the missing testament.

The light went out.

Carefully he found the stairs and reached the door at the top, but could not budge it. After a struggle, he ceased, fearing a loud noise would draw attention to him.

Despite inky blackness, his previous study of the entire room served him well, and he managed to locate a lantern, but nothing with which to light it.

Was the book of Joseph among the other documents he found? Or was its hiding place yet to be discovered? Was the book still in this house, or did someone take it?

The answers to those tormenting questions remained hidden in a vapor of darkness.

Sleep eluded him, leaving anxiety in its place. He forced himself to think methodically and searched his mind for solutions. His thoughts dwelled on the wars, violence, and treachery which saturated the ancestral journals.

Countless throngs of people in shackles came toward him, stepping over corpses of as many dead on endless battlefields. They wore apparel from another era. Some were personages of an ancient epoch. Some were familiar . . . Anahí's family! Her little sisters held their arms out to him. He reached out, but felt nothing.

"Papa!" he cried out. "Are you here?" His voice seemed to echo from another room.

Terrified, he again tried the door, but to no avail.

A great wind was blowing earth upon the unnamed bodies. Legions of ghosts limped and stumbled toward him. They came on steadily, row after row, dividing upon reaching him, then passing on either side. The look in their eyes made him want to weep. At last they emptied the fields. No, the fields were not empty after all, but golden with ripe wheat, as far as the eye could see.

Good. He could no longer endure the sight of those countless faces. But would they come back? What did those people want from him? What could he do?

At last he slept.

The wind whistled as it rippled through that wheat. No, it was a voice. Just a whisper. Ben. Ben? Someone was calling for help.

He awoke with a start. In the faint daylight, Ben saw he was alone. The panel door, though stuck, was barely ajar, permitting a pale strand of light to illuminate the room.

Immediately Ben went to the table, searching for the book of Joseph. Beside the sword, sitting in the light, there it was, with the cover torn off, as he remembered. Ben glanced toward the door. The light seemed brighter than at first. Chagrined that he had missed the book before, Ben started to reach for it, but stopped. Thick dust remained atop the book, but he could see fingerprints from a hand much larger than his.

Someone else had been there recently. Whether friend or foe he did not know. Of one thing he was certain: others sought possession of this book, and he must guard it with care. His father was counting on him.

He gently wiped the dust from the book, turned the pages, and began to read:

Behold, I speak unto you as though I spake from the dead; for I know that ye shall have my words.

And I am the same who hideth up this record unto the Lord. For none can have power to bring it to light save it be given him of God; for it shall be brought out of darkness unto light, according to the word of God; it shall be brought out of the earth, and it shall shine forth out of darkness, and come unto the knowledge of the people; and it shall be done by the power of God.

Therefore I write unto you, Gentiles, and also unto you, house of Israel. And I write also unto the remnant of this people. I write unto you all; for you must stand to be judged for what you have done, whether it be good or evil.

Behold what the scripture says — man shall not smite, neither shall he judge; for judgment is mine, saith the Lord, and vengeance is mine also, and I will repay. Behold, the sword of vengeance hangeth over you; and the time soon cometh that he avengeth the blood of the saints upon you, for he will not suffer their cries any longer.

In the light, a certain passage stood out, leaping into Ben's mind.

Behold, I speak unto you as if ye were present, and yet ye are not. But behold, Jesus Christ hath shown you unto me, and I know your doing.

Zephan was there. Ben knew it . . . and that ineffable, familiar feeling pulsed through him. *I feel as though I stand in the place of those who wrote these words.*

He was not alone after all, and he was no longer afraid.

Ben removed a small stone obstructing the door, then returned to the kitchen.

Juana and the child were gone.

5

Headlight beams probed a dark jumble of trees shielding his house from the road. As Ben crawled and ran through tall oats, a sluggish dawn inched over the field of grain. Reminded of his spectral experience in the secret room, he half expected those ghosts to reappear. Sounds of an approaching auto were barely discernible, and Ben glimpsed a figure which emerged brandishing a powerful search light. The visitor was no ghost.

Skirting claws of light that raked the field, Ben reached his car beyond the hill's crest. Its diminutive size, and being parked facing downhill, gave him a narrow advantage. He coasted down a horse trail and drove gingerly through an adjacent orange grove. Finally he rolled onto the paved road leading down into the valley.

The gas tank was nearly empty. He did not have enough fuel to get over the border, and the nearest gas station was past the hills in the opposite direction. Rather than risk getting stranded, he decided to go back to the house and take a horse. He could cross the mountains on horseback and thus avoid other human beings.

Fog lay dense in the valley and seemed to rise with him as his little car climbed the hill to return to his house. An oncoming car moved past him, like a pair of disembodied eyes floating in viscous fluid. He hoped he looked to passersby as they appeared to him, like the stare of nocturnal creatures into a campfire, gleaming orbs that were seen but could not see.

At the end of his driveway, an immense bamboo tree stood as a sentinel. It was more like a thicket of trees, with a kind of room inside. As boys, he and Abiram would hide there to escape their older brothers. They had often debated whether it was possible to park a car in there. Well, now he would find out. Turning off his lights, he rolled up to the widest opening in the clump of trees, where he got out and leaned against one of the thinner bamboo stalks. It resisted his weight, but inside were short, brittle reeds which he quickly broke with his hands so he could drive over them. No more time to waste.

He backed up on the grassy pasture and accelerated forward, forcing his way into the "room". It was very tight, but he made it. The pressure had bent the thin stalk, so he easily pushed it back to shield the entrance, viewing with regret the crumpled right fender and broken headlight. Sorry, little friend. Don't know when or if you will be found. But I hope it will be the good doctor who finds you, and not the enemy.

He ran for the stable, determined to escape under cover of the fog.

The horses were gone. He should have known. The stable was relatively clean, so the horses must have been stolen long ago. Fences were broken down and doors were hanging askew. Maybe the horses escaped. He hoped so. But how was he going to escape? Who else had horses? All his friends were long gone, and undoubtedly their horses were stolen or killed. Abandoned vehicles he had seen along the road were probably empty, as well. By now it was broad daylight and the fog was lifting.

From habit he started to close the door to the stable, but paused, hearing mewing sounds. At least rats were one thing that would not be in short supply in this country. The mother cat would feed her family well, provided she herself had not been killed by a predator. He reentered the dusty semi-darkness in the stable. Whoever had stolen the horses had left most of the hay. Bales were stacked to the ceiling. Plenty of places for a family of cats. But the sound was coming from the foaling area, which was several times larger than the other stalls. The wide gate was unbroken, and unlike the others, closed and latched. He opened it and stopped short. A car was parked in the foaling pen, and it was so encased in cobwebs it resembled a giant cocoon. It looked to be of pre-modern vintage. If only it would run. As he wiped away the clinging film, his astonishment grew. It was an antique — a brown station wagon with

424

wooden sides. Brother Joseba's car. Stacked to the ceiling in the back were framed pictures. Solano's art collection.

So this was why Anahí returned to Cumorah. She had continued to Granada, probably in search of the lost testament. He smiled, picturing the delight on her face when he returned with his treasures.

Only one small problem. Actually, a small problem and four tiny problems. Nestled behind the left front wheel was a calico cat, nursing her kittens. Ben removed a can from his backpack and tried to entice the mother with a sardine. She accepted his gift, rubbed against his leg to show her gratitude, and proudly showed him her brood. He stroked her, then backed away and called softly, but the cat returned to her bed and lay down for a long nap.

Good grief. He liked cats, but this was getting nowhere. Anahí would not want him to move them himself and endanger the kittens' lives, but the morning was nearly spent, and he had to get away from there.

Ben got in the car, and it didn't take him long to find the keys where Anahí had left them. He started the engine, and it purred. Brother Joseba, wherever you may be, you are still blessing lives.

A siren rent the air, echoing through a tunnel of fog up the hill. So the house was being watched. At least he had been warned. He gunned the engine while the siren screamed, then got out and observed the results with relief. Letting the engine warm up, he cleaned off the windshield and allowed the calico to move her family away from danger. He walked out into the lingering haze and stood to watch and listen, each of his senses intent and focused.

When all was quiet, he again took the bumpy dirt road through the orange grove, adding new battle scars to the faithful old wagon. Down off the hill, enough fog remained to require headlights. Anahí must be praying for him.

The tank was full, too. Anahí was a fanatic about keeping the tank full. Silently he blessed her wisdom and vowed never to tease her about it again.

6

"This is like Christmas," Anahí said as she helped unload the car, cleaned the paintings and set them up around the house. Some would go to Sarita, but Ben wanted to build a private gallery in memory of Solano.

"Why didn't you tell me about these, Ani?"

"I didn't want to add to your burden, Ben. Besides, I had given them up for lost, anyway. Why urge you to further endanger your life for what I was sure was a pile of rubble? This proves how puny my faith is!"

"Ha! Don't belittle thy faith, ma'am. It keeps me alive."

"It is a blessing you are returned safe to me, and with all these treasures, too. Look at this Friberg, Ben. It reminds me of your father." Instantly she regretted her words.

Ben took the large painting from her and leaned it against the wall. He stood before it, trembling.

"Forgive me, darling. How insensitive of me . . . " She stopped. Gradually the deep creases of agony flowed from his face, and his eyes reflected a peace and comfort she had not seen in years, as if he envisioned something she could not see.

Ben had not seen this painting, but somehow it was familiar. Far from a serene portrayal, it bristled with conflict. According to the ancient historian, the scene was the court of a decadent king. The king's corrupt nature was readily observed in his face, where a single black browline paralleled a thin, down-turning mustache and mouth. Fierce eyes, narrowly apart, bulged from their sockets, as if constricted by the per-unit pressure of his weight. He had no neck, and his preponderance of flesh, though draped in purpled silks and brocades and cinched by gaudily jeweled belts and buckles, yet overflowed a throne embellished with carved, leering faces of strange and seductive gods. His mammoth cape spilled over marble inlaid steps and onto the floor like creeping red power. At his feet lay vicious beasts, lightly harnessed, poised to tear apart the prisoner at the king's command. At the king's fingertips were heaps of food and jugs of wine for instant gratification, to satisfy a soul destitute of self-control and in abject servitude to lusts of the flesh.

To the king's right, in seats which were above all the others, were the soothsayers. They sat behind a breastwork ornamented with pure gold, described by the ancient historian as fit to "rest their bodies and arms upon while they spoke lying and vain words to his people." All wore tall hats, emblematic their lofty intelligence and permanent tenure.

426

This paragon of earthly power, this enemy of truth could, at the wave of his fat, bejeweled hand, snuff out the very embodiment of truth —— the prophet Abinadi. Abinadi alone stood upright among groveling sycophants, and thugs prostrate with drunkenness. In chained, ragged, snowy-haired dignity, the prophet cowed his foes, confounding petty and devious minds with simple truth. Abinadi warned them to repent of their iniquities or be brought into bondage and destroyed. He taught them to remember the commandments of God, and return to the ways of righteousness, for the safety of their souls. The prophet testified of his people's record which the Lord would preserve to the last day, and which would expose to other nations the enemies of Christ. Abinadi prophesied to the court the coming of Messiah, but his hearers defied him.

"I must fulfill the commandments of God, and because I have told you the truth, you are angry with me," Abinadi said. "Because I have spoken the word of God ye have judged me that I am mad." And his face shone with exceeding luster, even as Moses' did while in the mount Sinai, while speaking with the Lord.

Abinadi blistered the pride of petty magistrates with the pure white energy of his faith. And his accusers hated him.

"God executes vengeance upon those who destroy his people." When Abinadi had said these words, he was put to death because he would not deny the commandments of God, and he sealed the truth of his words with his death.

Ben stared at the Friberg masterpiece. The painting was not of a chance occurrence, nor the dabbling of a hallucinating artist. It was a pattern for all time, a motif on the endless mural of eternity. It captured the pivotal moment when men clashed, soul-to-soul, in the relentless struggle between good and evil.

One prophet, like unto Abinadi, had declared unto this generation:

"This is the last day in which the great consummation of God's purposes will be made, the only epoch in which the Lord has promised that sin will not prevail."

Again, as he had so many times, Benjamin reflected upon Dalton Mortfield's tapes of Zephan's trial. He had listened to those tapes dozens of times. But Mortfield had fled before recording Zephan's final words.

Ben closed his eyes. If only he could have known his father's last testimony . . .

427

Suddenly in his mind he heard his father's voice. *May God have mercy on you, but as for me, I forgive you.*
Oh, Divine Redeemer! I know that my Redeemer lives.

"Thank you, thank you," Ben said, over and over. For the first time since his father was killed, Benjamin wept.

The Book Of
GORDON

*"And I beheld the Sword of Laban,
and the hilt thereof was pure gold,
and the workmanship thereof was exceedingly fine,
I I saw that the blade thereof was of the most precious steel."*

THE BOOK OF GORDON

1

Mitchell Hunt emerged from Sarita's cottage and decided to walk the few blocks to the small house of Jaime Canosa, her kinsman. Since Zephan's death, Hunt had taken it upon himself to look after the prophet's widow. Despite good intentions to give Sarita moral support, somehow Hunt always left her presence feeling strengthened himself. Sarita was bereft of her husband and nursed a heart broken by her two eldest sons' wayward choices. In chronic pain from an arthritic hip and polio-stricken leg, Sarita continually amazed Hunt with her ability to carry on, serving long hours at the local hospital. To Sarita's relief, her son Benjamin had returned safely from "that evil place", as she called the Land of Cumorah.

Canosa, on the other hand, was eaten up with a desire for revenge. And who could blame him? Canosa had figured out the cause of his wife's death, and he struggled bitterly with the murder of two beloved prophets. Also Canosa seethed over the foul play which had slain forty innocent people he had known and loved. It seemed Yeshurun was in constant jeopardy of extinction. And why this

431

apparently relentless drive to eliminate the Canosa-Benamoz family in particular? Some type of conspiracy, perhaps?

He was getting paranoid, Hunt kept telling himself. Still, having grown to love this family, Hunt had vowed to keep further tragedy from befalling them. If some kind of plot did exist, it must be handled with extreme care. Propensity for plain, outspoken truth had gotten Canosa and the Benamoz men into a lot of trouble.

Yeshurun had difficulty fathoming the devious Egalitarian mentality. The Egalitarian elites were charming and likable, fantastically wealthy, citizens above suspicion, zealous in their utopian Voltairist beliefs. Thus the Egalitarians were capable of vast influence, usually overreaching with ease the straightforward, less subtle, and sometimes naive Yeshurun folk. When their objectives were not achieved through pervasive influence, or with seemingly inexhaustible financial resources, the Egalitarians would not hesitate to resort to raw power. After such brutal manifestations of their dark side, the Egalitarians would lie to the public with practiced eloquence, assuring gullible adherents that any means was justified to achieve their glorious ends. Thus Egalitarians had not only made their deadly practices legal, but also were daily praised and thanked by their victims.

Only Hunt's strict orders kept Canosa from launching a one-man crusade against faceless evil forces in the world. Such a vague cause could only end in futility, if not Canosa's own demise. The tough old veteran was not merely Hunt's trump card, but perhaps the only link to capturing the archenemy —— Rameses, ringleader of the powerful underground and elite Egalitarians.

Hunt followed a sound of machinery to Canosa's garage. There the old man worked his mechanical wizardry with various metal tools which Hunt was too ignorant to identify. This man's inventiveness was far more brilliant than any political "Intelligence". Hunt recognized farm implements, but elsewhere were piles of parts and mysterious but useful gadgets fashioned for Canosa's customers. The agent picked his way through strewn parts and constructions to a tractor chassis where his friend lay on his back tinkering with something.

"Any swords among these plowshares?" Hunt called.

Canosa stood up and wiped his hands with a greasy rag. "Is this a call to battle?" he said with a hopeful grin. "A word from you and I can turn this place into a weapons arsenal. Just point me to the enemy, and I'll mow'em down."

"That's your job, remember?"

Canosa's face fell. "Aw, what could Mortfield have been thinking? I wish I could help you, Hunt. Nobody wants Rameses' head more than I, but those POW years only showed me the web, not the spider." Canosa thought again of the concentration camps at Cumeni, and the man who had sent him there.

"Something is on your mind, Canosa."

"Same old dead ends. No proof, no leads."

"Well, if you find anything — anything at all, consult with me first. Don't do anything rash."

"You have my word."

Later Canosa received a phone call from the chief prophet: "*Hermano* Canosa, the Lord is extending a call to you, to labor in the mission field. Are you willing to accept?"

"Of course," Canosa said without hesitation. "With pleasure."

"The Lord is well pleased with your desires to serve him, for there are those, not a few, who criticize and rebel, who apostatize and lift their voices against this work. But they speak their piece as they walk across the stage of life, and then are soon forgotten."

"Some choose the gods of Babylon," Canosa said, "but as for me and my house, we will serve the Lord."

"Good for you, my beloved brother. I decided the moment has come that it is better to lean into the stiff wind of opportunity than to simply hunker down and do nothing."

Canosa chuckled. "And I shall follow the prophet. How can I serve?"

"You shall be further enlightened presently, under more secure circumstances. For the moment, suffice it to say this: It has been revealed to his servants that a forthcoming development in Babylon, though intended to thwart our progress, will present a glorious opportunity to go forward, marching as an army with banners emblazoned with the everlasting truth. You know, ——"

"The Lord works in mysterious ways, his wonders to perform."

"Precisely," the prophet said. "So, my good brother, prepare yourself to join your young kinsman in the mission field, and keep his machinery in good repair. His equipment has broken down, so it is urgent you depart at the earliest possible moment. Then we shall work day and night, and when the time arrives, we shall be ready to move forward in a major way."

"I'm ready."

433

"Your first assignment is to memorize Isaiah 2:3. It describes your mission. Goodbye, *hermano*. And *vaya con Dios.*"

Canosa took his scriptures from their safe place and promptly committed the verse to memory:

> And many people shall go and say, Come ye, and let us go up to the mountain of the Lord, to the house of the God of Jacob; and he will teach us of his ways, and we will walk in his paths: for out of Zion shall go forth the law, and the word of the Lord from Jerusalem.

That night Canosa left for Jershon and told no one of his plans, not even Sarita.

2

AVAUNT! AND QUIT MY SIGHT! LET THE EARTH HIDE THEE!
THY BONES ARE MARROWLESS, THY BLOOD IS COLD;
THOU HAST NO SPECULATION IN THOSE EYES
WHICH THOU DOST GLARE WITH.
HENCE, HORRIBLE SHADOW!
(MACBETH TO THE GHOST OF BANQUO)

Zarahemla

Gordon Slater hurried into the palatial lobby of *Chateau Versailles*, where Mitchell Hunt and Benjamin Benamoz already waited.

"I have little appetite for this banquet." Gordon frowned as the three men sat down to an elegant table with dainty settings. "A Dermucker Foundation Peace Prize for Kemen Ponte, destroyer of Cumorah. What a travesty!"

"I never eat anything whose name I can't pronounce." Hunt glanced at the menu and set it aside. "Even pronouncing *Chateau* sounds like a fancy sneeze. I hope the French are not as profligate with their finances as with their vowels. Could be worse. At least here the Award Committee Chairman can't drool on our food."

Gordon chuckled. "Hey! Comic relief is Dan MacRay's department!"

"Wish he were here," Ben said, his voice glum.

"Cheer up, young fellow," Gordon said. "Dan is out on bail, and the government will never win this case against him. The charges are absurd."

"We've got a good view of the head table." Hunt changed the subject. "Don't want to miss anything, like yonder FSB agent, Andrei Kovac. Good grief. That man is everywhere!"

"How about Haman Benamoz, sitting at Ponte's right hand?" Gordon shuddered. "Must be some kind of sadist to participate in an affair like this, honoring murderers."

"The villain Macbeth is reincarnated in my own family," Ben said.

"Hey, what is he doing?" Hunt whispered. "Looks as if he's seen a ghost!"

Ben focused the zoom lens on his camera.

Haman Benamoz was indeed acting strange. Through the lens, Ben could see great beads of sweat on his brother's face. That look of fright would fit any horror film. Inconspicuous in the din of conversing guests and clinking glasses, a little drama unfolded.

Haman addressed the vacant chair on his right, speaking nervously, "I never laid a hand on you, Papa . . .What do you mean, repent?. . .my beliefs? Ha! Just because I never agreed with you. You and your old repentance . . . The Egalitarian philosophy has caused the death of many?. . . Thousands?. . . *Millions?* Go away! Let go of my mind! How can you be talking to me? You do not exist! I refuse to believe this is happening. You're gone. Dead. Dead!" Haman's laugh was shrill and maniacal, filled with terror.

"As you can see, I am not dead," Zephan said. "This is what you get for believing Egalitarian lies about the afterlife. Why do you persecute your younger brother, Haman? Do you not know the Lord has chosen him over you, and this because of your iniquities? Satan has deceived you, my son, and I advise you to get out of his employ. Behold, the Lord will deliver Rameses into your brother's hands." And he was gone.

"I don't believe it," Haman said to himself. "It's not possible my brother could defeat Rameses. Rameses is the most powerful man in the world. At his command he could slay fifty. No, fifty thousand! Millions! How could my sissy little brother stand against him?"

435

Haman looked around. All was quiet except for cameras, snapping and whirring. All eyes were upon him.

"¿*Qué tienes*, Benamoz?" Ponte snapped, roughly grabbing his arm. "You're making a complete fool of yourself!"

"I, uh, I'm sorry, sir." Haman tried to smile. "I don't feel well. Must be jet lag!"

The committee chairman tapped his spoon against a glass and noisily began the ceremony.

Ben patted his camera. "Got it all here. The Benamoz Macbeth even has his own ghost of Banquo!"

"Probably for your benefit, Ben," Gordon said.

Ben smiled. "I hope Papa is haunting Haman. Papa never could resist a good joke . . . or a bad one. But my brother will never change." Ben's voice became bitter. "He could see an angel of God —— and he still wouldn't believe it."

Hunt leaned back, yawning his way through dinner and speeches. Finally as the crowd began to break up, and people jostled by, he felt a small paper pressed into his hand.

"I'll meet you in the lobby," he said to his friends, abruptly leaving the table.

Hunt discerned Andrei Kovac's form through clouds of smoke and weaved through milling people to the banquet hall's far side. Hunt felt for his weapon in case of foul play.

The FSB agent looked to be at least in his sixties. Mitchell was surprised when Andrei Kovac shook his hand warmly. "Mr. Hunt, thank you for responding to my request," he said, smiling, as they found a secluded room.

"I will get right to the point. When Benjamin Benamoz seized an Antionite vessel and confiscated its cargo a few years ago, I was on that ship. After the Skulls Island success, I turned myself over to Zephan and his people, informing them of cargo Zephan was not looking for, which was destined for the Zarahemla Republic. I showed him where a half ton of cocaine was hidden."

Hunt nodded, his expression guarded.

"I knew Benjamin as a little boy. I knew his grandfather in the old country."

Hunt was amazed at the evident emotion in the agent's face, but he was not prepared for what came next.

"During the months which followed," Kovac continued slowly, "Zephan's family converted me to Christianity. Until now I have guarded my true convictions with utmost secrecy. I continued gathering documentation on the Pyramid cartel, with which leaders from the Black Sea Democracies have been involved for thirty years. Mr. Hunt, I know the identity of Rameses."

3

With mixed emotions, Miles Potter watched former inmate Will Goodwin and his wife leave his cell. He stared at the Bible they had left in his hands. Perhaps those people had something.

"Potter!"

Hearing a key rattle in his cell door, Potter hastily shoved the book under his pillow.

"Today's your lucky day, man!" The guard grinned, leading the bewildered inmate down to an office. "Some big wigs in the gov'ment to see you, buddy, and there's money in it!"

After Potter shook hands with Skadden Wilkes, he resisted the urge to wipe his hand on his pants.

"Have a seat, Potter! " Wilkes removed some forms from his briefcase. "How would you like to get back at the guy who helped get you in here? That big mouth investigative reporter, Dan MacRay, is blowing the cover off the whole operation, ya know what I mean?"

"I want Hunt!" Potter said.

"Too risky. But tables are turned. The Central Committee says MacRay violated your civil rights!"

Miles Potter laughed, incredulous. "You're puttin' me on!"

Wilkes shook his head. "MacRay goes before the World Tribunal, and you get to be his judge! Committee pays you big bucks, and grants you liberty. All you have to do is pronounce MacRay guilty!"

Potter was skeptical. "That's the jury's job!"

Wilkes moistened his lips. "Nope! World Tribunal doesn't use a jury. What could be easier, man? Just sign here. Think of it as a political prisoner exchange!"

A stroke of luck. Potter returned to his cell to contemplate how to use his freedom. Freedom. "True freedom comes only when faith in Christ delivers you from spiritual bondage," Goodwin had said.

Miles had nothing else to do with his time, so he turned to the New Testament. The words of Jesus tugged on memories long buried.

Miles Potter's mother, seeing her son's remarkable intelligence, had worked herself to exhaustion, supporting him, not just through high school, but onward to a diploma from one of the country's most prestigious universities. He had taken her for granted. He could get A's without effort, even in college, and it pleased her. He soon learned the system — tell your professors what they wanted to hear, and you would get an "A".

The teachers loved him, too, and brought him to the attention of an influential professor named Cromwell. Miles Potter would be a leader among his own kind, Cromwell said. The world owes you a living, Cromwell had told him. Potter attended Egalitarian meetings and learned how to give rousing speeches. He acquired great wealth through public speaking. The famous Miles Potter flattered the political elite, and he flattered the poor. The wealthy Miles Potter believed it didn't matter how you got the money, as long as you made a better world once you became wealthy. Only the end result mattered. Every man of his race must do what was necessary to get ahead. Then, once he triumphed over his oppressors, he, Miles Potter could do good for the world, and his actions would be justified.

But somehow he, Miles Potter, had missed the lesson of his mother's life. "Seek first the kingdom of God. You don't have to be rich to get to heaven, Miles," she had told him, "but you do have to be good."

His mother had raised him with love and faith. She had worked two jobs during his college years . . . sometimes three . . . sparing nothing for herself, so he could have the best education possible. Where had he gone wrong? All her savings had been wasted by the very people she had paid to educate her son. The educators had corrupted him, or, to be honest, he had allowed them to corrupt him. He had become obsessed with wealth and power; he had become proud of his intelligence, because all his friends had flattered him. Smart he was, but he had been a fool.

His mother had gone to an early grave with the heartbreaking knowledge that her beloved son had turned out just like his derelict father.

Will Goodwin was right about one thing: he, Miles Potter, was a terrible sinner. Big time. How could he ever make restitution for all he had done wrong? He could not possibly pay the price. There was no way — no way at all. "There is no other way or means whereby a man can be saved," Goodwin had said, "only in and through Christ."

He desperately wished he were a child again, when he had declared his love for Jesus, but without understanding. He recalled Sunday School as a child in Sheffa. Days of freedom. Children.

Matthew 18:6 But whosoever shall offend one of these little ones which believe in me, it were better for him that a millstone were hanged about his neck,and that he were drowned in the depth of the sea.

Miles squeezed his eyes tight together, but could not shut out the faces of the scores of children he had corrupted with drugs. Potter drew in his breath sharply. He wrestled with an unfamiliar pain, the anguish of remorse.

4

Karl Devon and Elidor Redmund watched Skadden Wilkes leave the Executive Office with a gait somewhat akin to a scurrying rodent.

"There goes the shark of sharks," Devon said.

"Is he good enough, Karl?"

"The best that money can buy," Devon said wryly as he answered the phone.

"Karl? Gordon Slater here. Would you consider throwing out the MacRay case? You know your authorization of those tapes is illegal in Zarahemla."

"What kind of lawyer are you?" Devon snapped. "Under Pax Universalis, I have total authority!"

"I know it," Gordon replied. "But Pax was not in force at the time of the incident in question."

Devon laughed. "You can't get out of this so easily, Slater. Elidor just signed a directive today, making the Pax retroactive for fifty years." He slammed down the receiver.

"Quick thinking, Karl."

Devon frowned. "That's the problem. It was only a bluff, and it won't take Slater long to debunk. Cuddly appearances notwithstanding, the man has a formidable intellect, and he is a tough opponent in the legal arena, Elidor. He has won every case he's tried in the last seven years. Yet for all his successes, he certainly doesn't have the affluent lifestyle of such a thriving attorney."

"So why isn't he working for us?" Elidor demanded.

"He only takes cases against the Order."

5

On the office door was a small black label with the plainest of white lettering: "Gordon Slater". Ted Lipscomb walked in and took a hard wooden chair offered him and looked around this man's small, simple office. An uncomfortable chair. Not conducive to long, chatty conferences. No time piece in sight, no secretary to clock the minutes and seconds consumed in legal counsel and mail the notorious legal bills. The most elegant furnishings in the office were frames on a dozen family pictures. One or two framed official certificates on the wall seemed lost in a relative clutter of handwritten letters and numerous photos of many people, all of whom looked somehow familiar.

Here were the shelves stuffed with books . . . books written by European men who had been dead for centuries. This man Slater was really behind the times. Compared to offices of Ted's friends who were lawyers, this place looked like an old attic. The lawyers from the Anti-Hate Committee never used those old books. Modern lawyers said Zarahemla's constitution was outdated, and it was their duty to revise it. To do so, modern lawyers no longer needed to read those old books. Nor was it necessary to read the constitution, except to make it fit a desired objective. Lipscomb's friends relied exclusively on the case histories established by their peers. The only way to be fair was to take things case by case, and judge according to how one felt at the time, Lipscomb's friends informed him. It was obvious that Slater, here, was one of those rigid old fogies who were always harping old clichés. "It's the principle of the thing!" Slater and his kind would always say. How boring.

Lipscomb noted Slater had about a dozen copies of a slim paperback book named *The Law*, by Frederic Bastiat. How absurd. Slater probably couldn't understand those other books, so he really only read that one skinny little book. But why would he have so many copies? To give away to people? Nah. Why would anyone want to give a book as a gift?

The beat-up secondhand desk was probably newer than the antiquated chair behind it, which Slater occupied. Gordon Slater was. . . . well, quaint. His suit was outmoded but clean and neat, in good repair. This with his kindly face, silvered sideburns, whitish hair, and even whiter beard gave him the look of a man from another era. Like a character from a storybook. Hardly the appearance of a man who could win against a world body.

Lipscomb stifled the urge to squirm. His own perfectly combed hair, green contact lenses, fashionable suit —— and otherwise charming appearance created for him by Warner Brackenlaw's public image committee —— had given him a hard, confident shell before millions of viewers for many years. Why did he suddenly feel so small under scrutiny of this ancient old man?

"How long have you known Dan MacRay, Mr. Lipscomb?" Slater asked.

"We go way back. I went to school with him. He has always been this way."

"What do you mean?"

"Oh, you know. Boring. Big on history and such. But his biggest problem is inflexibility. He is radically religious, you know." Lipscomb sniffed. "Looks like his narrow views finally caught up with him. He deserves to go to prison as far as I'm concerned, even though he probably isn't really guilty of anything."

"Speaking of prison, your taped conversation between private individuals is illegal."

"Hey! I was only following orders."

"From whom?"

"Karl Devon, my boss."

"And the reason for making the recording?"

Lipscomb shrugged. "Who knows? It was all very boring anyway. Actually the administration is always looking for those who disagree with their policies."

Gordon wrote notes for several minutes.

Lipscomb did squirm. *What did I say?*

"So you heard nothing in the conversation which could incriminate Mr. MacRay?"

Ted rocked his head back and forth. "Nah. It was all obsolete stuff. Religion is so outdated these days, anyway."

"We may call on you to testify."

Lips shrank back, his face hot. "You want me to get involved? Oh, no. Not me. I could lose my job!"

"That will be all, Lipscomb," Gordon said, his manner brusque.

Gordon painstakingly organized the articles on his desk. Events of recent years had done much to unravel his hard-earned reputation of quiet equanimity. Switching off the light, he locked his office door and, rounding the corner to take the stairs, nearly collided with Dan MacRay.

"Dan! What brings you ——"

"We better sit down, Gordon," Dan said. "You're not going to believe this."

6

Slater and Beck secured an apartment near the immense Pax Universalis building where the World Court was to be held, in a suburb called Little Brussels. They purchased a few groceries and stocked the small kitchen.

A single phone call for Beck interrupted their meal.

"Hiya, O.D.," said a distant voice. "Verman, here. Are you scared about testifying at the trial tomorrow?"

"No!"

"That's my boy! Remember, O.D., when you get up on the witness stand, you owe your life to Rameses."

David clenched his teeth.

"You there, boy?"

"Yeah. I owe you guys my life."

"One more thing, O.D.," Verman went on cheerfully, "just in case you're feeling suicidal, and if you're thinking of ratting on me or any other club members, keep in mind I'm having your girlfriend Sonya watched. She doesn't breathe without my knowing about it!"

"Oh, come off it, Verman!" Beck forced himself to sound jovial. "You have been hobnobbing around the Eastern Empire for too long! Terrorism is outdated, remember?"

"Don't try me!" Verman's voice dropped to an ominous growl. "Rameses' credibility is so good he can't be touched, and he'll vouch for me. Besides, no one will believe you, anyway."

Beck faked a laugh. "Good grief, man. You think I want to spend the rest of my life in the pen? Listen, by the time I'm through they'll make you a saint!"

"Good, I knew we could count on you!"

When Beck hung up, he was trembling with rage. "Scum!" he spat out his words. "Verman would murder a defenseless woman!"

"He's also sloppy," Slater replied calmly, rewinding a tape. He patted the cartridge. "Since Elidor and company changed the rules so conveniently, we'll give them a taste of their own medicine! We have so much evidence against their pals in the Empire that they wouldn't dare convict our man!"

Slater put an arm about the younger man's shoulders. "Don't worry, friend. We'll protect the fair damsel. By the way, you always wanted Sonya to be a brunette rather than a blonde, didn't you?" He grinned.

7

Miles Potter fiddled with his collar. Despite an unseasonably cool October day, he felt warm. This trial was not shaping up at all the way his handlers told him. He expected this crowd, a record number, to be hyper and unpredictable. The assembly hall of World Tribunal in Little Brussels was immense, and people from the world over were pouring in.

Skadden Wilkes slithered over to the "judge". "Potter, we have made a few changes. We're not trying MacRay."

Potter cocked his head.

"Hey, MacRay has too many witnesses, and if allowed to testify . . . Well, not to worry. This one is a thought crime. Some idiot had the downright stupidity to criticize Elidor. Even made jokes about her. This case is nice and vague. We've got it in the bag."

"Who's the defendant?"

"Benjamin Benamoz."

Miles gasped. "You crazy, man? Son of Zephan Benamoz! Convict him, and that mob will take you apart!"

Skadden's smile was not pleasant. "I'm not going to convict him. You are!"

Potter stood up.

"C'mon Potter. Back out now and you'll only leave jail in a hearse. Relax. The payoff is worth it."

Miles sat down stiffly.

"Look." Skadden lowered his voice. "Benamoz knows too much."

"Yeah, like the Committee's role in drug trafficking?"

"Shhhh!" Wilkes' face was a mask of terror. "You know very well it would be best for us all if Benamoz is out of the way."

Potter's laugh was harsh. "Then why are we going to all this trouble? Why not just murder him like your punks did to Zephan?"

"No, it backfired. We're smarter now. Two martyrs in one family would only make it worse."

"Yeah, it could look like racism against the house of Yeshurun."

"Hey!" Wilkes scratched his head. "You're right. That angle had slipped my mind. But actually, Yeshurun is not one race as much as it is a vast religious movement which is getting out of hand."

Potter smirked. "So you want me to play the bigot and condemn this popular religious leader."

"Now don't worry," Skadden said. "The people aren't smart enough to figure it out. All we want to do is discredit Benjamin Benamoz in front of all these people, and we will effectively neutralize the entire religious movement. We know what we are doing. It will work!" Wilkes turned with an afterthought. "And thanks for the racist idea. That's a card I can play to the hilt."

Waving off Wilkes, Potter settled in his chair to study the crowd. Benamoz' attorney, Gordon Slater, looked like a pussycat, a cross between a plantation gentleman and a Christmas elf.

When Mitchell Hunt walked in, steady and unflinching, Potter could not stop the perspiration from flowing. He knew from experience that Hunt, though ordinary in physical stature, was a man not to trifle with.

Benjamin Benamoz strode in, dressed in faded blue jeans and a wind-breaker jacket. Potter studied the young man's tall, athletic frame, from burnished highlights in his wavy hair to the soles of his immense tennis shoes. This man would not be easy to condemn. Handsome kid. Something captivating about that face, not in a worldly way. Bold humility. A certain power, but from what? It was like gazing into a wide, blue-eyed innocence of future generations. The future of the free world. Remorse crept back into Potter's consciousness. He looked away.

The press was poised, each network prepared to doctor and rehash its own version for replay on the evening news. Horace Verman and Archibald Kingerman, Potter's coaches, sat at the prosecution table. To subdue his growing uneasiness, Miles tried desperately to summon his bluff and bluster from the old days,

With reluctance, Miles Potter rapped the gavel to bring the session to order, and read the charges.

"The Case of Zarahemla vs. Benamoz is now in session. The defendant, Benjamin Benamoz, will please come forward to be questioned by the prosecution. Mr. Benamoz, you are charged with Crimes Against the Peace and Security of Humankind."

Skadden Wilkes stepped toward the judge. "The Prosecution submits as Exhibit A, tape recordings of ghastly criticisms and degrading jokes the defendant has made against his own government leaders in general, specifically Elidor Redmund. Exhibit B contains, *in writing,* a litany of ideologically incorrect statements read by the defendant over international air waves."

"First witness for the prosecution, please."

Harvey Dermucker stepped forward and raised his right arm, saying, "I swear, by the authority of Pax Universalis, to tell the truth."

Beck leaned over to Slater. "They don't make an oath on the Bible?"

Gordon shook his head. "The World Tribunal does not accept the Bible. It is too absolute. For them, everything is relative. You know. I have *my* truth, you have *yours.*"

"The house of Yeshurun creates a constant climate of fear," Dermucker said. He was first in a stream of witnesses for the prosecution.

"The people of Yeshurun spread vicious lies about others who do not share their hypocritical faith," Horace Verman said.

"Members of Yeshurun are violent and murderous. Their political influence is becoming a cause for worldwide fear. These people are genocidal, and Benjamin Benamoz is one of their most outspoken leaders," Arch Kingerman said.

"Mr. Benamoz, a leader in Yeshurun, is racist, anti-Catholic, anti-Semitic, and pro-Nazi," said Rupert Banberg.

"Mr. Benamoz and his colleagues have done nothing but criticize and find fault with Elidor, her administration, and her entire agenda. Tapes of their conversations, made without their knowledge, prove it!" Warner Brackenlaw announced proudly. "I find their harassment very offensive."

445

Haman Benamoz was absent.

Karl Devon stepped forward and spoke with clear and relaxed self-assurance. "Your Honor, and the esteemed members of the Central Committee. The court has heard the tapes in question. As evidenced in Exhibit A, Benjamin Benamoz has spoken the unspeakable, and his jokes are no laughing matter."

"Zarahemla has no law against it," Ben said. "No one is exempt from criticism or satire."

"Furthermore," Devon continued, "Mr. Benamoz has purloined international air waves, owned and financed by citizens of the World, to openly and blatantly violate the Order of Voltaire's political code."

"What do you expect?" Ben cut in. "You control the press. You fired me from the newspaper. I have no other means of communication but correspondence, talk radio and television. By the way, my channel is privately financed."

"I will make the accusations here," Devon retorted. He fixed a dramatic glare upon Ben. "Now, my fellow citizens," he went on, mustering great pathos. "The poisonous hatred this man has poured out upon the world's children is inexcusable!"

"In what way, Mr. Devon?" Skadden Wilkes asked the witness.

"Mr. Benamoz' intolerant attitude, cultivated by orthodox religion and puritanical culture, persistently bruises our children's psyche!" Stepping down from the stand, Karl wagged his finger in Ben's face. "This man and his followers are selling out our children in the name of religion."

"Mr. Devon," Gordon Slater asked, "Have you any evidence that Mr. Benamoz has used any means whatsoever to force people to comply with his values?"

Devon nodded vigorously. "As long as the TV or radio is on, children might be forced to hear his point of view. This is a violation of their civil rights!"

"Try the off-button!" was Ben's blunt remark.

Potter ignored the snickers in the crowd. "Witness for the defense, please."

"The defense calls Mr. Ted Lipscomb."

"Mr. Lipscomb refuses to testify."

"Then we call Mr. Andrei Kovac to the stand."

"Kovac is not approved."

"Mr. Dan MacRay."

"Dan MacRay . . . is not approved."

Gordon Slater leveled a withering gaze on Potter. "Then, by tomorrow, we will make certain these witnesses are approved."

Momentarily flustered, Potter checked a list of defense witnesses approved by the Central Committee. Only one name was on the list: Oliver David Beck.

This man is a drug addict, was handwritten next to the name, *so his allegiance to the Committee is beyond question.*

"The approved witness for the defense is Oliver David Beck," Miles said, mouthing the words without feeling, like a wooden puppet. "Mr. Beck will please come to the witness stand."

"Mr. Beck," Slater began as Beck took the stand. "You were a hostage in Cumorah with Dan MacRay, a former employer of Benjamin. You have offered your testimony as a character witness for the defendant. But first, were you threatened in any way before taking the stand?"

"Your Honor," Beck stated in a solemn tone, "and all who are within the sound of my voice, however many millions you are. Every word I speak today is and will be the stark and unaltered truth, even though it is extremely dangerous for me to do so, as you will understand when my testimony unfolds."

"Your Honor," Skadden interrupted. "This man is a drug addict."

"Is this true?" Slater queried.

"The truth is," Beck replied, "I have been a drug addict. But I am clean now."

"How did you become addicted?" Slater asked.

Beck spoke out with ringing clarity. "My mother and I started asking questions about my father's activities, so Archibald Kingerman arranged to send me to the front lines in the Cumeni police action to get me out of the way. When I was a POW in the Tartarean Taj of Cumeni, my captors mixed cocaine in my food, purposely making me an addict, as they did many of my buddies. Later my father was killed by the mafia for revealing certain drug trafficking activities involving the Central Committee."

A deep rumble emerged from the audience. Ben glanced at Kingerman, sitting next to him at the neighboring table. Arch appeared to remain unperturbed by Beck's accusation. Arch had become quite chubby lately. The only slim thing on him was a pencil-thin mustache, which gave him an air of hauteur.

447

"What have you to do with Benjamin Benamoz?" Slater continued.

"The drug enforcement agency recruited me to go to Jershon and Cumorah with Dan MacRay to smoke out the rest of Horace Verman's rat maze down there. I was working for Verman, too, so I had orders to cover things up. A helicopter bearing a PAX insignia fired upon me, and I was wounded. Why would the Committee have me shot? PAX bullets missed their mark. They were gunning for Zephan Benamoz, Benjamin's father. I almost died, but Zephan Benamoz healed me. He prayed for me and healed me! We had several witnesses. Because of him I am drug-free today. It was a miracle."

"Only drug addicts are crazy enough to believe in miracles!" Skadden said.

"Out of order," Potter snapped.

"Benjamin captured and dismantled a narco-terrorist camp," Beck continued, "and confiscated a boatload of cocaine, run over our borders by a certain person which I will presently name. Benjamin's only mistake was to interfere with the drug cartel."

"Mistake?"

"Yes. Now the cartel wants to get rid of him." Beck paused. "But I ask you, who is really behind this cover-up?"

"What cover-up, Mr. Beck?" Slater prodded.

Beck produced a small black book which he waved above his head. "Ladies and gentlemen, in my hand I hold a log book retrieved from the drug-carrying vessel which Benjamin Benamoz confiscated. In this book you can find the handwriting of Mr. Horace Verman, revealing his membership code name in the infamous Pyramid drug cartel!"

The audience broke into bedlam, and Verman jumped to his feet, his face livid. Kingerman yanked him down.

From a corner near the judge, MBS's Brackenlaw screamed to the camera crew. "Stop the cameras!"

"Your Honor!" Skadden bellowed. "This man is an admitted drug addict. The prosecution questions the mental stability of this witness."

"Let the man speak!" A deep voice boomed into the mike, ringing over the din. Miles Potter rose to his full seven-foot stature, and his enormous frame towered over Brackenlaw. "And roll those cameras!" he thundered. In the absolute silence which ensued, Potter glowered at the vast assemblage, then sat down slowly. "A further outburst, and we shall clear the court! Continue, Mr. Beck," he said.

"So, ladies and gentlemen," Beck concluded. "If something happens to me, the Committee will pay the press to call it suicide. Know this. I will not commit suicide. It is against my religion. But whatever happens, remember what I said! That is all."

"Objection, your Honor!" Skadden Wilkes glared at Potter. "This testimony is irrelevant. Accusing the Empire does not vindicate Mr. Benamoz."

Potter read a scribbled note handed to him from behind and did not reply for several moments. At last he looked up, his face a study in fear. "Objection sustained." He slammed the gavel. "Court adjourned until 10 o'clock tomorrow morning."

8

For David Beck's own safety after his sensational testimony, Mitchell Hunt made certain the young man was secure in ZRI custody, safely guarded for the evening. Hunt arrived at his room to unwind, turned on choral Christmas music and pondered the day's events over a plain supper of soup and crackers.

When Hunt emerged from the shower, a ZRI official rang him with a message that instantly shattered his work of many years.

"Mitch, Beck is dead!"

"No!"

"No, wait . . . He's in a deep coma. His girlfriend Sonya visited him a few minutes ago. They had words. After she left, we found him totally out of it, with a suicide note on the floor beside his bed. "

"My soul." Mitchell groaned. "Signs of conflict?" He struggled for control, his mind racing.

"Not much. She struck him in the face, leaving a scratch."

"Under the circumstances, would we allow his girlfriend to stay in town? Sonya is out of harm's way! You bungling bureaucrats!" Hunt thundered. "That woman was an impostor! Keep Beck alive, you hear?"

Hunt immediately dialed Andrei Kovac's classified number. After giving an urgent message, he rushed to ZRI headquarters.

Ben sat at a kitchen table reading the remaining copy of the treasured book of Joseph which Anahí had smuggled in to him. He sipped his fourth cup of herbal tea and tried to count his blessings. Not being accused of a violent crime, he was only under "house arrest". He surveyed the large suite and modest furnishings. Considering the circumstances, it was quite comfortable. Security was moderate, he was given access to books and a word processor, and allowed to see his family. Dan MacRay, bless him, had spared nothing in exerting his influence.

But what would happen tomorrow? Would he, Benjamin Benamoz, son of Zephan the murdered prophet, be condemned to prison for the rest of his life?

He heard a soft knock on the door and glanced at the clock . . . well past midnight. Must be Anahí.

"Come on in, honey," he called. "You didn't come alone, I hope!"

Hunt laughed. "No, I didn't, lambcakes!"

"Oops!" Ben grinned. "You didn't?" He yawned.

Hunt was flanked by Dan MacRay, Abiram and his wife Alison, Gordon Slater, Sarita, and Anahí.

Ben embraced each of his family. It had been a long time since all had been together, except for Haman and Leb, of course.

"Things are not going well, Ben." Hunt was solemn. "I brought the family and friends so we could face this together." He thrust the evening newspaper before Ben.

TRIAL RECESSES ONE WEEK TO MOURN BECK SUICIDE

Ben sank into his chair. "Beck," he said, and his voice broke. Would this grief never end? "When is the funeral?"

"Tomorrow morning, limited to a simple, private grave side ceremony, down the road in Midbar," Hunt replied. "Eliminates further complications. We can rely on Father O'Donnell, an old friend, to handle things well. The Empire is pushing for immediate burial, to avoid investigation."

"It wasn't a suicide, Ben," Gordon said.

"The press cover up is quite a sorry attempt," Dan said. "Media anchormen are screaming that your mother harbored Beck when he was supposedly a fugitive from justice, and that your wife is calling public educators dirty names."

"Hunt, do you know who killed Beck?"

"Delia Matagorda. And without hesitation she labeled Haman as her accomplice. "

Ben turned to his mother, sensing her anguish. "This explains why Haman was missing today," he said quietly.

"Aw, but Haman is getting a little desperate now, Ben. He's moving fast, starting to make mistakes," Hunt said with a crooked smile. "He's following his little plan, but he doesn't know me, and he doesn't know he will lead me right to the man I'm looking for. Strange, isn't it . . . how the guards outside just up and got so friendly all of a sudden, and let us all in with . . ." He paused and handed Ben a shiny Colt .45. "Abiram has already armed everyone else. I require it until this is over, for your own protection. Now ladies, do you think you can find something for us to eat during our vigil? Unless you all feel like sleeping."

Everyone laughed nervously. Ben concealed the weapon in his shirt and passed around books and magazines for the men to read. He returned to the table to resume his study.

Alison began to paw through groceries she had carried in.

"My wife has become a marvelous cook already, just like you said, Mama," Abiram whispered proudly to Sarita. "She cooks for the missionaries."

"Remember how Papa always used to find positive things in the worst situations?" Ben recalled. "He sang when he was in prison. And the day our crops were burned, he took us all out for ice cream, to celebrate that no one was hurt."

"How well I remember, *hijo*," Sarita said with sad fondness.

Anahí headed for the kitchen, but stopped, her eyes widening in a stare, and fixed upon the door.

Slowly Ben turned and looked fully on the face of Beck's murderer.

10

If Haman noticed the others, he did not show it. His face, filled with loathing, was turned to Ben, shutting out all else. He was unarmed, but not without power. Somehow, wherever he went, death followed.

451

Ben shot to his feet, his hand closing on his revolver, his eyes steady on Haman's heart.

"Ben." Abiram's voice seemed far away.

For an instant Ben was back in the wilderness. *He did not look back to see the serpent close the gap and coil around his leg.*

Haman's face looked like wet clay, with fear embedded in it. His limbs did not, could not move. His eyes were locked into Ben's gaze.

For a moment Ben almost regretted having destroyed the snake which had threatened his own life . . . Fiery venom seared his heel, and a wave of weakness engulfed him. He urgently needed to . . . P r a y.

O God, the Eternal Father, I beseech thee, heal my heart of this poisonous venom.

All at once Ben felt no more disposition to do evil. In Haman he saw, not the arrogant monster who had tormented him all his life, but a lost man, empty of conscience, who no longer owned his soul. This man was to be pitied.

Ben lowered his eyes. His hand had not moved. He lifted it off the weapon. Suddenly he rushed to his brother's side and threw his arms around him. "Haman, Haman!" he said in a broken voice. "Give yourself up, *mi hermano!*"

Haman shoved him aside roughly. "How did you get here?" he said to the silent faces around him. "Why are you looking at me that way? You are all against me!"

"You're insane," Abiram said.

"No, he's not," Ben said. "He knows what he has done."

"Yes, I am totally sane," Haman said, ablaze with his own skewed reality. "Papa was insane. He was so judged in court. I saw it myself. Papa always was a crazy fanatic. I mean, he thought he was a visionary man."

"So you punished him for it. You killed him."

"No one killed him. He was treated with compassion. He was beyond help, and the doctors did what any sensible, humane person would do."

"You don't really believe that."

"Of course I do. Nothing in the world could bring me to believe such vile things as you continually imply about my friends. Are you accusing those good men of murder? How can you think such a thing? But of course, you of miserable Yeshurun. Always impugning good intentions of our leaders. Speaking hatred and lies. How can you believe such hateful things about wonderful men like Ponte, and Rames — I mean, it was all perfectly legal. We were only trying to help Papa. I was the one who arranged for treatment, so he would avoid a harsher sentence. How was I to know how bad his condition was? It's not my fault!" he wailed.

"It was all so unnecessary," Haman said into the silent room. He felt exposed. Why was Ben looking at him like that? What did he see? What did he know? Everyone was looking at him. The silence — it was unbearable. *Why didn't somebody say something?* "Papa brought it upon himself because he was so stubborn," Haman rushed on. "He only had to do one little thing. He could have denied the Bible just to avoid conflict, and they promised the book of Joseph would be published. But no, Papa wouldn't trust them. He backed himself into a corner, and, well, I could only do so much. He just kept quoting that awful book of Joseph, even after they told him to stop. You should have heard him. Papa really was crazy, you know. It's his own fault. He was incredibly rude to us, and we were only trying to help him."

"It is the law! For people of Papa's age and condition, it is the law!" Haman raved on. "The doctors were only obeying the law. Do you think Ponte's doctors are so cold and uncaring that it didn't make them sad to do it? And Papa died for nothing! It was that hateful, unproven, scientifically unsound little book of Joseph which caused his death. He believed in it beyond the bounds of common sense. It made him crazy. I tried to get him to compromise. We tried to tell him the book wasn't worth the bother. But he wouldn't listen. Now Papa is dead, and the book is gone anyway. And I'm glad. That book was nothing but trouble."

Ben stared at Haman. Fiercely he willed everyone else to keep their eyes off the sacred testament, lying there on the table, open, unprotected.

"I beseech you, Haman," Ben said quietly, inching over between Haman and the table. "Do not procrastinate the day of your repentance."

"Repentance!" Haman shouted. "Stop saying that. You act as if I did something wrong, as if my friends are wrong. You say the

453

whole world is wrong, and only you are right. Well, I happen to believe differently than you do. You can't kill a man for his beliefs."

"This is exactly what you did," Ben insisted. "Nehor killed a man for merely challenging his ideas. The man he killed was too old and weak to fight back."

"We don't do that," Haman said. "When people are sick, we treat them."

"It is the Egalitarian philosophy which is sick," Ben said.

"You are wrong," Haman said. "The Egalitarians will do anything to bring about a better world."

"I'm sure Nehor said the same thing when he enforced his doctrines with the sword. No matter what God you worship, Haman, if you shed innocent blood, it is still murder."

"Now you sound like Papa —" Haman stopped. "I mean . . ."

"Rameses killed a man, deliberately, just like Nehor did," Ben said. "Rameses killed our father."

"You are wrong about Rameses!" Haman shouted. "You don't know him at all. If you did, you would never say such a thing. He has done so much for me, more than any of you ever did. He is the kindest, most charming ——" His words froze in the still air. Outside, passing traffic sent beams of light gliding across the room. A stop light caught on Haman, dripping red reflection off his perspiring face. His mouth fell open, and he sucked in his breath.

Only a click was heard.

Hunt gathered up his tape recorder.

"You taped me?" Haman shrieked. "You can't do this. It's illegal!"

Hunt shrugged. "I suppose it was unnecessary. After all, I have all these witnesses. Haman, you've had your say. Now it's over. Since you know Rameses so well, you can answer some questions. You're coming with me."

"Rameses is the most powerful man in the world," Haman shouted, as if loudness would make his words true. "Against him, you are nothing!"

Hunt continued, unruffled. "While you're at it, tell me about Delia's little visit to Oliver Beck."

Haman shrugged. "Delia said she had a score to settle with him. What's Beck to you? Just another drug addict who lost his mind. I heard he wasn't even a credible witness. He even came out against the order of Voltaire, after all they've done for him! The world is better off without people like him, anyway."

454

11

"Life's but a walking shadow, a poor player that struts and frets his hour upon the stage, and then is heard no more." Dan had picked up Zephan's copy of *Macbeth*.

"Thank heaven we are all safe at last." Anahí stood encircled in the protection of Ben's arms.

Anahí saw the pain and desolation in Sarita's weary face. "Zephan is safe, too, dear one." She embraced her mother-in-law. "Do you think Haman will ever repent, Ben?"

Ben shook his head slowly. "I don't know, Ani. He has turned his back on the light. The truth makes him angry. Apostates often make the most relentless enemies."

Abiram moved to the window. The street was filling with PAX troops. "Tomorrow, as soon as the funeral is over, we need to get out of here," he said. "Let's go to Jershon. My home is yours."

12

With the Benamoz family and friends as passengers, Dan MacRay's plane left behind the velvety mist of green highlands and touched down in Bahia Verde, under warm sun cerulean Toltec sky. "I don't know how you managed to release Ben into your custody," he said to Mitchell Hunt, "but I'm grateful."

"No challenge," Hunt said. "With the goods I've got on Horace Verman, Haman, and the entire Pyramid investigation, Elidor and her crowd will be kowtowing to me for years to come."

"You're amazing!"

With a mysterious grin, Hunt bounced his eyebrows. "Just watch me. I'm full of surprises."

Dan accompanied the family into a cultural hall in the tiny chapel Zephan had built. Everyone arrived about noon, in time for the day's main meal. So great were the numbers whom Abiram and Alison had taught the gospel that an addition to the building was under construction. People with love in their eyes thronged around the family, while little ladies with busy hands and radiant faces carried tray after tray of steaming food to already laden tables and scolded their children to make way for the guests.

Hunt got a surprise of his own when he found Jaime Canosa on his hands and knees amid a flock of children, giving "horseback rides."

"So this is where you've been hiding!" Hunt said. "You could have at least told me you would be in such good hands so I wouldn't worry. Never mind. When you hear my news, nothing else will matter."

"All right. But first, let me take care of the important thing." Canosa bucked off a giggling cherub and walked to the stage, where he got the attention of all present to make an announcement. "With immense gratitude we introduce to you a fine family who has just joined our congregation. Alma Aguerros and family, will you please come up?"

A stunning brunette entered the room, guiding her husband's wheel chair. Though the man had dark hair, his reddish beard was peppered with gray. Even with a name like Aguerros, neither the man nor his wife looked to be of Zapotec descent. The boy, Pedro, however, was definitely native Zapotec.

Dan MacRay immediately recognized Pedro, an orphan whom he had met a year ago. These could not be the youngster's parents. The father's face looked hauntingly familiar.

As the guests from Zarahemla congratulated the family, Alma Aguerros, his wife at his side, wheeled his chair straight up to Dan and grinned lopsidedly at him. As if from a stroke, one side of his face drooped in weakness.

Dan gave the woman a warm handshake. "*Mucho gusto*, Señora."

"Just call me Sonya," she said, smiling.

Dan could not take his eyes off the man's face. "Forgive me for staring," he said. "You . . . look so much like . . . "

"Oliver David Beck?" Alma's hearty laugh was familiar.

The *familia* Benamoz could no longer restrain themselves. "Gotcha!" All exclaimed in unison, and joined in the merriment.

"I demand an explanation!" MacRay declared. "Are we seeing a ghost?"

"Same body, different name," Alma Oliver David Beck Aguerros said simply. "It's part of the witness protection program. Get this straight. Oliver David Beck died. But thanks to Andrei Kovac's sister, Anna, a world-class expert on drugs, an antidote was found, and I survived, like a bad penny. They flew me immediately here to Bahia Verde, where the nurses have been detoxifying me thoroughly with herbal oils native to this area. And I'm gradually getting stronger each day."

Dan finally found his voice. "So the funeral was just a —"

"Fake! You mourned the death of a dummy!" Alma laughed till the tears came to his eyes. "Boy, we sure fooled them, didn't we?" He patted Sonya's hand. "This beautiful lady has stayed by me, bless her. I still can't believe she'll have me for eternity!"

"Well, to give a long story a happy ending, my new name is Alma Aguerros. It's official on the records of the Church. Alma, in celebration of my conversion to the gospel, and Aguerros, because we are adopting Pedro. You remember Pedro, the one who nearly killed Benjamin. Oh, we are a frightful pair, aren't we?" He laughed again. "I guess we were made for each other. "He serves a mean ball, too, don't you, Pedro?"

"You have taught me well, Papá," the boy replied.

"We have great jai alai games now, *Hermano* MacRay," Ammon spoke up. "And Alma is our coach!"

Tears streamed down Alma's face. "The food is getting cold!" His voice was husky. "Let's eat!"

After the meal, Alison gathered all the children, who sang about their ancestors.

Book of Joseph stories that my teacher tells to me
Are about the Lamanites in ancient history.
Long ago their fathers came from far across the sea.
Given this land if they lived righteously.

Lamanites met others who were seeking liberty
And the land soon welcomed all who wanted to be free.
Book of Joseph stories say that we must brothers be.
Given this land if we live righteously.

The afternoon passed in warm camaraderie of good people who had endured much, and who had seen the hand of God in their lives. Anahí passed her brother-in-law on her way out, her arms laden with books, with Ammon in tow, carrying a tower of volumes which rose above his head. "Abiram, this is wonderful. Bookstores in Zarahemla have nothing good to read anymore, and the libraries are useless for research beyond the prevailing dogmas."

"Thanks to Canosa, we'll be doing even more in the future," Abiram replied. "When you are finished there, come with me. I want to show something to you and Ben, and Hunt, too."

Everyone followed Abiram in stunned admiration as he led them on a tour of the largest free press they had ever seen. Canosa ran the machines expertly, and every part, oiled and polished, seemed to sing at his command. Books of all kinds, but mostly Bibles, were stacked to the ceiling, filling bins and shelves in every room.

Abiram took the battered book of Joseph from Ben and leafed through it with care. "Now we will print this one."

"Why didn't you tell me, *hermano*? I would have brought it to you long ago if I had known," Ben said.

Abiram shook his head. "Only recently have we banished the last Voltairistas from our midst. Our preaching of the word has destroyed their priestcraft. By the people's choice, the Egalitarian philosophy has no more part in the government here; those savage Voltairistas who were not converted —— a third part of them —— have all moved elsewhere. Only now is it safe to print the book of Joseph. Even so, spies from Rameses might by now have informed him of our plan."

"Now I know who Rameses is," Hunt said, "but I haven't yet figured out how to capture him. Sarita told me your prophet says Rameses will be delivered into your hands." He shrugged. "I've learned not to take lightly the words of your prophet."

"Oh, Rameses will be at the trial, all right," Canosa added. "I know him to be an exceedingly proud and vainglorious man who will not pass up an opportunity to aggrandize himself. He won't be able to stay away."

"Starting tonight we will work around the clock and print as many millions of copies as we can this first week, in as many languages as possible."

"In *one week*?"

"Yes, Anahí," Abiram replied quietly. "I myself don't know exactly how it will happen. But we will act on faith and do as we are commanded. All I can say is, stand back and watch the power of God."

Canosa gripped the small, tattered copy of the book of Joseph. "By small and simple things are great things brought to pass," he said.

While Squanto added sticks to the campfire, Ben leaned back to look for the first evening star, paled by the setting sun.

Abiram stared into the fire, wishing his desolate thoughts could be carried out to sea with the relentless haste of the river below. He would never again see his father in this life. And now would someone take from him his beloved Benjamin?

"*Abuelo!*" Ammon whispered. "It's Grandpa. I hear him laughing."

"Can you see him, Ammon?"

"Not yet . . . He says to tell you to shut your mouths . . . that you look like bug-eyed guppies."

Everyone laughed, despite uneasiness. And then they saw him.

Zephan laughed again, but Abiram wiped tears from his eyes.

"The time for mourning is past, my sons. The work must go on," Zephan said. "How beautiful upon the mountains are the feet of him that bringeth good tidings, that publisheth peace —"

"It's peaceful here, Papa," Abiram said. "We should all stay here. Don't make Ben go back to that trial. Please!"

"Testify to them of the everlasting truth, Benjamin, and we will have the last word!" He laughed. "The last Word!

"The testimony of Jesus is the spirit of prophecy," he continued. "I saw heaven opened, and a white horse; and he that sat upon him was called Faithful and True; and his name is called The Word of God. And out of his mouth goeth a sharp sword, that with it he should smite the nations; and he shall rule them with a rod of iron."

Zephan paused to gaze upon his sons. "I see that your hearts are depressed. Do not be discouraged, my sons. Remember how the Lord comforted his ancient missionaries, saying: Go amongst thy brethren, and bear with patience thine afflictions, and I will give you success."

Zephan's look filled his sons with his overwhelming devotion to them, and they felt the love of God.

And he was gone.

"How do you get acquitted at a trial which is utter mockery?" Ben said to Gordon.

"Time to be wise as serpents. The prosecution will change its tactics, and so must we." Gordon perched on the edge of a log and peered over the cliff at the swirling waters.

Ben groaned. "Who would have dreamed the day would come when one's religion would be an international crime?"

"Pitched beyond politics and criminal law, this is a battle of the soul," Gordon said. "It is Zion versus Babylon. God's law is our only hope."

"Papa said something about a sword. Somehow, the key to victory is near, but I can't quite grasp it." Ben related his dream. "How could we use Abiram's sword in our defense?"

Gordon had no answer.

The wild olive tree still towered as sentinel over the unruly river below.

"This is not the lone tree anymore," Abiram said. "With all the influx of converts from surrounding areas, this wilderness is slowly being domesticated. Otherwise we would still be riding horses rather than jeeps out to this camp. And this tree has now become part of a small vineyard. When we first came here, we grafted it and planted others. Another seven years, and 'He shall cause them that come of Jacob to take root: Israel shall blossom and bud, and fill the face of the world with fruit.'"

"Nice touch, Abiram!" Ben said. "Isaiah?"

Abiram nodded. "Alison has got me studying it lately."

"Papa would be proud." Ben smiled. "He's still quoting Isaiah beyond the grave."

Ben savored the wilderness, its absence of entanglement. The olive tree stood free in bold relief against a golden sky. Would he ever see this place again? In a few short days, would his freedom be snuffed out, would he be cut off from his family for the rest of his mortal life? No matter what happened to him, that olive tree would still be there. And the river. How often Zephan had said that no unhallowed hand would stop the work of God.

Ben took some consolation that even if he alone were in bondage, the work would now go forward with unprecedented power. The word would go forth to every kindred, tongue, and people. The word ——

". . . *fill the face of the world with fruit*", Abiram had said. Somehow the answer was in his brother's words. Ben stared at the tree, and the river.

As a rushing tide, a wave of familiarity overpowered him, sweeping him inexorably from textured patterns of his past beyond infinite future horizons.

"That's it, Gordon! Not the sword of Abiram. The sword of God."

The Book Of
Joseph

THE BOOK OF JOSEPH

1

Two hours early, Miles Potter walked to the court house alone. The week's recess from court had been filled with doubts and confusion. Why should he care? Try as he might, he could not dull those increasing pains of conscience. More each day he dreaded his role in this entire farce the world was calling a trial. But it was his ticket to freedom. Sure. Forfeit the liberty of an innocent man. Why Benjamin Benamoz? Take Mitchell Hunt. Even Dan MacRay. No problem. He could lock them up, throw away the key, and walk away laughing. But not that innocent boy. Dear God, not Ben.

Miles stopped short. *Dear God?* Am I praying? What is happening to me? Do I actually care about one young man's life more than my own skin? Maybe after all the lives I've ruined, it's time to change. *Change?* Is it possible? Nah. What can I do? Go against the power of Rameses? No way. I must be rid of this responsibility. I'm not going to be responsible for throwing this boy to the wolves. Nope. Somebody else can help this kid out. Not me. But somebody has to help him. Who on earth . . . ? . . .*Me.* But I can't do it. There is no way . . . I'm almost to the court house. I can't turn back now. God, please help me. Yeah, maybe God could help me. No. Never mind. Don't help me. I don't deserve it. Dear God, please help Ben . . .

Someone was approaching him. A man of indeterminate age, slight in stature, who wore a business suit and outdated glasses. Miles felt the stranger's compelling blue-eyed gaze. Something was striking about this person's features — he seemed to be without guile. Morning sunlight on the man's thinning silver hair gave an aura of undeniable benevolence.

"Good morning, sir," the stranger said cheerily, extending toward him a pen and a small form. "Some of Mr. Benamoz' family members have traveled from far-flung corners of the earth to attend this historic trial, and will be here presently. To assure their entrance, after such a long and wearisome journey, will you kindly sign this pass?"

Potter stared, uncomprehending. "This trial is a sham." Though shocked by his own confession, he could not stop himself. "I. . .am not really a judge. I have no authority. Why are you asking me?"

"Because I am of Yeshurun, and you are my brother."

Potter's signature was a trifle shaky. "Who are the house of Yeshurun?"

The man handed Potter a small blue book. "Those who love the Lord and keep his commandments." Smiling, the stranger nodded at someone behind Potter.

Miles, fearing Kingerman had discovered him, spun around swiftly, but saw no one. When Potter turned toward the courthouse door, the stranger was gone.

Potter ambled slowly to his seat before the bar. *This trial is getting to me.* He turned the book over in his hands. The book of Joseph. On the first page, he read,

> To show unto the remnant of Israel what great things the Lord hath done for their fathers; and that they may know the covenants of the Lord, that they are not cast off forever —
> And also to the convincing of the Jew and Gentile that JESUS is the CHRIST, the ETERNAL GOD, manifesting himself unto all nations.

Miles Potter felt inexplicable, overwhelming peace.

Galleries were overcrowded and the entire court chamber was packed, with people standing in the halls. With flashing and rolling TV cameras, journalists seemed to have multiplied overnight like bacteria. Though the air was swollen with tension, the room was strangely quiet, except for rustling pages. Upon entering, every member in the audience had been handed a small blue book.

Benjamin Benamoz was wearing a suit today. He seemed somehow changed from last week. The boy looked more like . . . well . . . more like a man, and he walked with an assurance which Potter envied. Ben and his attorney made their way to their designated table. "Hi, Mr. Potter," Ben said. "How are you doing?"

Miles Potter nodded with a numb smile. He scanned the assemblage. All faces looked monochromatic, devoid of expression and distinguishable features, with the granular blur of an old gray newspaper photo . . . or some history book decades from now. Could he, Miles Potter, for just one moment in time, thwart the inevitable course of history's dark side?

Mitchell Hunt was there. Miles shuddered. Maybe Hunt could help the boy. He took his eyes from the ZRI agent and looked down at himself, dressed in a prissy suit and tie. He could go to a church, or something, dressed this way. What had come over him? And rooting for an officer of the law, even.

With Clarence Rook beside him, Hunt swept the vast hall with a devouring gaze; all Ben's enemies were again present in full force. Today someone else had joined the ranks at the prosecution table. Nils Cromwell was a portly, middle-aged man with a well-trimmed beard which gave him a dignified, professorial look. Thick graying hair spilled over the back of his neck, catching in his collar. His droopy-lidded eyes appeared kindly, or at least too sleepy to cause trouble, but his mouth wore that perpetual smirk characteristic in those of the Egalitarian persuasion. Despite his harmless appearance, Cromwell's open hostility for Benjamin Benamoz was well known.

And there, at Cromwell's table, was a massive human being, leaning back in a cushy chair evidently brought for his exclusive use; he surveyed the crowd with the expression of a lazy, overfed aristocrat. On a face sagging with years of obvious self-indulgence, a single black browline paralleled his pencil-thin mustache and mouth. His eyes, bulging from their sockets as if constricted by the per-unit pressure of his weight, gave the appearance of a hunted man to whom inner peace was totally alien. He had no neck, or at least his head seemed attached directly to an elegantly suited preponderance of flesh. With soft white, heavily ringed fingers he loosened his silk tie, which was clasped with a large gold Egyptian sphinx.

"There he is," Hunt said to Clarence Rook. "That's Rameses."

Rook stared in the direction Hunt indicated. Archibald Kingerman appeared to be enjoying some private joke.

"Huh?" Rook said. "Kingerman?"

"No, the big one, beside Kingerman."

Rook stared. "Kingerman looks like a smaller copy of the same model."

"Yep. Kingerman would be Rameses' son."

"How on earth does the man have nerve to come out of hiding?"

"He thinks he's going to witness the downfall of Yeshurun. He has worked for the destruction of Yeshurun all his life, and now he wouldn't miss the glory of this ultimate victory."

Rook gave a low whistle. "He must be very sure of his position."

"Yep. Of course, he believes the world media, too. Why wouldn't he? He controls most of it."

With a look of resignation, Miles Potter rapped the gavel. "The Case of League of Religions vs. Benamoz will now come to order."

Gordon Slater gave his client a knowing look. The prosecution had definitely changed its tactics.

"The Prosecution will now read from the Charter of the League of Religions, to present the charges against Mr. Benamoz."

Skadden Wilkes cleared his throat with an air of importance, rattled the document in his hands, and began to read. "Religion is an instrument of world peace. The sacredness of the earth is paramount. World peace is the supreme mission. Any person, group of two or more persons, or organization, using words, symbols, pictures, or any other means of communication, in an attempt to, or with the intent to: criticize, offend, undermine, detract from, defame, or in any way disrupt the universal peace and harmony in the world, interfere with the health of the planet, breach faith to the global spirituality, defame a League of Religions peace worker, deny the sacredness of the earth, or in any way not enumerated above, promote opposition to, or the destruction of the Universal Ethic which has been duly established by

468

world citizens, is guilty of criminal thinking and shall be prosecuted to the full extent of international law.

"The plaintiff finds Benjamin Benamoz guilty specifically of defaming a peace worker, namely Nils Cromwell, distributing hateful literature, using hate-words in public and private gatherings of two or more persons, writing ideologically incorrect literature, and in general purveying thoughts dangerous to the stability of the globally accepted and established Universal Ethic."

"Guilty?" Potter snapped. "You cannot declare this man to be guilty, Mr. Wilkes. That's my job. And he hasn't even been tried yet."

Someone in the audience brayed like a donkey.

For the first time in his life, Skadden Wilkes was embarrassed. "Correction, Your Honor. Mr. Benamoz is *charged* with all of the above."

"The defendant, Mr. Benjamin Benamoz, will take the stand to be questioned by the Prosecution."

"What have you to say in defense of your despicable acts, Mr. Benamoz?" Skadden Wilkes regarded Ben through half-shut eyes.

"Nothing," Ben said. "I have done nothing wrong."

"Listen to this, Your Honor!" Wilkes exulted. "He doesn't even know why he is guilty!" Wilkes fixed his eyes back upon Ben and said, "You have taught this following of yours —— "

"Not my followers. God's followers," Ben interrupted.

"—— whom you call the house of Yeshurun," Skadden went on. "You have taught your following that all of you, whom you call *meek*, shall be exalted, and that only you shall inherit the earth. By what authority do you claim this land is yours?"

"Not mine. The earth is the Lord's."

"This God of yours doesn't seem to hold the earth to be very sacred. Why should it matter to him? After all, this God of yours, does he live here?" Skadden enjoyed the laughter.

"No."

"Have you seen him?"

"No, sir."

"Then you have no proof that he exists, do you?" Skadden looked bored.

"Yes, sir. The Bible sets forth scores of persons who have seen God."

"Ha!" Wilkes scoffed. "The Bible does not hold up in the World Court. This God of your Bible is merely a God of an ethnic minority."

"The house of Yeshurun is not a minority, sir."

"You just made a racist statement! And you try to impose your God on the rest of us, which is a violation of civil rights." Smugness lay in comfort across Skadden's features.

"Compulsion is against our religion." Ben remained calm.

"In claiming the earth for your inheritance, you are imposing your religion, and you are defiling the earth."

"We claim no land nor empire," Ben said. "We have been burned out, flooded out, persecuted, harassed, and driven. But we are still here! The location of Zion is wherever dwell the pure in heart. But in the Lord's due time, He will grant many lands as inheritances for the faithful, and no one can stay the hand of the Lord in gathering his people."

"Prejudice!" Wilkes shrieked.

What paranoia. Aloud, Ben spoke with unbroken steadiness. "Lands and possessions are a temporal matter, in which, as in all things, we also obey God. As stewards of the earth, we respect all of God's creations. But the gathering is a spiritual matter."

Kingerman gave a fierce signal to the frantic Skadden.

"I can't shake this kid! His calm is maddening!"

"You would do well to follow his example," Kingerman replied. "If you don't change your tactics, he has you right where he wants you."

"This is all fine and good, Benamoz," Wilkes continued, "but your case cannot hold up. You admitted you haven't seen God, yet you claim He is a white male God, chosen by Israel, and father of the Christ. Under international law, your claims are no longer valid. You have no legal right to oppose the universally established religion."

"I am a citizen of Zarahemla, where the Law of God is the Supreme Law of the Land."

"Nationalism! All nations are subject to international law, and Pax Universalis *is* the Law!" Skadden said. "We have it in writing!"

"We have the Law of God in writing."

"The Bible is out! The Bible is not a credible witness."

"God told his prophet Ezekiel about another testament which is not the Bible. He said to Ezekiel, 'Write upon one stick for Judah, and another for Joseph. And join them one to another into one stick; and they shall become one in thine hand.'"

Mystified, Skadden glanced at the judge.

Behind Potter's stifled smile was the look of a man enjoying great entertainment. "Proceed, Wilkes."

Wilkes squinted with his whole face. "Why don't you just bring God over here to speak for himself? Is he afraid to show up at your trial?"

Laughter.

Ben felt confidence surge in him. "God is merciful. If He showed up, you and many others here would die from the glory of His presence. No unclean thing can enter the presence of God."

"Prejudice! See? Your God is a bigot! You have just proved our point, Benamoz." Skadden looked around at the crowd. Expressions were blank. He had failed to evoke the desired sensation. "All right." Wilkes concentrated on his opponent. "So your God doesn't bother attending this trial in your defense. How do you get his testimony?"

"Through His prophets. At Mount Sinai, God wanted to appear in Person to all the people, but the people refused, because they were afraid. So God sent His prophets, to whom He still personally reveals His word."

Wilkes made a sweeping gesture. "Do you hear this, ladies and gentlemen? This man is crazy. In this modern day, he still believes in biblical prophets!" He turned to Ben. "I'll bet you believe in angels, too."

"I do."

"Angels, ladies and gentlemen!" Skadden was giddy. "Have you seen an angel?" he asked Ben.

"I have."

"Did you ever hear anything so preposterous, ladies and gentlemen? Angels, no less! And prophets of a God he cannot prove!"

Ridicule reverberated throughout the chamber, long, loud, and intense.

"The Jews had prophets in their day," Ben said, "and now, during this last time, prophets are among the Gentiles."

"Yes." Skadden yawned. "I heard rumors about a prophet in Cumorah. During Solano's administration, wasn't it? Solano was a

471

deluded old man. Look at what happened to him! See what happened to Cumorah because of him. The whole nation had to be reformed by reasonable men." Skadden's laugh was harsh.

"Those days were a time of righteousness and prosperity, and many holy men were in the land," Ben said.

"Of course. Many holy men!" Wilkes said with impatience. "And where are all these holy men?"

"Killed. In thousands of years, little has changed. People still revile and kill God's prophets. Zephan Benamoz was an Apostle and prophet, like Joseba Bianco. Both were murdered by Voltairist agents."

"Ah, yes. A pity. Crime is rampant these days. But isn't another prophet around?"

"Yes, sir. He holds the keys of the kingdom."

"Who is he? Show him to me. I would like to see one of these holy men for myself."

"Reveal his name so people like you can murder him, too? Not a chance! But the Standard of Truth has been erected; No unhallowed hand can stop the work from progressing. Persecutions may rage, mobs may combine, armies may assemble, calumny may defame. But the truth of God will go forth boldly, nobly, and independent, till it has penetrated every continent, visited every clime, swept every country, and sounded in every ear. Till the purposes of God shall be accomplished and Jesus the Christ shall say, 'The Work is done!'"

"Racism! Treason! Prejudice!" Skadden's voice was shrill with emotion.

Kingerman hissed, and Skadden bounced back to his handler.

"I don't like where this is going, Wilkes. Get back to the Bible."

"Yes, yes. The Bible," Wilkes continued. "Merely a record of the Jews. The Jews are nothing but . . . " He checked himself. "The Bible speaks about earth being created in a week, the worldwide flood, the Red Sea divided, and all those irrelevant myths. I know all about it."

"The Bible is the testimony of the tribe or nation of Judah. But do you think God only speaks to one nation? The book of Joseph is a testimony from the nation of Joseph. Together, both testify of God's Law. Out of the mouths of two or three witnesses shall the

472

truth be established, Wilkes. This is a fundamental principle of law. You are familiar with the witness of Judah. To deny the family of Joseph the right to testify is an act of illegal discrimination, according to Item 3 in the Code of Human Rights." Ben directed a pleasant gaze beyond the squirming Wilkes to the sea of faces in the court room.

Potter rapped the gavel. "The court requests to hear the testimony of Joseph."

Kingerman grabbed a phone near his elbow. "Elidor?" Arch whispered softly into the phone. "Have you got this on your screen? Something is wrong. I thought you destroyed that infernal book of Joseph. Where did this come from?"

Rameses whispered something to Kingerman, who spoke to Nils Cromwell, who signaled Miles Potter.

Potter frowned, carefully avoiding the collective stare from the team at the prosecution table. "Mr. Cromwell will now testify."

With a benign smile which embraced the entire assemblage, Cromwell rose and took the microphone. His total self-assurance had a calming effect on the masses. "I have something you all should know about this so-called testimony of Joseph," he said gently. "I remind the court and the audience that it is illegal to speak about God in public forums, because this God represents a specific religion, and it might offend those who do not believe. I, for one, am offended.

"This is why the Bible has been outlawed. Well, ladies and gentlemen, this testimony of Joseph is also called the book of Joseph, and the house of Yeshurun esteems this literature as a testament of God, like the Bible. Furthermore, it even testifies of a specific Christ. This is obviously slanted. We all know Christ is but an idea, and we can make him anything we want him to be. The most objectionable parts of the book of Joseph deride and savage anyone whose ideas do not agree with Yeshurun. This should be classified as religious hate literature, which is precisely why the defendant is being tried. The defendant should not be allowed to use hate literature in his own defense. Therefore this testimony of Joseph, which is illegal, should be thrown out of court."

"He's right about it being a testament of Jesus Christ," Ben said to Potter. "It also exposes the enemies of Christ, which is why he doesn't want us to use it."

"See?" Cromwell said. "The man cannot speak a word without spewing hatred. He has used this book of Joseph to defame me,

473

assassinate my character, and smear me. He and this book are a menace to society. But Benamoz here has used his hateful book of Joseph to oppose me. He has called me a poisonous serpent, and railed on my religion. All this because I have a broader view of the idea of a christ than he does. Christ can be anyone, and could be anywhere.

My Universal Ethic would allow each person to decide his own destiny, without this pushy, arrogant, demanding, punishing God of Israel interfering in our lives. But Benamoz' dogma is pure religious hatred, the book is hate literature, and if there is anything I hate, it is these religious fanatics. I demand that this book be banned immediately ——"

"Enough!" Potter rapped the gavel. "This is irrelevant. I did not grant you a forum in which to push your personal agenda. I am the judge here, and since you folks refused to use a jury, and have made me the judge, then I, not you, shall determine what is hate literature and what is to be examined as part of the evidence." Potter was amazed at his own logic.

"Don't you see? Hate literature is not the issue here," Cromwell reversed himself. "The issue is, the God of the Bible: is he, or isn't he? That is the question. If the Bible is but a piece of ancient fiction, how are we to believe in its fictional God?"

Ben moved to speak.

"The defendant wishes to speak to the witness," Slater said.

"Permission granted," Potter replied.

"Don't you believe in God?" Ben asked Cromwell.

"I don't deny the existence of a God, or goddess, as the case may be. But I do not happen to believe in your silly and traditional God, just because your parents, and your grandparents, and your great grandparents believed in such a sexist and racist being. This unknown being, whom you say is God, offends me, and offends most people in this assemblage."

"I say to you, I know that God lives, and Jesus, his Only Begotten Son, is the Christ," Ben said. "And it was because God loves everyone so much that He sent His Only Son."

"There you are, being narrow-minded, again," Cromwell said. "Well, I just happen to believe in the sacredness of the earth. Who knows? Maybe the earth is our God . . . or goddess."

"It has come to this, then?" Ben said. "You are turning things upside down. We are but the potter's clay. And shall the work say of him who made it, He made me not? Did God *almost* create man in his own image, then change his mind, and leave it to chance?"

"Long before your silly Bible was even written — in fact, billions of years before the Bible began — some kind of human-like creature walked the earth. It just so happens those creatures didn't know how to write. But you can't deny it. We have scientific proof." Cromwell's voice was tight with impatience. "You are too vain to accept fact. Like everyone else, you evolved from primordial slime. Face the ugly truth, my boy. Of slime you evolved, and unto slime you will return. You don't want to believe it, do you? Because it means all your cherished theories about the creation, the fall, and the atonement look pretty ridiculous, don't they? You can't threaten us with sin anymore, can you? If we are children of the Earth, then we return to the Earth, and then the Bible is pretty pointless, isn't it?"

"What evidence do you have for this theory of yours? Were you present when the earth was created?" Ben asked. "You have no evidence, Dr. Cromwell, save your word only."

"My point, exactly. Nor can you prove your God," Cromwell said.

"I have all things as a testimony that these things are true," Ben said. "No decree banning the scriptures can alter their truth, and all things denote there is a God; even the earth, and all things on the face of it, and its motion; and also all the planets which move in their regular form. Yes, all these things witness to a Supreme Creator. And yet will you deny against all these witnesses?"

"I can't see your God. I *can* see living, breathing scientists, and I have seen and read for myself the volumes of scientific evidence those scientists have written. Your wisdom is pure foolishness, young man."

"You did not witness the birth of your grandfather, either, sir. Does this mean he did not exist? Else how would you be here?" Ben chuckled, and laughter bubbled through the audience. "Your scientists were not present for the creation. How can those scientists be sure about their theories? If you are so skeptical, do you trust human nature? Do you really believe every scientist is so honest that not one would ever yield to political pressure and alter reports on his experiments? Are you saying that matter, which is eternal, created itself out of nothing? Can a creature create itself?"

Cromwell did not reply.

" Dr. Cromwell, when any thing or creature is left to itself, will it not surely follow the path of least resistance?"

"Of course."

"And this path leads to chaos, not to order, does it not?"

"That is correct," Cromwell said uneasily. "But the elements obey the laws of chemistry and physics."

"Yes, the forces of physics can explain a star, but what about a rose?"

"What's the difference?"

"Who gives a plant or a person the very essence of life, or its purpose? Let's use your premise in an example," Ben continued. "Let us suppose that, rather than being born, babies were scattered in a field like so many seeds. Then suppose these babies are to grow to adulthood in the field, entirely by chance. By the time those babies reach adulthood, they are expected to know how to read, write, and sustain themselves. This the babies are to do of themselves, with absolutely no nurturing, teaching, or guiding hand. It must all be left to chance. Would such a plan be successful? Generations of illiterates streaming from our schools are proof, Dr. Cromwell, not that your assumptions are valid, but rather to the contrary."

"It is nice to assume that once upon a time a kind, benevolent Being decided to fashion you by an arbitrary whim, isn't it?" Cromwell argued. "But the laws of science cannot be ignored."

"Whose science? The infinite science of almighty God, or the finite science of man?"

"Young man, you cannot hide behind mysteries. We have proven knowledge. Everything you see has developed from the earth. There would be no fins if there were no water; no wings, if there were no air; no legs if there were no land. The light waves played upon the skin and the eyeballs came out in answer."

"You show contempt for the very power which gave you your brain to interpret what you see, and quickened your mind to devise the theories of which you boast. . ." Ben said.

"Permission to speak!" Skadden Wilkes interrupted as he scurried up to the judge's podium and thrust a sheaf of papers before Miles Potter. "Prosecution's research staff unearthed this evidence from a similar trial in the last century. These words of an unscientific ignoramus should put the matter to rest."

Potter scanned the item with interest. Unruffled, he read for several minutes. "Have you read this?" he said softly to Wilkes.

476

"I don't have to," Wilkes replied. "I know who wrote those words. Go on! Read it aloud!" he demanded.

Potter raised his eyebrows. "Very well. You are a deliberate man, Dr. Cromwell. Perhaps you can answer these questions which were posed over a century ago. How long did the light waves have to play on the skin before the eyes came out? Thousands of years? How can you be sure the light waves played all the time in one place or played in the same place generation after generation until the development was complete? Why don't the light waves play today, so we may see eyes in process of development? Why don't the light waves keep playing until there are eyes all over the body?"

Cromwell gasped.

The audience broke into waves of laughter.

Benjamin did not laugh. "People of Yeshurun, take heed!" He said into his microphone. His voice was not loud, but it was piercing, and the laughter stopped. "People of Yeshurun," Ben continued, "those words were written by a man defending his faith. At that time, Egalitarian advocates deeply humiliated him. How soon we forget the frequency and density with which we of Yeshurun have been shamed and maligned for our beliefs through the ages. We must refrain from ridicule. We are warned to repent of this wicked and prideful practice, for the Lord is not well-pleased."

He turned to Cromwell. "As for you, Dr. Cromwell, take heed also. History is no longer on your side. Science continues to expose the flaws in your logic. I suggest that you humble yourself before you are further compelled to be humble. When you are learned you think you are wise, but you won't listen to God. Can your speculations abide the truth? If so, then why do you despise the scriptures? Because if you were totally honest, you might have to forsake some of your theories. So, rather than face the truth, you must attack the revelations of God. Beware, Dr. Cromwell, if you are angry because of the truth of God."

"Do you deny the value in the scientific method?"

"Not at all. To be learned is good, if you listen to God," Ben replied. "Are *you* willing to search for the truth, no matter where it leads? What will you do when empirical evidence and your philosophy lead in different directions?"

"You say this because you are afraid the world's wisdom will liberate people from ignorance, which you use to keep them from enjoying their rights. It might free them from the power you hold over them," Cromwell said.

"Only the Truth, when applied, will make them free."

"Your so-called truth is based on ignorant assumptions. You have no credibility," Cromwell insisted. "You assume God exists, but you have no proof."

"The Bible is full of proof . . ."

"Everyone here knows the Bible is not a credible witness."

"The book of Joseph is another testament ——"

"Hah!" Cromwell scoffed. "You have even less proof for this ridiculous book of Joseph than for the Bible."

"You have placed me on trial," Ben replied, "but I do not need to prove anything. The book of Joseph is self-evident. And the existence of God is manifest in His creations."

"Humph. More assumptions."

"Dr. Cromwell, I believe in a perfect, omniscient, omnipotent God who knows how to use the laws which order the universe; who keeps the planets in their orbits; and who causes the sun to shine daily, without fail, on the just and the unjust. I believe in a gracious God who will not lie, whose only desire is to bring to pass the immortality and eternal life of all mankind. For these reasons, God has credibility, and I have faith in Him. Will the objects of *your* faith hold up under scrutiny?"

"I, uh . . ."

"Men can only make assumptions about the creation, because they did not witness it. God created the earth, and I believe Him, because He was present for the event. Whom shall you believe, a hypothesis, or an Eyewitness and Participant who gave us the account in writing?"

"The Bible is a book of fables!" Cromwell began to shout. "It is only the record of a single, small, obscure Jewish nation! How can the whole world accept the word of one tiny ancient tribe?"

"The tribe of Joseph is found throughout the world. It is more numerous than —— "

"The book of Joseph!" Cromwell's voice continued to rise. "That book is the whole reason for this trial! I tell you it is hate literature. You can prove nothing with it."

"I do not need to prove anything," Ben repeated calmly. "It's all in the book of Joseph. Why are you afraid of it?"

"All right," Cromwell said. "Since you think you're so smart, and if this God is all you say he is, you ought to be able to prove it.

Why haven't we had any miracles for so long? The reason is miracles are nonsense. Those fairy tales in the Bible never existed in the first place. If God did exist, we could have miracles at any time, couldn't we? Just show me a sign, and then maybe I will believe you."

"It is a wicked and adulterous generation that seeks after a sign."

"There you are with your sin and guilt talk, again!" Cromwell said angrily. "Why should I believe in God if I have to worry about silly traditions like adultery? Animals commit adultery all the time, and we are no different from animals. You are just saying this because you can't produce a sign."

"You have had signs enough, Mr. Cromwell," Ben said quietly. "Will you tempt God? Would you say, 'Show me a sign', when you have testimony from all the holy prophets? "

"Yep." Cromwell folded his arms, and *the* smirk seemed to be engraved upon his countenance.

Beneath Benjamin's gaze, a more sensitive man would have cringed. "God is the same yesterday, today, and forever." Ben stood, towering over the pudgy frame of his adversary. "Behold, I will show you a God of miracles," he said, "even the God of Abraham, Isaac, and Jacob; and it is the same God who created the heavens and the earth, and all things which in them are. Who can comprehend the marvelous works of God? And who shall say Jesus Christ did not do many mighty miracles? And if miracles were wrought then, why has God ceased to be a God of miracles and yet be an unchangeable Being? I tell you He does not change; if so He would cease to be God. Yet He does not cease to be God, for He is still a God of miracles."

"Then what are you waiting for?" Cromwell said. "Show me a sign."

"Signs only follow them that believe. In your eyes He ceases to do miracles, but it is because of your unbelief."

Cromwell snickered. "You are making excuses."

Ben persisted. "Do you think in that Great and Terrible Day when the Lord returns — that great day when the earth shall be rolled together as a scroll, and the elements shall melt with fervent heat; in that great day when you are brought to stand before the Lamb of God — then will you say there is no God? Will you still deny the Christ?"

"You talk in circles," Cromwell replied. "I only deny those issues for which I am given no proof. Now, if you would give me a sign, I might consider it to be proof."

"I know you believe it, but you are possessed with a lying spirit," Ben said, "and you have put off the Spirit of God so it may have no place in you."

"Skip all your preaching," Cromwell grumbled. "Just show me a sign. Don't you want me to be convinced? "

Ben felt infinite patience from a source beyond himself. "I feel sorry for you if you will not listen to Christ or His prophets. It would be better for you if you had not been born."

Cromwell puffed up visibly. "How dare you speak to me so, you fool?"

"Do you suppose you can get rid of the justice of an offended God?" Ben's voice was soft but piercing.

Cromwell assumed an expression of mock fright, but it did not eliminate the ever-present smirk. "Ooooh! Now I'm scared!"

Ben shook his head slowly. "I am grieved by the hardness of your heart. You would still resist the spirit of truth, even if your soul is destroyed."

Cromwell laughed. "Is that a threat?"

"It is the simple truth, but your conscience is so hardened you can't recognize the truth, or you refuse to do so. But it is better that your soul should be lost than that you be the means of bringing many souls down to destruction, with your lying and your flattering words."

Cromwell turned dramatically to the listeners. "See? This man utters hateful words, because this is all he can do. He is weak. He cannot produce a sign. But you must feel sorry for him. He looks very foolish, doesn't he?"

For such a large audience, the silence was intense.

"Of myself I would never attempt to give you a sign," Ben said. "I only endeavor to do God's will. It is you who have asked for a sign, not I. If you deny again, I say to you God will smite you. You will be dumb, so you will never open your mouth again, and you shall not deceive this people anymore."

"I do not deny the existence of a God," Cromwell said in his oddly contradictory way, "but I don't believe in your God. For thousands of years people like you have been trying to impose your narrow views on the rest of us. But we don't want it! When are you going to give it up? Everyone in the world is naturally good, and we are tired of being reminded that we are fallen. All these years we have survived by our own intelligence and wit. We have proven we don't need your ideas of sin and atonement. We have become strong and united. And now, just as we begin to create a new ethic which will at last bring world peace, you come along with your religious hatred and try to destroy my religion. You hate me because your church is as old as the Primitive Church, and it is weak, because it has never changed, even though those old apostles all died. But we are new and strong. Then when I challenge you to prove yourself, you threaten me. Well, the day of your demise has come. We now have the power to put you out of business, because the world will not tolerate fraud. I deny this God of yours, as I would deny any fraud. This trickery is perfectly obvious to any rational person, because you can't show me a sign. You're stalling."

"Then this is your sign." Steady and unwavering, Ben looked upon Cromwell. "You shall be struck dumb, according to my words, which I say in the name of God. You shall never speak again."

Cromwell snickered, and opened his mouth to speak, but nothing was heard. He stroked his beard and cleared his throat. He moved his lips; he licked his lips; he grunted, but he could not say a word.

But Potter found his own voice. "In whom did you think Benjamin would show this sign? You thought to afflict others, didn't you?"

Cromwell gestured wildly, and a word processor with an overhead projector was brought so all could see the words he typed: "I really cannot speak! I know now that nothing but the power of God could bring this upon me. And I always knew there was a God." He pointed to Rameses, shook his finger angrily, then typed faster, at a frantic pace. "But this man, Alger Rotcraft — he commissioned me to go and reclaim the people, who he said had all gone astray after the wrong God. He promised to pay me millions to start a world church and squeeze out all other churches. Rotcraft offered plenty of money for me to make everything right. I told people what they wanted to hear, so naturally I had great success. I had so much success that I began to believe it was true." Cromwell pounded his fist upon the computer table and glared at Rotcraft. He started to shout, but nothing came out. "I demand payment in full for my services," he wrote, "plus triple for damages." Suddenly he looked at Ben, then out over the audience. The smirk was gone from his face. "But as for this spectacle," he typed, "Rotcraft and I planned it all very carefully beforehand." Cromwell pulled at his hair and wrung his hands, then he clung to Rotcraft, sobbing.

481

Dermucker, who was sitting just behind the prosecution table, leaned forward. "Do something, Alger."

The big man scowled. "This is some kind of trick, I'm sure. It will wear off, like hypnotism." He shrugged his elephantine shoulders. "There is nothing I can do. He's an adult. Blaming me will get him nowhere."

Cromwell turned again to the keyboard and typed rapidly, heedless of his humiliation displayed for the entire viewing world to see. "Mr. Benamoz," he wrote, "I see the folly of my ways. I beg of you, pray to God to take this curse from me."

"It is in God's hands, Mr. Cromwell." Ben paused for a moment, his head bowed slightly. Then he said, "If this curse were taken from you, you would go right back to deceiving this people. This will have to stand. It will be unto you as the Lord wills."

Dermucker stood, incensed. He took Cromwell's arm and helped him to his feet. "Come with me, you poor man. I will help you." As he ushered the man out, he turned and glared at Ben. "You cold and heartless man, you! How could you do this to him? You are cruel and without mercy. I'll sue you!"

Several hundred people got up and followed them out.

But Potter said his next words so the retreating Cromwell could hear. "I must admit Mr. Cromwell's strong emotions about this book of Joseph have served only to arouse great curiosity. Before this interruption, we were about to examine this book. Mr. Benamoz, let us proceed."

3

"Very well." Ben turned to Potter. "With the permission of the court, the testimony of Joseph will be presented by three readers. I will begin, then Sarita, widow of Zephan Benamoz, will continue. The audience may follow along in their individual copies of the book of Joseph." Ben searched the audience. Where was the star witness?

Miles nodded slowly. "Permission granted." Potter settled in his chair with the comfort of a child being read to. He opened his book, noting the colorful illustrations.

"I am a descendant of Joseph who was carried captive into Egypt. And great were the promises of the Lord which he made unto Joseph," Ben began.

482

"What God? What promises?" Skadden interrupted boldly.
"Do not interrupt," Potter said.

Wherefore, Joseph truly saw our day. And Isaiah spoke about the people of Joseph, saying: out from Jerusalem shall go forth a remnant. And the Lord brought them out of darkness unto light—— yea, out of hidden darkness and out from captivity unto freedom.

"This is too political," Skadden said.
"I will put my trust in him, and he will still deliver me," Ben continued, ignoring the interruption.

For he has brought our fathers out from Egypt. He truly spoke unto the waters of the Red Sea and they divided here and there, and our fathers came through, out of captivity, on dry ground, and the armies of Pharaoh did follow and were drowned in the waters of the Red Sea.

"Hey!" said Skadden. "You can't use this. It's in the Bible!"
"Right," Ben agreed. "The record of Joseph verifies the Bible."
"I mean, uh . . . I didn't mean . . . " Skadden stammered.
"You are out of order," Potter said.
Nervous laughter rippled through the crowd.
Again, Ben continued.

Therefore, when you shall receive this record, you will know the work of the Father has commenced upon all the face of the land.

I write unto you, Gentiles, and also unto you, house of Israel. I write unto all the ends of the earth; and I write also unto the remnant of this people. And for this cause I write unto you, so you may know that all must stand before the judgment seat of Christ. Yes, every soul who belongs to the whole human family of Adam. You must stand to be judged, whether you be good or evil.

"Hey!" Skadden said. "We'll do the judging here."

"One more interruption without permission," Potter snapped, "and I will hold you in contempt." He turned to Ben. "Now, young man. Tell me about this remnant of Jacob."

And at this time Captain Moroni prayed that the cause of the Christians, and the freedom of the land might be favored. And when he poured out his soul to God, he named all the land, both on the north and south —— a chosen land, and the land of liberty. And he said: Surely God shall not suffer that we, who are despised because we take upon us the name of Christ, shall be trodden down and destroyed, unless we bring it upon us by our own iniquity.

And it came to pass that he rent his coat; and he took a piece thereof, and wrote upon it —— In memory of our God, our religion, and freedom, and our peace, our wives, and our children —— and he fastened it upon the end of a pole. And he called it the title of liberty.

And Moroni said unto them: Behold, we are a remnant of the seed of Joseph, whose coat was rent by his brethren into many pieces; yea, and now behold, let us remember to keep the commandments of God, or our garments will be rent, and we will be cast into prison, or be sold, or be slain.

Let us preserve our liberty as a remnant of Joseph; yea, let us remember the words of Jacob, before his death. He saw that part of the remnant of the coat of Joseph was preserved and had not decayed. And he said: Even as this remnant of garment of my son hath been preserved, so shall a remnant of the seed of my son be preserved by the hand of God.

Ben had the attention of the entire assembly, and he read on.

And thou shalt be brought down, and shall speak out of the ground, and thy speech shall be low out of the dust, and thy voice shall be, as of one who has a familiar spirit, and thy speech shall whisper out of the dust.

Behold, this is a choice land, and whatsoever nation shall possess it shall be free from bondage, and from captivity, and from all other nations under heaven, if they will but serve the God of the land, who is Jesus Christ.

"Kingerman!" Skadden whispered.
Arch held his finger to his lips.

> For as Joseph brought his father down into the land of
> Egypt; even so the Lord brought a remnant of the seed of
> Joseph out of the land of Jerusalem. Wherefore, the remnant
> of the house of Joseph shall be built upon this land; and it shall
> be a land of their inheritance; and they shall build up a holy
> city unto the Lord, like unto the Jerusalem of old; and they
> shall no more be confounded.

"See?" Arch said to the nervous lawyer. "Their inheritance.
These people are committing treason."

Ben glanced at the prosecution table, and Alger Rotcraft
returned his gaze with intense concentration, like an animal studying
its prey.

> Know ye not that the testimony of two nations is a
> witness unto you that I am God, that I remember one nation
> like unto another? Wherefore, I speak the same words to one
> nation like unto another. And when the two nations shall run
> together the testimony of the two nations shall run together
> also.

Ben's voice was deep, powerful, authoritative.

> And I do this so I may prove unto many that I am the
> same yesterday, today, and forever; and that I speak forth my
> words according to mine own pleasure. And because I have
> spoken one word ye need not suppose I cannot speak another;
> for my work is not yet finished; neither shall it be until the end
> of man, neither from that time henceforth and forever.

Ben's voice resonated through the vast chamber, not with a
force, but with a vitality of its own, an *influence*. Perhaps it was the
substance of those words — a quality of energy, much larger than
the young man speaking them.

It was as if Potter was hearing the voice of God himself. *This is weird. What is happening? I haven't touched drugs for years. But I have never felt like this before.*

He stared at Benamoz. The whole room seemed somehow lighter. No, light was brighter only where Benjamin was. That man he had seen outside the courtroom was the same way. Good grief. Maybe he hadn't even seen that old man outside the court this morning. He was imagining things. His eye fell on a passage in the book of Joseph: "Have you spiritually been born of God, and received his image in your countenance?"

Potter rubbed his eyes. What did Goodwin say to him? Something about a man of God being moved upon by the Holy Spirit. And God had written somewhere, "By my own voice or the voice of my servants, it is the same." Is young Benamoz a prophet? Nah. He's just a kid. A kid giving a message from God.

By the power of the Holy Spirit you can know the truth, Goodwin had said. *Do I have that spirit with me?* Potter looked down at his hands. Everything looked the same.

One thing is certain. I have never felt this wonderful before, and I'm not going to lose it. After all my mistakes, I'm going to do something right this time. If God really is speaking to me through this boy, I'm not going to reject it. I must not miss a word. But how will I know for sure?

Listen.

4

At the fifth hour, Sarita began reading.

Totally absorbed in the book before him, and oblivious to thousands of vacant seats, Potter had not called a recess. At least a third part of the audience had left, among them Horace Verman. Several of those remaining were asleep, while a few were following in their books, listening with rapt attention.

At length Potter announced a break for the evening meal. After dinner, restaurants, businesses, theaters, and concert halls for miles around were emptied. Fairgrounds, sports stadiums, parks, schools, ballrooms, party halls, and gymnasiums lay quiet and abandoned. Homes were vacated. For the evening meal, people had devoured everything from hot dogs to filet mignon, but all were still hungry.

Hungry for the truth. All their lives people had searched, but had been kept from it only because they knew not where to find it, until this moment.

People walked, rode bicycles, and drove cars. People arrived in buses, trains, helicopters, and private and commercial aircraft. People flooded into the great hall where the world court was held, swelling attendance far beyond capacity.

People of all races and religions flowed into the building as if gathered in a fisherman's net of infinite proportions. People filled balconies and poured onto broad staircases, with bakers, butchers, and bus drivers standing shoulder to shoulder with doctors, professors, and financiers. Foreign dignitaries offered their seats to barbers, grocers, plumbers, and their families. Children sat on laps and crowded two and three to a seat. Teenagers helped the elderly. Kings and princes made way for teachers, janitors, and carpenters.

Fathers in the overflow with children on their shoulders promised firemen and policemen in the audience that there would be no disorder. And they were as good as their word.

Not a person was pushed, not a speck of litter was dropped, not a word was spoken. Everyone was busy reading the books of scripture, so precious now, after being out of circulation for so long. And the children were gazing in wonder at the colorful pictures.

5

Outside the court, Jaime Canosa argued with the guard. "I must enter," he said. "My testimony is vital!"

"I have specific orders from the Central Committee," the guard said. "Benamoz supporters are to be barred entry."

"Excuse me," said a small, bespectacled silver-haired man, holding out a pass for the guard to examine.

The guard glanced quickly at the signature and nodded, but was unprepared for veritable brigades of young men who filed quietly past him, each holding a small but very thick book. Each of those books looked thick enough to be two books in one.

"Wait!" cried the guard, but he could not stop them.

One from the host of young men put his arm around Canosa, who melted smoothly into the crowd.

487

"And they were all young men," Sarita was saying in her concluding portion of the reading. "And they were exceedingly valiant for courage, and also for strength . . . they were men who were true at all times in whatsoever thing they were entrusted."

Sarita stared as hundreds of young men in dark suits, carrying Holy Scriptures, marched silently into the building. Persons close to the front, in deference to this obviously important company, vacated their seats.

Beside Jaime Canosa, Zephan, with a triumphant grin, was striding toward his wife. Outfitted in the armor, shield, and helmet of ancient Nephite military attire, Zephan nonetheless carried, not a sword, but a large, thick, book of Scripture.

The sword of God.

Miles Potter blinked rapidly, embarrassed by his tears. He saw, not his old enemy Zephan Benamoz, but thousands of youthful warriors, marching into his life from an era long past. Stunned by the power of their awesome presence, Miles rubbed his eyes, desiring to know the nature of their weapons. No weapons in their hands, only the Word of God.

"They were men of truth and soberness, for all had been taught to keep the commandments of God and to walk uprightly before him." Sarita's voice was barely audible. "They did not fear death; and did think more upon the liberty of their fathers than they did upon their lives."

Suddenly Miles knew the power of this people lay, not in their worldly weapons, but in their purity and faith.

"The young men had been taught by their mothers that if they did not doubt, God would deliver them." Sarita finished the last, tear-blurred words in her portion of the testament and handed the book of Joseph to Canosa.

Now the leader of those who were wroth against their brethren was a large and a strong man, and his name was Amalickiah. And he was desirous to be a king, and those who were angry also wanted him to be their king. And the greater part of those who wanted a king were judges and officials in the land, and they were seeking for power.

Now, this was grievous to the prophet, who said: Surely this will lead to captivity.

But because of their secret society and wicked abominations, the followers of Amalickiah rejected all prophets.

As the power of Canosa's voice carried throughout the chamber, the sleepers awoke with a start.

These were the flatteries of Amalickiah: that if they would support him and establish him to be their king, he would make them rulers over the people. And many were led away by the flatteries of Amalickiah.

Behold, this was the desire of Amalickiah, he being a very subtle man. He led many to seek to destroy the followers of God, and to destroy the foundation of liberty which God had granted unto them.

Thus we see how quickly the children of men forget the Lord their God. How quick to do iniquity and be led away by the evil one. And the pride of this nation, or this people, shall prove their destruction if they do not repent.

Therefore Amalickiah laid the plan in his heart to dethrone his enemy, who was the duly appointed chief of the people. And among Amalickiah's secret associates were those who planned assassinations.

Canosa had everyone's full attention.

And robbers filled the judgment-seats — having usurped the power and authority of the land; laying aside the commandments of God . . . letting the wicked and the guilty go unpunished because of their money; and moreover to be held in office at the head of government. And thus they might plunder, and steal, and commit whoredoms and all manner of offenses, contrary to the laws of their country and also the laws of their God. And these robber bands vowed to protect one another in whatsoever difficult circumstances, so they should not suffer for their murders and plunderings.

And it came to pass that as the chief came out to meet him Amalickiah caused his servants to go forth and meet the chief. And the servants went and bowed themselves before the chief, as if to reverence him because of his greatness. And it came to pass that the chief put forth his hand to raise them, as was the custom, as a token of peace. And it came to pass that when he had raised the first of Amalickiah's servants from the ground, behold, Amalickiah's servant murdered the chief, who fell to the earth.

Now the servants of the chief fled, and the servants of Amalickiah raised a cry, saying: See? The servants of the chief have killed him. He has fallen and the servants of the chief have fled. Does not this testify against them?

Amalickiah pretended to be angry, and said: Whosoever loved the chief, let him go forth, and pursue his servants to slay them. So all they who loved the chief, when they heard these words, pursued after the servants of the chief. Thus Amalickiah, by his fraud, gained the hearts of the people.

"Arch!" Skadden, near hysteria, clutched at his companion. "Must be at least two thousand of those men! We're being invaded! What does this mean?"

"Never mind them!" Kingerman said in a choking voice. "They're exposing us. How did Yeshurun find out about Amalickiah? Who else knows about this? Where did they dig up Canosa? He knew . . . I mean, knows everything. I mean, he's alive, and every person in here has a copy of that cursed book. So much for our secret plan. Yeshurun has it in black and white, and all those witnesses have it in their hands. They might as well broadcast it on every channel worldwide. We're trapped . . . " He glanced at his father.

Rameses was livid. "You and your clever ideas. What made you think someone among them would not do his history homework and figure you out? Of all the idiotic . . . Well, quit babbling and do something."

Canosa read on.

And now, my son, we see that the Jaredites did not repent, therefore they have been destroyed. And I will bring to light all their secrets and abominations, unto every nation which shall hereafter possess this land. And their lies shall you make known unto the people.

Now, behold, I, knowing these things must surely be made known, and that all things which are hid must be revealed upon the housetops; and also that a knowledge of these things must come unto the remnant of Jacob, and also unto the Gentiles—

Rotcraft's voice shook with rage. "Canosa. How did he get here? You told me he was rubbed out."

"Yeshurun got that cursed book published anyway," Kingerman said. "Where did they get it? How? Now that book is everywhere. At this very moment, the enemy will be filling massive orders worldwide for this book of dangerous ideas. This horrifying book of Joseph is pouring in everywhere, and Bibles are springing up out of nowhere. Where did they get them? Bad enough that the Jewish Bible is back in circulation, but now this other testament, from a remote corner of the house of Israel — a relatively unknown entity. This could be the most terrifying of all. Now everyone will know the truth . . . "

"Shut up!" Rotcraft said. "I can see all these things for myself."

"For behold," Canosa read on:

. . .they murdered all the prophets of the Lord who came among them to declare unto them concerning their iniquities; and the blood of those whom they murdered did cry unto the Lord their God for vengeance upon those who were their murderers; and thus the judgments of God did come upon these workers of darkness.

"Where is Devon?" Rotcraft asked.

Kingerman shook his head. "By the time he figures out what is happening, any hope of an advantage will be lost. Already it might be too late. Verman is gone, wallowing in his own problems. Dermucker went somewhere to blubber with Cromwell. Even then, he will do nothing until after the cocktail hour."

Rameses, squirming? Potter never thought he would see it.

The man was actually losing his grip. For nearly a century, Rameses' forces had built the City of Man, fortifying it with an impermeable levee of censorship, regulation, extortion, and deception. Now his enemy had thought the unthinkable, done the impossible, penetrated the impenetrable — tiny Yeshurun had driven a wedge into the dike. The damage would be irreparable. Once the truth began to leak out, it would gush forth at a blinding speed.

Rotcraft would never stop it now. Who could stop a deluge? The world would be flooded by the knowledge of God. Alger Rotcraft, the mighty Rameses, self-appointed leader of all which was wrong with the world, the most powerful man on earth, the chief of all liars, now faced a sea of truth. Suddenly Rameses, despite his physical immensity, looked very small. Potter had to smile.

"Arch, you take over," Rotcraft said. "I must escape while I can." He waited until a trickle of people passed by, then began to make his exit.

Rotcraft ducked flashing cameras and inquisitive reporters by the door, but it was no use. Mitchell Hunt was waiting for him.

Arch Kingerman stared at his father's retreating back. He clenched his fists. But he was not surprised at his father's betrayal. Somehow he had known the day would come when his father would not support him in a time of crisis. Of all Rotcraft's children, legitimate and otherwise, none could rely upon him. Alger Rotcraft would save his own skin first.

Canosa was concluding his portion of the testament.

Wherefore, I, Moroni, am commanded to write these things that evil may be done away, and the time may come that Satan may have no power upon the hearts of the children of men. But that they may be persuaded to do good continually, so they may come unto the fountain of all righteousness and be saved.

And all this shall stand as a testimony against the world at the last day.

And now, if I have no authority for these things, judge for yourself, for you will know I have authority when you see me, and we shall stand before God at the last day.

For thus saith the Lord God: I shall speak unto the Jews and they shall write it; and I shall speak unto the descendants of Joseph and they shall write it; and I shall also speak unto the other tribes of the house of Israel, which I have led away; and I shall also speak unto all nations of the earth and they shall write it.

For I command all men, both in the east and in the west, and in the north, and in the south, and in the islands of the sea, that they shall write the words which I speak unto them; for out of the books which shall be written I will judge the world, according to that which is written.

"Elidor!" Kingerman was back on the phone, his agitation intense. "Things are getting out of hand. This was not done in a corner. These people are organized in all nations . . . A major authority is here which I do not recognize . . .

"No, stupid! Of course you won't find this on your computer. It's much bigger. This power must be reckoned with. It's worldwide . . . No, it's even worse. It is a crisis of international proportions. Now listen carefully. This is what I want you to do. Order all the communications satellites jammed. All telephones are to be tapped . . .

"Yes, even telephones in non-Yeshurun households. No one can be trusted. Have Banberg freeze all accounts worldwide. Close all banks, businesses, and schools. Dispatch PAX troops to guard the food supplies for the governments of member nations. Troops are to arrest any and all who try to buy food or weapons without proof of loyalty to the order of Voltaire. All travel is forbidden, effective immediately. But the threat is from the nonmember nations, those who oppose PAX. We can't penetrate their borders with our control. The only thing to do is . . . uh, call up all PAX troops immediately and all the reserves. Their first command is to crush all revolt within our own borders and the borders of member nations . . .

"What do you mean, the troops might balk at killing their own countrymen? They'll do it. All are trained soldiers, and thoroughly indoctrinated. This is the moment we've been preparing them for. I just hope they're prepared, because this is far worse than even I imagined . . .

"Why? You're asking me why? At this very moment, the enemy is gaining control over millions of minds. This is not conventional warfare. We're fighting an idea, Elidor! An instant of

493

truth can ruin us! Don't you see? All we can do is exterminate the opposition on the home front. Then prepare all the troops for a universal uprising against the order of Voltaire . . .

"Elidor?. . .Elidor!"

Kingerman swore.

He looked at the vast audience. At Devon's suggestion, this audience was multi-cultural. Devon had been so sure about the outcome of this trial that he had invited kings and princes from every nation on earth to witness the demise of Yeshurun. He had underestimated the cunning of Yeshurun leaders, who promptly had all their so-called scriptures printed in hundreds of languages.

Elidor would be indisposed for hours. It was a race against time, and he had no one to help him. It was like one man trying to stop a tidal wave.

For the first time in his life Kingerman felt panic. He stood weakly and felt himself swept along, against his will, by a surge of stifling horror.

At the tenth hour Canosa gave the book back to Benjamin. With eyes riveted to the speaker, Potter did not budge. Of the original ten thousand spectators, the remaining half were submerged in waves of newcomers.

"Wherefore, by the words of three," Ben read, "God hath said, I will establish my word. Nevertheless, God sends more witnesses, and he proves his words through his prophets.

> Now we have seen in this record it is by faith that these things should come unto us through the Gentiles; therefore the Lord, even Jesus Christ, hath commanded me.
>
> And I said unto him: Lord, the Gentiles will mock at these things, because of our weakness in writing. Thou hast made our words powerful and great, even that we cannot write them; wherefore, when we write we behold our weakness, and stumble because of the placing of our words; and I fear lest the Gentiles shall mock at our words.
>
> After I said this, the Lord spoke to me, saying: Fools shall mock but they shall mourn; and my grace is sufficient for the meek. They will take no advantage of your weakness. For I will show unto the Gentiles their weakness; and I will show them that charity brings them unto me — the fountain of all righteousness.

494

Skadden Wilkes noisily shoved his chair under the table and stalked out.

> Verily, verily I say unto you, he that has the spirit of contention is not of me, but is of the devil, who is the father of contention, and he stirs up the hearts of men to contend with anger, one with another. Behold, this is not my doctrine, to stir up the hearts of men with anger, one against another, but this is my doctrine, that such things should be done away.

Warner Brackenlaw and his corps left. Devon, agape with stupefaction, stumbled out on their heels like a lost cur. Out with them went the spirit of contention.

Ben read on.

> I will give power to bring forth my word— not to the bringing forth my word only, saith the Lord, but to the convincing them of my word, which shall have already gone forth among them.
> The writings of Judah, and also the writings of the descendants of Joseph, shall grow together, unto the confounding of false doctrines and laying down of contentions, and establishing peace.

All was quiet, except for the turning of pages in the audience.

> Now I, Nephi, write more of the words of Isaiah, for my soul delights in his words. For he verily saw my Redeemer, even as I have seen him. And my brother, Jacob, also has seen him as I have seen him; wherefore, I will send their words forth unto my children to prove unto them that my words are true.

Midnight, and with it a hush, an uncommon respect. "For as sure as thou livest, behold, I have seen my Redeemer." Ben looked out over the multitude. He saw their humility and felt the power of their faith.

> And it came to pass that the Lord stood in a cloud and talked with Moriancumr for the space of three hours. And then Moriancumr finished building ships for his people whereby they could cross the great waters to the promised land,

and he conversed with the Lord, saying: Behold, O Lord, will thou suffer us to cross the great waters in darkness?

And the Lord said to Moriancumr: What will you have me do to have light in your vessels?

And it came to pass that Moriancumr did molten out of a rock sixteen small stones; and they were white and clear, even as transparent glass; and he carried them in his hands upon the top of the mount, and cried again unto the Lord, saying: Behold, O Lord, thou can do this. I know thou art able to show forth great power, which looks small unto the understanding of men. Therefore, touch these stones, O Lord, with thy finger, that they may shine forth in the darkness, and light our vessels while we cross the sea.

And the Lord stretched forth his hand and touched the stones one by one with his finger.

And the veil was taken from the eyes of Moriancumr, and he saw the finger of the Lord. And Moriancumr fell down, for he was struck with fear.

And the Lord said unto him: Arise, why hast thou fallen?

And he said unto the Lord: I saw the finger of the Lord, and I feared lest he should smite me.

And the Lord said unto him: Because of thy faith thou hast seen it. Sawest thou more than this?

And he answered: Nay, Lord, show thyself unto me.

And the Lord said unto him: Believest thou the words which I shall speak?

And he answered: Yea, Lord, I know thou speakest the truth, for thou art a God of truth and cannot lie.

And behold, the Lord showed himself unto him, and said, because you know these things, you are redeemed from the fall, and brought back into my presence. Therefore I show myself unto you.

Behold, I am he who was prepared from the foundation of the world to redeem my people. Behold, I am Jesus Christ. Do you see that you are created after mine own image? Yea, even all men were created in the beginning after mine own image.

At length, Ben came to stand before the "judge", and quoted from memory, directly to the big man.

"Wherefore, my beloved brother, take heed you do not judge that which is evil to be of God, or that which is good and of God to be of the devil. For behold, my brother, it is given you to judge, that you may know good from evil; and the way to judge is plain. You may know with a perfect knowledge, as the daylight from the dark night.

"For behold," Ben continued, "the Spirit of Christ is given to every man, that he may know good from evil; wherefore, I show you the way to judge. Everything which invites to do good, and to persuade to believe in Christ, you may know it is of God.

"And now, my brother, see that you do not judge wrongfully; for with what measure you mete, it shall be measured to you again."

Potter tried to look away from Ben's earnest face, but could not.

"Therefore, Brother Potter, I beseech you. Lay hold upon every good thing, and condemn it not."

Miles was astounded, but it must have been love which he felt for this innocent young man standing before him. *How can I resist an appeal like that?*

Finally, the reading had continued for a total of fifteen hours, and Ben turned to the audience and concluded the testament.

Now I speak boldly, for God has commanded me. And I exhort you to remember these things; for the time will come speedily that you shall know that I lie not, for you shall see me at the judgment bar of God; and the Lord God will say unto you: Did I not declare my words unto you, which were written by this man, like as one crying from the dead, yea, even as one speaking out of the dust?

I declare these things unto the fulfilling of the prophecies. And they shall proceed forth out of the mouth of the everlasting God; and his word shall hiss forth from generation to generation.

And God shall show unto you: that which I have written is true.

And it came to pass that I prayed unto the Lord that he would give unto the Gentiles grace, that they might have charity. And now I bid farewell unto the Gentiles, yea, and also unto my brethren whom I love, until we shall meet again. And then shall you know I have seen Jesus, and he has talked with me face to face. And now I would commend you to seek this Jesus of whom the prophets and apostles have written, that the grace of God the Father, and of the Lord Jesus Christ, and the Holy Spirit, which bears record of them, may be and abide in you forever. Amen.

Miles Potter remained silent, enjoying the wondrous spirit of peace which rested upon every soul in the assembly. *If I do not convict this man, I shall go back to prison. No matter. I will choose to be a prisoner for Christ.* He lifted his head. The prosecution table was empty.

Miles felt as if he would never be cold or thirsty again. It was a warm, sacred feeling, but he was trembling. He could not stop himself. He stood. "God lives. Jesus is the Christ." Potter's voice filled the chamber. "By God's law, Benjamin Benamoz is innocent."

"Rejoice, the Lord is King!" someone said.
"Rejoice, the Lord is King! Your Lord and King adore!" A handful of those young men began to sing, and soon all those youth were singing.
"The Lord, the Savior reigns, the God of truth and love.
His kingdom cannot fail: He rules o'er earth and heav'n."

Faintly, as from a great distance, a fanfare sounded. Where did it come from? Perhaps one of those youth had an electronic instrument. Whatever the source, the two thousand youth all began to sing. This had to be the biggest choir Miles Potter had ever seen or heard.

God of our fathers, whose almighty hand
Leads forth in beauty all the starry band
Of shining worlds in splendor through the skies,
Our grateful songs before thy throne arise.

Thy love divine hath led us in the past;
In this free land by thee our lot is cast.
Be thou our Ruler, Guardian, Guide, and Stay,
Thy word our law, thy paths our chosen way.

From war's alarms, from deadly pestilence,
Be thy strong arm our ever-sure defense.
Thy true religion in our hearts increase.
Thy bounteous goodness nourish us in peace.

Miles Potter imagined the immense hall of the World Court had never been used for this purpose before; nor had such a possibility ever occurred to the building's architects or the world body called Pax Universalis. In fact, they would probably oppose such a thing. Potter looked out over the vast assemblage. No objection was heard. And none could be heard, for everyone was singing. Not a single news video camera was present to capture the scene, but the hymn caught on, until thousands of voices filled the air with this expression of joy and praise.

"Mortals give thanks and sing
And triumph evermore.

Lift up your heart! Lift up your voice!
Rejoice, again I say, rejoice!
Lift up your heart! Lift up your voice!
Rejoice, again I say, rejoice!"

6

Potter checked his ticket at the counter and searched the airport anxiously. No sign of Verman or Kingerman. Too late he saw a mob of reporters swarming toward him. He jammed his hat over his eyes, but to no avail.

"Judge Potter! Judge Potter!" The mob literally tugged and pulled at the big man's coat.

"Your honor!" Ted Lipscomb's whine rose above the others. "You ruled in favor of Yeshurun due to a technicality. But tell me, sir, don't you feel, personally, that the views of Yeshurun are, uh, shall we say, exclusive?"

Before replying, Miles noted a scribbled statement on Lipscomb's note pad. "Judge Potter personally offended by Benamoz racism . . . Y N"

499

Pitiful. "Nonsense," Miles spoke quietly, edging toward the departure gate. "I *am* of the house of Yeshurun."

"Uh-huh." Not hearing over the din of reporters, Lipscomb hastily circled the "Y" and hurried on to his next question. "Do you plan to file suit against Benamoz for defamation?"

Incredulous, Potter shook his head.

"One more question, sir. Some people say the ghost of Zephan Benamoz was at those proceedings. Do you believe such things, sir, or is that the ravings of a sick mind like Beck's?"

"Believing is seeing." Miles winked at someone behind Lipscomb.

Laughing, Lipscomb turned to see who was behind him. No one. All the reporters had mobbed Benjamin across the corridor. "Believing is seeing," Lips repeated to the camera. "Seeing is believ . . . what did you say, Judge?" Lips spun around. Potter was gone.

7

Sheffa
A Year Later

Ben retrieved his guitar from the old station wagon and made sure the twins, Amoz and Libertad, were with their cousins. He returned to the side of his wife, who was gazing up toward a mountain and the House of the Lord.

Anahí drank in fragrances of plumeria, orchid, and orange blossom. "Today, at the wedding of Alma and Sonya, I felt closer to home than I have ever been in my entire life."

"It has been said someone searched for Eden all his life, but found it more each day right in his own land."

"The land is more scarred and torn than ever, with these endless wars," she said.

"I was not prepared for Voltairism's brutal reaction to the outcome of my trial," Ben said. "During the past year, so many people have suffered."

"But even more have gained an unshakable faith."

A vast fountain pool reflected a red sunset. Against a blazing sky, water shot high into the air, each droplet like a soul in desperate flight to escape the furnace of affliction to which it was born. But the thrust of mortality impels each to the battle front, and there is no turning back. Succumbing to gravity, the droplets returned to the pool and plunged to the elemental salts on its floor, to learn, like the journeying soul, that the only path to immortality is, not over or around, but through the valley of the shadow of death. But in the end, buoyed up by enduring obedience, to emerge on the surface somehow cleansed from the evils of this generation — it was all part of the eternal plan, and therein was the miracle.

The Book Of

Joseba

THE BOOK OF JOSEBA

1

*T*hink of —
Stepping on shore, and finding it Heaven.
Of taking hold of a hand, and finding it God's hand.
Of breathing a new air, and finding it celestial air.
Of feeling invigorated, and finding it immortality.
Of passing from storm and tempest to an unbroken calm.
Of waking up, and finding it Home.

Zephan read the words on the great window. "My wife had that saying posted on the refrigerator for years!" he exclaimed.

"Whoever wrote it was surely inspired," Brother Joseba said.

"Sure is familiar." Zephan remembered Sarita and felt a wrench in his heart.

"Nothing is going to startle you more when you pass through the veil than to realize how well you know our Father in Heaven and how familiar His face is to you."

"The veil is gone, now?" Zephan asked.

"For you, it is."

Overwhelmed by the light, which exceeded that of the sun, Zephan fell to his knees, and with his tears bathed the nail-marked feet of his Savior.

The Lord took Zephan's hand and lifted him to his feet. "Well done, Zephan. Enter into the presence of our Father."

2

Like a child learning to walk, Zephan tottered a few feet before again falling to his knees. "*Abba!*" Reaching at last the waiting, outstretched arms, he was engulfed in the bosom of God.

"Welcome Home, my son!"

"And it came to pass"

SUGGESTED TYPES and PARALLELS

in

ANCIENT and MODERN HOUSE OF ISRAEL

STICK OF JUDAH	(Ancient America)	STICK OF JOSEPH	(Modern America)
Genesis Dissension, Bondage	Dissension	Nephi	Revolutionary War
Exodus Moses, a type of Christ liberates Jews	Self-Government	Mosiah	Founding of Free Government
Receive covenants from God	Receive Covenants	Alma	Restoration of Eternal Covenants
Scattering of Israel	Wickedness, prelude to destruction	Helaman	Wickedness, Evil of Last Days
Deuteronomy Law of Moses typifies points to Christ	Visit of Christ to America	3 Nephi	Millennial Return of Christ

PARALLELS TO PONDER
(Topics for Family Discussion)

BOOK OF AMOZ

1. Compare the suppression of speech and press in Eastern Europe in the mid-20th century to the current political correctness movement in the U.S.

2. In your opinion which is more effective in combating crime, controlling guns or controlling criminals? Explain.

BOOK OF CANOSA

3. What do you think Isaiah meant by grinding the faces of the poor? How do you think the Lord's way differs from a welfare state? Is it righteous to enjoy the fruits of honest labor? (Isaiah 3:10)

FIRST BOOK OF ZEPHAN

4. In Shakespeare's Julius Caesar, consider Marc Antony's funeral oration. How did he manipulate the crowd? Is mob rule ever justified? Give examples of other demagogues in 20th century history, and today. What techniques do they use to manipulate people?

5. Show how class warfare and the politics of envy are a collective violation of the tenth commandment. Express your feelings concerning God's wisdom in giving the ten carnal commandments.

6. Is the United States a democracy? What opinion did the Founding Fathers hold of democracy? (See Federalist Papers)

BOOK OF DAN

7. Discuss how the philosophies and politics of men differ from the teachings of God and His Son. How can we improve our ability to discern between truth and error?

8. What fundamental flaw in United Nations policies so endangers our personal liberty? Our national sovereignty?

BOOK OF AMMON

9. Why did ancient peoples practice human sacrifice? For what reasons do people support this practice today? What heavenly commandments are violated before such persons ever arrive at the clinic? In what ways does rationalization threaten an individual's spiritual progress?

10. What is idolatry? Why does God abhor it so much?

BOOK OF GORDON

11. Summarize Macbeth's encounter with the ghost of Banquo and give examples of current coverups in our society today.

BOOK OF JOSEPH

12. Understanding typology. What are semantics and why do they often lead to confusion in today's society? God often communicates to His children by using types, or symbols and patterns. In what ways is this beneficial? Look for types in the novel, *Remnant*.

ACKNOWLEDGMENTS

Grateful acknowledgment to the following for their valuable assistance and unwavering support:

Carol Johnson, Richard McClung and family, Don and Mildred Davidson

Dr. Thomas R. Valletta, for a greatly enhanced understanding of typology

Alan Gudmundson, for meaningful insights into the life and teachings of Christ

Dr. Jean Campbell, Cathy Gileadi, Mary Lofquist, and Manja Midgley for editorial assistance

Much appreciation to the writers at American Opinion Publishing, whose research and analyses have been an immeasurable help. For insight into the pro-human sacrifice rationale, and the demographics, I am indebted to the writings of Harold O. J. Brown in *The Religion and Society Report.* For understanding of the guiding principles of the tribe of Joseph in the house of Israel, special thanks to Joseph Fielding McConkie, Robert Millet, and Brent Top for their doctrinal commentary. The character type of Cromwell/Korihor is authentic, and visualized in part from their writings. Additional information on various human philosophies was found in excellent articles by Samuel Francis, William Norman Grigg, and William Jasper.

Final remarks of Joseba Bianco in Ammonihah are quoted from Ezra Taft Benson. Zephan's rebuke in the prison paraphrased from the writings of Parley P. Pratt. Ben's epistle on chastity quoted from Spencer W. Kimball. "Hand-in-glove" warning attributed to Dr. Peter Jones, author of *Spirit Wars: Pagan Revival in Christian America.* Parts of the phone conversation with the prophet quoted from the writings of Gordon B. Hinckley. Ben's rebuttal to Cromwell concerning Water Puppy Day and the effects of light rays, etc., are paraphrased from the writings of W. J. Bryan. The author was unable to identify the author of the lovely quotation in the Book of Joseba. Whoever you are, thank you.

Battle scenes in the Book of Abiram are taken from actual episodes in Cuban Bay of Pigs invasion, as portrayed in the excellent account, *The Russians Stayed*, by Nestor Carbonell. Canosa's retreat paraphrases the words of Pepe San Roman, as recounted on pages

172-3. This twentieth century parallel to incidents in the ancient stick of Joseph is included in honor of valiant men and women who struggled for freedom throughout the twentieth century but were victims of many bureaucratic betrayals. Their stories have been kept under wraps by powers and principalities, depriving the rest of the world of the truth. It is hoped that this literary offering will be instrumental in bringing more truth to light and thus give long over-due tribute to those who gave the ultimate sacrifice for liberty.

Also helpful were the writings of H. Verlan Andersen, Richard Grenier, Eugene Hansen, David B. Haight, Thomas A. Holt, Robert W. Lee, Philip E. Johnson, John F. McManus, Keith McMullin, Boyd K. Packer, George Roche, E. Merrill Root, W. Cleon Skousen, Joseph Sobran, and Fr. James Thornton.

Map and geographical settings adapted for fiction from an extensive compilation of research and writing by Dr. Joseph Allen. The fiery serpent artifact, found in Teotihuacan, Mexico, is actually from a much later period than the Mulekites. The figure is also called the "plumed serpent", referring to the plumage of the quetzal bird. Thus the native name of *quetzalcoatl.*

All fictional characters in this work are composites. Any resemblance to specific living persons is coincidental. The longstanding American tradition of satire is still legal in the United States. The perspective given in this story, though based on authentic ancient history, is a fictional creation of the author. Some historical quotations have been modernized for use in fiction, but care has been taken to preserve original meaning. This novel is strictly a cultural statement, and the author does not claim representation of, or endorsement by any specific religious body or political organization.

Information, inspiration, and influence were obtained from the following works: H. Verlan Andersen, *Great and Abominable Church,* and *Many Are Called, Few Are Chosen;* Nestor Carbonell, *And the Russians Stayed;* Dennis Laurence Cuddy, Ph.D., *The Road to Socialism;* Chuck Colson, *Why America Doesn't Work;* Jack Cox, *Requiem in the Tropics;* Joseph Douglass, *Red Cocaine;* Russell Evans, *The Panama Canal Treaties Swindle;* G. Edward Griffin, *The Creature from Jekyll Island;* William Norman Grigg, *Freedom on the Altar;* Milton R. Hunter, *Christ in Ancient America;* William Kilpatrick, *Why Johnny Can't Tell Right From Wrong;* David O. McKay, *Communism and the Constitution of the U.S.,* James Michener, *Mexico,* and *The Source;* Monte S. Nyman, *Great Are the Words of Isaiah;* James Perloff, *The Shadows of Power;* William Shakespeare, *Julius Caesar,* and

Macbeth; Joseph Fielding Smith, *Man... His Origin and Destiny*, Aleksandr Solzhenitsyn, *The Oak and the Calf*; Anastasio Somoza, *Nicaragua Betrayed*; James Strong, *The Comprehensive Concordance of the Bible*

Hymns by Frederick W. Faber, William Fowler, William Phelps, Daniel C. Roberts, and Charles Wesley; children's songs by Elizabeth F. Bates and Eliza R. Snow, and adapted for the novel

Also for encouragement, feedback, meaningful insights, useful information, and help with the multitudinous little tasks that go into a project like this, thanks to Todd Allen, Reed Benson, Ron Blue, Glenn Both, Audrey Carlson, Dale Carr, Dr. Bryce Christensen, Jim Clawson, Jeff Davidson, Cheryl Delavan, Keith Eschmeyer, Dr. Thomas Fleming, Dr. and Mrs. Avraham Gileadi, James Giometta, Paul Gottfried, Vicki Hultgren, Brian and Jackie Josephson, Glenn Kimber, Rebecca Larson, Gail Lee, Gerald Lund, Peter Lundquist, Laurie and Jim May, Jordan, Deon, and Casey McClung, Narelle McClung, David Midgley, Bob Mortensen, Paul Neuman, Jan Noble, Gerald Pointer, Wade Provo, Kenneth Robbins, Larry Sarver, David Skousen, Dr. and Mrs. W. Cleon Skousen, Frannie Smith, David Soderberg, Scott Spencer, Melanie Spurgeon, Kathy Stonehocker, Donna Thomas, Ralph Westberg, Karen Winebrenner, Brent Yorgason

All that this work has become I owe to the Lord Jesus Christ, through whom all good things are possible.

ABOUT THE AUTHOR

For more than twenty years, Beth has studied typology and patterns of history, particularly that pertaining to the house of Israel. She spent two summers in Mexico on student tours and lived in Argentina for two years in the late sixties. In July Of 1994 she investigated archaelogical sites in Central America. Beth and her husband currently reside in Rockford, Illinois, where they schooled their four children at home from 1984-1994.

Remnant

A Book You will want to tell your Neighbors about

ORDER FORM

Please send _____ copies of *Remnant* at $19.95 each, plus $3.50 per book for shipping and handling. Canadian orders must be accompanied by a postal money order in U.S. funds.

Name_____

Address_____

City/State/Zip_____

Enclosed is my check ____money order____ for a total of $_____

Payable to:
Atitlán Publications, PO Box 5567, Aloha, OR 97006

For information on Quantity Discounts, write to Atitlán Publications at the above address.